HAND OF VENGEANCE

Shane L. Coffey

N
W
E
S
BURN THE MAP
PUBLISHING

This story is dedicated to my mother, who first
helped me to spin tales
And to the loving memory of my father, without
whose support I could never have continued

Table of Contents

PROLOGUE

Two men stood in a barren field, silent shadows amidst rising, twilit mist. Their silhouettes stood apart from a dozen-strong contingent of friends and allies a few yards ahead as they watched the eastern stars wink out one by one in the van of the coming dawn. One man was clearly the elder of the two, but they shared eyes too haunted, hands too bloodstained. The older, thicker of the pair broke the silence first.

"I thought ye might go yerself, milord."

"You've seen her eyes these past months, my friend," the younger, more refined man replied. "She's not been the same since he fell. All the rage that was in her when first she came to us, it's consumed her all over again."

"An' ye think one stroke'll change all that?"

"That, she must choose, but I'll not rob her of the chance. Vengeance is her nature, after all."

"An' 'er name."

"Of course."

So it was that Baraxis, Lord of Sutherset and Major of the Storn River Bridge Battalion, had sent his Hand of Vengeance to do her work.

A fiery dream melted into darkness as the sleeping orc snapped open his eyes, quickly absorbing all around him. Everything at the edges of his vision was as it should be, his gear, weapons, and trophies showing dimly in the dawn light that filtered through the seams of his tent. In the center of his view, however, staring straight into his bleary eyes, stood a vision of terror, a nightmarish demon spat up from the bowels of hell, or so his people believed. Still, it bore a human shape, a lithe woman with a mass of hair falling down her back, red and wild as flame. A heavy cloak of green and black shrouded her form, but the dull glint of mail beneath gave proof to her violent intentions. A flash of gold-trimmed scarlet tied about her right arm and the bloody gleam of a garnet in her cloak clasp matched a hellish, inhuman glow behind her piercing green eyes, eyes that held the orc's even as they cowed him. It was the battle light, sparked by the imminence of blood. For all the many rumors of this demon, the light in her eyes was unknown to all who faced her, for no enemy seeing that glint had lived to tell the tale. To the orcish captain, prostrate, unarmed, helpless beneath that burning stare, nothing could provoke more terror. His mind screamed for flight or battle, but those eyes held him, searing away his courage and replacing it with the certainty that any movement could only hasten his death.

"You know why I'm here, who I am," asserted the demon in a fair mimicry of the orcs' brutish tongue.

"I know *who* you are, Hellwitch," he grunted, biding his time while his mind scrabbled for anything that might save him, "but not *what* you are. If I'm dead anyway, tell me that secret."

The orc was denied even that, for the answer, the last words he would ever hear, came in a tongue he did not understand. The woman straightened to her considerable height, pointing a great sword at the prone orc's throat.

"I am *Gwyn et Sheevasa*," she proclaimed. "I am the Hand of Vengeance."

She swung her blade once, severing the orc's foul head from its body. Lifting the skull by the horsehair adhered to its bald pate, she stepped silently out of the tent, turning her gaze to a shoulder-high spear buried haft-first in the ground: a trophy pole, lashed with crossbars from which hung the trinkets and pieces of the orc's human victims. She slammed the orc's head onto the spearpoint, then, with a decisive jerk, removed a single ring of silver and crystal from the pole. Drawing her cloak more tightly about her shoulders, she mounted her gray stallion and rode slowly out of the sleeping orcish camp, sitting proud in the saddle, a ghostly figure in the gray light and mist that rise with the dawn.

After a few long moments she reached the line of soldiers in the field and their commander, Baraxis, a man she had grown to trust and respect over the past eighteen months, months which weighed like years. As Gwyn drew abreast to them, an older sergeant threw her a red towel on which she cleaned her gore-stained blade before wiping her bloodied hands. As she finished, she looked up to meet Baraxis' coal-black eyes, reading the unspoken question behind them.

She nodded her head, silent at first, then said, "It's done. I have avenged our fallen brother, as I swore I would the day he fell and every day thereafter. But there are more deaths unanswered, more scales yet to balance." She cast a backward glance at the orcish camp, her eyes narrow with contempt. "Burn it."

As fire arrows arced through the dawn sky, searing trails through the mist like deadly rainbows, Gwyn watched the first canvases of the small tent city ignite. Most of the orcs fled, but she had put an end to the one they came for. Baraxis looked sidelong into Gwyn's eyes, watching the reflection of the flames that danced there, wondering what she would do next and, after she'd done it, whether either of them could find their way again.

CHAPTER I

Years, leagues, lives, and worlds before, other flames burned, candles and hearth smoking into the cold night in a well-furnished longhouse. Cozy as the place was, for the past few months it had always seemed inexplicably cold; gladness and laughter were now strangers here. A tall, broad man, his sandy hair unkempt, leaned against a windowsill, facing grimly into the west and watching the tops of the nearby forest pines whip and sway under the force of a harsh northern wind. *Bia Creg*, the Little Wanderer, rose quickly in the west, a faint glimmer through the treetops, while the larger moon, *Aridan*, the Faithful One, rode high and full, shedding its brighter light over the surrounding village. Glancing back into the house, he scratched his head while gazing at a strange contraption of levers, counterweights, and slowly flowing sand, doing his best to reckon the hours since sunset. Timekeeping devices were foreign to him, for he had been born into a poor family that followed the old traditions, and to whom such amenities were not destined. Still, he was clever enough and figured another three hours before the dawn. Even for her first child, it was beyond the realm of hope that Lischa's labor would take that much longer.

With that very thought, a tiny but forceful cry ripped through the sound of the howling wind, carrying all the power only such a cry could. Strength, pain, love, confusion, courage, fear, the burning desire to survive as a new soul wills itself into existence, proclaiming boldly to the world that it has a new master.

Despite all this sublime beauty, the man by the window felt a chill tear up and down his spine as though the fingers of Death had raked his back, for in his heart he heard only the cry of a frightful creature, the cry of a Windborne child. And in that cry, his mind could focus only on that which he did not hear, that which gives purpose to the newborn will, a note absent from the birth cry of all Windborne children: the sound of hope.

Sometime later, the man leaned against the same windowsill gazing at the Wind as the midwife approached him softly from behind. "They're asleep," she said flatly.

"I told you this would go badly, Midwife," the man replied, spite edging the brusqueness in his voice.

"What badly?" the midwife replied. "Mother and child are both alive and healthy…and the babe may be the strongest I've brought into the world, and that's a large group."

The man looked sidelong at the midwife, the pain of a wife and newborn lost under her care still fresh in his eyes these years later, though the rage was left behind. "Strongest maybe, and maybe that's my fear," he answered. "The Windborne need no strength to power their madness."

"Windborne, Tehgil? I know your family had always followed the old ways, but I thought you greater than that superstition."

"It's no superstition. I've been in battle with Windborne, both beside and against. Trust my experience; the Windborne are mad."

"Well, it's all moot," the midwife replied with a tired sigh. "There shan't be much of battle for this child. Lischa had a lass."

"The women of Atlund are free to rally to arms if it suits them."

"Aye, they may, but why should they? They learn early from their own mothers the rewards of bringing new life into the world. Only Death rewards the soldier. I don't expect Lischa will teach any differently."

"You've not heard then?" Tehgil inquired, at last turning fully toward the small woman.

"Heard what?"

"What she'll name the child."

"You know it's bad luck for a midwife to know before–"

"And you lecture me about superst–"

"Get on with it, Tehgil."

The large man paused, then, "The child's to be called *Gwyn et Sheevasa.*"

"*Gwyn et Sheevasa*? That's no name for a lass. That's no name at all!"

"No, it is not," Tehgil replied. "She isn't the same, Midwife. Since Girahl was killed, there's been naught in here but anger and hate, and the guilt of the living. I know it's only been a few months, but... She doesn't grieve as one must grieve."

For a moment, Tehgil's words called back the midwife's pain over each child and mother she had lost. Though the number was small, smaller indeed than it might have been under less skilled hands, each face was a wound on her soul.

Her next words were measured with care. "You came through that dark better than most who have wandered it, and your counsel would be wise, but take care how you give it. You know each must weather that storm in his own way, and Lischa must weather it in hers."

"Until tonight, I would agree, but now there is the child to consider."

"It would go better…with the right father." The midwife laid her hand on Tehgil's right arm.

Tehgil recoiled from the touch in disgust. "I'll not marry my best friend's widow!"

"And I'd never suggest such a thing, though you must know he'd not blame you if your hearts tended that way. I only meant that you could watch over the mother and child, and see that little *Gwyn* grows up well."

Tehgil shuddered at the word. "I love Lischa as a sister; I've barely left this house since we lost Girahl. There's always been work to do, old chinking, bad patches in the thatch. I didn't risk my life bringing Girahl's blade back to this home only to watch it crumble. I'd die before I'd leave Lischa to fend for herself. More important, taking care of the child was the last thing Girahl asked me to do, and I will, like she was my own. But I'll never get used to that name."

Eight years later…

Gwyn darted between market stalls, listening for the sounds of clumsy, grownup pursuit behind her. Her stepfather was hunting for her again, and she hated him. Even here, in the chaos of Clanmeet, he seemed to be everywhere, insisting she help herd her stupid half-brothers or, worse yet, play with them. Or trying to make her "presentable." He insisted these orders for grooming came from her mother, but Gwyn knew he was lying. She slid under a wheelbarrow and lay still, holding her breath.

Ages crawled by as she waited for the coast to clear. People laughed and haggled all around, a good joke for a mug of ale, a better one or a few pieces of copper for mead, a bushel of apples for a tunic, a horse for a fine sword. Warriors bragged over new scars, a new wife, a new baby, not necessarily in that order. The sun warmed the ground, but here in the shadow of the barrow, the autumn air was cool, the soil damp. Gwyn loved the Clanmeet. The descent of cold from the mountains meant the grip of winter and her birthday were both coming nearer. Better still, the Clanmeet meant contests against children from other families and clans, boys and girls she hadn't already bested a thousand times over as she had the ones in her own village. She knew all the northwestern tartans: next year she'd be big enough to carry the Candon standard herself in parade. Kart was everywhere as their village hosted this year, Dunree and Dekschra had arrived yesterday noon, Andisch and Bardren last evening, and Vassin just this forenoon. Maybe after she won at wrestling tomorrow morning, she'd ask to do foot races with the ten- and eleven-year-olds so she could show her mother how fast she'd gotten.

Suddenly a boot, one Gwyn knew too well, smote the ground before her eyes. The shade of the wheelbarrow erupted into dazzling light, and Gwyn braced her feet to bolt away. Before she could move, a meaty hand grabbed a fistful of her smock and hauled her upward, the uncoiling springs of her legs pushing against nothing but air. She windmilled her arms but could not reach her abductor. "Put me down!" she shrieked.

"Little Gwyn, where in all the hells have you been?" Tehgil sighed from behind her.

"Under the wheelbarrow," she answered, her hands still grabbing for some purchase on Tehgil's arm or shirtfront.

"I can see that, but where before? *Ugh*, by Terillah, you *stink*." Tehgil put her down, still holding one of her little hands in his great paw, and led her through the crowds as she gawped at swords and hauberks of mail.

"I went to the stables to see Clan Kart's best horses," she finally answered.

"Went to them or *rolled* in them?"

"One of the stableboys challenged me to a duel, so—*whoa!*"

They had reached the edge of a nearby stream, and Gwyn suddenly felt herself heaved off the ground and into the water, flailing as she broke the surface with a mighty *splash*. She heard laughter as her head came back into the air and looked toward the sound to see two women washing clothes at the bank, chuckling at how she'd been dunked. She stuck her tongue out at them.

"Now scrub the worst of that off while I go find your mother," Tehgil ordered. "If you don't get cleaned up she won't let you go to the feast tonight. I ought to tell Adric I finally ran you to ground, too."

"I hate Adric," Gwyn pouted.

"Gwyn of the Family Candon, I don't want to hear you talk like that. What harm has Adric ever done you?"

"He locks me in the storeroom."

"Your storeroom hasn't got a door!"

"Some other storeroom," Gwyn mumbled. "Besides, he's just a dumb farmer, not a warrior, like you."

"And who do you suppose feeds the warriors…and the saucy little girls?" he called over his shoulder as he left.

Gwyn began scrubbing at herself with her hands as she waited for the inevitable soap bar and hairbrush. Why couldn't Tehgil be her stepfather?

Gwyn loved the Clanmeet feast. No hall in any town could hold everyone, so they spread out on trestle tables around roaring bonfires on the village green. The food was the best any of them would eat all year. The speeches were boring, of course, and the other children mostly babbled about stupid things, but the best warriors would stand and tell tales of their deeds long into the night. By the end some of them were always drunk, which a few of the grownups would scoff at, but sometimes they flailed about too much and fell down, and that was funny. Even better, every few years the king would attend; he was a distant kinsman, but Gwyn didn't particularly care about him. What she appreciated was his bodyguard. The best fighters in all the land, almost as good as her father would have been, and with the best weapons and mail. She was getting too old now to clearly remember the last time they'd come to her Clanmeet, and every year she hoped *this* would be the next time.

Bia Creg sailed dimly overhead, but *Aridan* didn't shine that night, leaving the green to no light but the bonfires as the children all sat around a trio of tables at the foot of the long feasting area. Gwyn was used to the order of serving at regular meals: women with child, then warriors, then children, then other grownups. At the feast, though, there was so much food everybody just took and ate what they wanted all at once. Most of the serving platters were too big for the children to pass themselves, so parents or older siblings would take it in turn to fill the plates of the young. Her half-brother Aldrin was a few chairs down; Gwyn was supposed to be sitting next to him, but she managed to shift away once the littler ones started getting bored and running around between plates. A few tables away, on the left side of the green, she could see her mother sitting with Adric and the new baby, Lirisch. Adric played with and fed his son as Lischa held him. Adric's love for the boy was plain on his face, as plain as Lischa's vigilance over him, but Lischa didn't smile. Gwyn thought she seemed to be enjoying the feast, but she never smiled. Except when Gwyn won things. Tehgil sat farther away on the right with some of the older warriors, listening and nodding his head.

A woman, maybe older than Gwyn's mother and with soft, brown hair, approached the table from the light of the bonfires. Bearing a tray of meat, she started at the left end of the children's tables and began placing cuts on each empty plate. Some with other food left uneaten clamored for more of the juicy roast, but she always refused them with a "Tut, tut. Finish what you have first." She stopped in front of Gwyn, noticing a pastry still on her plate.

"I never asked for that," Gwyn insisted. "Meat makes you strong, sweets make you fat."

"A child as rawboned as you could use a little fat, young Gwyn."

"How do you know my name?"

"Oh, I know all the children hereabouts," the woman answered with a dismissive wave of the hand that wasn't under the platter. "Someone has to keep you little scamps from getting into mischief in the woods."

"I can't go in the woods by myself," Gwyn pouted. "There's a bad wizard that lives too close."

"Yes, I know," the woman acknowledged with a solemn nod of her head. She looked to either side and saw the children nearest were distracted with talk or play. "Here, I'll make an exception for a growing warrior like you." She set a piece of braised beef on Gwyn's plate as the girl made her most savage war face. The older woman moved on down the table with a clear, free laugh, one that made Gwyn wish, for just half a heartbeat, her mother would laugh that way sometimes. She turned back to her food, as a warrior from Dekschra stood to tell a tale.

The young ones all around her made so much noise she had to strain to hear the burly man as he swung his ale mug about like a war mace, recounting his deeds against the nomads far to the east when, being a bachelor in a quiet town, he had traveled there to help repel raids. Gwyn barely noticed when something bumped her left knee; she jabbed back in that direction to knock away whatever nearby child encroached on her space. When something brushed her left foot, she had to look under the table to see what was going on. A boy, a little older than her, crouched on his knees and tried to lift up the skirts of the older girl to Gwyn's left. "Hey!" Gwyn called, stomping hard on the boy's left hand.

The boy howled and scrambled away, but Gwyn stood up, putting all her weight on her left foot, trapping the hand. She could now just see the boy's right arm on the other side of the table as he pulled hard to free himself, his hand wrenching from under the leather sole of her shoe. As the boy tumbled back, Gwyn jumped onto the table and climbed over, standing above him. "Don't be looking up girls' skirts, you cur!" she yelled as the taller boy stood.

He looked her once up and down. "Don't worry," he said, "I wouldn't have bothered looking up yours."

Gwyn swung her fist faster than an eyeblink and with accuracy that belied her few years. The boy reeled back, holding his hands over his nose as blood ran down his chin.

Children nearby yelled, "Fight! Fight!" Others farther down the table, likely too far to have seen anything, took up the call until it became a regular chant.

Gwyn stood with her feet wide, left forward, and her tiny fists balled in front of her. "C'mon, you snake! Rat! Bastard!"

The final insult seemed to spark enough rage to overcome pain, and Gwyn waited for the charge, grinning for the chance to wallop the older boy. Before anything else could happen, Adric burst in between the two youngsters, spreading his arms to hold them apart. "Gwyn, what are you doing?"

"He was looking up girls' skirts."

"I was not!" the boy insisted.

"No more lies and excuses, Gwyn," Adric demanded. "You apologize."

"Why should she apologize for winning?" Lischa asked, strolling up from behind with the baby on her hip. "Is your hand alright, Gwyn?"

"You know Tehgil taught me how to punch right," she answered with defiance.

Other grownups started gathering. Two separated from the crowd and took hold of the bleeding boy, pulling his hands from his face to look at his nose. "I don't think it's broken," one of them muttered. The man stood up and stared at Adric, his hand pointing at Gwyn.

"Are you going to whip this sassy brat, or should I?"

Before Adric could say a word, Lischa had handed him the baby and squared up with the larger man. "Nobody lays a hand on my girl for winning a fight. If your little milksop wants to see her beaten, let him do it for himself. If he can."

Gwyn could see the father's eyes flashing in the firelight. He was about ready to make a challenge. Maybe he would whup Adric; that would be fun to see. "If she's not punished, then it's between us," the man growled.

"And me," came Tehgil's voice as he shouldered through the crowd of adults. "This girl is my oath-daughter. Did anyone really see who started things?"

"She started it," the boy cried.

"Anyone else?" Tehgil asked.

"Are you calling my boy a liar?" the father demanded.

"Are you calling my oath-daughter one?" Tehgil's voice was flat and cold; it held no bravado but brooked no argument unless it were backed by a challenge.

The other man went quiet, the tension in his body dissipating. "Shake hands," he finally ordered his son.

"But Papa…"

"Shake hands!"

Gwyn was a better winner than loser; she knew she would have refused if the situation was reversed, but she extended her hand and waited. The boy gave the briefest of squeezes, then hurried off under custody of his mother. "Back to the tent, Little Gwyn," Tehgil ordered.

"But–"

"No 'buts.' The next father whose son you beat may not be so easy to talk down."

"Now, Tehgil," Lischa soothed.

"He's right, Lischa," Adric muttered. "She needs at least a shred of discipline."

Lischa relented with a nod, but she flashed Gwyn one of her rare smiles before Tehgil ushered the girl away.

The woman with the meat tray looked on from the far end of the children's tables, her face impassive.

Two years later...

Gwyn sat at the foot of the heavy table in her house, bouncing her heel on the floor. Tehgil sat at her left with a mild smile; Lischa was at her right, her hands hidden under the table. Adric was off farming someplace.

Gwyn's stomach ached from her birthday breakfast, but she had one more bite to finish before she could have her present. She picked up the piece of bacon with greasy fingers, exhaling a weary breath before shoving it into her mouth, chewing a few times, and swallowing. "Now?"

Lischa revealed the secret she had been holding, a narrow bundle of dark plaid more than a foot long. Gwyn unrolled it gingerly, revealing a short hilt protruding from a hard leather sheath. Her eyes lit up as she saw it, her smile broadening into a grin as she drew the single-edged dirk and examined it. The grip of dark wood was polished to a smooth luster, a joy simply to hold. The handle was wider at the blade and pommel; it would give a secure grip when her hand grew into it a bit more. The furniture was brass, the blade with a wide spine and narrow taper, perfect for stabbing. She gave a few experimental swings.

Tehgil smiled. Though Gwyn had begun to take after her father's towering height, the knife still looked more like a short sword in her hand. He feared she was still a bit too young, but Lischa insisted the time had come for her to have a proper weapon.

Lischa's eyes shone at Gwyn's glee for the deadly instrument. "It's from both of us," she explained. "I decided to give you a good fighting knife for your tenth birthday, and Tehgil chose all the particulars to tell the smith. Do you like it?"

"I love it," Gwyn exclaimed. "Thank you, Mama. Thank you, Papa."

Gwyn's right cheek exploded with fiery pain, her head whipping to the side. Tears sprang to her eyes of their own accord as Tehgil cried out in alarm. Gwyn's jaw trembled, more with rage than hurt, as she looked back to her mother, her eyes aflame.

"That is *not* your father," Lischa declared, pointing across the table. Her face, so pleased only a moment ago, was twisted with anger. "Girahl is your father, murdered over ten years ago by the wizard Kellgore. How dare you try to replace him? I hope when the time comes you're still *fit* to avenge him." She stood and stomped to the narrow hall that led back into the bed chambers.

"I'm sorry, Gwyn," Tehgil muttered.

"It's my fault," she answered. "I shouldn't have said it."

"Not in front of your mother, anyway. I know it just came out, but…it still meant something to me. I don't think your father would mind. It hurts your mother, though, so best not to say it again. I'll just know from now on."

Gwyn nodded.

"Do you want to go get some training with your new knife? I don't have to patrol today."

Gwyn hesitated, then squeezed the hilt tighter in her hand. "Yes," she answered. "I do love it." She had to train hard enough to ensure she was, indeed, fit when the time came.

Three years later...

Gwyn sat in the crisp air of the Clanmeet feast. From her position at the far right end of the children's tables, she could see Tehgil with the other warriors, but her mother and stepfather were invisible behind the glow of the nearest bonfire. She had no idea where her half-brothers were; the adults had long since given up asking Gwyn to supervise them. Gwyn did love the Clanmeet. Last year she had won wrestling and mock sword within her age group and had come in second and third overall in horsemanship and tracking. She competed in hunting but didn't care about her place; it was judged on the quality of the game harvested, and she only practiced it to hone her stealth. This year she would do better in all events. Despite her love for the contests, she loathed the feast. The food was fine, but the other children her age hated her because she always won, and the old warriors' boasting over ancient victories was tiresome, sometimes even a little pathetic. Not one of them had the courage to lead an attack against the wizard that had murdered her father. Of course, that was for the best, since Kellgore was hers to kill. Tehgil would have had some decent stories from defending the village against the wizard's minions, fell beasts, and such, but he was too humble to tell them.

A boy about Gwyn's age approached with a full plate. She paid him no mind until he asked, "Can I sit here?"

"Why?" she retorted.

"There's a lot of empty chairs around you," he answered.

"What's that supposed to mean?"

He shrugged.

"Do what you want." She looked at him as he sat and realized she'd never seen him before, even at Clanmeet where she could meet people from farther villages. She certainly would have remembered him if she had since he looked quite different from other Atlunders. His eyes and hair were dark, the latter a mass of tight ringlets. He had skin a couple shades darker than was common in the north, and his frame was at the narrow end of masculinity, even for his age. "Where do you come from?" Gwyn asked.

"Clan Baldor," he answered as he picked at his meal. "My father's brought us west on some trade business, and the Dunree elder invited us so we wouldn't miss out on Clanmeet altogether. And yes, my mother's from the nomads east of the mountains."

"I didn't ask about that."

"People always do."

"People should mind their own business," Gwyn grumbled.

The boy looked over at her. "I'm Sudro," he announced. "You're Gwyn?"

"How do you know that?"

"Everybody talks about you. They told me not to bother coming over here. Well, some told me to try, but then they laughed."

Gwyn snorted. "They can go to hell. None of them is worth a damn in a fight, anyway."

Sudro coughed. "No wonder you're so popular."

"You don't need to be liked when you're the best." Her plate was empty, so she went to find a platter of something to bring back for herself and the little children. With any luck, some of them would follow her example closely enough to be useful when she needed them some day.

The next morning began with horsemanship competitions. Gwyn took first place at maneuvers but lost at jumping to none other than Sudro. "Stranger from Baldor," she grumbled as she led her sorrel courser to the next event. "Shouldn't have even been allowed to compete."

Gwyn's family was well off, but not wealthy, certainly not enough to afford a second horse for her. This put her at a disadvantage against a few of her peers in the final event, a four-furlong sprint, since her mount would be tired from the previous efforts. Still, she would take her animal over any ten of their beasts, anyway, and she knew how to ride him to ration his strength for the race. She stood with him on the starting line, waiting to mount until the last possible moment, chewing her lip as other competitors gathered at the line. Sudro's win at the jumps had been the more decisive, putting him ahead on points. In order to win overall, she had to take first place in the sprint.

In a few more minutes all the competitors had gathered, and the judges came down the line with stepstools to help the children mount. Gwyn refused such a crutch and half-jumped, half-heaved herself into the saddle. Sudro, to her left, raised an eyebrow. Gwyn was sure this was for her unexpected strength and not at how it torqued the horse's saddle.

Once everyone had mounted, a judge walked the line and moved horses forward and back to ensure an even start. Gwyn watched his progress to the far end, where a younger boy struggled to control his animal; the unruly gray kept pushing forward over the scratch despite the child's best efforts. "Hurry up!" Gwyn shouted first, and a few of the less patient riders joined her. After three failed attempts to correct his horse, the judge disqualified the boy, who led the gray stallion away from the line with a brooding air.

At last the competitors stood ready, and the second starting judge, standing just to Sudro's left, slapped two planks of wood together with a *clack*.

Gwyn put spurs to her sorrel and took off like a bowshot. Her horse was an eager sprinter; she knew her best strategy was to let him take an early lead before any sense of tiredness could reach his equine brain. In the right edge of her vision, she saw two riders almost keeping pace, but Sudro, to her left, dropped away quickly. She smiled. What her opponents couldn't know was how she had trained for months with forty pounds of sand strapped to her saddle in anticipation of the day this horse would carry her in full mail hauberk. Now with only her slight frame to bear, he continued to accelerate over another fifty yards, leaving the nearest challengers a few lengths behind. She laughed as the wind whipped her hair behind her, allowing the joy of her inevitable victory to surge up when she finished the third furlong. She could now see the crowds gathered at the finish line, growing larger in her vision every moment, as her courser threw turf into the air behind her.

The dull, rhythmic thuds of another horse's hooves barely registered in her left ear as she continued forward. The nose of Sudro's piebald mare just entered her vision with a hundred and fifty yards left to run. She pushed her beast, but already he gave everything he had left. The finish line was moments away, and now Sudro's horse was even with her stirrup. Her eyes and brain churned, judging distance, time, and speeds; it would be close. Closer than she would allow.

Gwyn made a subtle lean and twitched her reins. Her horse, prepared by long hours of training, executed Gwyn's intent with a hard cut to the left, taking Sudro's mare completely off guard. She reared up in shock, tossing Sudro to the ground. Gwyn flew down the last hundred yards unopposed, her nearest competition barely making up any of the few lengths they had lost at the start.

Gwyn threw her arms in the air, cheering herself and turning to the crowd. The applause came in sparse and weak, and she frowned as many in the crowd already dispersed. She saw Adric shake his head as he walked away with Aldrin and Lirisch.

The finish line judge walked from the crowd, threading a strip of the Candon tartan through the ring on a carven medallion, but his tone was not congratulatory as he yelled, "Winner," and handed the medal to Gwyn. Tehgil and Lischa came only a few steps behind. Lischa wore a broad smile, but Tehgil scowled.

"That was wonderful, Gwyn!" Lischa called, clapping her hands. "Nobody can best you in the wrestling and fighting tomorrow; you're sure to take at least three first place medals this year."

Gwyn beamed at her mother's approval until she turned to see the judge's backslapping and congratulations in awarding the second and third place medals, placing them around the winners' necks after they'd dismounted. She looked down at her own medal in her fist with a frown.

"That was a dirty play, Gwyn," Tehgil scolded.

Lischa protested as Gwyn replied, "I didn't do it. My courser doesn't like any horses sneaking up on his left; he just cut over on his own."

"See?" Lischa put in. "That other boy shouldn't have tried to come up so close."

Sudro, meanwhile, now crossed the line, leading his mare.

"Congratulations," he called over, his voice flat. "Too bad I won't be at your Clanmeet next year. I'd love a rematch."

"Why wait?" Gwyn challenged.

Sudro shook his head. "My horse is tired. She needs rest, not another sprint."

"Hang the horses then; I'll race you on foot!"

Sudro shook his head with a snort. "You win."

"Coward," Gwyn spat.

Sudro kept walking. "If you say so, Candon."

Gwyn finally dismounted. Lischa looked over her shoulder at a call from Adric in the distance and walked away. Tehgil walked with Gwyn as she led her horse to the corral where the Candon animals were held. "Girahl would have been prouder of a second-place finish than knocking an opponent out the way you did," he admonished.

"I told you," Gwyn complained, "it was the horse." Her control of the mount had been subtle and Tehgil's point of view had been from afar. As importantly, her voice carried no hint of deception.

"I hope that's really true," Tehgil replied. "Only you know for sure. There's no rule against what you did; it's meant to be training for warfare, after all. I've been the first to teach you not to fight fair when the fight is real. There's a place for honor in your life, though. Never forget that, Little Gwyn."

Tehgil hurried away before Gwyn could protest. Neither noticed the older woman with soft, brown hair listening from a respectful distance.

True to Lischa's prediction, Gwyn dominated the combat events the next day, and with tactics none could gainsay, though her savagery, as always, caused tongues to wag. She'd hoped to best Sudro, but he was knocked out early by other fighters in mock weapons and didn't compete in wrestling at all. Two older boys, both sons of master trackers, were in their last year of competition before attaining manhood and kept their places in the tracking event, relegating Gwyn to third. Several youths took better game in the hunt, but none as quietly as she did. Of course the clans held a host of other events in logging, agriculture, husbandry, and crafts, but Gwyn ignored them all. Tehgil's words still nagged at her. When she returned home, she hung her fighting medals, and even her third-place tracking award, on the wall with the others, but she threw the first place horsemanship medal into a trunk and rarely looked at it again.

CHAPTER II

Three years later…

Gwyn sat in Tehgil's simple home on her sixteenth birthday, coughing over an empty whiskey tumbler as she absently fingered a cloak clasp of pewter and garnet, a gift from the older man. This had been her first drink of liquor, a passage into adulthood better celebrated with friends, but Gwyn had none.

In her final years of childhood the early growth spurts had not slowed, and having reached nearly six feet she now towered over others her age. She had, nevertheless, kept her mother's narrow frame save for broad shoulders. Gwyn appeared thin and hard as flint, her back stiff and face unreadable. Her muscles had matured into whipcords capable of lashing into action in a blink and striking like hammers when directed in violence. Indeed, her slight build only made her feats of strength seem the more terrible. Even growing into adulthood, she combed out her hair but little more often than she had as a child; it sprayed out from her head like a fiery mane and trailed down her back in tangles styled only by the wind and her constant activity. Likewise, training and the elements sculpted her taut body and darkened her skin just half a shade more than other Atlund women. To most eyes, this rugged strength was something short of alluring, but the flower of young womanhood bloomed in her features, and some of the young men noticed. Gwyn noticed them, too, but didn't think about them much, fearing dalliances would blunt her edge and fail to impress her mother.

Tehgil remained her only consistent companion, but even their conversations had become forced as Gwyn stumbled her way into adulthood, and his house was mostly quiet even as they celebrated her birthday together. "Tehgil," she finally asked, "I've always known you were the last one to see my father alive, how you bore his sword back to the village. Nobody would ever tell me the whole story. 'When you're older, when you're older.' Well, I'm not a child anymore. How did it happen? What did he say as he died? Why did he... Did he even know about me?"

Tehgil stood from his modest table, taking another glass of whiskey as he went. He paced to the window and stared out at the tree line to the west, as he had done countless times since Girahl was lost to him, letting his mind drift back to the time when his best friend was alive. A moment before Gwyn could speak to force or withdraw the question, he spoke.

"Understand, Little Gwyn, that Girahl was more than a friend or comrade to me. He was my blade-brother, a bond even greater than family or clan. I still have scars I earned saving his life in battle, but no more than he had for me. I never went to war without him. When I married, I asked him to assist the Priest of Terillah, and he was to be the oath-father to my son, had the little one not been taken from me. I would trade my life for his even now. All these years later, if my death could bring him back to you, I'd call my life forfeit. And yet, that day, he chose to ride into battle alone. He'd been gone for hours when rumor reached me that he'd ridden into the forest, and the wizard Kellgore's minions were growing in strength and number.

"Between us, Girahl was the better fighter, but he could never match me for speed on a long ride. I picked up his trail and tracked after him faster than I've ever done, but he was moving with awful speed. The closer I came to Kellgore's stronghold, the easier it got, though. His trail was marked by the bodies of slain minions lying thicker with every league, enough I could pick up some ground even after sunset. It was summer, and the days were long.

"I was still miles short of Kellgore's keep when I saw him stumbling into a clearing–"

"Where?" It was the first sound Gwyn had made since Tehgil began his story.

"Along the stream that runs through the north side of the village," Tehgil answered, his voice still distant. "Twenty miles or so upstream there's a clearing surrounded by white birch. That's where I saw him, bleeding from a dozen wounds, stumbling, his left arm hanging limp at his side."

He turned from the window to gauge Gwyn's reaction. He hesitated, loathe to cause her pain, but for so long he had carried this memory alone. Now that he had begun, he could not easily hold back.

Gwyn sat, staring past Tehgil out the window, her face blank and jaw set. She nodded, bidding Tehgil forward. She had been raised on the legend of Girahl, and the time had come to hear that legend's end.

"I sprang from my horse and ran to him," Tehgil continued, "to catch him as he fell. I was much sprier in those days. His great sword, covered in minion blood, dropped from his fingers. 'Girahl, are you mad?' I cried to him. 'Why did you do this?'

"'Kellgore must be stopped,' he said. 'His spells blast armies, but I thought one man might slip through.' I wanted to ask him 'Why now?' but already I could hear the snarling of the minions as they came crashing through the brush just moments behind. 'Hurry,' I said, and tried to pull him toward my horse.

"'You'll never make it out,' he told me, 'not with my weight. I won't last anyway. You were the truest friend. I'm sorry. Take my blade. Bear it back home. Tell her and Lischa, tell them both that I love them. And watch over the girl. You know you were to be her oath-father. You shall be her only father, now.' And then he…"

"And then he died." Gwyn's voice was flat, though Tehgil's had grown hoarse through the tale, hoarse from holding back tears.

Tehgil was silent for a moment, then nodded stiffly. "I barely managed to mount before the minions broke into the clearing. I flew from there faster than I've ridden before or since, nearly rode the life from my horse in the doing. Not for myself. After I'd lost my family a couple years before, watching Girahl die drove all the love of life out of me. But he had set me to a task, and I would finish it, whatever it cost. A day later I snuck back, hoping to at least bring back his body, but…"

Gwyn was quiet, and for a few moments Tehgil watched her jaw bunch as she stared into infinity. Finally she asked, "He knew Mother was with child? With me?"

"He knew. Somehow he even knew you'd be a lass. I never could ask him how." Pain still strained through Tehgil's tones.

"He knew. Then why did he do it? Why did he go off to die and leave me without a father!?"

Tehgil stood silent for a long time, wrestling with an understanding of Gwyn's bitterness and offense at her accusation of Girahl's selfishness or irresponsibility or whatever she believed it was. "I don't know, Little Gwyn," he answered at last. "That's just one of the questions that has haunted me these sixteen years. But it couldn't have been pride or greed; that wasn't his way. Whatever it was, it must have been very important."

"More important than raising his own daughter?" Gwyn spat.

By this remark Tehgil was angered and pained, but to it he had no reply. Gwyn awaited one only a moment, then stormed from the longhouse.

Tehgil gave no thought to following her. There was no reasoning with her when she was like that, anyway. Hours passed before anyone began to fear something must be amiss, for dusk was fast approaching. Wondering if she'd snuck back home already, Lischa checked her room and only then found the note.

She rushed immediately to the parchment on Gwyn's pillow, picking it up with trembling fingers. After scanning it only a moment, however, she returned to the main room and held the note out to Tehgil. He watched as her shoulders sagged forward and she seemed to shrink somehow, as though something holding her up and quaking under the strain had finally snapped.

On accepting the parchment, Tehgil saw a clue toward Lischa's reaction, for the note was not addressed to her. He puzzled through the words with head-scratching difficulty, for he read but poorly and Gwyn's penmanship left much to be desired, but in time he reached the end.

Tehgil,
     I apologize for my behavior in your home. I am
a grown woman now and must leave childish fits

behind me. You have treated me better than anyone, have loved me as a daughter even though I am not your blood. I know, by your praise, that my father really was a great man. I love him, even without ever knowing him. I know his reason for striking against Kellgore when he did must have been a good one, and he kept his quest secret to save you, to leave me a father if he failed. Now, I am his only legacy, and his memory deserves better treatment than it got today. He shall have it.

Tehgil puzzled only for a moment at Gwyn's last sentence before rushing past Lischa to Gwyn's bedroom, pinning his gaze on a pair of new pegs in the wall, now empty. Upon gaining adulthood, Gwyn attained her birthright as a warrior and, with it, her chief tool of that trade: Girahl's sword, the ancestral blade of the Candon line.

Now it was gone.

"That little liar," Tehgil hissed, his tone of longsuffering frustration rather than rebuke. Gwyn hadn't needed the story of Girahl's death, Tehgil realized. She could have pieced most of it together from overhearing things through the years. All she required, because Tehgil had never spoken it aloud since reporting it to the clan elders, was the location. Had her outburst even been genuine? The note implied so, but who could tell now? The result was the same, that no one would miss her for a few hours at least. Now that Gwyn had stepped into the rights of her birth, she would waste no time in taking the responsibilities as well. She would avenge her father immediately or die in the attempt.

The notion was madness, a slip of a girl taking a five-foot sword into the wilderness to kill the most dangerous sorcerer in living memory. Still, thought Tehgil, what but madness could be expected from the Windborne?

Now, however, Gwyn's Windborne status was more than superstition or temperament. It complicated pursuit, her birth during the weeks of Wind preventing any nighttime search around her birthday. The winter days were brutally cold, of course, but Atlund blood and breeding were Gwyn's; enduring their frigid homeland was as much her birthright as blade or croft. The Wind that ruled the dark, though, was another matter. Even Tehgil, dearly as he loved the girl, would not brave the Wind, for it could not be conquered. He could only pray Gwyn would find shelter until morning.

Dawn came with still no sign of Gwyn. Tehgil mounted a search party while riders sped northeast to the Citadel, to King Vassin VI, Chief of the Vassin Clan and King of All Atlund, who was also Gwyn's second cousin, once removed, on her father's side. These riders bore messages beseeching the king to send his most skilled trackers. Unfortunately it had snowed during the night, just heavily enough to cover any tracks Gwyn might have left. Dogs were dispatched, but these were not the great Hounds of old, and between the snow and whatever steps Gwyn had doubtless taken to cover her scent, they could pick up no trail. Even along the stream leading to the place of Girahl's death, they found nothing. Tehgil had taught her woodcraft too well.

This fruitless endeavor continued for two full days after Gwyn's disappearance. Glimmers of hope came in the form of a mark here or a scent there, but all led to nothing. Deeply pained, Tehgil sent the search parties home on the third day to rest and see to their families after he had spotted sign of Kellgore's minions the day before; he would not risk the lives of many to save the life of one, no matter how dear. *His* life, however, was his own to spend, so Tehgil went out alone on that third day. Though he slew a pair of minions who picked up his trail and tried to ambush him, still he found no sign of Gwyn. He did discover another pair of minion bodies, but they had been savaged as if by wolves or an angry bear, or perhaps had turned their teeth on one another.

Racing back to the village as dusk approached, Tehgil mounted the western lookout tower, determined to stand as he had for the past two nights, watching and refusing shelter until the first gusts of Wind stirred the trees. After a few minutes, he saw movement in the foliage at ground level, followed by the wraithlike emergence of a single figure. Tehgil's heart leapt as the spotters on the walls cried out their recognition and ordered that the wicket gate be opened.

Gwyn staggered toward the open door in the wall of rough-hewn timbers, the village suddenly ablaze with torches, bathing the area just inside the gate in guttering, orange light. As Gwyn limped into view, the crowd let out a collective gasp.

Her father's great sword dragged limply behind her, its point leaving a shallow furrow in the dirt and pine needles. Her clothing was covered in blood, her hair likewise and matted with leaves and twigs. Through a handful of rents in her thick, winter garb, her own crusted blood could be seen holding together ragged claw wounds. Her right ankle, twisted and swollen, dragged behind her awkwardly. About her neck was a crude necklace of minion fangs laced on a bloody sinew.

Desperate and macabre as this was, none of it stunned the witnesses like her eyes. They stared straight ahead in their sockets, perceiving without seeing. Even a large bruise covering most of the left side of her face stole no notice from the horror haunting those eyes. More chilling still, despite their lifeless aspect, the green irises sparked with a hellish madness.

Tehgil took one step toward her; Gwyn tried to come to defense by reflex, her grip tightening slightly on the great sword, but, lacking the strength, instead she collapsed in a disheveled heap at his feet.

The watching townsfolk, shocked into stillness throughout her entrance, sprang suddenly to action, Tehgil pitching forward in an attempt to catch the girl as others quickly slammed shut the gate and threw fast the bolts and bar against the baying of minions now heard in the forest fringes. Archers bounded up the steps to the ledge that ran along the inside of the wall, loosing flaming arrows into the watchfire wood piles that dotted the strip of cleared land between the forest and the village, hoping to drive the minions back or even pick off a few before being forced into shelter by the Wind. Lischa, nearby during Gwyn's staggering entry, rushed forward, cradling Gwyn's head in her lap and feeling for breath from the cracked and bloody lips. With difficulty Tehgil pried Girahl's sword hilt loose from Gwyn's right hand and passed it off to Aldrin to be taken back to the house. A few townsfolk bolted off to the north edge of the village to fetch the physician from his evening meal, while others chose spirit over body, or perhaps realism over optimism, and sought the Priest of Terillah. Tehgil, waving off a pair of stretcher-bearers, hoisted Gwyn in his thick arms and bore her toward Lischa's house. "The Wind quickens," he bellowed. "Let them bring the healer and the priest, you rest get back to your homes, while you can."

Tehgil laid Gwyn down on her bed just as the doctor and priest rushed through the doorway. Anxiety covered both their faces. "Has the Wind taken her?" asked the priest. "If she's Windtouched, there's nothing either of us can do," he added, indicating the physician.

"Won't know that 'til she wakes up," Tehgil replied. "Meanwhile, I suggest you perform your duties while she has breath, at least."

The night passed slowly and sleeplessly for all in the home, the physician and priest eventually declaring they had done all they could and taking it in turns along with Gwyn's stepfather to watch over her. This was a grim duty from which Lischa and Tehgil were excused by their closeness to Gwyn, for each watcher held a sturdy cudgel with which to brain the girl if she was found to be Windtouched when she awoke. The men bore the burden unhappily but without complaint.

Relieved from this obligation but still unable to sleep, Lischa found Tehgil sitting at a small table near the hearth, diligently cleaning Girahl's sword of dried blood and redressing the edges with a flat stone, a steaming mug sitting untouched beside him. Lischa collapsed with exhaustion into a chair across from the weary warrior.

"I love this sword," Tehgil said as much to himself as Lischa. "It has its scars, but the love of generations is in this blade. Strange, though. It feels colder somehow."

Lischa ignored him, then after a few minutes stated without preamble, "Adric thinks she's Windtouched. He won't say it, but I can tell."

"Adric always thinks more than he says," Tehgil answered. "That doesn't mean he's always right."

"There's something else he won't say that *is* right. He thinks this is all my fault."

Surprised, Tehgil laid the Candon blade on the table, his work now finished, and at last looked up to meet Lischa's gaze. In it he saw a pain he hadn't noted before, finally realizing the change Gwyn's disappearance had wrought. "Let's say Adric does think that. You agree?"

"Why shouldn't I? All these years I pushed her, for what? To gain a vengeance that won't return my dead husband to me. And later, after Adric, to find a vengeance that won't ease the guilt I feel for marrying again, looking to someone else for contentment. The last year I've doubted myself, wondered if I should change my way with Gwyn, but I was so proud of her strength and her fearlessness, and I love Girahl so much, I thought maybe, just maybe, she really could avenge him. So I held onto the anger and the grief and pushed even harder. Why? We don't know what happened out there; maybe she killed Kellgore, by some miracle. Maybe she found vengeance for Girahl and finished what he began all in one stroke. And if she did, is it worth the price? She *is* probably Windtouched and as good as dead now, and even if she isn't she may be just as mad after what she's been through. By Terillah, you saw the chain of fangs around her neck. She didn't get those by asking…"

Tears streamed down Lischa's face, and her speech became inaudible at the thought of what Gwyn had become, of what *she* had made her.

Only on seeing Lischa broken did Tehgil truly realize how much he blamed her, for even in her regret he had no words of absolution. Training Gwyn as a warrior, as was her desire and right, while trying to temper her undue aggression had been an impossible feat, and one in which Lischa had offered no support. "We all do what we feel is best at the time," he finally muttered. "Sometimes we realize we were wrong soon enough to do some good. Sometimes not." Tehgil picked up his mug and, sliding his chair noisily back from the table, turned to leave the hearth.

Dawn stole quietly into the Candon house, finding Gwyn still drifting in feverish sleep. She mumbled softly, her eyes darting wildly beneath squinted lids, as though she tried to rise into consciousness which eluded her like a shadow. At midday she became just lucid enough to ask brokenly for water, but after drinking three large tumblers dry, she sank back into her nightmares. The priest and physician both whispered to Tehgil outside Gwyn's room.

"Still too soon to be sure," the doctor equivocated, "but she didn't try to murder anyone straight away. Maybe she's not Windtouched, after all."

"What of her body, then, the wounds and fever?" Tehgil replied.

"One of the deeper wounds in her side seems not to be healing properly," the physician responded. "This is the cause of the fever; her body tries to burn out the sickness. In a weak person, this would mean certain death, but Gwyn is young and strong. If she wakes up by tomorrow and starts eating, I think there is a good chance. If not…" he ended without saying what needn't be said.

Tehgil's jaw was set, his face grim. "Is it too soon yet to say how her mind will be? Even supposing the Wind didn't take her, I mean, clearly she's done things."

"She won't be the same, if that's what you mean," the priest finally spoke up. "She's a killer now. You know yourself you can't go back."

Tehgil silently nodded.

"What she went through must have been more terrifying and savage than any fight I've known," the priest continued. "Alone, untested, beset on all sides by creatures that would gladly eat the flesh from her bones, or worse. She's reliving it all right now, in her tortured dreams. She can't bear this alone; when she awakens, she'll need to tell everything, and the sooner the better."

"I'll be here," Tehgil started to assure.

"It won't be you," the priest interrupted.

"What do you mean?" Tehgil demanded. "Why not?"

"She's done brutal things, Tehgil, dishonorable things. Just look at the fetish of teeth she's made. She's carved up the dead to adorn herself. We can't know why, may never know, but it isn't how you raised her, and Terillah alone knows what else she's done out there. She won't talk to you. She'll be too ashamed."

"Who then?"

The priest shrugged. "I may be able to help. I wasn't always a priest."

"We'll see," Tehgil sighed. "I'll be surprised if she'll talk to anyone. She's always carried her burdens alone."

"This one will be her heaviest yet. Possibly too heavy for one so young. It may break her."

"If she isn't broken already, it would be a miracle worthy of Terillah himself," Tehgil sighed.

The priest looked at Gwyn as she tossed, mumbling in another nightmare. "It would, at that."

The watch continued with only slightly less tension. The little moon sat low in the east while *Aridan*'s crescent sunk into the west, and starlight filtered into Gwyn's window. Her older half-brother, Aldrin, had been watching over her before finally drifting off to slumber in the silence of the house. A gentle snore escaped his lips, and at that barest noise Gwyn bolted upright in bed, her hand flying toward her calf where she normally strapped her dirk. Finding it missing, she cursed under her breath, at which Aldrin began to stir. Gwyn was on him like a panther, throttling the boy with her bare hands as he gasped her name, trying to make her recognize him.

The door boomed open, Tehgil's bulk framed in the opening as the old warrior quickly assessed the situation. He leaned forward to grab Gwyn in his massive hands, but she darted off Aldrin, around Tehgil's grasp, and into the great room where the rest of the family sat. As Lischa screamed from the corner for Gwyn to come to her senses, the wild-eyed girl bounded to the table before the hearth where rested the sword of Girahl, its steel reflecting the guttering flames. Whipping the blade up with such speed it seemed almost to leap into her hand, Gwyn dashed out the door into the chill night.

"She's Windtouched!" Adric shouted.

"Maybe not," Tehgil challenged, striding to the door.

The doctor, nearing panic, shouted, "If she wasn't before, she will be. You've got barely a minute to get her inside."

Tehgil was halfway out the door, the priest, roused from his prayerful vigil and remembering his soldiering days, right behind.

Gwyn sprinted into the night, her feet slamming the ground and driving her forward despite her barely healed ankle, pursued in her mind by unseen demons, bellowing "Kellgore!" with all her strength. She flew through the darkness like a scream, Tehgil and the Priest losing ground with every stride behind her. Tehgil, knowing he was no match for the Wind, counted the seconds since his exposure began, ready to turn on his heel and flee back to the house at the halfway mark as his hope of catching Gwyn vanished like windblown smoke.

Then, as suddenly as she had begun her mad dash, Gwyn stopped dead in the center of the town square beneath the wan light of the moons. The name of her enemy finally catching in her ragged throat, she slammed the point of the Candon great sword into the frozen earth, gripping the guards and sagging against the blade as she wept, "Father, I'm sorry. I've failed you. Kellgore lives."

Arriving just in time to hear the last of her hushed confession, Tehgil scooped the girl up around the waist in one giant arm and swept her over his shoulder as the Priest collected the sword of Girahl. Gwyn pounded Tehgil's back, screeching, "Put me down, Tehgil. I'm no use; I've failed us all. Do as I deserve. Let the Wind take me!"

Tehgil, his feet smashing the frosted grass back to Lischa's longhouse, shot back, "Over my frozen corpse, you foolish brat. And stop behaving like a child," he added as he skidded through the door, "you're a woman now. You embarrass yourself."

Adric slammed the door shut behind the Priest, who entered two steps behind Tehgil, and the rescuers collapsed to the floor, shivering with cold but otherwise unharmed. Gwyn extricated herself from Tehgil's grip and started toward the hallway. The rest of the residents moved out of her way and watched as though a hungry wolf stalked the house, waiting to see what horrors the potentially Windtouched girl might commit. Tehgil, however, stopped her with a withering shout.

"Where in the hells do you think you're off to, lass?"

"To be alone," she shot back, not turning.

"Oh, no. Explain yourself, young lady. What was in your head, running out there like that?"

Now facing him, she ordered, "Stop talking to me like a child!"

"I'm not. I'm talking to you like a grown woman who I expect to be responsible for herself. By all rights you should have been left out there to die. Have you any notion how many lives have been risked since you went missing?"

Lischa stepped in, yelling, "You can't talk to her like that. You're not her–"

Tehgil turned toward Lischa, and the steel in his stare silenced her. "Do not," he grated, "say I'm not her father. Never again."

"He's right, Lischa," Adric said, his voice low. "I did the best I could with Gwyn, but she never accepted me. That's alright. Tehgil was better for her than I could have been. Still, you did neither of us any favors trying to bring her up right."

Finally breaking from the distraction, Tehgil looked up to find Gwyn gone from where she had stopped at the edge of the hallway. Fighting a sense of momentary panic, he saw the priest still guarded the front door and noticed the curtain to the storeroom askew. Slowly, he turned back to the main room, addressing Lischa once more. "I have to attend to this. Unless you'd like to…"

Lischa shook her head and fled, as her silent tears broke out into choked sobbing, to her bedroom. Adric shook his head. "The last few days have been hard on her."

"Maybe the last few *years, we* haven't been hard enough," Tehgil rebutted.

"I can coax a crop from the most infertile soil in the north," the younger man answered, "but working a change in a stubborn woman so full of pain…that's a miracle beyond me. Maybe this is the proper season." He nodded to Tehgil and went after Lischa.

Tehgil found Gwyn sitting on a water barrel in the storeroom, her back to the curtain, chin on her chest. In her hands was the minion-fang necklace which she passed between her fingers, rubbing one of the larger fangs like a worry stone. Tehgil rested a hand comfortingly on her shoulder, but she recoiled as if burned, blocking the gnarled hand away with her left forearm and visibly fighting the urge to counterattack. Her eyes gleamed, pupils dancing around the small space, searching for possible danger with twinkling anticipation. That anticipation, Tehgil thought, was not concern but eagerness, suddenly giving him the impression he shared the storeroom with a coiled serpent looking for its next meal. Slowly, with concentration, Gwyn relaxed her guard, as though it required more effort to be still than to attack.

"I'm sorry I put you in danger, Tehgil," she finally said. "Since I failed, I suppose I'm sorry about everybody else, too. To me, it would have been worth all their lives had I succeeded, but I'd not see them wasted on a failure like me."

Hesitantly, Tehgil searched for words of forgiveness or encouragement, or even rebuke of Gwyn's self-loathing, but found none. Still awed the girl was even alive, all he could do was give voice to that shock. "What happened out there?"

After a brief silence, Gwyn stammered, "It was…" Finally, she turned toward Tehgil once more, her eyes rimmed red with unshed tears. "You shouldn't ask questions you don't want the answers to."

"But I do," Tehgil replied, his voice soft with compassion. "Gwyn, you're not alone. No warrior walks out of battle without memories of things he wishes he hadn't done, hadn't *had* to do. Whatever happened, I'll understand. And your father would understand."

Gwyn just shook her head, rising from the barrel and pushing past Tehgil into the hallway, picking up speed as she headed toward her bedroom. "Gwyn!" Tehgil shouted after her.

"I'll be fine, Tehgil," she croaked back. "Just leave me alone. Please, in Terillah's name, just leave me alone." Her door closed fast behind her with finality, banishing the house to silence.

The hours to another dawn crawled by, and the first shafts of wan light found Tehgil on the green in front of the Candon longhouse, stretching his aging muscles as his breath fogged in the frigid air. The activity and movement of the day had cleared the roads, but snow still covered the rooftops. Tehgil could only guess how few hours he'd slept in the past several days, but the man had reserves of toughness that belied his age. In truth, he hadn't passed his forty-fifth year, but those years had been hard ones. He remained alert as, from the northeast quarter of town, he heard the approach of rapid hoofbeats against the hardpacked earth of the streets. Moving his hand to the hilt of the short sword he always wore at his hip, he sauntered over to the house's front door and leaned in the frame, waiting for whatever would come. The rider sped into view within a few moments, and Tehgil instantly recognized the royal livery and moved out to greet him. "Hail, Courier! What news of the king?"

"He has responded to your summons. I am sent ahead of the entourage to inform you that they will be here by midmorning."

Tehgil inhaled sharply. "Blast, the riders." In the chaos of Gwyn's return, Tehgil had utterly forgotten the messengers sent to King Vassin requesting aid in the search. "I deeply apologize," Tehgil said to the courier. "You may inform the king's men that the girl has been found and that the trackers are no longer needed."

The courier grimaced and cleared his throat in obvious annoyance, but he kept a civil tongue. "I've been unclear. His Highness is almost here, now. *Personally*. Certainly you could spare him a meal for his trouble."

Now understanding, Tehgil responded with more courtesy. "Of course, of course. As His Highness pleases, we would be honored. Again I apologize for not sending word that Gwyn had been found. Things here have been confused."

Softening, and now with genuine concern, the courier asked, "She wasn't Windtouched, then? His Highness will be eager for news as well."

"No," Tehgil replied, "she's not Windtouched. Though perhaps something nearly as bad." With difficulty, Tehgil related the incident in brief to be relayed back to King Vassin VI.

~ * ~

Vassin was an unusual man and an even more unusual king. Still young, only in his thirty-fourth winter, he had inherited the throne a few years earlier when his father died in a brutal raid by crazed nomads from east of the mountains. In ages past, when the many independent clans that inhabited the north confederated into the Nation of Atlund, the chieftains and elders formed the Conclave to manage joint affairs. In time the Conclave created the monarchy to serve as a supreme executive, holding a Kingmoot with the passage of each king to determine whether his heirs would retain power. Arrogant leaders tended to fare poorly, and the Kingmoot typically handed the throne to another clan after such a king died. Indeed, a small bloc of oligarchist elders, its size and influence waxing and waning with the generations, always seemed willing to abolish the monarchy altogether. A successful king of Atlund was one who could lead without resorting to power, and by this measure Vassin ruled well. He was loved almost universally and trusted even by his detractors, for he was a man whose deeds followed his words. Through this trust he directed his people, guiding where others might command, and in this lay his greatest strength, for while the Conclave might limit the power of the king, they could do nothing to deny the charisma of the man.

Midmorning had passed into late morning when the king appeared before the Candon home, accompanied by only four of his bodyguard. The entire household, save Gwyn, stood arrayed in the small yard outside the house in preparation for their monarch's arrival, Tehgil in the lead. As soon as Vassin's horse rounded the last corner, the assemblage bent to one knee except for Tehgil. The law declared that the King of Atlund could raise no army, save a guard for his person and demesne, except in times of crisis. Warriors swore fealty only to their clans and, in token of this, bowed to royalty only in times of war. Still, Tehgil's eyes were respectfully downcast as he waited to be recognized; he noted at the edges of his vision the king's well-chiseled features, close-cropped hair, and carefully trimmed beard presiding over a physique that was fit, though small for an Atlunder.

"Tehgil, yes?" the king inquired with confidence as he dismounted from his horse and approached the waist-high wooden gate separating the yard from the road.

"Yes, Highness," Tehgil replied, unsurprised at the king's memory. "Respectfully, I expected a larger entourage. We have begun preparations for twenty."

"They should arrive by the time the meal is prepared, or not much after." Vassin absently motioned for those assembled to stand, a slight but genuine distaste for the formality edging into his body language. "You know," he continued, "when I was a boy, my father's stable masters were always careful not to give me too fast a horse, lest I fall and hurt myself. Now I am king, and I can have as fast a horse as I like, but they've tied me down with so much baggage and freight in the train, and so many guards and advisors looking after, that I have to sneak out of my own caravan to make good time."

"Please, Highness," Tehgil replied, "don't take undue risks on our account."

The King frowned. "I'm more than capable, Tehgil. I was only attempting to lift all your sour spirits with a light jest, but perhaps it is too soon for humor. Or the jest wasn't funny."

At this Tehgil did show at least the beginnings of a smile. "I'm sorry your effort went to waste, Highness. I'm afraid the house of Girahl is in too much sadness for even the jest of a king to cheer it."

"Don't apologize, friend. I've not been to this house before," Vassin pressed on, deftly changing the subject, "though I did meet Girahl when I was a boy, and he was in his prime as a warrior then. I remember liking him almost immediately, as most did, I'm told. Some even say that Father had tried endlessly to entice him into moving to the Citadel to join the Royal Guard, but Girahl would have none of that."

"This village was our home," Tehgil replied. "He could no more leave its defense than stop his breath. But you may be comforted to know he struggled with the decision almost as endlessly as your father offered it."

"Well, as far as I'm concerned I've stood out here holding my horse's bridle in the cold like a fool for long enough, so if none of you good folk are prepared to invite me and my guards inside, I'll have to seek a more willing abode."

By this time the presence of the king was beginning to draw a crowd, so Tehgil, sheepish at his lack of manners, ushered the king and three of his bodyguards into the house while the fourth led the horses away to see to their stabling.

The rest of the King's entourage arrived just before the meal was prepared, and they humbly took it in turns to enter the Candon home and eat, as it would not contain them all. A steward, meanwhile, went door to door to arrange overnight lodging as the small village had no inn. The meal passed in a combination of awkward silence and forced conversation. Gwyn appeared at the start and offered her respect to the king. After that she ate quickly and wordlessly, then retired as politely as she could to her bedroom. The knowledge that all the commotion was happening on her account seemed to grate on her. When the gathering began to wind down, King Vassin took his leave and wandered the main room, eyeing curios and decorations, warming himself at whiles by the hearth. As the final rotation of his entourage entered, causing commotion around the table, he ducked down the back hallway toward Gwyn's room. Finding the door which he had intently watched her enter after leaving the meal, he rapped softly.

"Go away," Gwyn shouted.

"I've grown unaccustomed to taking orders, lass."

"I'm sorry, Your Highness. *Please* go away."

Over the general hum of conversation in the main hall, none could hear the king as he proclaimed, "You'd best be decent, Gwyn of the Family Candon, because I'm coming in."

It took several minutes for the group around the table to realize where the king had gone, but once they did, a crowd quickly formed around Gwyn's door, every ear bent toward the unyielding barrier in the hope of catching some elevated word or phrase. Gwyn's impertinent shouts, they believed, must begin soon, allowing them to hear quite clearly at least half the conversation. All the eavesdroppers perceived was a trade of indistinct murmurs, however, until there came the slightly louder clearing of a throat and King Vassin stating apologetically, "Just a moment."

The door swung open with some violence, and every face was cast to the floor by the withering stare of an annoyed King Vassin. "Hells' teeth, you lot! Can't you figure out I'm trying to accomplish something here? Busy yourselves somewhere, *elsewhere*, if you don't mind."

Tehgil chuckled, "I think we'd all best clear out. I wouldn't like it very much if His Highness had to open that door again."

"No you wouldn't," came the muffled reply from beyond Gwyn's door.

~ * ~

After fifteen minutes the king emerged from Gwyn's chamber and sought one of his pages. "Dorain," he said, "go into my supply wagon and bring me the package I laid out after the advance messenger returned, before I rode ahead here. You know the one?"

"Yes, Highness."

"Good. Fetch it for me and set it on the floor in front of Gwyn's room. Knock to announce it's done, then retreat back here to the main hall. It wouldn't do to have anyone hanging about when I open the door to retrieve it. Understood?"

"Yes, Highness."

"There's a good lad. Now, off you go."

Dorain scurried off to do his king's bidding, and Vassin smiled. "A good lad," he repeated to himself. "Mother was the best cook in Atlund," he said to the half-dozen listeners who had wandered nearby. "Pies so delicious grown men were known to weep at the taste of them. You all might as well find something useful to do. As Tehgil told my messenger, she's in a state, and I have a feeling it's going to take a bit to do anything about it." With that, he turned back to the hallway and Gwyn's door.

The various snoops in the Candon home were staring intently when Dorain returned with the package Vassin had sent him to retrieve, but it was wrapped securely, and the only clue to its contents was a faint tinkling of glass from within.

Adric approached Tehgil with a wary eye. "Tehgil," he started, "shouldn't one of us be in there. I mean, I know he's the king, but they're both unwed, and it's not proper."

"Believe me, Adric," Tehgil answered, "if it was any other man I'd have the door off the hinges and one of his elbows going backwards by now, king or no king. Vassin's a good man, and he could talk the antlers off a summer elk. We should let him try."

Adric nodded and started toward the front door.

"Adric, thank you," Tehgil offered as he left, "for thinking of Gwyn."

It was two hours later, more or less, when the door finally opened again, and King Vassin emerged holding a small earthenware jug in one hand and a pair of glass tumblers in the other. Casually he tossed the jug to Tehgil, who stood nearby. "Split the rest of that with whoever wants some," he said.

Tehgil, catching the jug, looked at the writing pressed into the clay, then rubbed at the covering dust in disbelief. "Can this year be right?" he asked the king.

"Far as I know." Vassin paused for a long time as word of his emergence trickled outside and folk started drifting in. Oblivious to this, he appeared deep in thought for a few long minutes as he took a seat by the fire, angling it so he could see the room. Vassin VI was never known as a great orator, but people listened when he spoke, and he had every ear in the Candon home.

"Gwyn has suffered greatly," he began. "A consequence of her own rashness, to be sure, but her intentions were honorable. I hope she will choose to tell her story to others, but let none pry at her for it, or it's no less than myself you'll answer to. She's a woman grown, by law, and a strong Atlunder may keep her own counsel about many things. Her sense of justice and fearlessness do credit to all our people. Perhaps she is more an Atlunder than I am." The listeners waited for explanation of this last statement, but it took time for Vassin to continue. "It's my fault," he said at last. "What happened to Gwyn, to this village, it wouldn't have happened if I had done my duty. I knew

Kellgore had been carving a personal state out of our western forests, had been doing it all my life and before, but I let it go. He didn't have enough power to threaten all Atlund, and the woodland he was taking was too wild to be used for much. I didn't think it was important, and so I traded the honor of my people for peace. Well... *This* is important. The lives Kellgore takes *are important*. And I will cringe from him like a craven dog no longer. I will not shrink from my duty while one of my people, an Atlunder barely into her womanhood, takes upon herself the responsibility of avenging her father's spirit."

While King Vassin spoke, Gwyn had emerged from her room, Girahl's massive blade steady in one hand. Seeing her, Vassin stepped through the gathered crowd and dropped to one knee before her, earning a gasp from the more conservative onlookers. "Gwyn," the king began again, "you have shamed me. You have reminded me what it means to be a true Atlunder. We should seek peace, but if we don't thirst most for justice, peace is only submission. I'm sorry you had to suffer to put me back on the right course."

"None here blame you, Highness," Gwyn replied. Her voice was steadier than it had been since her return, despite the accompanying hint of brandy, but the renewed clarity only made its continuing hollowness the more chilling.

"I know," Vassin replied. "The people trust me too much to blame me for such a thing, and this is the trust I have broken. So my failure is double." Rising back to his feet, the king's eyes fell to Gwyn's sword.

It was a massive, two-handed weapon, its five feet of length making it the height of Gwyn's shoulders. A foot of that length was hilt, wrapped in black leather and a single spiral of braided wire, capped with a wheel-shaped pommel, not hollowed or set with a gem, but convex and heavy, the better to balance the blade. The guards were simple and straight, extending four inches on either side and angled slightly toward the point to keep them clear of the forearms in tight maneuvers. Just beyond the guards, a further six inches of the blade were unsharpened, wrapped in black leather bindings, and protected by triangular protrusions forged on either side of the blade itself—a secondary grip for improved point control or close-in fighting. The blade proper was dull in luster, casting back the sunlight in the diffuse, matte fashion of steels which are polished for use, not decoration, with a broad fuller running most of its length. The taper of the four-foot blade was only slight until the last six inches, when the two edges flared back apart almost imperceptibly, then began symmetrical arcs toward one another to end in a wicked thrusting point. This was a blade without ornamentation or adornment, a warrior's weapon crafted to a purpose, made beautiful not by an artist's frills, but by the love of the generations that had carried it into battle; sanctified not by a priest's censer, but by the blood it had spilled in defense of home and kin. Like the legendary blades of old, it had no magic, no glowing enchantment, but seemed to have developed something greater, a protective spirit and life of its own, born from the faith of numerous warriors who had trusted it with their very lives.

"I've no idea where you find the strength to swing that tree-axe of a sword," the king muttered.

"You've never seen me in a rage," Gwyn responded flatly.

Now that he knew her full tale, Vassin, brave man though he was, shuddered almost visibly at the thought of Gwyn battle-mad in all her Windborne fury. Still, he respected the girl, and she *was* family, even if distantly. He could not deprive her of her birthright. Turning to put Gwyn on one side and the audience on the other, he asked, "Will you continue what you began, *Gwyn et Sheevasa*?

Will you go back into Kellgore's lands, this time with an army of Atlund at your side, and mete out justice for your father's killing? Will you take his sword to strike at the heart of the sickness that infects our western border?"

"If your army can but get me to him, Highness, I swear my father's sword will drink deep of Kellgore's blood." Gwyn's voice was thick with a hatred beyond her years.

A rustle of fabric and scrape of foot against floorboards signaled a motion from Tehgil as he lowered his aging bulk down to one knee. King Vassin regarded him with a puzzled look.

"Duty demands it, Highness," the old warrior answered.

After a moment of hesitation, the King replied heavily, "Yes, Tehgil. We are now at war."

CHAPTER III

The next few weeks were a riot of activity. While moving troops and supplies was difficult until the Wind ceased, Vassin spent the remainder of deep winter setting up Gwyn's village as a forward command post for the coming campaign. The Wind still ruled the night, but the days grew less frigid, and Gwyn used this opportunity to resume the training her wounds and fever had interrupted. After a vigorous sprint around the village perimeter in a padded jack and mail hauberk, Gwyn stopped on the green inside the gates and shed her armor, sitting against the hadun tree that traditionally faced the gates in any Atlund town as the heat of her exertion radiated from her. She slowly regained her breath, amazed at the difference thirty pounds of steel could make, not only in effort but in inertia; changing direction and stopping were both surprisingly more difficult than normal, making tight maneuvers and turns a new challenge. As Gwyn sat, panting, and pondered how this new learning would impact her abilities, a mailed and helmeted man rode a sleek white horse through the timber archway of the eastern village gates. Removing his helmet to show his middle-aged face, weathered and pocked, with flecks of salt beginning to show through his rough-cropped black beard and hair, the man swept his steel gray gaze once across the village before spotting Gwyn sitting against the tree.

"Lass," the man said in a voice meant to be heard, "tell me where I find the house of this brat, barely out of her diapers, who drags a nation to war."

Tired as she was, Gwyn's speed was impressive as she growled inarticulate rage and launched herself at the mounted man.

Bracing himself and yielding by a sideways step of his horse, the older man extended his right arm to full reach, grabbed a fistful of her tunic, and shoved downward as he let go. Gwyn tried to hang on his arm but couldn't find a good grip, her attempt only barely slowing her as she slammed rump-first onto the ground.

The rider maneuvered his horse so he could lean directly over her. "Gwyn of the Family Candon, I presume?" he inquired with disgusted amusement.

Undeterred, Gwyn responded harshly as she picked herself up. "You presume too much. And who are you to come into my village and insult me?"

"*Your* village? It's the clan's village, isn't it? Or your family's village, maybe. This certainly doesn't look to me like a village that belongs to a little girl."

"I am *not* a little girl."

"If you called yourself a maid, I'd say you were one. But you call yourself a warrior and you aren't one, so you must still be what you were before. Until you have some proper blood on your hands, you're just a little girl to me."

Gwyn's hand went instinctively to the necklace of claws and fangs under her tunic but did not remove it for display, for while it proved her mettle, it also evinced her shame. "You still haven't answered my question. Who are you to decide whether I'm a warrior or a child?"

Finally, the rider dismounted, showing he stood only an inch shorter than Gwyn. "I am Nafar of the Family Hradash, Captain of the King's Guard."

Gwyn paused. A shade of anger and arrogance still colored her face, but tempered now with a grudging respect. If any man in Atlund had a greater reputation as a warrior than the man standing before her now, she couldn't name him. When Vassin V had died, it was said Nafar and the royal guard could not be made to quit the field, intending to give their lives avenging the king that had been too bold to be defended, to protect his body by allowing their slain forms to fall over his in a final shielding heap. This they tried to do with a full measure of valor, except they had been too skilled, too ruthless to die on that day. Forming a ring around the King's remains, they battled tirelessly; the tales said the two-dozen guardsmen slew more than a hundred of the nomadic invaders before reinforcements arrived to rout the enemy. For a moment the memories of the little girl, marveling at Nafar's image from afar at Clanmeet, resurfaced to quell the pride of the young woman.

Gwyn's silence pacified Nafar. He took a few graceful steps in an arc to the left, moving clear of his horse and giving Gwyn space enough to maneuver as he spread his arms wide. "Care to try again…*girl*?"

Gwyn lunged once again in her rage, Nafar sidestepping left and leaving his right foot planted to trip her as he dealt a heavy clout between her shoulder blades. Gwyn went sprawling, face-first this time, into the half-frozen mud. Growling, she lashed out with her feet, tripping Nafar in return. His years of experience did him credit, however, as he controlled his fall, hit the ground rolling, and came to rest with his knee on the small of Gwyn's back. Finding her flailing wrists with his gloved hands, Nafar pulled her arms back and pressed with his knee until she was forced to cry out in pain. Still, he was impressed by her toughness; another inch and he'd have been forced to stop for fear of cracking something.

Tossing her arms to the ground, he stood. "You have the heart of a warrior, lass. I'll give you that. But you go into battle without the head of one to match, and the next time you find yourself face down in the dirt, it'll be soaked in your own blood."

Gwyn had no time to retort as she pushed up off the ground, for Tehgil had heard the commotion and strolled out to investigate. "Nafar," he shouted, "well met, but I'll trouble you to stop pummeling the girl."

"The king has instructed me to train her," Nafar yelled back as Tehgil leisurely closed the distance between them. "Let's call this lesson number one," he added to Gwyn as she shot him a venomous look at the implication.

"I can fight!" she spat.

"There's no denying that, Gwyn," Nafar said, perhaps a touch gentler. "My job's to make sure you can *win*."

Gwyn's second lesson commenced the next day. Nafar began simply, calling attack and guard maneuvers for Gwyn to execute. She wielded the great sword while wearing her mail, and to her extreme annoyance Nafar waited agonizing seconds between each call, forcing her to hold every position like a pose. Tehgil had taught her these forms not long after she could walk, and she'd drilled them constantly ever since. Nafar, however, was an exacting teacher, correcting every lapse in her structure down to the eyelash. The tension of his observation tightened her muscles, and by the end of half an hour she gritted her teeth as sweat rolled down her temples in the chill air. Her shoulders burned and arms shook.

"That's enough," Nafar called at last, and Gwyn let the weight of her sword rest on the ground. "Put that away," the captain ordered, tossing a wooden waster to the ground at Gwyn's feet, in length and proportions like her real blade. As she sheathed her sword and set it aside, Nafar picked up a shield and wood sword of his own. Gwyn began to complain any contest wouldn't be fair since she could barely move her arms but decided not to give him the satisfaction.

Gwyn charged in, aiming a diagonal downward slash at Nafar's right side. He blocked with his blade and slammed the edge of his shield, which was full weight and iron banded, into Gwyn's mailed and padded ribs. "The weight of a real sword would have crashed that guard," she protested.

"Maybe. Maybe not," Nafar replied.

This time Gwyn attacked his shield side, knowing he would block, and prepared to sidestep past his counter and launch a new attack. Instead the captain spun to his left, taking the slash on his blade and clouting Gwyn again, backhand, with his shield. The move had exposed his back for an instant, a dance of footwork such a veteran would never risk in a real fight. Nafar was showing off and not even trying to hide it.

Next Gwyn thrust her weapon straight at Nafar's sternum to take fullest advantage of her long blade and force him to choose how to parry so she could respond. He batted the point aside with his shield then drove forward, keeping the banded edge in contact with her weapon to protect himself and crossing his own sword over the rim to thrust at Gwyn's neck, tagging her lightly.

"What is this teaching me?" Gwyn growled.

"I have a feeling what I'm teaching and what you're learning will hardly ever be alike," Nafar answered.

Gwyn half-sighed, half-growled, launching another attack which Nafar parried and riposted just as easily.

"You overcommit to everything," Nafar answered at last. "Your weapon's advantage is reach, but you close too quickly and give that advantage away. That tactic will never defeat a man with a shield."

"It's worked for me every time in the ring," Gwyn argued.

"I said a *man* with a shield. Not a boy. You are reckless and hasty." He paused. "When I gave you the training sword, I never even instructed you to attack me. You just assumed. Think on that. We're done for today."

Gwyn trained almost daily with Nafar. The relationship was tumultuous. Tehgil had taught Gwyn well, and the king's captain managed early on to show the young warrior how the techniques she had learned so carefully had been corrupted, in a sense, by her own emphasis on winning points in competition instead of looking ahead toward battle. Once she opened her eyes to this reality, Gwyn hungrily consumed every point Nafar would show her on form and technique, eager to transform her skills at winning into expertise at killing. The blood of beast and minion alike, slain in her brief sojourn through the deep forest, still lingered in her senses, quickening her pulse with desire and shame entwined.

But why did he challenge her attitude as well? He railed against her unchecked aggression, insisted she see how and when to make a tactical withdrawal despite her heart's every instinct to attack. Repeatedly his counsel was toward defense instead of dauntless attack, and she hated him for it. She would learn everything he could teach of skill, but he would *never* change who she was. And damn him for trying. Just as he tried right now.

They both sat on horseback, Nafar with shield and blade and Gwyn with her great sword. "You'll take a spear for the charge–" Nafar argued.

"Under protest," Gwyn interrupted.

"–so *why* do you insist on using only that giant sword afterward?"

"This is my weapon," Gwyn answered for what felt like the thousandth time. "It served all my ancestors, and it will serve me."

"Why did the old Atlunders even invent such a big sword? It took the best of materials and smiths to make them; more failed and were ruined than were finished. Do you know why they thought it worth the effort?"

"Of course I do," Gwyn spat back. "In the old days great beasts still roamed the lands, beasts that could snap a spear haft in their jaws as easily as a twig. Shields were no use against such a huge monster. The great sword can reach deep to the vitals, with the cutting edges to help open up thick hides better than any spear."

"And do you expect to confront any giant beasts out in the forest now, on this campaign?"

"This is my weapon."

"Fine," Nafar growled. "I don't have all day to argue with you. There's a trick, though, to riding past a body you've spitted with a sword, a way of passing by while turning the arm so the motion of your horse hauls the blade free. With a sword that long, if you don't get it perfect, and I mean *perfect*, every time, there's a list of things longer than the Sharai that will go wrong.

Gwyn smirked. "I guess you'd better teach me how to do it perfect, then."

"I'll teach it," Nafar grumbled.

"I know, I know, 'but I have to learn it.'" Gwyn mimicked.

More weeks passed, the seasonal ending of the Wind allowing for a rapid muster of troops to the new front around Gwyn's village. Dawn was an hour past when she finished her morning jog around the village perimeter in full raiment, sharpening her endurance day by day.

As she stopped to breathe under the hadun tree, she stretched and considered the change in herself. Her whipcord muscles, previously raw and wild, were growing lean and honed. She wore her sword across her back almost everywhere, and its weight felt so natural now she noted only its absence. In addition to polishing her fighting skills, Nafar had taught her awareness and observation; already the practice of sweeping her gaze periodically to all sides, of stopping to listen and identify sounds before ignoring them, had become instinctive to her. Her heart remained in turmoil. As soldiers had arrived for the muster, many had sought out the tale of her sortie into the forest. She had refused them all, revealing her brutality to none but the king himself. Her silence only inspired others to tell the tale for her, and some of what they invented was more heinous than anything Gwyn had actually done. Despite this violent embroidery, none recoiled from the supposed details, instead seeming to view her with all the more awe. Why should she be ashamed, then, for what she'd actually done? Where was the place for honor between enemies and survival? Having lived through it, the margin seemed vanishingly small. She rubbed her gloved knuckles over the mail at her sternum, pressing through steel and padding on the fang necklace until she could feel its familiar digging at her skin.

Many of the men, especially the younger ones but some of the veterans, too, looked at her in a way she couldn't understand. At first these seemed only the gazes she occasionally got from boys, but the more fighters arrived to bivouac around her village, the more she realized these looks were different. The intensity was there, but something replaced the desire, something like awe. The label of "Windborne" that had followed her all her life as an insult, muttered when people thought she couldn't hear, now came with an honorific hush as people speculated what she would really be like in battle. Nafar seemed to think she had become some kind of symbol. She'd overheard him asking the king to relegate her to that role, holding her back when the fighting began. She thought she'd heard the king protest such a plan as she ducked out of sight and earshot, but she didn't care. Hold her back? Let them try.

Another cadre of warriors approached the gate under the tartan of one of the central clans Gwyn couldn't remember. This would be one of the last to arrive, she considered, before they began their attack. Some from farther east might mobilize for a reserve, but any more distant would have to stay in their own lands in case the nomads east of the Qachar range decided to launch a raid.

Gwyn almost turned away to continue her training before she noticed a face she recognized in the riding column. Sudro remained lanky for an Atlunder, but he had filled out in the last three years and sported a fuller beard than any fullblood northerner could muster at his age, though he had it trimmed very close. His brown eyes gazed into the far distance, missing Gwyn entirely.

"Sudro," she called. "Have you come for that rematch?"

Startled, the young man looked toward Gwyn's voice, then shook his head with an eyeroll. "My horse and I have more important business, Gwyn. Yours, too, I think."

She shrugged. "You want to let my victory stand, that's up to you."

He seemed to ignore her as the company rode past. Vacillating for a moment, Gwyn finally followed them to one of the corrals where travelers' horses were being kept, growing more crowded with each passing week. She waited at the gate while the men settled their animals, watching for Sudro to exit as he carried his saddle on his back.

"Why won't you race me again?" she asked when he walked past.

He kept walking, loosely following the rest of his group as they made their way to the side of the village where they were to camp. He looked at her with a raised eyebrow as he moved. "By Terillah, that was three years ago. Who cares?"

"*You* said you wanted a rematch," Gwyn argued.

"Sure, at the time. Who wouldn't, after that move you pulled? That was a long time ago, and obviously it meant a lot more to you than it did to me."

"You don't care about winning?"

Sudro walked a few paces. "Not overly."

"That's the stupidest thing I've ever heard."

"I've heard stupider."

"What's that supposed to mean?" Gwyn challenged.

Sudro shrugged.

Over the next two weeks Gwyn observed Sudro when she could. Talking to him caused an odd reaction in her: she felt warm and anxious. She was quite certain it wasn't love. That, after all, was the province of starry-eyed girls, not sword-wielding warrior women, and more importantly, she wasn't even sure she *liked* the lad. Still, there was something about the way his almond eyes held hers underneath those black, curly locks that she didn't understand and was more than a little afraid to. At last she had the chance to watch him spar and found his fighting style was different as well. Sudro, inferior in strength to his peers, tended to dodge and misdirect rather than block, to seek carefully for openings rather than batter down defenses. This style usually frustrated his opponents, though his defeats, while few, were more decisive than his victories.

One morning after her run, Gwyn ducked under the raised flap of Sudro's tent, thankful for some shade after her exercise. The air was still crisp, but the mid-morning sun shone bright and hot on her armor. Sudro's tentmates were all out someplace, but he sat inside, looking up as the young woman crossed his threshold. His eyes betrayed no surprise, nor the awe so common among the men. "Good morning," he said, his voice infuriatingly nonchalant.

Assuming his fellow fighters had already begun daily practice, Gwyn asked, "Why aren't *you* out training, Sudro?"

"If you paid any attention to orders, you'd know."

"Churl!"

Sudro shrugged. "We're supposed to rest today. Captain's orders. You know what that means?"

"Not really. Where's the rest of your tentmates, if we're supposed to be resting?"

"Out getting into trouble, I imagine. If they knew you were coming here, I'm sure they'd have stayed around."

"And what is *that* supposed to mean?"

Sudro shrugged again. "You can act like you don't know if you want to, but you see how they look at you."

"'They'? Not '*we*'?"

Sudro shrugged once more. "Sorry to disappoint you."

"And who said it disappointed me?"

"Nobody."

Gwyn sighed. She paid little attention to the stares and whispers of the young men of the camp, and she didn't want them from Sudro either, but *some* kind of acknowledgement would be appreciated. He never sought her out but never asked her to go away when she appeared, as though he found her presence or its lack completely inconsequential.

"So what does it mean?" Gwyn asked, changing the subject for want of a rejoinder.

"What's that?" Sudro asked, having lost the thread of the conversation.

"The captain ordering a rest day. You asked if I knew what that meant. If you're so smart, what does it mean, then?"

"I didn't mean it like that. I just heard some of the older men talking, and they said–" A horn blast broke the morning stillness, the rhythm calling all warriors to assembly on the green. "Looks like we get to find out for ourselves," Sudro concluded as he stood, following Gwyn out of the tent.

The King's announcement was brief and clear. Advance scouts had located a minion camp close and large enough for a worthwhile first strike. The army would ride forth with the dawn.

Gwyn roared excitement at the news, a cry joined by cheers from all quarters. Everyone in the camp had grown restless, but Gwyn felt something deeper still, her blood stirring with the knowledge that her need for battle would soon be met.

Captains were ordered to report to Nafar for specific orders. Everyone else was to make ready all the gear and supplies they would carry. Additional orders were shouted to wagon masters and similar noncombatants, but Gwyn ignored them. Within a minute, the village green emptied as the young and seasoned alike went about their preparations in a flurry of activity, methodical in some quarters, frantic in others, but universally quick. Tehgil, his kit long since prepared, walked the lonely green and watched Gwyn from afar.

A woman with soft, brown hair approached him as he neared the gate. "Do you think she'll be alright?" the woman asked.

So aligned was the question with Tehgil's thoughts, he answered it before noticing its source. "I don't know," he said. "I've taught her all I can, and Nafar's lessons will help. Anything can happen in the clash." He finally looked at the woman.

"How do you know Gwyn?" he asked.

She smiled. "Don't you realize by now *everyone* around here knows Gwyn?"

"Of course," Tehgil answered with a nod as he started away. "Keep yourself safe, miss. Most of the defenders will be gone soon."

"Thank you, sir. I'll be careful."

The minion camp lay quiet beneath a westering sun, the slovenly conglomeration of crude tents and hide blankets resting in deep shadow as the burning orb dipped behind the peaks of the Tunari range. At this darkening, one minion began to stir, reaching to his left for a half-eaten chunk of carcass so mangled its species couldn't be guessed. Paying no heed to the flies, it sank its short fangs into the corrupted flesh, tearing off a strip and slurping it down after a few perfunctory chewing motions, movement taken more in lingering devotion to some old and dimly remembered habit than out of any real need. This minion was fairly "young," recognizable even to a casual observer as something that was once a man. It's trousers had long since been discarded, the better to relieve itself without hassle, but the tattered remains of a shirt still clung about its shoulders, eerie reminder of the human soul trapped inside the hairy, magic-twisted flesh. It's hunger temporarily sated, it lurched to its feet, shaking the fog of sleep from its head. Slowly, it picked its way through the sleeping forms to the edge of the clearing to empty its bladder.

Suddenly its nostrils flared, hungrily drinking the air as the scent of horseflesh washed over the reek of rot and offal that filled the clearing. It is doubtful the beast had even a moment to wonder why the smell was so sudden and so overpowering before an iron spearhead ripped through its chest and drove it to the ground. All at once the thunder of hoofbeats shattered the afternoon silence, a rumble punctuated only by snarls and growls as a greater part of the minion troop began to awaken under the onslaught. The surprise now broken, a mighty war cry arose from the throats of charging Atlunders, a challenge no less savage for its humanity, drowning the bestial noises of their enemy.

Gwyn had grown apprehensive as the long, slow ride through the deep woods wore on, a laborious process in which the sleek, cagey horses of the Atlund cavalry negotiated the forest by paths that would have confounded larger breeds. More and more often her hand inched to her neck where the fang necklace hung under her tunic. Most of the young riders on the sortie feared for their lives, but not Gwyn. She feared what she might do.

At the first sounds of steel and terror, though, it was not her mind or muscles that reacted, but something in her soul. The bloodlust burned awake within her, and she urged her sorrel stallion forward into the fray, desperate to feel life ebbing around her blade once more before the day might be carried by lesser men. Ten yards ahead, a minion sprang to its feet and snarled at the Atlunders charging into the camp's southern edge. At a light tap of Gwyn's heels, her mount sped forward as she couched her spear according to Nafar's instruction. The jolt through her body was amazing as the point struck the center of the minion's chest, but her horse barely slowed, the feeling of raw power thrilling Gwyn to her core. She let go the spear haft not a moment too soon as she rode past, reaching down to the foregrip of her great sword to pull it through the lashings that held it to her saddle. Filled with confidence, she adjusted her grip and leveled the blade's sharp point at another minion that had just dodged a charge from one of her comrades, holding the sword out spear-like before her. The minion turned just in time to accept the point through its left shoulder, but everything else went wrong. Out of habit, Gwyn pulled her arm back to withdraw the blade after delivering the point, but by then her horse was well on its way past the target. Too late, she tried to turn her wrist and elbow as she'd been taught, but the angle was wrong, and the weight of the minion fell on the blade like a lever, popping the hilt cleanly from her grip. By reflex, she reached backward for it, and the sudden shift of weight confused her horse, which checked suddenly, destroying Gwyn's balance. She flopped lamely from the saddle, still grappling for her sword which now lay impaled in the minion's shoulder. The minion, though knocked supine and gravely wounded, was still alive, thrashing dangerously with disease-ridden claws. Gwyn approached cautiously, her eyes fixed on the flailing nails as she sought an opening to either take hold of the sword or finish the minion with the dirk she had pulled from her boot.

A sudden snarl from behind caught her attention; she whirled, but too late. Another minion was bare inches from her with its hooked claws outstretched toward her throat. She had not even a moment to cover her eyes before twin gouts of blood sprayed her face as the clawed hands disappeared in a pale, twilit flash of steel. The snarl first turned to a howl of pain, then ended suddenly as a sword point erupted from the beast's right side. Gwyn stood numb as Nafar roughly grabbed her dirk. *"Stupid girl!"* he growled, throwing her knife through the throat of Gwyn's thrashing minion on the ground. "Go get your thrice-damned sword. It's over."

Gwyn looked about in mute awe. The battle had ended in barely a minute. Sounds of crashing and baying could be heard from the west heading swiftly away, but a half-dozen bowstrings twanged, and after that only silence reigned in the clearing. After Gwyn's days of terrible hiding and lone skirmishing in the forest, the swift and sudden brutality of a whole company of her countrymen was somehow thrilling. Her desire to snap back at Nafar lost out to the shame over her failure, and she reclaimed her sword without comment. She knew from repeated experience she hadn't heard the last about her mistakes.

Gwyn was unsettled, though, when Nafar did not appear that night, nor the following morning, to berate her failure, even after the forward camp was established in a clearing about a mile from the first battle–the previous minion habitation having fouled the battle site beyond use. Finally her impatience bested her sense, and she sought the captain herself to dispense with the punishment sooner than later, carrying her sword on her shoulder. Nafar looked up from his breakfast of dried meat and biscuit and stared for a moment before swallowing. After what felt more like minutes than seconds, he finally spoke.

"Gwyn," he began, a sigh underpinning the word, "I've trained hundreds of men in my years. I've trained old men and young, deft men and clumsy, bright men and dull, farmers and warriors, and, yes, more than a few lasses of all those stripes as well. Every one of them I've been able to instruct on at least the rudiments of how to stay alive in a fight. There is always somebody out there faster or stronger, but I'm proud to say none of my recruits was ever slain in a novice mistake. But you? You are easily the most thick-headed creature I have ever been unfortunate enough to *meet,* much less try to teach. At first I blamed myself, but after yesterday… How many times did I show you the care you must use if you insist on using your sword that way? You *know* the right thing to do, you just don't *care.* If I didn't know better, I'd think you *wanted* to die out there." Nafar paused and gazed piercingly into Gwyn's eyes. She shifted her feet. "And maybe you do," he concluded quietly. "Whatever the case, I surrender my responsibility over you. Your training is finished. I've taught you everything you'll learn. You are a warrior. How long you remain one, whether by choice or by death, is up to you now, Terillah save you. Now I've used enough words for a week, so leave me to my breakfast."

Gwyn stood silent a moment, then turned and stalked away. She was at once glad to have completed her training and outraged at being dismissed with such scorn. The outrage she could deal with, or any other emotion if her feelings were clear, but the internal conflict rankled her all the more. It was by unhappy chance that Sudro wandered near as she brooded over her ambiguity.

"Something wrong?" the young man asked, innocently enough.

"Go to hell!" Gwyn shouted, shoving him out of the way.

"You first," the boy retorted, keeping his balance and hooking his foot around Gwyn's ankle.

He truly thought she would drop. He wasn't prepared when she didn't. He felt an impact, then an odd weightless sensation, and the next thing he knew he was sitting on the ground, holding his hand to a throbbing jaw and blinking the spots from his vision. As the starbursts cleared, he suddenly saw the long, fearfully sharp shaft of metal that was pointed at his face, wavering only slightly with Gwyn's ragged, furious breath. Sudro's eyes flicked up to hers, and for a split second he thought he saw something there that couldn't be, a quick flash of green and crimson like an animal's eyes catching torchlight in the dark. He blinked again, and the impression was replaced by a more usual twinkling, barely less frightful, set as it was in an expression as hateful as any he had seen. Still he held her gaze. Though she could slit his throat even with an accidental move, there was no cowardice in him, and he'd done nothing wrong. He would not relent.

Before he could decide what to say, the song of steel hastily drawn filled the air; like lightning Gwyn was forced to whip her blade away from Sudro and into a hard block that stopped Nafar's sword only inches from her neck. Gwyn's focus now solely on Nafar, Sudro scrabbled backward a few feet before standing.

"How dare you?" she spat. "You could have killed me."

"If you were any slower, I would have."

Incensed, Gwyn deftly turned Nafar's blade and launched her counter. The calmer fighter easily blocked her wrathful swing while stepping forward inside Gwyn's reach, forcing her sword down and grabbing her right wrist. With a twist of his left hand and a sudden downward shove of his blade, Nafar disarmed Gwyn, then laid his blade across her throat. Even in her peril, Gwyn couldn't help but remember their first engagements, weeks ago. Gone were the flair, the arrogance, the artful flourish. Nafar engaged her now not as a student but as an enemy: efficiently, dispassionately. It was an attitude he had tried to teach her to no avail. She finally felt a grudging respect for it, even with the realization she could never mimic it.

"This is not a game, lass," Nafar half-growled, half-whispered. "What in the name of Terillah were you thinking of, drawing on a comrade? You could face exile for that, or worse."

"She didn't," Sudro finally spoke up.

Nafar turned his head, keeping one eye on Gwyn as he regarded the lad dubiously. "Explain that."

"She didn't attack me. We were just sparring. I lost."

Nafar sighed. "That's the way you want to tell it?"

"That's the way it was, Captain. Sorry if we startled you."

The captain shook his head, slowly stepping away from Gwyn and finally sheathing his blade. Gwyn reached for her sword, but Nafar took a sudden step back toward her, pushing her off-balance. He grabbed a fistful of Gwyn's tunic to drag her ear down to his mouth. "What do you expect a commander to do with a savage like you? For all your faults, I thought you better than this. Even for a Windborne."

Suddenly a horn blast filled the clearing, accompanied by the sounds of yelling and baying from the western edge of the clearing. The horn's report was cut short, and all in the camp knew the war had claimed its first human life. Nafar still blocked Gwyn's reach to her sword, and she stared at him with a deep anger but an even deeper longing. In that instant, Nafar knew there could be no cure for Gwyn's bloodlust. His choices were clear: he had either to put her out of her misery without further delay or to use her as the weapon she was. The veteran fighter took a step backward as he re-drew his sword.

"Go," he said, not without resignation. "Go and kill."

Ravenously Gwyn grabbed up her sword and ran toward the sounds of the battle. She didn't try to locate her unit, didn't wait for an order, didn't hesitate to choke down the rage rising up in her heart. When first she saw a minion, she launched herself at it, cleaving it's torso almost in half. She felt its tainted blood spatter her face, and for the first time she ignored the pang of shame and let the heat of her hatred surge through her. As she hauled her sword free of her first victim, another minion leapt at her from a low hillock to her left, but she merely stepped to one side and swung upward with all her might. The beast was in two pieces when it hit the ground. An unearthly scream ripped its way free from Gwyn's throat as she drove at the flank of a quartet of the enemy. Two looked up in time to see their deaths. The two remaining howled and ran in abject fear, mindlessly plowing into spears leveled by two younger warriors. The pair looked up at Gwyn with awe, but she barely saw them. Already she was charging at the next knot of minion flesh, now with the two young spearmen at either arm. Two more Atlunders had joined them by the time the next foes were dispatched, and at that moment Gwyn heard a long, ululating cry, a battle wail common to the eastern clans.

Looking toward the sound, she saw Sudro surrounded by three minions. His artful footwork and agility were keeping him alive for the moment, but even as he slew one of his assailants, Gwyn could see three more moving in. Pointing her great blade in that direction, she led her newly formed team on the offensive. Halfway to their beleaguered comrade, a gang of minions crashed into their flank, disrupting their loose formation, but Gwyn charged on, running one minion through from behind as Sudro killed another with his quick, curving blade. Now the pair stood back to back, turning in concert as minions charged in from every side, ever falling to the superior reach and deftness of the Atlunders' weapons. At last the space around them was cleared of attackers, and the horn blasts from the forests reported the enemy in retreat. Without thinking, blood still pounding hotly through her veins and bereft of anything else to kill, Gwyn turned toward Sudro and grabbed the back of his head, kissing him with an aggression that was not quite lust, swollen jaw and all. The taste of blood sparked metallic on her tongue, from when she'd punched him or some subsequent wound she didn't know. Satisfied, she pushed him lightly away, his stunned eyes wide and uncomprehending. Gwyn felt something grab her ankle and spun quickly to face the new threat. A minion, bleeding heavily from the stump of one arm, had clasped at her boot with its remaining hand. Gwyn prepared to defend herself, but the creature's almost-human eyes merely gazed up at her beseechingly. The difficulty was clear as it reached back into its distant past to conjure a human word. "M...mercy?" he begged. Then, more strongly, "P, please! Mercy!"

Gwyn looked into the depths of those eyes but felt no surge of sorrow or pity, only contempt. The warrior scoffed and held the beast's gaze as she raised her sword to cut off its final plea.

Across the battlefield, Nafar watched as Gwyn slowly, with relish, drew her fang necklace out from under her tunic, letting it dangle freely for all the world to see.

CHAPTER IV

By nightfall the camp was secure, and King Vassin's train arrived to join the forward command post. Desperate as Nafar was to move the focus of the campaign to anything other than Gwyn's dramatics, his conversation in the king's pavilion that evening inevitably turned to his erstwhile pupil.

"I've been on the battlefield most of my life, Highness," the old campaigner said solemnly, "and I've seen many heartless things, but that cold decapitation was among the most cruel I can remember."

"Surely that can't be," Vassin replied. "I recall my father's tales from the eastern campaigns, men cutting–"

"That's as may be, my lord," Nafar interrupted, "and I've seen acts more creative in their brutality. That's true enough, but always done by men in grip of the madness of battle, full of emotion. Gwyn was clearheaded, intentional. For Terillah's sake, she'd just kissed a boy!"

This revelation gave the king pause, but with some effort, and a nervously cleared throat, he ignored it and continued. "And what would you have done differently, Nafar?"

Nafar looked at the king and raised an eyebrow.

Vassin looked back quizzically for a moment. "What?"

"For starters I wouldn't have kissed the boy."

"Dammit, Nafar, don't make light. You know what I mean. We've been trying for the better part of a decade to turn minions back to their former lives; you know as well as I that it can't be done. You'd have just watched and let the creature bleed to death?"

"Not likely, I'll admit. But to put it out of its misery, and I doubt that was on Gwyn's heart. It's admirable you try to defend her, Highness. She is your kin, after all. It's just a feeling, a look in her eye I can't trust. If I had a dog as savage as her, I'd put it down. Meaning no disrespect."

"Take care, Nafar."

"I'm sorry, your—"

"No, that isn't what I mean," Vassin interrupted. "You know you can always speak your mind to me. You're no hypocrite, though. If she lives out this campaign and slays in every skirmish, she won't have a tenth of the blood on her hands that you do. Why do you begrudge her the same choices you've made for yourself?"

"You're thinking I don't like it because she's a lass?"

"I don't know, but you did have that answer at the ready."

"Because I've considered it. A man has to know his own heart, as best he can. She isn't the first woman I've trained, though, not by a long stretch. It isn't that."

"What then?" the king pressed.

Nafar wrestled with his thoughts long before replying. "Atlunders love our warriors. It's a belief that keeps our nation alive, but it has its cost in lives…and in sanity. Good training can reduce the one, but there's naught I can do about the other, and I fear Gwyn will pay it. It's a shame for one so young. What of you, though? If you think it should trouble me less, I'd think it would trouble you more. As I said before, she's your kin."

"I'm not *un*troubled; I think you miss my motive. You see in her every warrior you've known who was ruined by a life of war. I see a girl twisted up inside by a mother who couldn't stop grieving. Give her a chance to test this life for herself without anyone over her shoulder, and I think she'll find her way."

"I pray you're right, Highness."

"You doubt my decision about Tehgil, then?"

"No, that was best," Nafar replied. "Our force here is moving slow and cautious, clearing the minions as we go, but if we do need the reserve force in the end, then we'll be needing them quick, and none alive know these forests like Tehgil of the family Tarach. And as for Gwyn, Tehgil shielding her will only delay the inevitable, or worse."

"Shielding her is just what he'd have done, had I let him come along. He didn't like being left behind. I fear I've gone down in his estimation," the king worried aloud.

"I doubt that, Highness. Tehgil is as loyal as the Wind is cold."

"That much I do know, but if Gwyn falls he'll never forgive me."

"So…what then?" Nafar asked.

"So nothing. Cousin or no, her life is in her own hands now."

Gwyn's frustration at her dismissal from Nafar quickly dissipated, replaced with satisfaction. While she had to admit, if grudgingly, such an experienced warrior *could* show her more, she convinced herself she'd seen all he *would*.

A week later Gwyn sat with her troop around a roaring fire, roasting meat and yearning for the next battle while Nafar explained tomorrow's plan of attack.

"Our position will be the right flank," he explained. "We'll be at the head of a small ravine; if the enemy flees after the first clash, they'll likely be forced toward us, so we'll hold position and– *Sheevasa*, are you listening?"

People rarely used Gwyn's full name and never the latter part alone. She found great appeal in simply being called "Vengeance." She had not, however, been listening. "Show me the minions and I'll go kill them, Captain."

Several of the nearby soldiers chuckled. Nafar shook his head and continued his briefing. Gwyn went back to eating and running through prior battles in her head. Her relationship with command, she considered, always worked best when they did the planning and she did the killing.

The next morning Gwyn stood at the center of a dozen men on foot, blocking the top of some ravine. Another dozen stood behind and farther up with bows at the ready. All their horses were picketed some thirty yards back, their liabilities outweighing their advantages in a static, holding action–particularly given minions' unfailing love of horseflesh. Nafar was off somewhere, giving orders to another company, leaving in charge a sergeant whose name Gwyn no more remembered than cared about. At the moment she could see none of the enemy, though she could hear the horns of a charge over a ridge to her left. Her muscles twitched with anticipation.

Since minions carried few weapons and never wore armor, relying on numbers and savagery, no sound of clashing arms carried over the ridge. Instead, shrieks and snarls echoed up the ravine, occasionally punctuated by the scream of a wounded horse or shouts for help from a surrounded man.

Gwyn didn't belong here, waiting for cowards and stragglers to flee toward her. The assault, the slaying, these were her destiny, and she couldn't even see them. Seconds dragged by like hours, but in barely a few minutes a knot of minions rounded a bend in the ravine, sprinting uphill with desperate glances over their shoulders. Gwyn charged down at them, her eyes flashing.

"Hold!" someone yelled, but she paid no heed.

Churning dead leaves and pine needles, Gwyn sprinted toward the enemy with a mighty roar, drawing their attention and wide stares of dismay. Timing her charge and sweep with the edge of her reach, she slashed her blade in a mighty, flat arc. Two minions leapt back, but a third, too slow, took the edge across his naked belly, spilling his guts to the ground. Gwyn let the momentum of her slash carry her in a pivot to the right and drove at the minions on that side, spitting one through the chest and withdrawing her blade with a backward step.

By then the remainder had surrounded her in a loose ring about a foot outside her standing reach. She charged the direction she faced, knowing her steep advantage in equipment would allow her to break through and renew her attack. With quick maneuvers and good footwork, she disabled two more of the enemy before the rest could close on her back. She heard a *thunk* and a scream from behind her. Apparently the rest of the indecisive novices in her troop had finally charged after her, though she felt surprised she'd missed the sound of their footsteps. She pivoted free of the ring of minions and turned back toward them to see not eleven men hewing and stabbing, but a hail of arrows darting down the ravine, their barbed heads and heavy shafts punching through minions to her left. None flew too close to her, but she pulled away regardless; she trusted her armor more than the skill of her comrades, but neither enough to stand fast under their barrage.

Realizing they were doomed, two remaining minions turned to flee back down the ravine. Gwyn caught up to them and impaled one through the back without ceremony. Before she could free her weapon, an arrow whistled past her ear and took the final enemy through the neck. She turned, her stare smoldering, to see Nafar on horseback handing a bow back to a soldier on the ground.

Horns sounded recall over the ridge. Gwyn gave a look down the ravine to ensure no more minions would run this way, then stomped back up the hill. "What in all the hells was that?" she demanded.

Some of the men yelled down at her, a mixture of praise and rebuke, but Nafar said nothing.

"Captain," she called again.

"I'm not explaining myself to you, Candon," Nafar replied. "I haven't survived this long wasting time or breath." He looked to a man in the front rank. "Get the men back to camp, Sergeant. We aren't advancing today." With that he turned his white charger and trotted away.

Gwyn had seen nothing of Sudro in the past week, but she knew the warriors from Baldor were camped less than a mile away down secure trails, so after taking her evening meal she walked in that direction to seek him out. She found herself in the rare need of someone to talk to, and though she hadn't been particularly friendly with any of the men in her troop to begin with, since her defiant charge that morning they had actively avoided her.

She spotted Sudro in his camp, hurrying between tasks, and called his name. He turned and saw her, then walked over. "Hello, Gwyn," he greeted. She hadn't remembered until seeing his face that their last meaningful encounter had been giving him a full-mouthed kiss on a bloody battlefield. If it had left any impression on him, he didn't show it, though this might be for the best. She'd been so caught up in the heat and blood she hadn't thought about what it might mean after, and though it had felt pleasurable in itself the emotion that drove it was not romance or even lust, at least not in the sense she'd heard people speak of it. She hoped it had sparked some desire in him in the moment, but if he was willing to leave it behind them it would simplify her life.

"Can we walk a little?" she asked, her voice low and halting.

"Alright," he agreed, turning back up the trail and setting a leisurely pace.

Gwyn explained the events of the morning, and by the time she finished they'd walked about halfway between camps. Sudro sat on a fallen log and sighed. "Why do you have to push that man?" he asked. "By Terillah, Gwyn, he's probably the second-most respected leader in all Atlund; would it kill you to just listen?"

Gwyn looked into the forest and ground her teeth. "It might."

"Then you aren't leaving him much choice. If you ignore orders, he can send you home. Keep doing it and he can exile or execute you. Or he can let you get surrounded by minions so he can shoot them down with arrows. I can't fathom why he's letting that be your choice instead of his, but…" He shrugged. "So what's it to be, Gwyn? Retirement, death, or bait? Or actually follow orders?"

She sighed and looked back at Sudro. "Some of the orders aren't so bad. I'll at least try a few. If I don't like them, I can always choose 'bait.'"

Gwyn never asked Nafar to explain himself again, and he never offered to. Gwyn did as she liked as often as not, and though the captain never punished her he also never risked a man to protect her. She might have been hard-pressed to credit her survival to skill rather than dumb luck if any ever argued with her, but none ever did. In time she began to notice how her position in skirmishes often benefited from some measure of barely restrained havoc, and she thought too much of Nafar's tactical wisdom, at least privately, to assume this was a coincidence.

After reaching this uneasy peace with Nafar, Gwyn's fight against Kellgore wore on for three bloody months. The wizard seemed to have minions in endless supply, orders of magnitude more than the people who had gone missing to be twisted into them, leaving the Atlunders to wonder with revulsion at what horrors the sorcerer used to create his forces. The closer the army came to the wizard's stronghold, the more desperate grew the defense. Soon Gwyn and her people found themselves fighting not bands but whole hordes, all ravening for the flesh of horse and man alike and frenzied by the enchantments of their dark master. During the last month the Atlunders found that, undisciplined as the beasts were, they would no longer route or even retreat. Minion ranks would collapse beneath a charge, but before the cavalry could reform more enemies swarmed over them, even those wounded in the first clash, driven by some sorcerous craving that overmatched their fear. At long last the Atlunders' casualties began to climb, and while morale remained high in its way, it cooled from the exuberance of a seemingly easy victory to the grim determination of warriors who had buried too many friends to quit the field except by lack of argument.

Blood and gore covered the ground, the horses, the men. Kellgore's stronghold lay just a few miles away, and if anyone told Gwyn the minions formed a solid block between it and her, she'd be forced to believe them. The battle had raged back and forth for hours; any time one side withdrew to lick its wounds the other had likewise been too damaged to press the advantage. Here, at last, Gwyn's rebellious initiative served rather than hampered the battle, for commanders fell and orders failed everywhere throughout the day. A man who couldn't decide quickly marked himself for death.

The immediate effort called for a cavalry charge at the enemy center while infantry surged forward on either side to guard the flanks. Gwyn had worked her way to the front rank, happening to find space at the far right, and spurred her sorrel mount to keep pace with her comrades. Without warning, a line of Minions leapt to the attack from a hidden defile. A few Atlunders failed to get their spears on target at the unexpected enemy, but most of the minions fell easily. Still, the sudden adjustment caused more than half the line to lose their spears to fumbling or breakage, and Gwyn was no exception.

From the right corner of her vision she saw mobs of minions attacking the flanking infantry while the cavalry struggled to rearm themselves; a few yards away Sudro stood a bit out in front of his fellows, as did Gwyn, and there she hesitated. She had lost her momentum, and whether to spur her horse forward and do the best she could or dismount to fight properly with her great sword wasn't clear. She heard the call for fresh spears from the reserve, but to wait for them would condemn the infantry. Now the main horde of minions directly ahead, the cavalry's original target, surged forward in a snarling wave. Checking her mount, Gwyn fumbled for her blade, watching to her right as Sudro's curved sword became lodged in a Minion's ribs. Letting go his weapon, he took up a spear from a fallen comrade just as he saw another Minion drop from the trees in front of Gwyn's horse. Somehow Sudro saw it and hurled the spear without hesitation. Before it could even strike Gwyn put spurs to her charger. She was forced to watch in utter shock as the Minion caught the spear from the air, held its point directly in her path, and braced its butt against the earth.

Gwyn tried to rein in her mount, but too late. The hardened spear point pierced her chain mail and drove into her right shoulder, pain exploding through her body and drowning her senses with fire. The impaling point lifted and pitched her backward from the saddle as her horse continued straight at the minion, which leapt at the frightened animal's throat with terrible savagery. The sorrel's screams filled Gwyn's ears as she lay on the ground and desperately fought to remain conscious. She touched the spear point and immediately felt a greater wave of dizziness surge through her at the strangeness of the sensation; she was certain the weapon had lodged in bone. Finally her horse fell with a heavy crash beside her, and with her one working hand she reached for the hilt of her sword still lashed to the mount's tack. Before she could draw, the Minion leered above her, horse blood dripping from its fangs. Crashes in the woods from the west revealed the arrival of enemy reinforcements.

Suddenly the Minion's nostrils flared, and it looked sharply to the right just in time to see Sudro swing his now-freed blade through its throat. The beast looked confused for a single stunned moment before collapsing. As Gwyn's vision began to blur at the edges, she saw Sudro motioning to either side, seemingly to figures out of her sight, before charging toward the west with his bloody sword at the ready. A thunder of hooves broke through the fog that billowed in her brain before she finally succumbed to the blackness.

She awoke in a tent, confused and frightened. Suddenly Gwyn knew she was dreaming because she could see Tehgil standing watch in the far corner, and he was still back home. As her senses slowly fought back to life, she felt a cavernous hunger gnawing her belly. More importantly, she realized she couldn't move her right arm. Fear overcoming her pride, she cried out through taught vocal cords, "Tehgil! My arm!"

Stirring, the large man knelt immediately at her side. "Yes, Gwyn, what is it?"

"I can't move my arm!" Panic edged her voice.

"Of course not, child, it's strapped to your chest."

"Why?"

"Why?" Tehgil retorted. "Your collarbone's busted, and your shoulder blade probably cracked up, too, not to mention a hole halfway through you." He paused. "What do you remember?"

She squinted, concentration lining her forehead. "We were riding into another battle. Minions ambushed us. I was stabbed!"

"'Impaled' is more like. Anything else?"

"No. Except Sudro. He, he saved me. Where is he?"

"Gwyn…Sudro's dead."

"What? How?"

"He led a charge against the Minion lines, trying to hold them back until reinforcements could get there. The horsemen were breaking, and most of the infantry was committed to the flanks. If the Minions had broken through our rearguard, which was light, they'd have been among the supply lines and the wounded."

Gwyn might have been upset by news of Sudro's death, but at that moment she still struggled to piece everything together. "If Sudro was killed, then I'd guess his charge fared poorly. So why am I still alive?"

"Nafar and the king's guard were right behind. They managed to hold the Minions until the rest could redeploy."

"They were too late."

"Not too late to save you."

Gwyn remembered Sudro's honest, unawed eyes, involuntarily imagined them blank and dead. "They were too late," she repeated.

Tehgil didn't reply, but she caught the perfect empathy of experience in his expression.

"How did you get here?" Gwyn asked. "You're supposed to be back home."

"King Vassin called up the reserve for the final assault."

"What? Final assault? No, we were still days of hard fighting from Kellgore's stronghold."

"Five days, as it turns out."

"I've been unconscious for five days!?"

"Six. Though you've been in and out the whole time. You lost a lot of blood, and you went feverish again. One of these times you're going to get yourself wounded and not wake up. You know that, don't you?"

Gwyn ignored his remark. "If we're ready for the final assault, I've got to get my arm out of this sling! Help me up." Gwyn tried to push herself to a sitting position but quickly slumped back down to her bed of furs as the tent began to whirl around her.

"Gwyn, you haven't understood me. We aren't 'ready' for the final assault."

She glared at him. "Make yourself clearer, Tehgil."

The old warrior stood and paced back to his corner of the tent, putting some distance between them before he made his report. "The final assault was made yesterday, Gwyn. Kellgore is dead. The campaign is over."

"No!" Gwyn shouted. "It was supposed to be me! *I* was supposed to kill Kellgore! My mother–"

"Your mother misses you, Gwyn," Tehgil interjected. "She wants you to come home. She's had yet more time to think since you joined the campaign, and she's found little but regret. There's a lot she wants to amend where you are concerned. I even think Adric misses the, ah, color you brought to his household."

"It was supposed to be me," Gwyn repeated, now with resignation. "Who was it that killed the sorcerer? Who stole my birthright?"

"Now, Gwyn–"

"*Who?*"

"It was the king. Nafar and I tried to hold him back, but he has too much of his father's spit in him. It was a magnificent battle. We'd stormed the fort and breached the throne room. Vassin demanded Kellgore turn over his staff and submit to the clans' authority, but of course the warlock refused. He should have been quicker with his spellcraft."

A cold fire burned in Gwyn's eyes. "This was *my* war, Tehgil. The vengeance was to be *mine.*"

"It was justice, lass, and that doesn't belong to anybody," Tehgil replied, his words carrying more authority than usual. "Your father never would have wanted vengeance, not the way you see it. He would have hated to see you lust for it as you do."

Gwyn's head fell back once again to the furs, her staring eyes transfixing the canvas of the tent. Her muscles felt relaxed, but her pulse pounded restlessly in her veins. After a moment, Tehgil spoke again. "Be glad, Gwyn. Don't you see? It's over." A taut weight was gone from Tehgil's voice, and for a moment Gwyn realized how Kellgore's existence must have eaten at him, though he controlled himself better than she. "After all this time," he continued, "it's finally over."

Gwyn thought before replying, and her voice was thick and bitter when she did. "Then what now, Tehgil? *What am I now?*"

Gwyn's return home was a dark and silent trek as reality of Sudro's death seeped into her. Whether or not she had loved him was a question she stubbornly refused to contemplate, but she could not deny, try as she might, that he had been a friend to her, or at least the closest to it she'd ever had.

King Vassin ending the campaign while she lay in fever cut deeper still, and she refused to speak to him during the entirety of the week-long march back to her village. The army was welcomed to a hero's feast, but the food and wine tasted as ashes in her mouth. Even tales of her bravery and ferocity sounded as empty to her now as the repeated boasting of old warriors at Clanmeet.

On Tehgil's advice, the family left Gwyn alone for the next two days except to wait on her needs while she continued to heal. Lischa touched her hair and shoulders more than Gwyn felt was normal, but otherwise everyone was inoffensive enough. On the third day Lischa came into Gwyn's room at midday with a wooden tray of bread and cheese. "Do you mind if I sit with you awhile?" she asked.

"You should," Gwyn replied, bringing a smile to her mother's face. "I need to talk with you." Her voice cracked.

"What's wrong, Gwyn?" her mother asked, setting the tray aside.

Gwyn's eyes sparkled with moisture as she choked, "I'm sorry, Mama. I couldn't kill Kellgore. I failed again. I tried, I swear I did."

"Gwyn, Gwyn," Lischa soothed, taking her daughter's hand, "don't apologize. Don't even think of it again, not for an instant. How could you think I still care about that?"

Gwyn stopped, her mouth slightly ajar. "Still care? Mother, it's all you've *ever* wanted from me, as long as I can remember."

Lischa closed her eyes and took a deep breath. "I know," she answered. "It was wrong. Even if you'd wanted to train as a warrior, I suppose I'd have had to let you, but any decent mother would have met that with fear, fear I'd lose you, too. All I could think of was your father, the pressure of raising you alone, the hate for his killer." Tears sprang to Lischa's eyes as she continued. "I lost so many years with you, Gwyn. I don't know if you can ever forgive me, but I *am* sorry."

"Sorry!?" Gwyn barked, sitting up in bed with a wince. "You're sorry? For what? For making me this way? Like there's something *wrong* with me? What do you think I am, some kind of Windborne monster?"

"What? No, Gwyn, please, I didn't mean that, I just–"

Gwyn pointed her good arm at the sword hanging on her wall. "*That* is what I am, Mother. It's too late to want me to be something else." Lischa began to speak again, but Gwyn wouldn't allow it. "Just get out. And take the food, I'm not hungry."

Lischa made no effort to hide her tears as she followed Gwyn's commands.

Gwyn could get up and about by the end of the week and shed the sling altogether a month later, though she'd experimented without it for some time by then. By the end of summer she was fully healed.

Tehgil, hoping to offer Gwyn any sort of renewed purpose, stepped down from his role as the village's chief warrior and awarded it to Gwyn, her birthright as Girahl's heir. As she showed no interest in organizing patrols, taking reports, or planning for armaments, though, Tehgil's actual work remained the same, save a little less guard duty of his own.

Gwyn's life fell into a dissatisfying pattern: Wake, patrol and guard, guard and patrol, eat, sleep. Wake, patrol and guard, guard and patrol, eat, sleep.

"Anything to report today, Gwyn?"

"Killed a couple minions that wandered down from Kellgore's old land."

"Anything to report today, Gwyn?"

"Took a kill from some poachers and gave it to the clan council to piece out to the widows. Only one poacher fought back. He'll live."

"Anything to report today, Gwyn?"

"Game must be getting scarce up north. Some fell wolves encroached from the ice and tried to whip up the local packs. The tanner should be done with the leader's hide in a couple days if anybody wants it."

"Anything to report today, Gwyn?"

"No."

It was with little surprise that Aldrin went to raise Gwyn one morning in the early spring, a week after the Windcease Festival, to find her clothing, gear and sword all missing. In their place was a note he almost feared to touch. He wisely summoned his father first to read the message, hoping he might find some gentler way to break the news to Lischa. Adric read the note with a falling heart.

Mother,

    I cannot remain here. I have no wish to cause you pain, but that is all I will do if I stay in the village and waste away or go mad before your eyes. I have no place among peaceful folk. Battle is all I can understand any longer. Gone south to the orc wars. Expect me when you see me.

    –Gwyn et Sheevasa

Adric did all he could to soften the blow, even trying to conjure some hope that Gwyn might soon return, but at length he had no choice but to show Lischa the brief letter, after which she sobbed inconsolably for hours. She could bear the thought of Gwyn leaving home, could even bear the idea of never seeing her again if it would truly make her daughter happy, even if that meant she could never be forgiven. It was not for Gwyn's disappearance that she wept. She wept because the woman who had written that note, who had, for the first time, even signed her full, meaningful name, was not the daughter she had hoped to win back, but the daughter she had already raised: the savage, the bloodthirsty killer, The Hand of Vengeance.

CHAPTER V

So it was that Gwyn took up the three-month journey to the Southern Kingdoms, a nation of humans who had long ago emigrated from Atlund to found their own states. For a century or more they maintained close ties, but when the young race of elves sprang up in the vast band of forests between the two countries, the smaller beings took on a role as intermediaries in trade, and in time the human peoples had become sundered, now barely able to understand one another's tongues. Of course, there was a darker reason for the Southerners' estrangement, and it was this reason that lured Gwyn thither over four-hundred leagues of dangerous and sometimes trackless wilderness.

For generations the Southerners had been distracted from any relations with the friendly north by a fearful enemy on their southern border. The orcs were primitive by any standard, and savage. Not since the time of ogres had any race been so brutish or so strong, but while that older people had been an insular and failing species almost from the beginning, the orcs thrived and grew in number, driven by some unknown ambition to conquer and slaughter all before them. Long ago the conflict had forced the many Southern Kingdoms to unite under a single High King who eventually consolidated all royal power, leaving only the plural name as legacy of the confederation that once existed. Rumors had filtered back to Atlund that many in the South had even given up their faith in Terillah, forsaking any creator that could spawn such a murderous and hateful species.

The blood war between the two races had lulled at times, but all rumor from the south, coming mostly through elven traders, suggested the current state of affairs was as pitched and violent as had been seen in perhaps fifty years. Indeed, if the rising trade price of arms was any indication, the Southern Kingdoms were growing desperate. In the central regions of Atlund, where neither Kellgore nor eastern nomads provided an immediate threat, many warriors had traveled south to sell their blades and skills to whomever could afford them. Few came ever back, but whether that was due to a fateful end or a Southern lass was always in debate. Like those before her, Gwyn rode due south, but from her western home; thus, unlike them, she would end her journey not at the great capital of the Southern Kingdoms, but rather in its midwestern regions, where it was said sell-swords were sparse, but the battles even more vicious.

Gwyn's journey took her first down the roads of Atlund to the western bridge over the great Sharai, the nation's southern border. Next she passed through the dense Elven Forest, but most elves' travel was for trade, and most of that routed through their only major city, far in the east. Save for a few fleeting glimpses of their passage or catching the odd glow as their eyes reflected her firelight like a cat's, she saw none of that elusive people, and she knew from every tale she had heard not to stray from the main roads in search of greater contact. It was widely known that elves of the wood rarely killed, but their magic was strong and their love of nature unrivaled. It was not unheard of for disrespectful travelers to fall suddenly into an unnatural slumber, only to awaken disoriented and dozens of miles from their last known position, usually in the completely wrong direction and, on occasion, stark naked.

Compared to the woods of Atlund, the Elven Forest was less ancient but sported denser undergrowth thanks to the milder climate and lack of regular management, and Gwyn found it to be claustrophobic and unsettling. Her new horse, a young, spirited gray, did not seem to agree, however, thriving even on the forage in woods that few doubted were laced with enchantments of growth and renewal. Even Gwyn had to admit a drink from its streams never failed to refresh wholly, even when little could be taken.

Gaining the southern edge of the forest represented only the first third of Gwyn's journey, and there she was forced to rest. From here, the western regions were crossed only by a few trade roads and peopled by frontiersmen and bandits. Traveling such regions alone challenged the line between arrogance and foolishness, even for Gwyn. Fortunately the route she had followed through the forest came to a crossroads within sight of the trees, the southward trail meeting with another that stretched from the blank sky in the farthest east to the foothills of the Tunaris in the west, a hazy smudge just peeking above the distant horizon. She camped for a day in the forest, the cool shade and easy foraging making a pleasant rest. Even still, by sunset she dreaded how long she might be stuck here and cursed herself for passing up a pair of wagon trains she shunned at the crossing of the Sharai, opting instead to make better time on her own through elven lands.

She lit her fire within sight of the road and roasted a squirrel she'd snared earlier in the day, holding the meat strips over the fire on a spit of green wood. Suddenly she saw movement on the road and reached for her sword, then peered more closely in surprise rather than fear. A lone woman walked the path coming up from the south, her gait and manner unhurried. As she entered the fringe of the forest she turned toward Gwyn's fire and called, "May I approach?"

"Uh, yes," Gwyn answered, glancing about her in case the woman's appearance was meant to distract her from some threat.

As she neared the fire Gwyn saw the woman's features; she was a generation older than Gwyn, at least, and had soft, brown hair with a few noticeable strands of silver. Narrowing her eyes, Gwyn asked, "Do I know you?"

The woman smiled. "No. I only hoped to warm myself a little."

Gwyn nodded and began to stand so her elder could sit on her bedroll, but the woman declined with a wave of her hand. "Do you need any food? Water?" Gwyn asked, seeing the woman carried no supplies.

"Not at the moment," she answered, settling in on the ground.

Gwyn's intuition didn't read cause for fear, but the woman's appearance unsettled her. If she was more than she seemed, it would not be the strangest story Gwyn had heard of these forests by any measure. Caution tempered her impertinence. "Do you live nearby?" she asked.

"At whiles. You're of the northern blood. What brings you hither?"

"I'm headed south. To the war."

The woman's eyes narrowed ever so slightly. "Do you think that's wise?"

"I'm a warrior, so war is my trade. I can't practice it in my home, so I go where I can. I'm not sure wisdom enters into it."

"Wisdom always enters in when we allow it," the woman claimed. She sat for a few minutes, looking into the forest and occasionally at Gwyn, who said nothing. At last the woman gazed up at the half-circle of the Faithful One shining down in the twilight. "Well," she said, "I know our visit was brief, but my bones are warmed and ready to be on their way. I'd normally wish safety to a traveler before taking my leave, but I won't wish something you don't desire for yourself."

"It's nearly dark," Gwyn cautioned. "Let me offer hospitality until morning."

The woman laughed freely, a sound that triggered some yearning in Gwyn's memory she couldn't pin down. "These woods are friendly to me, child. My way will be much less fraught with danger than yours, I assure you."

Her words, in the unnatural current of the encounter, gave Gwyn a shudder. "Do you curse me?"

"Not at all," she answered with a smile as she stood, "nor prophesy. Only observe what is clear. If not safety, I wish you life and success. Farewell."

"Farewell," Gwyn answered, her voice bewildered.

The sun had begun to drop toward the earth on the second day when Gwyn spotted a dust cloud on the western road. She stayed hidden until the line of half a dozen wagons arrived at the crossroads and began circling to camp. Many of the men looked rough, though from all she'd heard this was to be expected. As the caravan vehicles disgorged their occupants, she saw two of the finer wagons exited by a woman and children. Praising her good fortune, she threw together her kit and jumped on her horse, keeping her sword resting against her shoulder as she rode forward in the dusk.

"Hail to the camp," she called when she came within earshot.

"Who's there?" several of the men called back.

"I'm a traveler from Atlund. I would ride south with you, if you'll let me." She continued forward at a cautious pace.

"What can you do for your keep?" a single voice asked.

"I fight," she answered, by now close enough to be heard without shouting. She stopped her horse outside the ring of wagons but close enough that the firelight illuminated her through a gap.

A short man came to the open space. He wore dun trousers and tunic and had a hardscrabble beard and a brush of tan hair. "That's quite a sword," he commented. "I know how things are up north, but women don't really fight where we're going."

"Only because I've never been there," Gwyn retorted.

The small man chuckled. "Fair enough. Let's see what you've got." He turned back to the people around the fire. "Who wants to test her?"

"I'll do it," a tall, solid man volunteered as he stood.

"That's not quite fair, Borse," the small man countered.

"Why not?" Gwyn asked. "Is he crippled or something?"

The small man shook his head at her impertinence. "He's the best fighter in the caravan."

"I'll fight him, then."

"Suit yourself. We don't have sparring weapons here. Can you pull your strikes?"

"Of course."

"That goes for you, too, Borse," the small man called as Borse went for his weapons. "Behave yourself and pull your strikes."

"He won't have to," Gwyn assured as she dismounted. She pulled her dirk sheath from her boot and tucked it into the front of her belt.

The man scoffed. "I'm Adezavax," he said then, "captain of these caravan guards. Somebody bring some fire over here," he called out to the rest of the group.

A pair of men walked out on either side of Borse, each holding a burning torch. Borse carried a round, boss-grip shield and a mace. As soon as he appeared ready, Gwyn charged forward without waiting for a command. Borse stood behind his shield, his mace cocked back and ready to strike. Gwyn sidestepped to her right and slashed at the big man's back. He pivoted to his left to catch the attack on his shield and began to swing his mace around. Gwyn dropped her point faster than Borse could react, leaving the bind with the shield and laying the edge of her blade against the back of his left leg. "That's your hamstring cut," she announced, moving back out of range.

"Dammit!" Borse yelled. He glanced at Adezavax, then looked back at Gwyn. "Best of three?"

Rather than answer, she rushed in again, thrusting her great sword in quick jabs like a short spear. She kept Borse at a distance, suspecting he wouldn't fall for her first trick again, and looked for an opening. Instead, Borse suddenly beat aside one of her jabs harder than before, knocking Gwyn's point offline and startling her. At least that's what she let him believe. Instead of fighting to get back into guard, she took her left hand off the hilt and burst in under his mace swing, whipping her dirk from her belt up to Borse's throat. "You're dead."

"My mace is still going right for your skull."

"Maybe," Gwyn admitted as she backed away from the clinch. "Even if I'm dead tomorrow, you're dead tonight."

Borse let his mace dangle from the thong about his wrist and rubbed the back of his neck. "Best of five?"

"That's enough, Borse. I wouldn't bet against you once you get her measure, but she's capable enough, has good gear, and we could use another man, or woman, as the case may be. You three go back; I have business to discuss."

Once the others were out of polite earshot, Adezavax asked, "What's your name?"

"*Gwyn et Sheevasa*. Just 'Gwyn' is fine."

"And you can call me Dez, unless we're under attack, and then my name is Captain. Understand?"

Gwyn nodded, though she didn't expect to be any more diligent about Adezavax's orders than she'd been about Nafar's.

"You got trouble up north? Somebody after you? Kill someone?"

"No."

"What are your terms?"

"Safe passage and provender," Gwyn answered.

"Done," Adezavax agreed, shaking hands to seal the bargain. "Next time hold out for more."

For three weeks they saw only occasional scouts in the distance on the scrubby, broken plain, whether nefarious or from one of the far-flung frontier settlements they couldn't tell. In the fourth week a handful of brigands rode closer and loosed a few arrows at maximum range. The caravan men, of which there were eight, shot back. Afterward the enemy turned and rode away.

"Why don't they attack?" Gwyn asked.

"They're just testing our strength," the captain explained. "They'll come back tomorrow with more men."

Gwyn flexed her hands, then balled them into fists. "About time," she grumbled.

"You do understand we win by the caravan *not* being attacked, don't you?" Adezavax asked.

"I haven't had a decent fight in months."

"Sleep well tonight, then. Tomorrow may be the day."

The sun stood high and bright the following day, and though spring had not yet passed into summer, Gwyn's southward progress already brought more heat than she liked. She rode toward the front of the caravan on the west side when a cry of "Bandits!" went up from the east. Assuming these were the same that had harassed them yesterday, they'd switched directions on her. Spurring her horse, she looped around the foremost mule team and cantered to the knot of activity halfway down the column.

A dozen men on horseback stood at the crest of a hill a furlong away, bows at the ready. The other guards had strung their own bows as soon as experience told them the road would grow dangerous, and kept them so. Now they pulled bundles of arrows from their packs and took cover positions behind pavises they unstrapped from the wagon sides or simply ducked behind convenient corners.

Gwyn had no bow, but Adezavax produced an extra. "Are you any good with one of these?" he asked.

Gwyn was loathe to admit a weakness, but she knew any empty boast would be immediately exposed. "Fair…at best."

"Well, don't waste too many arrows, but give them something to think about."

Other guards began shooting, so Gwyn did the same. She found the bow both too short and too light for her, and even shooting high into the air its arrows would not reach halfway to the enemy. Half the bandits started down the hill but in long, zig-zag fashion, running nearly parallel to the caravan and forcing the guards to make difficult cross shots. So far no one had hit anything on either side. Growling frustration, Gwyn threw down the bow and snatched a spear from a rack on the side of a wagon, then leapt into the saddle and charged off toward a gully to the south. She barely heard someone yell, "Where the hell is she going?" before distance and the beat of her horse's hooves drowned all sound.

Her Atlund-bred horse was a master of forest ridges and ravines. He dove into the gully without a pause and, at Gwyn's direction, turned to the east and set off at a gallop. In half a minute she chose the gentlest section of gully wall she could find and urged her horse up the slope, leaping upward in great, bucking surges. Her estimate of the distance had been good; she now flanked the bandits still on the hill only fifty or sixty yards to the south. Her horse tore up the rise, and Gwyn couched her spear. The nearest bandit barely had time to turn toward her before she impaled him, his horse spooking and bolting down the hill, taking his rider and her spear with him.

Pressed for time, she drew her dirk and slashed the throat of the second bandit in the line before he could draw a hand weapon. As he held his hemorrhaging neck and began to slump sideways, Gwyn reached forward and pulled the short sword from his belt and immediately hurled it at the next enemy. It tumbled harmlessly off his arm, but it bought her just enough time to grab the foregrip of her great sword and haul it free.

The bandit horses, apparently not well-trained, had already become unruly, and the sight of Gwyn's great sword was more than their riders could bear. They turned and rode back to the north, though Gwyn managed to stab one through the shoulder before he could get out of reach. Rather than give chase, she turned her mount down the hill and charged the remaining brigands. One had started to flee with an arrow in his thigh. Instead of his comrades at the top of the hill covering his retreat, he saw *Gwyn et Sheevasa*, her eyes flashing jade fire, swinging her sword at his neck. The blade cleaved through flesh and bone, decapitating the man in a gout of blood. The other guards had slain another of the six by the time Gwyn reached the fighting, and her arrival fell like a falcon among pigeons. All four scattered, but only one managed to get out of range before being grievously wounded.

Gwyn's chest heaved with breath as her pulse pounded in her temples. None of her comrades had been seriously hurt. The merchants with their families, as well as their noncombatant employees, cheered and clapped. The guards argued over whether Gwyn was fearless, mad, or both and began placing bets on whether any bandits would try again. Adezavax regarded Gwyn with new respect, but she noted something not unlike fear layered beneath the appreciation in his eyes.

The merchants dispatched riders, with Gwyn and another guard as escort, who managed to chase down five of the robbers' horses and add them to their goods for sale. In only a few more minutes the caravan rolled on, knowing the vultures they occasionally saw making their lazy spirals over the plain would find the refuse soon enough.

That night, as she spread out her bedroll, Gwyn realized the threshold she had crossed that day. She'd never killed a human being before, and in a single skirmish she'd killed three outright and wounded more. She remembered the words of the warriors all around her during her childhood, those who had gone on sortie against the eastern nomads or other human foes. Some spoke of regret or even shame, others of a sort of survivalist determination, but all alluded to a cost, a change the act wrought in the killer. Gwyn remembered the stunned eyes of the first archer she'd killed, the gasping panic of the second, even the weirdly leaden way the head of her last victim had tumbled to the ground.

She felt no revulsion and no pity. They were evil men, intent on plunder and whatever murder such plunder might require, and she had killed them. Priests and philosophers might debate the morality, other warriors may regret the necessity, but for *Gwyn et Sheevasa* the matter was simple. She wondered if there would be another fight the next day and slept well that night.

By midmorning Gwyn had become fed up with waiting. The other guards predicted the bandits, at least those in this particular gang, would either not come back at all (the most common theory) or, if they did, would come back with every man they could throw. Neither scenario encouraged them to stray too far from the caravan, but Gwyn insisted on it. She borrowed a shield and another spear, made sure her sword hung loose and ready in its straps, and rode off west.

The terrain offered little cover either for her or potential enemies, but she took advantage of what she could, riding briefly to the top of hills and ridges to get a look about, then descending into depressions and defiles to get back out of sight. An hour after noon she spied two scouts riding parallel to the caravan behind a screen of hills. Moving farther to the west, she looped around and found a cutting between two hills in which to await them. She could hear their idle chatter as they approached and rode out into plain view just twenty yards away. So far Gwyn couldn't be sure they had barbarous intentions, but as soon as they spotted her they reached for weapons. She spurred her horse and took one through the chest, managing to wrench her spear free as she passed, then quickly turned her mount to face the remaining brigand. He stretched his bow, and Gwyn crouched behind her shield, praying he would shoot at her and not her horse. She needn't have worried, horses being far more valuable alive than dead. Gwyn felt and heard the arrow *thunk* into her shield as she charged, then thrust her spear into the second man as easily as the first. She left both of them there, neither yet dead but beyond any hope of mending, and rode one of their horses back to the caravan since she had tired hers with the hours of uphill and downhill riding. Returning to the merchants with two more free horses cemented their favorable opinion.

In a way, Gwyn fell victim to her own success. All she wanted was battle, but no more outlaws would attack. The following day she spotted another pair of scouts, but these fled as soon as they saw her. Even after they left the territory of the first gang and traveled into another, the brigands would threaten attack only until one of them marked Gwyn's visage, then the caravan was allowed to pass unmolested.

Two more weeks after the first skirmish, the caravan stopped for an extra day at a timber-walled outpost erected by the Southern Kingdoms' border patrols.

After stabling her horse, Gwyn found the corner of the mess hall the civilians had converted into a tavern and took a table for herself. She bought a glass of mead and, for a few coppers, rented a cushion stuffed with down and a southern crop called cotton. Though the lack of battle had rankled her, she didn't hold equal enthusiasm for the simple hardships of the road and considered those few coppers the best money she had ever spent. The mead, on the other hand, disappointed.

Left with nothing in particular to do, she sat quietly in the tavern and listened to the speakers as closely as she could, working to acclimate her northern ears to the southern dialect. The merchants and caravan men had bridged the gap well, but the farther south she traveled the more trouble she had understanding the locals, so she took every opportunity she could.

She strained her ear toward a pair of travelers a few tables away, catching only every fourth word or so until one stood out: "Windborne." It was a pure Atlund word, one forgotten in the southern speech, and it struck her as clearly as someone speaking her name in a noisy, crowded room. The speaker glanced at her and saw her looking, quickly shifting his gaze elsewhere.

A moment later Adezavax ambled into the tavern and ordered something at the bar. Looking for a place to sit, he spotted Gwyn and asked her leave. Eager for a translator, she raised her boot to push back the chair across from her by way of agreement, and the captain sat down.

"Can you hear what they're saying, Captain?" Gwyn asked before the wiry man could bring up any other topic.

"It's just 'Dez' in here, Gwyn," he corrected, then turned his ear subtly to the speakers. In only a moment, he smiled. "They're talking about you. 'Red-headed northern devil, sword the size of a pikestaff.' Doesn't sound like anybody *else* hereabouts. Wait, what's that Atlund word? Windborne? What's that?"

"It's…a long story. How do they know anything about me? We just got here?"

"Some outlaw gangs are enemies, but others talk. Word spreads. And they're 'business' doesn't work without people who will buy goods without asking questions, and those people hear things, too."

"Even so, why won't they fight?" Gwyn demanded. "They have the numbers, especially if a couple groups joined together."

"You can't spend loot when you're dead," Dez reasoned. "They're used to a violent life, but only up to a point. They *aren't* used to losing half the men in a sortie or getting their heads chopped off."

"You can't really get *used* to getting your head chopped off."

"*Collectively*," Dez clarified. "I and my guard troop didn't exactly have the worst reputation when it came to fending off bandits, and now with you on the team? We're untouchable. Which brings me to: What are your plans when you get south, Gwyn?"

"Sell my sword, as you guessed from the start."

"To who?"

Gwyn shrugged.

"Stay on with me," Dez offered. "It's safer work than the front, and you could make a lot of money. The owners of this caravan are already talking about offering you a sum up front to convince you to stay, a bigger bonus than I've seen them give in a long, long time. What do you say?"

"I'm looking for something else."

"Just think it over. We'll talk again when we get back into real civilization."

In another month the wagon train quickly crossed into that "real civilization." Three days in a row they passed through crossroads that added to the traffic. A day after that they stopped in an actual town. Now free from the possibility of being ambushed by more brigands than she could handle, Gwyn knew her time had come to part company with the caravan. She woke early and found Dez stowing weapons and armor for a planned passage through a guarded city later in the day. "Captain," she called. "It's time."

If Dez had any doubt of what she meant, her belongings all packed on the horse she led behind her dispelled it. "Don't be hasty, Gwyn. If you stay on, none of us will have to fight but once or twice a season the way you put the fear into outlaws. That's a money proposition, and my employers know it." He gave a quick look left and right, then pulled a small bag from his belt pouch and hefted it, jingling. "That's gold you hear, not silver. Full value for the horses you brought back and half up front for the next trip, well over the going rate, too. That's more money than a tradesman could make in two years or a farmer in ten. How do you walk away from that?"

Pride swelled Gwyn's head that men of wealth placed such value on her skills. Still, she thought of the long, dull rides with barely any combat. "It's a fine offer," Gwyn replied in the Southern dialect, which she'd practiced enough to be serviceable, "but I can't accept. You're turning east toward the Capital, and I'm still bound south to the front. It's war I'm after."

"You're daft, I think, lass, or maybe something worse," Adezavax answered. "I'd never heard of a Windborne before you came along, but I've learned enough of it since. I don't hold to such notions as a rule, but I can't explain it any other way when one so young as you looks me level in the eye and says she's *looking* for a war. If you'd never seen a real battle, I'd just figure you didn't know any better, but I don't think that's the way of it."

"Look to the bright side, Captain," Gwyn said as she swung up into the saddle. "If I have the same effect on the orcs as I've had on the bandits, I may just win this war for you." With that, she tapped her heels, and her horse started away south at a canter.

Adezavax grunted humorlessly before calling after her. "You'll need more than brash arrogance down there, lass! If you didn't learn anything else from me on the road, I hope you learned that."

Gwyn did not turn back to answer.

CHAPTER VI

$\mathfrak{N}$ow that she had returned to civilized lands, the population grew denser the farther south Gwyn traveled. She found this strange at first, since the fighting lay in that direction, but the Southern economy relied heavily on river trade, and the Storn River that flowed down from the southern Tunari Mountains was the greatest water in the region. The river also represented the high-water mark of the orcish advance, and it was said they were dangerously close to that mark again. In any case, Gwyn was glad to be on well-kept roads once more, and she made good time through the Southern Kingdoms. Based on directions from the locals, she believed she was only two days of hard riding from the river when she stopped at a crossroads inn to pass the night and find stabling for her horse.

Southern inns were strange to Gwyn. In her native Atlund, common houses were unusual; travelers rarely found themselves outside the lands of their clan, and almost any home could spare a bedroll and a spot near the hearth for a member of the extended family. Those inns that did exist evolved from simple shelters built to protect royal dispatch riders from the Wind when urgent news required winter travel, and those utilitarian roots ran deep. Eating and sleeping all occurred in one large room, tables and benches simply being pushed out of the way when the evening meal was done, a curtain pulled down the center to allow for some privacy between genders. There was little security, but the laws of hospitality were strict and the penalties for violating them severe. A traveler could be assured of a safe night's sleep, if not a particularly comfortable one.

The Southerners, however, did not seem to trust one another, at least in Gwyn's estimation. Their inns relied on private rooms, with only the lowest classes relegated to sleeping in the common areas which, since Southern women of low station rarely traveled, were not segregated. This forced Gwyn into the private rooms to preserve her decency, and that taxed her money pouch heavily.

The inn she now entered was no exception. Gwyn stood just inside the door, dripping from the recent rain. The humidity brought a dull ache to the old wound in her shoulder, and she reached across to rub at it with her left hand as she waited for the proprietor to finish serving a nearby table. He turned to her then, a stubby sort of man, wiping his hands on his apron. "How can I serve you, miss?" He asked.

"How much for stall and fodder, and meal and room?"

At hearing her accent, the man raised an eyebrow. "Atlund silver?"

She nodded.

"Five."

Scowling, Gwyn reached to the bottom of her purse and scratched out the required payment. Only one real coin and a few scraps of trade silver would be left. The innkeeper thanked her for her patronage and motioned to a lad sitting on the nearby stairs, a figure Gwyn had learned quickly must be the stable boy. "I'll board the horse," she insisted.

"Suit yourself," the proprietor replied, hurrying off to serve another customer.

Gwyn walked back into the rain and led her gray mount around the back of the building to the attached stable. Atlund custom admonished warriors not to leave the care of their horses to strangers anyway, but by observation of others she'd realized the stable boys also expected gratuity she could ill afford.

The rain had blown over as she rubbed down her horse, and she looked up to see the clouds scattering in ragged scraps, revealing *Bia Creg* making her backward transit against the stars. Still, the heavens gave no useful light, and the illumination of the stable's lanterns barely reached to the glow from the windows flanking the front door. Gwyn tripped over a barrel stave in the dark and stumbled through the front door, cursing. The innkeeper saw and caught her eye from the back of the room, nodding toward the empty end of a long table to the right. She sat, and in a moment the man appeared before her with a steaming bowl of stew, a farl of bread, and a mug of small beer.

Before he could scurry away again, Gwyn asked, "Do you know what noble hereabouts wants mercenaries?"

"Couldn't say," the man replied, and was gone.

Knowing laws to be generally more strict in the south, Gwyn had expected innkeepers to object to her sword at every turn; however, this hadn't proven to be a problem. While Atlund had a culture of battle, the Southern Kingdoms, it might be said, were in the constant business of warfare. Armed men going to and fro on unknown errands made a substantial part of the traveling population, if still technically the minority, and trying to disarm them all was work without profit. Still, wearing the blade often proved cumbersome due to its sheer size, and anytime she encountered a chair with a back Gwyn found herself turning it the wrong way around and straddling it. Here, though, the long table was served by a simple bench, offering no obstacles to her weapon.

The darkness outside left the inn to the honeyed glow of candles and lamps. A dozen other diners and drinkers sat scattered in groups of twos and threes, and though the conversation was quiet, it was enough to create an inarticulate drone to Gwyn's ears as she sat alone and apart from the rest. Still, she was wary enough to note a bubbling of mirthless, drunken laughter from behind and to her left. She caught Southern words for northern women, and not the kindest, and the hairs on her neck stood up. As readying her sword from its back sling was not a quickdraw affair, she pulled the shoulder strap over her head and laid the weapon on the table, loosing the ties around the guard so the scabbard and trappings would fall away if she pulled it. This elicited no reaction from patrons; none were close enough that the blade encroached on their space, and removing any burden at mealtime was hardly worth notice. These strangers couldn't know Gwyn felt more comfortable wearing the sword than not. The words from the other table had gone softer, and she could make out nothing more until the sounds of scraping chair legs and the uneven thuds of boot leather on floorboards put her every muscle on the alert.

"Hey there, lass," a gruff voice on her left tried in vain to purr, "you don't look like these local whores. Suit the eyes a sight better, I say. What brings you into these parts?"

"I'm no lass," Gwyn responded, "and my business is my own." She didn't want trouble and tried to keep her voice neutral, but she knew she had failed.

"Oh ho, she's a tart tongue on her," the man slurred to a comrade who now approached from the right, "and a fine, big sword as well. Maybe too big for such a narrow girl, but she'd probably be grateful for a lesson or–"

As the first stranger was speaking, Gwyn felt his hand fall on her left shoulder, but she batted it away with a quick forearm block, interrupting his speech. "Don't touch me." Her voice brooked no further advances.

Whether the pair missed her resolve or simply doubted it, she felt a hand on each shoulder now, but they made the mistake of pressing too lightly, still foolishly hoping for their encounter to end with anything other than violence. With raw strength Gwyn grabbed the rightmost wrist and spun as she leapt from the bench, throwing one opponent into the other and clearing herself from their attempted pincer. As the two regained their footing, Gwyn placed one hand on her sword hilt, but did not lift it, and moved around the end of the table, her blood quickening, suddenly just as eager for a fight as she'd previously been to avoid one. There was no fear or disappointment in her as the closer assailant whipped a short sword from his belt. Still Gwyn didn't lift her sword; she had learned a smattering of Southern culture and knew they gave short shrift to strangers, and the intervening table gave her an extra moment for prudence. "Drawn blade," she shouted to the room in general. "Witness!"

"I witness," the innkeeper spoke from a doorway leading into the attached kitchen, his voice more interested than shocked. "Loser's purse and rig forfeit for any damages." Gwyn had learned that this custom long ago replaced an insistence that fights be taken outside as it produced fewer crippled innkeepers. Still, the combats were usually with fists, not steel. All such history was cogitation for another time, however; she hefted her own blade and watched in confusion bordering on embarrassment as her first attacker tried to lunge at her across the table. With such a short weapon, he had little hope of reaching Gwyn, and the awkward maneuver left him indefensibly committed. With a cleaving strike, Gwyn claimed his sword arm below the elbow, then turned her attention to the second attacker as the first screamed and bled.

Gwyn half-expected the remaining foe to give up the battle and was pleased for further testing when he swatted her bowl up into her face, relying on the distraction to leap onto the table. This enemy had a longer blade and aimed it in a downward strike at Gwyn's skull which forced her into a rushed parry. Knowing any traditional counter at this range might expose her head to the enemy, she quickly stepped onto the shorter bench and inside her opponent's attack, maintaining her overhead guard with her right hand while reaching forward with her left to grab the drunkard's belt. In a moment he was on the floor with Gwyn's boot on his sword arm, the point of her blade at his throat, her eyes wild and breath ragged as she resisted the urge to take the kill she felt was her due.

"I witnessed," the innkeeper spoke out again, "but if you kill him like this, I'll witness to murder."

"Come get his weapon, then," Gwyn growled, choking down her anger, "and the rest of your claim for the damage." Taking a cautious step back as the man did as she'd bidden, she added, "Though I'll expect a fresh meal and a better room out of your profits." She was not shrewd but wasted no opportunity for intimidation, suspecting how the innkeeper had fleeced her with the exchange rate of her coins and reckoning that the blood on the table would make him more income from curious patrons than it would cost him to plane away.

The attackers now relieved of their weapons and valuables, Gwyn addressed the more coherent one again, and harshly. "Go," she said, "and take your friend with you before he bleeds to death. If I ever see you again, pray it's somewhere the law is at least as good as here, else I *will* kill you." She watched the pair leave as they both tried to staunch the blood flowing from the one's stump of an arm. She wondered briefly if he would survive, but realized she did not care. Minions, after all, had once been human as well, and she didn't consider these predators' chances of rehabilitation any greater.

She sat down again, not bothering to return to her original side of the table, and shoved the dismembered hand onto the floor with her sword point. The attacker's short blade had already clattered down to the rough planks, and as part of the proprietor's claim, she didn't touch it. While she waited for her replacement meal she first cleaned her blade with one rag, then wiped the stew from her face and hair with a second. When the innkeeper set down her new meal, he said, "Go to Sutherset."

"What's Sutherset?" Gwyn asked.

"Name of a fief near here, held by Lord Baraxis. He needs swords."

Gwyn thought 'Baraxis' had an evil sound to it, but she thought it without judgment. Returning her attention to the innkeeper, she asked, "Why didn't you say so in–?"

"Didn't reckon you could really fight," the man interrupted. "Now I reckon you can."

"How do I get to this 'Sutherset'?"

"Go east a day, then start asking about. Folks there'll put you on the right road."

Two days later Gwyn had reached the Storn River and the small, aged castle of Lord Baraxis, or so the local residents told her. The sun was at its zenith but lost in heavy clouds as she rode across a short drawbridge toward a high, stone wall, her straight back and mien covering her deep unease. In Atlund, only the king and the richest clan chieftains had stone forts; she had seen them only rarely and never had occasion to go inside one. Something about the gray stone and dark arrow slits of the towers on either side of the gate seemed cold and foreboding, but she resisted the urge to pull at her cloak in the gray light. In a few moments Gwyn had crossed the bridge and reined in her horse at the wall. The portcullis was open, but she expected there to be a challenge and waited for it.

She had only just paused when four guards, all as young as Gwyn, emerged from chambers on each side of the opening. Two of them crossed spears a few paces before her; a third aimed a crossbow from behind them while the fourth came forward almost even with her horse's head on the left side. Their stances and expressions suggested less confidence that Gwyn expected of guards, and she surmised they had less training and testing than they needed.

"Who goes there?" the leader questioned, his voice just short of cracking.

"*Gwyn et Sheevasa,*" Gwyn replied.

The young man's eyes went wide. His throat bulged as he swallowed hard.

Gwyn growled, "What's the matter with you?"

Now offended, the guard plucked up his courage. "I react badly to foreign troublemakers. We don't need your help here!" There were murmurs of assent from the other guards.

Gwyn backed her horse a step and sensed a cautious relaxation easing through the guard's stance. She smiled to realize he thought she was retreating; she'd only wanted space to look the young man up and down. "How many battles have you been in?" she asked.

The guard cleared his throat. "Ah…two." He pulled himself up straight and squared his shoulders before continuing, "You?"

"More," Gwyn growled as she urged her horse forward and leaned in toward the guard. "Many more." Now she was close enough for the youth to see the truth of her words, for her bare forearms were a patchwork of scars both smoothed and fresh.

"Daramis!" came a shout from the wall.

Gwyn straightened and threw a hand to the dirk in her boot, and the young men shuddered at the confidence in her speed. The face on the wall was not addressing her, however.

"Yes, Lord Major!" the young guard, Daramis, replied.

"Let her through, son. I want to see this one up close."

Once inside the high wall, Gwyn leapt from her saddle as a solidly built man descended steps from the wall top. He nodded once to her and passed on into the keep while a younger man with short, blond hair came towards her. He had gentle, blue eyes, but his expression was more suspicious than kindly.

"I am Captain Shon," he said, extending his hand in the Southern custom. Gwyn clasped his hand palm to palm, knowing only those who had shed blood together gripped wrists in warrior fashion. She felt a painful snap in her hand, the kind that sometimes happens touching metal things in winter. This one was strong and sent a tingle up her arm.

"I am *Gwyn et Sheevasa*," she responded, her voice as suspicious as Shon's expression. "I am here to sell my sword-arm."

"So said the rumors," Captain Shon acknowledged. "You are becoming known in these regions."

"I hope this will make your decision easy."

"It isn't mine to make. You're to be reviewed by the Lord Major immediately. Our men will stable your mount—"

"Captain," Gwyn interrupted, "if there are rumors then surely they say where I come from. Atlunders see to their own horses when they can, and we never allow them to be stabled by strangers."

"As you will. Daramis here will show you the way to the stables and on to the strategy room after that. Be swift about it, though. The Lord Major has too many responsibilities to be kept waiting on the customs of a mercenary."

Gwyn scowled at the captain's retreating back before allowing herself to be led to the stables. She felt her prospects for employment dwindling, along with her respect for her potential employers. There was something strange about this Shon, or about the feeling he inspired. She was regularly aggravated by other people, but rarely so wanted to strike them with so little provocation. She shook her arm, realizing it still tingled oddly from the shock of his handshake. Still, she followed the young Daramis to the stables without further complaint. "Why do you call your master 'Lord *Major*'?" Gwyn asked as they walked.

Now away from the judgment of his peers, the guard's manner toward Gwyn relaxed. "Noble title and military title. Some have one or the other; many, like Baraxis, have both."

"The people I talked to on the road only called him by the noble one," Gwyn challenged.

"Military only gets used on duty. Though in Sutherset, we're all on duty so often we pretty much just say 'Lord Major' all the time."

Gwyn wasn't sure what to make of this, but she asked no more, entering the stables and leading her horse to the stall Daramis indicated. After a moment of hesitation, she began removing the beast's saddle and tack. She preferred to leave herself the option of a quick getaway, but the tired gray was in need of proper rest.

"Is it true?" Daramis asked while she worked.

Exasperated by the tendency she had noticed for Southerners to begin a conversation in the middle, Gwyn sighed before asking, "Is *what* true?"

"That you killed two men just for looking at you."

"They did more than look, and they were still alive when I last saw them. It was better than they deserved."

"But, you *have*… I mean, you've killed *men*?"

"You haven't? You said you'd been twice in battle."

"Only against the orcs," Daramis answered with averted eyes, "and I'm not sure I acquitted myself well enough to count a kill. I've surely never fought men. Why do humans fight each other when there are so many orcs at our throats?"

The faces of the bandits Gwyn had killed and even some of the more human-looking minions flashed briefly in her mind. She felt as little for killing them now as she had at the time and shrugged at Daramis' question. "People will do most anything if they think there's profit in it. Even without gain, some are mad or desperate or just evil. Still, they all look alike when they're charging you, and they all bleed the same. As far as I can see, they all die the same, too, at least on this side of the veil. What Terillah does when he takes them is his own affair."

Gwyn didn't think Daramis would answer, but he spoke again before she could leave the stable. "You seem to know a lot about killing."

"It's become my trade."

"Have you ever seen an orc?"

"Not yet."

"You may find your match. Killing–for orcs it's not just a trade. It's everything."

Gwyn nodded once before leaving. Daramis stood for a moment in the familiar stables, breathing the comforting scents of leather and horseflesh, before remembering his assignment and racing after Gwyn to show her to his lord.

~ * ~

Gwyn saw a bit more life on the walk from the stable to the keep. The stables led to a corral where a trio of black horses stood, watching her as she passed. Against the back corner of the keep itself was a vegetable garden, and behind it ivy grew thick up the stone walls. Once inside, Daramis retreated quickly after leading Gwyn to what she assumed was the "strategy room" the captain had referred to, or, more precisely, to a bare hallway outside it, dim in the cloud-choked light that filtered through the windows. Two older guards stood flanking a heavy door, and when Gwyn reached for the latch, the one on the right cleared his throat while the other caught her eye and made a small but insistent shake of his head. Gwyn frowned and backed a few steps away, still facing the door with her arms crossed and her eyes on the men. Both were middle-aged and looked strong enough, but something about their air seemed lacking. Atlund warriors were solid and rugged and stood with a subtle confidence; the guards she saw before her now were too heavy and nervous of eye. Captain Shon did not hold his bearing like a warrior either. To be a "captain" in Atlund was as much an honorific as a proper rank; it meant a man was a true leader of men. Whether a dozen or a thousand, they would fight, kill, and even die for their captain. It was a duty that required equal measures of experience and gravitas, and this Shon seemed to be lacking in both.

Before she could ponder him any further the door opened at last, revealing the visage of the small man himself flanked between the guards, and that visage already frowning. Gwyn did not speak, but her expression must have said, *What now?*

Shon cleared his throat. "I'm sorry to have kept you waiting. Further, Daramis should have seen to a matter and saved you some delay and embarrassment; since he did not, I must. Please remove your sword and present it to one of the guards for safekeeping."

Gwyn's eyes narrowed. "No one takes this blade from me."

"And no one here would try to *take* it," Shon replied, "but if you wish to see the lord major you are required to *give* it. Our rules are not open for debate, and we cannot let armed strangers into the lord major's presence. These are dangerous times, as you must surely understand, or you would not be here."

"I am here, and you know *why* I am here. How impressed will your lord be at my mettle if I disarm myself at every request?" She stammered on the less common words and knew her northern accent was thick and rustic. Anxiety overcame pride as hot blood flushed her face.

"We're confident that the orcs will not *request* anything of you. The rule is simple. You cannot approach my lord with a weapon. Leave it here or leave this place."

Gwyn crossed her arms again and looked hard into Shon's eyes, pondering whether it would be prudent to seek employment elsewhere. She was mulling regret over unsaddling her horse and only a heartbeat from turning on her heel when a smooth, baritone voice resonated out of the room behind Captain Shon.

"Shon," the voice soothed, "let her keep it." Now the voice took on an edge, becoming once again the commanding tone Gwyn had heard earlier from the wall. "She may try to kill me if she likes, but she would be disappointed. I've been spilling blood for some time longer than she has. Probably longer than her heart has been pumping it."

Gwyn grimaced at the jab toward her immaturity, but by then the lord major had come to stand behind Captain Shon, gazing at Gwyn from over the smaller man's shoulder. His eyes were a brown so deep they were almost black on black, but there was a sparkle in them, a warmth that Gwyn couldn't help but absorb somehow. There was jest in the eyes, true, but no malice and no challenge. This realization gave Gwyn pause, for she saw challenge almost everywhere. More striking was the thing replacing the challenge: a cold, steady confidence Gwyn had rarely encountered before. Baraxis' statement that he could best her in combat was no threat or bravado, just a fact he was pointing out, like the season or the time of day. It was a confidence Gwyn could respect, if she could somehow judge it was warranted.

"Let her in," the man continued, "and then leave us. I will review her alone."

"As you wish, Lord Major," Shon replied, walking past Gwyn down the hallway.

"Please, come in," the older man said, stepping backward into the room. Gwyn took two steps inside and stopped as the door was closed behind her at a nod from the lord major to one of his guards. The room was sparsely furnished, dominated by a large table, its surface invisible under layers of maps and charts, surrounded by simple, wooden chairs. A low fire burned in the hearth, and a pair of antique swords hung crossed above the mantle under a plain banner of crimson trimmed in gold. "I am the Lord Major Baraxis," the man continued as he paced to a high-backed chair behind the table and sat, sliding a dripping candle forward to adjust its light.

"You have an evil-sounding name, Lord Baraxis," Gwyn declared.

Baraxis betrayed no offense or hesitation before replying, "So do you, *Gwyn et Sheevasa*, and a perilous way in a fight, or so I hear. Word reaches my ears of a certain tavern two days north of here–"

"They drew first," Gwyn retorted flatly.

"So I heard it," Baraxis replied. "Why didn't you kill them?"

"Too many witnesses."

The corners of Baraxis' lips turned up slightly, and his jaw dropped in the beginnings of a laugh, but he stifled his mirth as he realized Gwyn was serious. He cleared his throat. "Fair enough," he finally said. "You'll have to forgive me if I misunderstand your manner at first; we don't get many Atlunders in these parts. In fact I've only seen any of your people once before, when I was traveling with my king in a delegation to the elven capital in the northeast, on the fringes of the Elven Forest."

"You were fortunate to have seen any of my people there–" Gwyn replied.

"I don't know about *fortunate*," Baraxis interrupted, but Gwyn kept speaking.

"–we don't frequent the Vale."

"Atlunders are not the friends of elves?"

"We trade with them, but spend little time on their side of the river. We prefer to stay among our own kind."

"You speak *my* language well enough, and find yourself far from home, for someone preferring her 'own kind.'"

"The languages are much alike," Gwyn said. "They sprang from a common root before your ancestors came on this mad quest to found an autocracy, which of course you would know if you read better histories."

"You *ass!*" Baraxis shouted, though laughter shook his voice. "You don't have much of manners, do you, Atlunder?"

"Where I come from, manners don't require false flattery. I don't suspect the orcs will require it, either."

Baraxis nodded. "You are a strange one, Gwyn, but I've heard enough to know your value in battle, and seen enough myself now to know you are no traitor or blackguard. I will admit more than a passing interest in employing you, but there are a few matters to be addressed."

"Go on."

"You have to understand that we can't afford confusion or lone heroics in the heat of battle, which is why our law makes no distinction between bound men and paid men, or paid women for that matter, in the chain of command. If you sign on, you must follow my orders, and those of my captains and sergeants, without question."

"In battle, you mean."

"In battle and in related endeavors."

"I'll kill where I'm told and stay my blade when I'm told. When the battle ends, I am my own woman and follow my own orders. I'll not have you or your men taking liberties with their authority."

"That would never happen," Baraxis reassured.

"If it does—"

"It won't."

"*If it does*…witnesses won't stop me a second time."

Baraxis' eyes narrowed at the threat as he weighed Gwyn's words for a moment. "There is bravado in you," he said. "Today I deem it more a danger to you than anyone else. If it ever gets any of my people hurt, there will be trouble between us. Fair?"

"Fair. What other matters are there?"

Baraxis cleared his throat again, and for the first time in the encounter Gwyn thought he looked ill at ease. "I, ah… I can't pay you much. I hope I haven't wasted your time, and I know from rumor of the caravan guards that you can probably name your price at any keep near—"

"I don't care," Gwyn interrupted. "I will fight for a roof, even a canvas, over my head and food in my belly, the same for my horse, and enough free access to your armorers and smiths to keep my weapons and gear in good repair. That's all I need. I didn't come here to grow wealthy."

Baraxis couldn't help but give in to his curiosity. "Then why *did* you come here?"

"To kill. People say the fighting here is the bloodiest."

Baraxis shook his head. "And so young. How did you come to be this way?"

Gwyn scowled. "My motivations are mine. Is your lack of mercenaries because you are poor or because you are judgmental?"

"Because I'm poor, at least in coin. None of the prior suppliants have baffled me so."

"Well, I've said what I will. Make your decision. Give your first orders or leave me to find a different employer."

"Very well. So there is no misunderstanding, I will have my scribes draw up an agreement. Can you sign your name, or do you have a mark?"

"I can sign," Gwyn growled, frustration building throughout the encounter now unleashed by the implication she was probably illiterate, "and here is my mark!" With that, she pulled the dirk from her boot and rammed it through some of Baraxis' maps an inch deep into the heavy oak table.

"Full marks for the zeal," Baraxis said, chagrined, "but I should tell you this table has been in my family for generations."

"I…" Gwyn stammered. Regret was strange to her, but she respected family history more than most things. She'd assumed the Southerners too modern or shallow to care about such traditions, and the challenge to her prejudice was jarring. "I didn't…"

Surprisingly, Baraxis smiled. "Don't worry so much," he said, sweeping the parchments off the tabletop, with the exception of a few held in place by Gwyn's knife point, to reveal a nearly solid expanse of burn marks and cuts. "This table may well have been used for a barricade more often than for dining or planning. Each scar is a tale, and now it has one more to tell. Perhaps we'll even survive long enough to see how it ends."

CHAPTER VII

After signing Baraxis' papers, something she considered little more than a distrustful Southern formality, Gwyn toured the lord major's keep with Daramis, just relieved from guard duty. While they walked past the kitchens and smithy, the younger guard struck up idle conversation.

"You're the first to agree to fight for what little our lord could pay," he began.

"Is that so?" Gwyn asked, uninterested.

"It is," Daramis pressed on. "It'll surely be a boost to morale when you join us on the line."

"I thought you didn't like 'foreign troublemakers.'"

"If you're good enough for the lord major, you're good enough for me. Most everybody else will feel the same."

"And who is 'everybody else,' if Baraxis is struggling to attract fighters?" Gwyn had wondered who her comrades would be, and this seemed a good opportunity to ask.

"That's, well, *us*. All the Sutherese, as Baraxis' people call ourselves."

"Surely not everybody," Gwyn countered, skeptical.

"All the men over fourteen years," Daramis replied. "A few skilled tradesmen are excused, but only those whose craft serves the war. Armorers, smiths, masters of horse. Everybody else fights."

"I understood that in the Southern Kingdoms, the farmers gave a measure of their crops and freedom in exchange for a lord's protection. It seems a bad bargain if you're doing the fighting as well."

"The south is a big place," Daramis replied. "Things aren't the same all over. In the days before the orcs attacked, there wasn't much fighting to be done. Nobles would band together and skirmish on their own, and if they needed more men they'd whip up their tenants, then whoever they attacked would whip up theirs, until fighting for the noble turned into an obligation. Then the orcs came, and the need for farmers and laborers to feed the war effort was as great as the need for soldiers. Around the Capital where there's plenty of trade and profit, nobles started to pay and equip standing armies so the working folk didn't have to fight. Once those in the poorer regions got wind of that, they refused to bleed for land they didn't own. We're freemen now, for generations. We could leave, but Baraxis is a good lord, and this is our home. We fight for it as best we can."

"So you have no warriors?"

"I said we all fight," Daramis insisted.

"No, I understand. What I mean is: Are there none here who fight by trade? None who practice at arms as their life's work?"

"Not to speak of."

Gwyn shook her head as they stepped outside into the summer heat. "It's no wonder you couldn't defeat the orcs in two hundred years."

"Now that you're here, I'm sure you can show us how it's done," Daramis shot back, his eyes exasperated. Gwyn smiled as she followed the shorter boy out toward the main gate.

Lord Baraxis' keep stood north of the Storn River, but his land extended on the other side, at least in name, and the stone bridge he commanded was the only such crossing for twenty leagues in either direction. Over the years it had been coveted by men and orcs alike, and the orcs tried daily to purchase it with blood. Just on the other side of the bridge, Daramis found Captain Shon and turned over his charge, dismissing himself with a salute. About a hundred yards distant was a timber barricade. Shon nodded toward it and began walking. Gwyn took his meaning and followed.

"I see you've managed to impress the lord major," Shon mused.

"I don't know about that, but he did hire me on," Gwyn replied.

Every time Gwyn spoke her tone carried notes of argument. Shon stopped and crossed his arms. "You're going to be trouble for me, aren't you, Atlunder?"

Gwyn scowled. "You 'Sutherese' are the rudest lot I ever heard of." Slowly, his words sunk in. "Trouble for *you*? *You're* the leader of the mercenaries."

"Well, mercenary, anyway. And the rest of the fighting men."

"Then, please, tell me at least *you're* a soldier," Gwyn insisted.

"Of course–"

"Thank Ter–"

"–when I'm not on my ranch."

"Ranch?" Gwyn growled. "I'm to be taking orders from a rancher?"

"You *will* take orders from a rancher, if that's what the lord major decides. And he has."

Gwyn's eyes narrowed. "*You're* going to be trouble for *me*, aren't you, Southerner?"

Shon's eyes gleamed.

Gwyn sighed. "Fine. So now wh–"

A horn blast cut across the afternoon, and like a herd moving toward feed, men in every corner turned and ran south.

"Now we fight," Shon replied. "Hurry." They continued to the barricade at a jog.

A few moments later, Gwyn stood on a waist-high step on the inside of the log palisade, its top set with iron spikes, outward pointing and barbed. Many were crusted with blood or worse, others wrenched downward or missing altogether. A hundred yards away, arraying themselves near a line of trees, milled a throng of orcs, the first Gwyn had ever seen. She gasped, despite herself.

Shon looked over. "A mite better control than most first-timers, I'll give you that."

Gwyn nodded but did not take her eyes off the savage horde before her. Most were larger than a big man, but as a species the orcs were far more varied than humans. Their skin was scaly but smooth, like a snake's, and ran in shades from pale green to almost black. Their weapons and armor were clearly scavenged and in poor repair; some of the smaller fighters wore only furs for protection and wielded hatchets made of stone. Still, that was their only disadvantage. Their ferocity was daunting as they shoved and gnashed at each other, each striving to be foremost in the horde when the charge began. Gwyn's brothers-in-arms in Atlund had never been cowards, but she had never known them to actually fight for the front rank, and even *she* showed more restraint when the blood scent was on the air than these creatures. She shuddered, then replaced her apprehension with hatred. The beasts confronting her now reminded her too much of Kellgore's minions.

At last the charge came, the hundred vile fighters pounding across the turf in great, loping strides, trampling over the bodies and bones of what must have been dozens of prior charges, smashing them ever deeper into mud that might once have been green with pasture or golden with wheat. The men around her were already armed with tall bows, but Gwyn still hadn't acquired one. Shon noted her lack of armament and shouted to the soldier next to him, a ruddy-faced man in his middle years. "Ardos."

"Yes, Captain?"

"Let me have your bow."

"Aye, sir," Ardos replied, handing him the weapon. Shon promptly turned it over to Gwyn, shifting Ardos' quiver from its place leaning against the wall so it was also within her reach.

"There you are, Atlunder. Let's see what you can do. Nock!" At Shon's command, three dozen men drew arrows and laid them across their bows, their broad, barbed heads dark and pitted. Gwyn wanted to protest her lack of skill but had to struggle just to catch up to the more experienced men around her. She could swear the bow was as thick as her wrist and noticed the one called Ardos watching with a vaguely amused expression. "Hold!" Shon shouted as the mob hurtled toward them, now barely sixty yards away. "Stretch! Aim! Loose!" In virtual unison thirty-six arms drew back, bows raised slightly, and strings twanged out through the evening air. Gwyn was a step behind, and her eyes bulged as, for all her great strength, the longbow refused to move after three-quarter stretch. Even lacking its full potential, the arrow sprang swiftly from the bow, and Gwyn was confident it had struck something; it was hard to miss when shooting into such a mass of charging bodies, now so close. Most of the first rank fell and were trampled, but now the second rank turned, and for the first time the Southerners realized these orcs had stout wooden shields strapped to their backs. They held fast, sheltering those behind, at least momentarily. The Southerners looked at each other, bewildered, except Shon, who had taken a few paces back north, and Ardos, who was still looking at Gwyn. Now that she had a moment to regard him, she saw that though his years hung thick about his middle, he had arms like small tree trunks beneath broad, dense shoulders. "Don't feel bad," the Southerner chuckled, "the captain was just playing. Nobody in Sutherset can stretch that bow but me. You did well enough. You've longer arms to start with, so it surely felt worse than it was. I think you were only a couple inches short of the mark."

Gwyn knew he was being kind and felt wary of his motives.

"What are they playing at?" boomed Lord Major Baraxis suddenly, thundering across the bridge on a great, black stallion, half again as large as the biggest riding horse in Atlund, his chest and arms covered in light plates and a bearskin cloak flapping heavily from his shoulders. He reined the beast in next to Shon, a few steps behind them, and it tossed its head and snorted. Gwyn recognized it as the largest of the three she'd seen earlier and admired its spirit.

"I don't know, Lord Major," Shon answered. "This is a new trick, and no mistake."

"Don't let the savage looks fool you, Atlunder," Baraxis said to Gwyn. "They aren't bright, but they're cunning in their way. Don't forget it. Shon, get the men shooting again. I don't know what their game is, but they'll have a harder time holding those shields up with their legs full of arrows."

"Aye, sir. Loose at will, men!"

Arrows began hissing out along the wall, and a few orcs fell. As the men continued to loose shafts, though, a heavy mist spilled ominously from the forest behind until it nearly enveloped the orcs on the plain. Moments passed as a few more orcs fell, the line contracting to take their places.

Suddenly a bolt of darkness lanced forth from the mist, crackling and forking like lightning over Gwyn's head to pass mere inches from Baraxis' face. He leaned back and raised his arms over his eyes as his horse bucked in fear, throwing him heavily to the ground. Shon immediately dropped down beside him, trying desperately to revive his fallen commander. By now the mist completely obscured the orcs, but Gwyn could hear the tramp of their booted feet slowly advancing.

Scowling at the distracted captain, Gwyn looked over at Ardos, who quailed against the wall. "What in the hells is going on here?" she growled.

"A zil'bast," Ardos shuddered, "it must be. Orc sorcerers with the power of death. We've never faced one. We're finished for sure."

A second bolt flashed out and struck the barricade ten yards to Gwyn's right. Two defenders were thrown back like reeds as a six-foot section of wall detonated with unnatural force, showering Gwyn with slivers. The remaining defenders were looking back, indecisive and growing more fearful by the moment. Gwyn had never been *in* a route, but she had *caused* her share of them, and she knew the signs.

"Didn't you hear me, lass?" Ardos repeated. "We've got to fall back, we're done for here!"

Gwyn's eyes burned. "Not while *Gwyn et Sheevasa* still breathes, you're not!" Dropping Ardos' bow, she unslung her great sword and hoisted it over her head. "To me, men!" she cried, "To me!" She sprinted to the opening in the wall, gathering defenders as she went. Soon a knot of fifteen or so had formed behind her. Some looked at her with distrusting eyes, but Shon still knelt over Baraxis, and the men were desperate for any kind of orders. Fearful as they were, Gwyn was impressed that so many had rallied.

"We can't even see them," one of the men protested.

"Then whine less and listen more," Gwyn reprimanded. "Hear their feet. They're ahead and left, and haven't begun the charge. Wheel out to the right, not too far. Follow me, and we'll drive into their flank."

"What about the zil'bast?" someone insisted.

"It's mine!" Gwyn rebutted, breaking into a trot. The men followed. She had no idea what a zil'bast was, but she hadn't met a thing yet she couldn't kill.

Only a few seconds passed before she heard the orcs bellow their charge, and Gwyn waved her sword forward to signal her men to advance. All at once the shadows loomed up in front of her as she and her force approached the third rank of orcs at an oblique angle, and she only now fully appreciated their daunting size. Unfazed, Gwyn picked out an orc at the outside edge and threw her shoulder into him, knocking him back into his compatriots and disrupting the charge as the first ranks thundered on. She felled him with a quick slash before he could recover. In the same instant she felt the impact of the Southerners behind her, and so did the orcs. The left flank of the charge dispersed, no longer protecting those further to the right. Gwyn could see the creature that must have been the zil'bast a few paces behind the charging lines, an orc-like figure, though twisted and gaunt, its bony limbs out of proportion to its body, sitting astride a rangy horse, and it had turned to face her. Gwyn understood little of the ways of magic but thought her attack must have broken its concentration, for already the mist was breaking up in the face of a rising southerly wind. Gwyn hacked down another orc and was clear of the charging mass, now sprinting straight for the sorcerous, mounted creature. Suddenly panicked, the zil'bast raised a thorny staff and growled some strange, broken syllables; suddenly the air started to shimmer around it like waves of heat.

At that moment, the mist must have cleared enough for the few defenders who stayed behind to see the zil'bast, for arrows began racing from the wall toward the enemy. Those that came within a few feet of the sorcerer burst into flame and incinerated almost instantly as though under some impossible heat, their melted heads causing irritation but no apparent harm as they struck their target awkwardly. Indeed, as Gwyn approached, the heat of a bonfire washed over her, though she could see no flame. Gripped in her rage, the battle light flashing in her eyes, she ignored the heat and drove forward, straight at the zil'bast's horse. The animal reared up and tried to strike with its hooves, but Gwyn darted to the side and swung her blade mightily at the horse's hind leg, shearing flesh and shattering bone just below its knee.

The horse went down with a horrendous scream, the rider pinned beneath its side. The zil'bast managed to free its staff and pointed it at Gwyn, the heat still blazing around it, but Gwyn swung her sword once more toward the creature's head. The moment it touched that shimmering barrier, the leading edge grew red hot, but Gwyn did not relent. Though the edge was nearly molten by the time it struck, still there was force enough to crush the zil'bast's skull.

Their charge was disrupted, their leader was dead, and the hail of arrows was only growing as archers from farther down the wall redeployed to the defense. Demoralized, the orcs broke and ran back to the trees, arrows and Southern cheers chasing them the whole way. Ardos came to Gwyn's side and, thankfully, put the zil'bast's horse out of its misery. Gwyn could not; she knelt in the bloody field, cradling the bent and misshapen remains of her father's sword.

Ardos helped Gwyn up. "It'll be alright, lass. Baraxis has a fine smith. He'll get your blade fixed up if the steel's strong."

"She's strong," Gwyn replied, straightening, but remained unconvinced. Ardos provided only a faint glimmer of hope in the yawning pit the loss was opening up within her.

"Can I ask ye something, Atlunder?" Ardos hazarded as they began their walk back to the wall.

"You can *ask*," Gwyn replied.

"Yer name, that the rumors all brought ahead of ye?"

"*Gwyn et Sheevasa.*"

"Aye, that one. I don't know much o' the northern speech, but it means 'Gwyn the Savage,' don't it?"

"It means Hand of Vengeance."

"Oh." Ardos cleared his throat. "Well, I thought sure there must be 'savage' in there somewhere. The rumors told it true enough, any case. Ye don't hold back much, do ye?"

"I wouldn't know how."

By then they had returned to the breach in the wall, where others already stood to roll a large cart into place until more permanent repairs could be made. A few yards away, Shon helped a revived Lord Major Baraxis back onto his horse. The captain caught Gwyn's eye for a moment and glared before turning and accompanying Baraxis northward across the bridge. Gwyn ran her finger along the ruined edge of her sword. "I hope your lord's smith is better than his captain," she mused.

"What was that?" Ardos snapped, grabbing Gwyn's arm to stop her short.

Gwyn wrenched her arm free, secretly surprised at the strength in the older man's grip, and took an aggressive step toward Ardos before he raised his other hand, open palmed, in a staying gesture. Other men happening by moved closer, their eyes suspicious. Ardos looked at Gwyn levelly. "Yer new around here," he said, "so we'll let that pass, fer now. Give ye some time to sort things out. The next time ye speak ill o' Shon, you'll like as not find yerself fightin' every man here."

"Then every man here will get a beating!" Gwyn shot back.

Some of the other men scoffed angrily, but Ardos stayed calm. "Maybe, maybe not," he replied. "I certainly wouldn't best ye, but there's men here better 'n me." He shrugged. "Don't matter. Once ye get to know 'im, ye'll come around."

Gwyn took a pace back and eyed the crowd, then turned her critical gaze back to Ardos. "You *love* him, don't you?" Her tone was bewildered.

Many nodded, and several voiced their assent. "There ain't a man here," Ardos continued, "that don't owe 'is life, 'is *family's* life, to Shon an' the lord major. I can see ye don't like 'is manner and I s'pect he don't care much fer yers, but take my word, ye'd rather him an ally than an enemy.

"Now, you go and take yer sword to 'em. They'll make it right, ye count on that."

As Gwyn departed, she heard Ardos take the conversation back to his fellows. "Well, except fer the zil'bast, it was a light day. We should be thankful."

"Aye," another replied, "we should have known something strange was up when they only sent a hundred."

Gwyn remembered the image of the savage horde and thought of facing double that number. Within her, bloodlust warred with sense on whether to be grateful or terrified, and slowly she came to remember that these men, whose bravery she'd presumed to insult, marched out to face them every single day.

~ * ~

Gwyn found Shon and Baraxis arguing in the bailey as Daramis led Baraxis' horse away to a corral. They hadn't noted her approach.

"Shon, you know I admire your loyalty, but I'm just one man."

"One *lord*, you mean, and that without an heir," Shon corrected.

"I *have* an heir," Baraxis replied, placing his hand on Shon's shoulder.

"I don't want it!" Shon hissed back, shrugging the hand away.

"I know you don't. Hell, most days *I* don't, but leadership isn't a privilege. Not here, not with the orcs at our throats. It's a duty, and one I know you can carry."

"Still, do you blame me for trying to keep you alive?" Shon pressed.

"For that, no, but..."

Finally they saw Gwyn. "By Terillah!" Baraxis gasped at the sight of Gwyn's weapon, or what was left of it. "What happened out there?"

"That creature, the zil'bast, Ardos called it? Whatever its name, it was...well protected."

"May I?" Baraxis asked, holding out his hands. Gwyn handed over the mangled sword, surprised at the lord's humility. "This will be righted at once," he ordained. "I assume you would prefer it repaired rather than replaced."

"I will *require* it to be repaired. Perhaps remade if that isn't possible. It cannot *be* replaced," Gwyn answered.

Baraxis nodded, holding her eyes but smiling faintly at her imperious manner. "Please, go and rest. I only have one master smith, but many skilled enough to assist him, and they will work through the night if need be. If repair is possible, that should be enough time. I will find you myself when the work is done." With that, he strode off toward the smithy.

Gwyn stood with Shon, eyeing him sidelong, relieved there was hope for her ancestral weapon but none the less puzzled. She sighed. "Why does he trouble himself? I'm just a hired sword."

Shon kept his eyes on Baraxis as he answered. "It's just his way. He practically *raised* me. If he has other reasons for his favor toward you, they aren't for me to say. I'm still not sure they are wise."

Gwyn started to argue, but Shon interrupted. "No, Gwyn." It was the first time a Southerner had used her name *as* a name and not some alien sobriquet. It was a troubling realization that something in her liked the way Shon said it. "There is a danger in you still," Shon continued, "but on the whole I may have, *may have*, misjudged you. You acquitted yourself well today, your *first* day, by Terillah...better, perhaps, than I did. You probably shouldn't have taken command, and Baraxis probably won't like it, but I'm glad you did. Thank you." He extended his hand, and Gwyn grasped it palm to palm. They had not yet shed blood together, though they should have, and Gwyn could see the weight of that awareness in his eyes as they shook hands. She felt no shock this time, but a strange kind of compulsion took its place.

Gwyn looked into Shon's averted eyes, carefully, for the first time, and saw something there un-looked-for. His gaze was distant, almost sad; she did not see the love for battle that she met in her own reflection, but something else was there, something she now recognized in Baraxis, even Ardos. It was resolve: deeper, hidden courage she was shamed to think might be stronger than her brash fearlessness. Atlunders were raised to glory in battle, but in this place men fought hard even though they hated fighting. She nodded slightly, understanding Ardos and the

Sutherese a little better, and made a hard decision. "Captain," she said, summoning Shon's eyes back to hers, "one day soon we will share the warrior's grip, and I hope we'll find one another worthy."

Shon nodded as he released her hand. "I hope for the same." He left to attend to his duties, leaving Gwyn to rest and try to clean off some of the blood.

Many of Baraxis' fighters lived in their own homes, near enough to his keep to come and go daily. Those living farther away stayed in a barracks within the walls during their rotations through the guard but, of course, these were all male. Gwyn, therefore, was given an empty room and a decent mattress in the south tower of the gatehouse, but sleep eluded her that night as her mind cast about for understanding of her place in Sutherset.

Dawn found her in the bailey, leaning on the corral fence where the three black horses spent most of their time. By now she'd learned the big warhorse was called Storm Cloud. Also in the corral were a big, black mare, barely smaller than the stallion, and a two-year-old colt that would soon fill out to be the very image of his father. All three looked at Gwyn again as she stood there, their expressive eyes curious.

"Gwyn," came Baraxis' shout from behind her. "Gwyn, good news!"

The warrior turned to see Baraxis, again wearing his crimson, lordly robes, striding across the green, her blade in his hand. Two other men were with him, one the smith by the look of his build and garb, the other, she guessed, some kind of steward or scribe. He was perhaps the smallest grown man she'd seen, barely over five feet and thin, though the latter was obscured somewhat beneath heavy blue robes that matched a skullcap pulled down over his black hair. Gwyn's eyes, however, were mostly for her sword. Baraxis was still some yards away, but she could see that the leather wraps were missing from the hilt and foregrip. Still, the blade looked straight and true once more, and her heart leapt hopefully. Baraxis extended the hilt to her as he approached.

Gwyn took the sword and made a few experimental cuts, testing the weapon's balance. The smith spoke up as she did. "I told the lord major, nine times in ten repairing a blade like that is naught but a tale for minstrel's songs, but that weapon o' yours... There was no magic in it, I'd swear to that, but the steel moved to my hammer like to a lover's kiss–eh, begging your pardon, miss. Say it how you want, and I won't try to suss out the 'why' of it, but that sword *wanted* to be whole again."

"Of course she did," Gwyn replied, finally resting the blade point-down after a heavy, downward hack. "It'll cost more than a little sorcery to take this blade from a Candon hand. You are truly a master at your craft, smith; I have to admit it's even better than before."

"Oh, that's no work o' mine, miss."

"What do you m–" Gwyn's eyes suddenly flicked up at Baraxis, then down at her sword again, where one flat of the blade faced her. "What are *these*?" A line of seven strange characters ran vertically down the flat of the foregrip, etched or stamped into the surface and pulsing with a dim, purple glow.

"I'd best be on my way. Long night an' all," the smith muttered, retreating hastily.

"Ah, perhaps I'll join you," the blue-robed man added, beginning to turn away. Baraxis, however, put his arm around the narrow shoulders, encouraging him to stay.

Gwyn's eyes still bore into the lord major. "Elven runes," he replied proudly.

"Elven *what*?" Gwyn spat.

"It's magic, Gwyn!" Baraxis announced. "Master Drax, please explain."

As the little man cleared his throat, Gwyn looked at him more closely. His nose was finer, his cheekbones higher than most men, but not enough to cause surprise. He'd arranged his straight, black hair to hide the tall points of his ears, but not enough to conceal them from a careful view. His eyes were gray, but not without a subtle wash of violet Gwyn had missed at first in the dawn light, and even in that relative dimness his pupils were tiny. Gwyn was certain she'd never been this close to one of the diminutive people. The wizard wore rings on most of his fingers and a small, silver ear cuff just peeked through the hair covering his left ear.

"I'm Drax of the Western Vale," the elf began. He moved his right hand forward only an inch or two, then his glance fell on Gwyn's hands both squeezing her sword hilt, and he stopped. "I'm an enchanter, mostly. For magic on an object to have permanence, it has to be modified in some way, and the more the change is incorporated into its making, the better."

"The timing was a rare stroke of luck," Baraxis cut in. Master Drax happened by, looking for a bed and a bit too light on coin for the inn. Your blade had just been quenched and was going back for the temper."

Gwyn's expression was baleful, and Drax spoke carefully. "The first three runes work together to protect the weapon from the effect of any future magic. The next two make it more resilient; with proper care and protection from great abuse it will serve your family indefinitely. The sixth rune reduces the felt weight to the wielder; the seventh inversely affects the impact to the target. That means–"

"I know what it means," Gwyn spat. She turned to Baraxis. "Why did you even hire me if you felt I needed such *assistance*."

"I never said you *needed* it, though a smarter fighter wouldn't turn it down," Baraxis added as Gwyn snorted at the insult.

"You should have asked me first, Baraxis." There was threat in Gwyn's tone.

"Ah, that's likely my fault, miss," the wizard Drax piped up. "By the time we'd concluded our negotiations the temper was half done, and I told the lord major it was sort of 'now or never' if he wanted a great result."

Baraxis' eyes narrowed. "Gwyn, this is a rare and valuable thing, and don't think for a moment this elf didn't know it."

"It was a fair price," Drax protested, but Baraxis talked over him.

"This magic was at no small cost to me, and freely given to you. I'm not even looking for gratitude, but I'm not going to stand here and take your scorn, either. Whether or not you appreciate it, it *is* a gift. Don't commit the insult of spurning it."

Baraxis' unrepentant attitude pushed Gwyn's frustration past the point of reason. Leaving her left hand on the sword hilt, she stepped forward, aiming a savage right fist at Baraxis' nose. "You pompous-*hunh*!"

Gwyn found herself half gagged and raised to the balls of her feet by Baraxis' dagger at her throat, drawn quicker than her eye could see. Drax hurried away. "*Don't*," Baraxis whispered. "You're fast, you're strong, and you've got spirit. Given the choice I'd have you on my side in a heartbeat, but I warned you yesterday that I've been killing for longer than you've been alive. I may not like it, but I'm damn good at it, and against you I have the best edge of all."

                    Shane L. Coffey

"And what's that?" Gwyn rasped against the blade at her throat. Despite her position, her voice was filled with skeptic venom.

Baraxis lowered his dagger, allowing Gwyn to relax, and sheathed it. "When I fight," he replied, "I still care that I make it out alive." He turned on his heel and walked away, leaving Gwyn speechless. She hadn't read her contract with care, but she imagined assaulting her employer was probably grounds for termination, so she had started toward the stables to saddle her horse when Baraxis stopped and turned back. "Gwyn," he said, his tone oddly strained, "don't think that I dislike you. Quite the contrary, in fact, you…" He shook his head. "My own feelings aside, there is a chain of command here, and you are its bottommost link. If you ever presume to lead my men in an unsanctioned counteroffensive again, I'll have you hanged. Is that understood?"

Gwyn sensed his sincerity and nodded dumbly.

"Good. You are excused from combat duty today, but refit the furnishings of your new weapon and train with it. The edge still needs a final grind as well; see the smithy for tools. And don't stray too far from the barricade. That sword of yours is the only weapon I know about that can cut through a zil'bast's defenses. I don't think they'll spare another against us so soon, but if they do, it's yours. Report to Shon or Ardos tomorrow at dawn for your next assignment." With that, he walked away, and this time did not turn back.

Gwyn started her walk to the smithy, mulling over the fact that for the second time in little more than a year her commanding officer had put a blade to her throat. This was the beginning of a troubling pattern.

CHAPTER VIII

For the next two days the orcs sent only probing forces, and arrows turned them back. Though archery little excited Gwyn, she felt compelled to do her part, now that she fought for pay, and borrowed a bow suitable for her height. Her eyes were sharp, and she improved quickly at figuring range and angle. Ardos told her another week would see her capable enough to compete with her fellows against orc-sized targets as long as the wind was calm.

On the third day a larger body of orcs emerged from the distant trees, maybe seven or eight score, and with decent shields. The orcs bellowed their throaty war cry and charged forward with the same loping strides Gwyn had seen the first day, chewing through the yardage with frightening speed. Gwyn struggled to adjust her range against such fast-running targets, and she hesitated until the enemy was close enough to loose with a flat trajectory. She had time for only a single shot, to her comrades' three, and didn't even have time to mark what it struck before dropping her bow and grabbing her sword from where it leaned against the wall.

The orcs clambered upward, some leaning their tall shields against the wall as a makeshift step, others bending low to boost the next in line. Between the fog and her focus on the zil'bast during her first close-range encounter, Gwyn hadn't taken in much detail, but now she got her first proper look at orc faces, which were no more uniform than their heights or coloration save that they all had two slit-pupiled, yellow eyes. Most had short but pointed noses and long, pointed ears; however, many were missing some or all of those features. Some bore the scarred stumps of them, but others seemed never to have grown them in the first place. For the most part, their lower jaws jutted forward and sported two protruding tusks, and when they opened their mouths to bellow or even bite, their jaws parted disturbingly wide to accommodate them, giving Gwyn a clear view of the sharp, slicing teeth that crowded their gums farther back. Their breath blasted hot and foul in her face.

Out of every thirty or forty orcs, one had a shock of hair atop its head, and these varied in size and color. One such orc leapt up the wall in front of Gwyn, at a gap in the iron spikes she thought would give her the best chance at a real fight. Half the orc's left ear was missing under a short crest of red; this close she could see the crest was formed of dyed horsehair stuck with animal glue to what she realized, with revulsion, was a human scalp. She thrust her point at the hideous face, but the orc grabbed the blade with its bare hand and shoved the thrust aside as it worked one leg over the wall. Gwyn shouted in alarm as she pulled the blade back, ripping through scale and sinew, and shoved her crossguard forward into the enemy's face. Perhaps she surprised it back, or perhaps it was simply too slow, and it took a quillon full in the left eye. Even reeling back, it swung a human-made blade toward her right shoulder, and she leaned her torso and tucked her arm so the blow glanced lightly off her mail before finishing the orc with a downward slash.

To her left, Ardos had been caught in a grapple by a smaller attacker, pressing him too close to bring his blade to bear. Gwyn stabbed straight into the orc's flank, knowing from his width it must have erupted from the other side, then quickly pulled it free. Ardos felt the creature go slack and shoved it back over the wall. In the same heartbeat another orcish face appeared in front of Gwyn, so closely she had only to adjust her withdrawing motion to slam her pommel into the side of its head. The head whipped to the side, but the brute managed to stay clinging to the wall until Gwyn swung down, splitting its skull in a spurt of black blood. She roared with laughter as it fell back at last, then leaned over the wall to thrust down at the next wave of climbers, slicing heads and faces as they clambered to reach the top. Most bellowed or growled and pulled back, but one batted her thrusts aside with a hatchet and managed to gain the top. Grinning, Gwyn stepped slightly to the side and moved one hand to her sword's foregrip in the tight quarters, giving the orc space to get both feet on the wall and stand straight. "Come on!" she yelled, preparing for his attack. It swung the hatchet, but instead of parrying the weapon Gwyn stepped even closer and parried the arm, cleaving halfway through its wrist. As the orc screamed she leaned back and threw a mighty kick in the center of its chest, driving it over the wall to land with an awkward snap on the dirt below.

Only moments had passed, and an orc off somewhere began bellowing in their growly, guttural language. Those not already at the wall top began to pull back, picking up the large shields for what cover they could. Those Sutherese not still embattled or wounded reached once more for bows, and some of the better archers managed to fell a few more before they made it to the cover of the trees. Gwyn looked down the line and guessed a couple dozen of the enemy had been slain in the melee.

Ardos turned to Gwyn and saw the grin on her bloody face. "Yer mad, Gwyn the Savage. Mad. But thank ye." Despite its incorrectness, Ardos' moniker for her had stuck.

She laughed again as she pulled a rag to clean the gore from her sword.

"That first one ye killed, with the horsehair? Those are the elites," Ardos explained. "We aren't too sure o' the lengths or colors, but they're all some kind o' battle award. That was a good kill."

She smiled at the older man. "They're all good kills to me, Ardos."

The next day Gwyn sat in what had become her customary place on the wall, wondering if the orcs would come close enough for a proper fight again. Once the other defenders had settled into their places, she noticed younger men filling a few spaces on either side and recognized the guard, Daramis, on her right.

"Thought you were a guard in the keep," Gwyn commented.

"Everybody takes a turn on the wall," he answered. "The younger men less often, but still. Heard you got my dad out of a spot yesterday."

She squinted. "Ardos? I see the resemblance, I guess. Except you're a lot skinnier."

Daramis laughed. "Mother's a fine cook." Then he sobered. "And there's less of us now to eat it."

"How's that?"

"I had two older brothers, but…"

For all the battle in their culture, Gwyn was hard pressed to think of an Atlund family that had lost two of three sons in battle. "Damn," she finally said, considering nothing in Ardos' manner pointed toward that depth of grief. "I never would have guessed."

"He's the strongest man I know. Don't tell him I said; he'd never let me hear the end of it."

Gwyn nodded. "Just be glad you knew him."

"What do you mean?"

"Never mind."

Captain Shon rode by at the base of the wall atop his bay stallion on an informal inspection of the defenses. "Daramis, don't you think your squad is a bit bunched up here?"

Daramis cleared his throat as Gwyn looked to either side and realized the other men had been sliding in their direction, overhearing. Now chastened, they spread out again. "Sorry, Captain," Daramis answered. "After Sergeant Ardos' story from yesterday, I guess we figured this was the safest stretch of wall to be found."

That day the orcs were turned back by arrows, and the following day they didn't attack at all. The day after that, Ardos was back at Gwyn's left, but one of Daramis' friends was on her right.

"…the prettiest girl in all the south, meaning no disrespect to you personally, of course," the boy rambled. "I hardly get to see her, though, on account of her mother took her a few miles up north away from the fighting while…"

"Gwyn," came a call from the base of the wall. Shon was there, not on his horse at the moment. "Climb down; walk with me a bit."

Offering no parting to the lovelorn fighter, Gwyn picked up her sword and bow and shoved herself down from the fighting step, landing lightly. "Thank you," she sighed grudgingly.

"I didn't call you down to rescue you, sometimes it's just easier to move *you* than to keep spreading out the men."

"I don't mean to be a distraction," Gwyn offered, her respect for the necessities of battle greater than for the man. "I guess I didn't think about how strange it would be to have a woman on the line down here."

"No," Shon mused, "I mean, it is, but I'm not sure it's that. And they're still fighting well. I–" Cries went up from the wall, sighting the orcs' daily sortie. "They never let you finish a thought. Let's to it, then," Shon ordered, clambering up to the step with Gwyn on his heels.

She crested the wall to curses from either side and swept her eyes over the orcs taking position on the field. "I know I'm new here," she muttered, "but that looks like a lot."

"It is," Shon confirmed, not making light of the horde, at least two hundred strong, even now beginning their charge. "Concentrate on the center, loose at will, quick as you can."

Gwyn grabbed arrows from a bundle and nocked as fast as she was able, this time managing two shots before dropping her bow. Shon called for a spear and was handed one, thrusting down over the wall along with his fellows. Gwyn stuck with her sword, and though shorter, if any orcs believed this would offer an advantage in assailing her particular position, they found it a lethal, final mistake.

Gwyn couldn't help noting Shon's demeanor as they fought. His movements were smooth and unhurried, almost mechanical in nature, his strikes well aimed. Between fighting his own opponents, in every safe moment he glanced left and right, giving orders to men by name to shore up a section or help a comrade. Gwyn couldn't see the results of these commands in the midst of her own bloody work, but she little doubted they saved lives that day. When orcs finally gained the top of the wall, Shon shortened the grip on his spear and kept fighting. When a burly orc managed to break the haft, he smoothly drew his sword while using the broken end to parry.

The nearby orcs started to flag, and Gwyn looked to the east to see the fighting raged hotly there. She turned from the palisade and made to move toward the thick of battle.

"Hold, Atlunder," Shon ordered.

"You hold," she shot back, taking a step.

Shon grabbed the back of her sword sling and spun her about, glaring up into her eyes. "I said *hold*, damn you!" She fought the urge to strike him as his icy blue eyes bored through her, demanding obedience. In their brief time together she had never imagined him capable of such wrath, nor such mettle. She made no reply but the grinding of her teeth as she turned back to the wall. Shon leapt down and sprinted to the east.

"What do we do?" a young man asked.

Gwyn looked to see a soldier speaking down to where an older man wearing a sergeant's armband sat holding a bleeding wound in his armpit.

The sergeant nodded toward Gwyn. "You heard the captain's order. We hold here."

The orcs had grown too exhausted to come within the range of Gwyn's sword, so she set it aside and picked up the sergeant's spear, thrusting downward as orcs neared. None made serious attempts, only keeping the men occupied. Gwyn saw how sporadically the orcs challenged the defenders here and silently lamented the waste of strength. "Maybe you should check on your sergeant," she muttered to the young man next to her.

He looked down to see what Gwyn had; the man had bled through a second wad of bandages and was looking pale. "Sergeant," the soldier said, "we've got to get you to a surgeon."

Gwyn could see the sergeant had no desire to die needlessly on that wall, but he hesitated, finally looking at Gwyn. "Keep them fighting here, and by Terillah don't you move without orders."

She'd hoped to sneak away to the thicker fighting as soon as the only command authority had been carried away, but now, to her shock, she found herself put in charge, however informally. The surrounding men looked to her with that weirdly innocent awe she'd seen before, and suddenly she knew her responsibility was more than to herself. "My word," she answered. "Go get patched up."

The heaviest blood and slaughter never returned to Gwyn's portion of the wall, but with great reluctance she stood her post. She later learned the sergeant survived and would even keep his arm, finding with surprise that a part of her was glad.

Two days later another six score orcs reached the wall, though they did not commit as heavily as the previous assault had. Gwyn stood next to Ardos, shoving a spear down the wall at the timid orcs below that refused to make any real effort to climb up.

"Why don't they really attack?" she griped. "I can see them seething up the wall not thirty yards away."

Ardos peered in that direction, squinting, then surprised Gwyn by saying, "Go over there and see what they do."

Gwyn turned toward him with a raised eyebrow. "I couldn't stand another lecture about orders."

The veteran pointed to the sergeant band on his arm. "It's an order, then. Go."

Gauging the situation from where she was, she switched spear for sword and made her way down the line, hacking an orc off the wall top with a twohanded chop as she arrived. A second she stabbed through the neck, and the weary men about her pulled back a step to breathe and give her room. Two more orcs stood near, but as soon as they looked upon her they turned and scrambled back down the wall. A moment later the orcs in the field bellowed their recall order, and the mob began pulling away.

Bewildered, she looked at the men nearest her, but they only shrugged back. She barely realized what she was doing as she vaulted over the wall in frustration, landing on broken orc bodies, and charged the pair that had fled from her. One she overtook and cut down as it ran. The second, sensing her behind him, turned to accept the challenge. It growled a mass of syllables Gwyn felt sure represented words in its guttural tongue. Then it launched itself at Gwyn with terrible fury as several of its fellows, farther away on the field, paused in their flight to growl savage cheers. The beast's rage burned almost as hot as Gwyn's, but hers was the superior skill. The battle-light flashed in her eyes as she thrust, and the orc fell dead. The others continued their cries of triumph for a few moments before continuing their retreat.

Jumping over the wall had been easy from the defender's step on the north side, but Gwyn needed help to get back over. Ardos was there with another of the Sutherese to lend a hand. "Yer a madwoman, Gwyn the Savage, an' no mistake," he chuckled as Gwyn's feet found the step. I'm sure some o' the boys didn't mind the sport, though." That much was undeniable. Men up and down the wall applauded and cheered, and some were making their way closer to clap Gwyn on the back.

"Does anybody speak their tongue?" Gwyn asked. "What did he say?"

Shon, pacing past from farther down the line, called out, "What in the hells was that?" He turned to the other men. "Stop your cheering." Turning back to Gwyn, he said, "We've been over this enough; why shouldn't I hang you this time?" She wasn't sure he was joking.

"I gave orders, Captain," Ardos piped up. "Honest."

Shon grimaced. "Fine. What did this orc sound like?"

Eager to avoid the subject of capital punishment, Gwyn replied, doing her best to phonetically copy the sounds the orc had made at her.

Shon puzzled for a moment, then nodded to himself. "Loose translation?" he offered.

Gwyn nodded back.

"I think the first part was an epithet. Then he said he was 'earning' his death from you."

"What kind of epithet? Loose translation."

"…Hellwitch?" Shon replied, looking to Ardos for confirmation.

"Hellwitch," Ardos agreed after considering for a moment. "Well, it… No, yer right. Hellwitch."

"Hm," Gwyn answered. "I've been called worse."

"Comin' from them, it's kind of a compliment, in its way," another Southerner offered.

"And he said he was earning his *death*," Gwyn puzzled. "He knew I would kill him?"

"Just like they fight for the first rank, even knowing the damage our archers can do," Shon replied. "Just like they felt it was worth opening with a charge last week even when the zil'bast would do more than they ever could. We don't know a lot about their beliefs, but we think those not strong or quick enough to kill many of the enemy would rather die fearlessly than be thought a craven."

"There's a fine line between bravery and stupidity, I guess," Gwyn mused.

Ardos and Shon exchanged looks at the comment, and Ardos couldn't suppress a chuckle.

"What's funny?" Gwyn asked.

Neither spoke, but their faces were expressive.

"You can both go to hell," Gwyn snapped, walking away, but already the fire was gone from her insults. She had shed much blood and learned much of the men fighting on either side of her in the past ten days. The greenest recruit in Atlund could best any one of them in the dueling ring, but in battle the Southerners fought together in ways Gwyn had scarcely imagined. She had been raised in a nation of warriors, and she respected their skill and drive, but the Southern Kingdoms were a nation of soldiers, men who fought not for love of glory but for the necessity of defending their homes. When the battle came they toed the line, swallowing their fear and dispatching the enemy with good fundamentals and grit. When one fell, they fought on relentlessly, only later grieving a man who had been a brother, a friend, even a son. She wondered if she would have heard more of this attitude from the warriors of her own land if she'd really been listening.

Her first uninterrupted week of duty came to a close, and Gwyn still hadn't spoken again to Lord Major Baraxis. At last she grew weary of delaying the encounter. Having been granted another day of rest, she sought him out in the evening near the same corral where they had come to violence before. Wordlessly she took a place next to him on the fence and watched the colt play for a few moments. Baraxis said nothing. He wore his own colors of scarlet and gold, but a simple tunic and breeches instead of lordly robes.

Finally, without meeting his eyes, Gwyn managed to whisper, "Thank you for mending my sword, Lord Major." She heard the smile in Baraxis' voice when he replied.

"Learned to respect our elders, have we?"

Involuntarily rubbing her throat, Gwyn answered, "My betters."

"*Ha!*" Baraxis snorted. "Time and Terillah will tell on that score, I suppose. Until then, let's just say I have the burden to lead, and you have the burden to follow. Fair enough?”

Gwyn looked over to see him painting her with a wry half-smile, and she nodded once. Baraxis handed her a small pouch. “What’s this?” she asked.

“First week’s pay,” Baraxis answered, taking his foot off the lowest rail and stepping away from the fence. “Come on, you can buy me a drink.”

Gwyn narrowed her eyes suspiciously and hesitated.

“A drink,” Baraxis urged. “People drink them when they want to, you know…have a drink.”

“Is that an order?” Gwyn asked.

“Damn it to all the hells, lass–” Gwyn sighed and started to protest. “*Fine*, fine, damn it to all the hells, fully-grown, orc-slaying warrior-woman, must *everything* be a fight with you? *No*, it’s not an order, it’s not a threat, it’s not a flirtation, it isn’t any other untoward thing you might want to fear it is! Shon says you’re doing well on the lines, you seem to be fitting in with the men, and I’m *thirsty!* Are you coming or not?” Baraxis started walking away without waiting for her answer.

Gwyn followed, and for a few steps the pair walked silently as they left the castle and headed toward the nearest tavern. Just as they cleared the drawbridge, Baraxis asked, quietly, “You’ve never had somebody ask you to go for a drink after a fight, have you?”

Gwyn hesitated and tried to feel offended, but for once she was too unprepared and weary to succeed. She also wasn’t sure if Baraxis meant a drink to amend an argument or celebrate a battle, then realized the answer was the same, either way. She shook her head. “Not really.”

“That’s a real shame,” the lord major said with sincerity. “Sorry if I overreacted.”

Gwyn shrugged, and they entered the tavern without further conversation.

Once inside, they saw a half-dozen fighters were already there, Captain Shon sitting at a table to one side, alone, nursing an ale. The men brightened at the lord major's entrance, and Baraxis shouted, "Good news, boys! Next round's on the Atlunder!" The group raised their glasses and cheered as Gwyn grimaced at Baraxis. The men parted to make space in their midst, and the barkeep turned to face Baraxis. "What'll it be, m'lord?"

"One of your best wines, on the Atlunder's tab. Don't worry, I'll vouch for her."

"And you?" the barkeep asked Gwyn.

"One of your cheapest ales, apparently," she replied. "I'm a petty sellsword, and it seems my employer has expensive tastes."

Baraxis was quiet as he drank his wine but asked the men probing questions to encourage their stories. After one drink, he bowed out gracefully, so gracefully, in fact, that Gwyn didn't notice his departure. She was deep in trading stories with the men, and deeper in her third pint, when she realized he was gone.

"Where's Baraxis?" Gwyn asked.

"He's always like that," Shon answered as he came to the bar for another mug. "Says he's afraid if he makes a show of leaving the men will take it as a hint and break up the party."

"Speaking of that," one of the men answered, draining his last tankard. "Daydis," he continued, calling the barkeep, "can I settle up with you at the store tomorrow? I've got to stop in for a couple boxes of nails, anyhow." The barkeep nodded, and one by one the men drifted away, some paying their tabs before they went. Left suddenly alone, Gwyn followed Shon back to his table.

"So what do you think of Sutherset now, Gwyn?" Shon asked. He wasn't drunk, but ale had made his demeanor easy. Gwyn wasn't drunk either, but more ale had made her demeanor even easier.

"It takes some getting to know," she said, "but I think I'm getting to like it." She looked over the rim of her mug into Shon's ice-blue eyes, and his flinched away as he raised his pint. "Baraxis says you told him I was doing well," she pressed.

"That I did," Shon said, only meeting her gaze intermittently. "Well, specifically, he asked if you'd been any more trouble, and I said, 'Surprisingly little.'"

Gwyn should have been affronted, but a strange warmth inside her made Shon's barb feel more like friendly banter. Moreover, the strange provocation she felt from Shon that first day had never gone away, but as she overcame her dislike of him the feeling had changed into an urge to be near him, to learn more about him. "I can be more reckless if it would help make your life more interesting," she replied coyly. "I mean, we all know the orcs are dangerous, but they get a bit predictable, and–"

"You know you remind me of someone," Shon cut her off, an odd urgency coloring his tone.

"Who's that?" Gwyn asked, uncomprehending but undeterred.

"My wife," Shon replied.

A song that had been building softly in Gwyn's head died with a screech as she choked on her ale. "Your wife?" Gwyn repeated.

"Yeah," Shon said innocently. "You don't look alike or anything, but she's tough, like you. Speaks her mind. They're good qualities, too rarely valued here in the Southern Kingdoms, especially from women. I know it's hard on you having to take orders from someone who isn't as good a fighter as you."

Skillfully diverted, Gwyn replied, "I was raised to it. I can show you some pointers, if you like."

"No, but thanks for the offer. I'm not sure our fighting styles are a match."

"Suit yourself," Gwyn replied, draining her mug. "I should probably find my bed. I'm starting to feel my ale."

"Have a good night, Gwyn. Take an extra hour before you report in the morning, in thanks for stopping by and drinking with the men. Swilling ale builds at least as many bonds as spilling blood, you know?"

"I'm learning," she answered, and left the tavern.

The next morning, sobriety had returned the edge to Gwyn's reason, and she found herself mortified at her feeble attempt at flirtation with Shon. "And married, anyway," she growled to herself as she dressed. "Stupid!" She dreaded facing him at the barricade, but she had her orders. The only way out would be to claim illness, but that would only delay the inevitable by a day or two, and the other men might think she was weak. Steeling herself, she crossed the bridge and took her usual place next to Ardos, thankful Shon was nowhere in sight. After a few moments, however, a voice called from behind her.

"Gwyn," Shon said, "a word."

No orcs in evidence, Gwyn left the wall to approach Shon in the lee of a supply cart.

"Gwyn," Shon began before she could speak, "you're late to your post."

"What?" she exploded, taken off guard. "Last night, at the tavern, you told me, very clearly–"

"Ah," Shon interrupted, clearing his throat. "I fear I must have had one pint too many last night. I remember we spoke, just not anything we spoke *about*. I trust I didn't say anything…unbecoming?"

Gwyn's eyes narrowed suspiciously. "You've all your teeth, still, so nothing to fear on that score. You really don't remember?"

"Just bits here and there. What did we talk about?"

"Nothing important. You mentioned your wife, I believe."

"Did I? I hope I didn't get too morose. Two weeks ago I was able to get a few days leave to see her, and it may be months before I can go back."

"Months?" Gwyn questioned. "She doesn't live nearby?"

Shon shook his head. "When we were wed, Baraxis gave us the small ranch that had belonged to my parents, a day and a half from here. With the demand for horses being what it is, I could afford good hands, and I'd leave them in charge for stretches of time so my wife, Tira, could stay in the keep with me. Then last year the orcs pushed harder at us than ever before. It looked like we'd lose the bridge and be overrun, so we sent the women and children away, at least those that would go. We were tough. Mostly we were lucky. We held the enemy long enough for the king to send reinforcements. Most of the families returned, but on account of our little one, Karon, I convinced her to stay away. He's only a toddler, and I couldn't bear the thought of him growing up so close to the fighting. She'll keep him safe, until the war is over or he's of age to start training." As he spoke, he started gazing down at his hand, where a ring of silver and crystal sat on his finger.

"What's that?" Gwyn asked.

"This is the ring she put on my hand the day we were wed," Shon replied wistfully. "It seems ages ago, now. Do brides and grooms not trade tokens in the north?"

"We do not," Gwyn replied, "but I've heard of the custom. I thought it was usually necklaces or bracelets."

Shon nodded. "Family heirlooms, mostly. Both Tira's family and mine were lost in a plague when we were small, and the physicians ordered everything burned, so we had no such trinkets. Baraxis insisted we have something. By then I knew money was scarce, so I told him we liked silver over gold, and the smaller the better, so he had these made. So it's a token of his humor as much as our marriage. Tira has a matching one. I even use a symbol of it to brand my horses, a diamond atop a circle."

"Lovely. You really don't remember telling me this whole story already, last night at the tavern?" Gwyn asked, dissembling.

"I told you," Shon said without a pause, "I only remember bits and pieces."

"You are either a much weaker drinker or a much stronger liar than I would have guessed," Gwyn said accusingly.

"Perhaps both," Shon replied, betraying nothing. "Now, best take your place back on the line and help Ardos keep watch. His old eyes aren't what they once were. Be on time tomorrow."

"Aye, Captain," Gwyn replied, returning to her place.

Chapter IX

Days and battles came and went, and Gwyn's reputation grew more quickly than her purse. Little changed for a month. Then, unexpectedly, the men of Sutherset saw no orcs for four consecutive days. Gwyn was off duty on the fifth and took her horse from the stable in the early morning, for the animal sorely needed exercise. As she rode toward the drawbridge, Baraxis happened to be standing nearby. He called her name, so she turned from her course and approached him. He hadn't donned his plates, but he wore a light mail shirt and his heavy, bearskin cloak as if wary of a fight. "I know it's your off day," Baraxis began, "but please stay close."

"Something wrong?" Gwyn asked.

"I can't say," the older man replied. "Just…something in the air. I'm uneasy."

Gwyn's compunctions about remaining her own master while off duty notwithstanding, Baraxis' ominous manner, so unlike him during their brief association, influenced her even beyond her eagerness for a fight. Still, keeping her mount in fighting shape wasn't to be ignored. "I'll still ride about the town a bit if that's alright."

"Of course. We'll ring the chapel bells if there's trouble."

Gwyn took her leave but, still unsettled by Baraxis' tone, she returned to her room to buckle on her sword before beginning her ride.

The Sutherese all referred to the collection of eight buildings outside the keep as "the town," but this was merely shorthand. Even in Atlund such a settlement wouldn't be considered a village, and the Southern Kingdoms boasted a much greater and denser population. Rather, most of Baraxis' subjects were spread throughout surrounding crofts, but as the area around the bridge drew men to the defense, a handful of services had grown up to support them: a tavern, an inn, and various craftsmen's shops.

Rather than the several-mile ride along the roads Gwyn had planned, she took her steed on laps around and through the town, working on his various gaits. She pushed him to longer runs at canter and gallop than he wanted. As a forest-bred horse he showed excellent maneuverability and surefootedness but rarely had clear enough terrain to stress endurance at faster paces, a potential weakness Gwyn hoped to gently mitigate.

She had tired the horse well and was growing hungry herself, so she led the animal toward the inn. Despite her meager pay, Gwyn could afford a better meal than the daily ration from time to time, and now seemed a good opportunity. She was less than thirty feet from the tavern door when the twin bells in the keep's small temple began clanging furiously, their high and low pitches in tonal harmony but pealing without rhythm in panic.

Gwyn jumped back into the saddle and spurred her mount. He snorted in protest but dug deep, galloping back cross-country toward the bridge over the Storn. As the hoofbeats on the stones rattled to her ears on the near side, a trio of soldiers on the other waved her forward, shouting something she couldn't yet hear. Halfway across, the sight of their mouths moving and their voices registering faintly above the thunder of hooves combined to convey their message: "Zil'bast! Zil'bast!"

Gwyn didn't slow, indeed would have coaxed more speed from her animal if she believed he could give it. In less than a minute she'd reached the wall. Under Shon's direction, a squad of soldiers pushed a wheeled frame bearing a steep ramp of timbers to the barricade; another squad stood ready to carry a lighter ramp up to the top.

"I need a fresh horse," Gwyn yelled.

"Take Cinnabar," Shon ordered, pointing several feet away to his rested bay.

Gwyn had no idea what commands the horses of the south were trained to, but she had little choice and switched horses with haste. She doffed her sword sling and cast off the sheath, flinging both to the ground. Meanwhile, a squad of young men on horseback approached, led by the sergeant Gwyn had seen wounded during her first week.

Men ran to and fro, yelling orders and questions as the wheeled ramp *thunked* into place and bearers started up with the carried one. Orc battle cries fell in waves over the wall. Seeing the approaching horsemen, Shon yelled over the din, "Get her to the zil'bast, understand? Whatever it takes!"

The sergeant shouted confirmation. Now understanding the plan, such as it was, Gwyn turned to her escorts and added without thinking, "If I fall, somebody take my sword and kill that thing."

The second ramp slammed down, the soldiers that carried it hastening back down and out of the way. Gwyn charged up the timbers, cresting the wall and seeing the enemy for the first time. The orcs had not spared defenders for their sorcerer as they had in the first attack. Ten score stood in a solid block between Gwyn and her target. No fog billowed out to hide them so she could clearly see the zil'bast's stretched, skeletal form sitting bent on its mangy horse. The Sutherese on the wall had started ranging bowshots, but the zil'bast, as yet, had thrown no spells. Even the orcs defending it gave a wide berth.

"Throw the ramp down behind us," Gwyn yelled back as she crossed to the downward timbers.

"No, leave it up!" Shon countermanded.

She made no argument as she descended, waiting for her escort squad, each man holding a long, kite-shaped shield and a spear pointing skyward, to form up on her left flank. Once organized, they took off at a gallop forward and to the right, hoping to curl around the orc defenders and strike the zil'bast alone. As soon as she rode clear of the ramp, Gwyn heard a mob of voices screaming "For Sutherset!" and the cadence of boots charging down the planks onto the field, their full-throated defiance, and the set jaws and steely eyes of the men riding with her, a complete transformation of their cowering despair just weeks before.

Perhaps the zil'bast would have blasted the wall as its counterpart did in the previous encounter, but the defenders had now gone on the attack and given it something else to consider. Gwyn stared death at the beast across the field, her focus showing its shifting body and roaming gaze; she believed Shon and his footmen had taken the zil'bast by surprise. The orcs, surprised or not, didn't hesitate. Given the chance to get straight at their foe with no barricade in the way, they charged forward in barely organized frenzy. Gwyn could see Shon's small company outnumbered four to one, a threat as deadly as any magic. The zil'bast recovered from its unease and launched from its twisted, gray staff a blast of scarlet fire that detonated in the midst of the defenders and scattered half a dozen of them.

A platoon of orcs on the flank stood firm and hurled javelins at Gwyn's escort as she rode forward. Most fell short. Gwyn heard as much as saw two strike shields. A third found the flesh of the fourth horse's thigh, and it slowed suddenly. The last rider in line managed to swerve away, but the fifth crashed into the horse's shoulder as it checked, then reared in shock, exposing its belly to another orc javelin. Both riders managed to jump clear but were forced to abandon the poor animals and try to retreat to Shon's company. Gwyn could spare no attention on whether they made it, still charging forward. Her fears over controlling Shon's horse proved groundless; Cinnabar showed great intuition to his rider, seeming to need no direction but Gwyn's shifting weight and tapping heels. She saw one more blast of fire from the zil'bast as her remaining escort pivoted around the block of orcs. Gwyn held back, giving the riders a chance to reform their shield wall in front as they now charged the zil'bast and its defenders head on. This they did with some jostling and hesitation, and Gwyn reckoned this was their first time fighting ahorse.

The zil'bast now faced them, and Gwyn saw its eyes. Her heart hammered her ribs, and a strange tension seized the back of her head and wormed behind her eyes. As she charged forward one, two strides, she wrestled with this alien sensation as she realized the riders before her had slowed, forcing Cinnabar to do the same. Suddenly she knew the name of the feeling clawing through her: fear. She laughed aloud at the realization. She hadn't feared such a creature even before she'd slain one with few comrades and a battered sword; she certainly didn't fear one now. This emotion could not be true, and with that realization the weight of it slipped from her mind and body. Laughing again, she called to the men before her, "Charge on! If you can't stop fearing that thing, then at least fear me more. Charge!" The riders renewed their speed, and Gwyn smiled at their courage.

The zil'bast snarled and slung a bolt of black lighting in their direction. Gwyn ducked and leaned, and Cinnabar swerved to the right, the bolt passing between the center escort riders and missing her by a hair. A moment later, a second bolt lanced forth and took the rider in front of Gwyn full in the chest. The strike flung him backward from the saddle, and Gwyn was forced to cut back left immediately to avoid him. Time seemed to slow as his body spun past her, and she saw the gaping jaw and lifeless eyes before he crashed into the mud behind; his horse, bracketed by its herd mates, ran on.

The riders, now three, lowered and couched their spears. The defending orcs braced but, never having faced a cavalry charge before, had no long pole weapons to deploy. The riders impaled the first rank and trampled them asunder, then continued, they and the riderless horse plowing through the second rank, the third. Gwyn's way opened before her. The zil'bast raised its staff, but it was out of time. Gwyn roared as she leveled her blade. She expected the wave of heat as it washed over her, but her sword remained icy cold in her grip. The point punched through the zil'bast's chest and exploded out the other side. She tightened her fist and wrenched the blade free as she passed, the friction and leverage dragging the foul creature from the saddle, it's mangled body splitting nearly in two as it struck the ground. The zil'bast's horse shrieked as though burned and dashed toward the trees, eyes wide with madness and fear.

Gwyn reined in Cinnabar and turned him so she could see her escorts. Another had been pulled from the saddle by enemies after losing his momentum, but his comrades had rescued him. His horse, unfortunately, had bolted back to the wall, and the other riderless mount had followed. A few other orcs in the zil'bast's guard still lived, but seeing their master killed, they cut and ran back to the forest. Gwyn raised her eyes northward to the battle by the barricade. Shon led a fighting retreat back toward the ramp. Gwyn knew he had only meant to draw away the main orc horde, and he'd succeeded. She raised her sword and waved it, hoping he would at least see her work was complete. She looked to the sergeant and one other of her escorts who now rode double. "Go back the way you came," she ordered. They nodded and rode off. Addressing the last rider, she asked, "Ready for more?"

"I'm with you, Captain."

"I'm no captain," she corrected before urging Cinnabar toward the orcish right.

Gwyn had no desire to put herself on the path between the orcs and their retreat, so she rode hard to the right and came obliquely at the flank. Though she and her companion were only two, they hit hard enough to cause notice. Knowing her comrade's inexperience, she led him away from the enemy after striking to avoid becoming bogged down and putting their horses, and thus themselves, in danger.

Upon turning her horse to attack again, Gwyn saw the lord major atop the wall in his raiment, commanding a dozen archers. Now that Shon's company had retreated almost to the ramp, men could shoot into the mass of orcs without fear of hitting their own.

Gwyn rode forward and struck again, and this time several orcs in the flank saw her face. As she turned for another charge, she saw them look over their shoulders at where the zil'bast should be, where it, indeed, was, only broken and dead. With that, they turned and ran. As Gwyn neared for her third strike, another half dozen routed.

Baraxis ordered a volley there, and the right flank collapsed. The center felt it and pulled back. The left saw the center waver and hesitated. Another volley fell. Gwyn struck again. Shon ordered a countercharge. The orcs broke and fled.

Gwyn rode up the ramp to a thunder of applause and weapons pounded on shields. Sensations not unlike the zil'bast's spell rippled through her as she alternated between pride and embarrassment at the attention.

"Why, Gwyn, are you blushing?" Shon asked as she handed off the reins of his horse.

"Shut it, Southerner," she grumbled, then walked the wall toward Baraxis. She tapped her sword against her gloved palm. "You were right."

The lord major smiled. "I usually am."

Shon ordered sergeants to the retrieval of the wounded and dead, and the silencing of wounded orcs. The enemy would not trade for them, and they were wild creatures at heart; the cold mercy of a dagger blade seemed easier for all than taking them to waste away in the agony of captivity.

Before she left the wall, Gwyn stopped the last rider in her escort. "Why did you call me 'Captain'?" she asked.

The young man shrugged. "You were the leader on the mission and, well, I guess it just came out."

Gwyn pondered this as she collected her horse and walked back to the keep. As she left the north end of the bridge, a woman with soft, brown hair worked in its shadow, collecting wild herbs from the shallow edge of the Storn. Gwyn did not see her, but the woman watched Gwyn until the young warrior had passed out of sight.

Baraxis hoped such a demoralizing defeat would push the orcs away from Sutherset for good, or at least for a long time. Alas, that was not to be, and after a few days licking their wounds the enemy returned to their constant harassment.

After the second zil'bast, the orcs went to even greater lengths to avoid the "Hellwitch." Shon believed Gwyn's killing two of the wicked sorcerers, and that without taking so much as a scratch, led the orcs to believe she could wreak destruction even into the next world, from whence the zil'basts' power was said to derive. He could offer no other explanation why even those orcs eagerly seeking death would not seek it from Gwyn the Savage. In little time Shon and Baraxis learned to turn the enemy's fear to an advantage by sending Gwyn out on more sallies against the enemy instead of keeping her behind the palisade. Ardos or Shon always led the party, wielding Gwyn like a weapon. Gwyn appreciated the battle, but after a time the inclusion of an officer seemed wasteful. The maneuvers Shon and Ardos employed were simple, and she couldn't help but realize the men were beginning to trust her. Shon had no trouble filling squads for their sorties, and after her first few such counterattacks the rotation of faces suggested men were waiting in turns to come along. Two months after her arrival in Sutherset, Gwyn decided the time had come to discuss the matter with Baraxis. That evening she stood by the corral, waiting for the lord major to appear to hand over the smattering of coins that passed for her salary, as had become their custom over the past weeks. Gwyn was relaxed, despite ongoing disdain for the southern heat, leaning against the fence when Baraxis approached. He pulled an apple from the sleeve of his robe, smiling.

"Nicked this from the kitchens while the cook wasn't looking," he laughed.

"Don't you already *own* all the apples in the kitchen?"

"Gwyn, life is exactly as fun as you decide it's going to be, and what fun is there in *asking* your sour, old cook for an apple?" He made a face as though he'd just tasted something foul. Pulling the same dagger he'd held to Gwyn's throat just weeks before, he took a slice from the apple, holding it between the blade and his thumb as he offered it to Gwyn. She took it and ate, enjoying its ripeness. Fresh fruit was a rare luxury in her colder homeland.

"There," Baraxis said after taking a bite. "Tell me larceny doesn't improve the flavor."

Gwyn smiled as the black mare, Cirrus, cantered over, drawn by the sound or smell of the apple. She had to admit, the thought of Baraxis sneaking about his own kitchen like an ornery boy made the apple a bit sweeter. At first it had been strange to her that these people with the orcs always at their throats could be so often jovial, but she finally put it down to one of two possibilities: either the fear was so constant they'd become inured to its influence, or the weight of it had just cracked all their wits. Then she considered the only times she felt truly happy came when someone or something was trying to kill her and decided she had no place to judge, regardless.

Finally, as Baraxis fed Cirrus the last half of his apple, Gwyn cleared her throat. "Lord Major," she hazarded, "I wondered if I could discuss something with you." Gwyn's Southern was all but perfected by then, but speaking seriously in any language made her timid when she wasn't too mad to think about it.

"Say on, Gwyn," Baraxis responded easily, "no need to be so cautious."

"Alright," she nodded. "I want to start leading the men when I go out on sortie. Ardos and Shon are too valuable to expose to the risk, and too needed on the wall if something should go wrong. I think the men will follow me, those that know me best, and our maneuvers are easy." She drew herself up, unable to ignore how much her attitude had changed since her arrival. "I believe I'm ready, sir."

Baraxis was rubbing the mare's muzzle and didn't look over at Gwyn. "It's about time," he grunted.

"Excuse me?"

Now Baraxis did meet her eyes. "You really don't see it, do you?"

"Damn Southern conversations," Gwyn growled. "Why do you always start out in the middle?"

Baraxis thought a moment, then chuckled. "I suppose we do. What I meant was, you don't see the way the men respond to you. Before I thought you just didn't care, but hearing you now I suspect you aren't even aware of how they've changed since you joined us."

"I must not be," Gwyn replied. "You're right that I didn't care what they thought of me at first. In some ways, maybe I still don't, but I'm glad they've accepted me. I guess fighting men have always seemed to like having me around. Apart from that, I really don't know what you're talking about."

"Morale hasn't been this high in years, Gwyn" Baraxis went on. "The men don't just 'like having you around,' they see fighting with you as a privilege. At first I assumed the obvious reasons; after all, you may be a bit, or a lot, more rugged than most Southern lasses, but you aren't without your charms. Before long I could tell their admiration was more than that. You've an inspiring spirit, Gwyn. I know no other way to say it. I can't put my finger on the reason, but your fearlessness, your strength, even your bluntness, all combine into something that drives the men, makes them fight harder than they have before. I don't say that to undercut their bravery, most have lands and families behind the barricade, and they risk their lives to protect them every day. All I can say is that since you've come to Sutherset, they do it *better*. So when you say you *think* the men will follow you, you are more right than you know, and I say, 'It's about time,' because it's *past* time, in my reckoning, that you started developing your greater talents instead of just slashing your sword around."

"You're the lord major–"

"Thanks so much for the reminder."

"–if you wanted me to do more, why not order it?"

"Fair question. Ardos wanted to, but I believed you should ask for it. It isn't enough that you're able to do it, you have to *want* to. Being a leader of men is a heavy burden. It can be done for duty to another, but I think it is only done *well* out of duty to yourself."

"So you agree to my proposal?" Gwyn asked.

"Not remotely."

Gwyn scowled, confused.

"Gwyn," Baraxis continued, "I have no doubt the men would follow you, but when you say you think you are *ready* to lead them, there we disagree. You didn't learn to wield a sword without training, and neither will you wield a platoon. The good news is this: Word from the Capital says the orcs have taken heavy losses there in recent weeks, and scouts report most of the bands in this region are pulling to the east to shore up the attack. We should have some breathing room for a while, and I will use that time to teach you what you need to learn."

"I had a teacher once before," Gwyn said glumly. "It was a quarrelsome arrangement."

"Oh, don't worry about that, Gwyn," Baraxis replied, his voice bright. "If I don't like your manners, I'll just dock your pay." As if in punctuation, Baraxis handed Gwyn her weekly coins, then retreated toward the keep before she could protest his comment. "We'll start tomorrow at dawn," he called over his shoulder.

Gwyn arrived at the green outside the corral a few minutes before dawn, and Baraxis was already there, unarmored but with a sword on his belt. "Attack me," he said without preamble.

Gwyn, having begun to lean her sword against the corral fence, paused. "Armed?"

"As you will," Baraxis replied impatiently. "Attack me!"

Baraxis' apparent irritation decided Gwyn. She held her sword in guard and rushed in, aiming a horizontal slash at the lord major's elbow. She hesitated at the last instant, though, as Baraxis had drawn no weapon to defend himself. In that instant, the older man stepped forward and right, grasping the leather-wrapped foregrip of Gwyn's sword with his left hand as he drove his right palm up into her chin, leaning her backward awkwardly as her knees buckled. Just then Baraxis let go of her sword, and too late did Gwyn realize their mutual grip on the blade had been the only thing holding her up. She crashed down onto her back as Baraxis danced away.

"Why did you hesitate?" he asked as she rose.

"You ordered me to attack, but not to chop you in half."

"So you *can* hold back if you choose to. I wasn't sure you knew how."

"Holding back in a real fight will only get you killed," Gwyn argued.

"Sometimes. Sometimes blind aggression can get you killed, too. It takes instincts to know the difference, but all you want is to kill."

"And you don't?"

"Orcs? I've never had a personal quarrel with one," Baraxis answered. "I have to keep them from killing me or my people, that's all. If I thought there was a way to do that which didn't require killing them, I would. But you: You *choose* to hate them so you can enjoy killing them, is that it?"

"You think too much," Gwyn shot.

"You think too little," Baraxis shot back. "But I suppose I should expect that from a northern barbarian."

Gwyn had baited enough fights in her youth to know when it was being done and ignored the jibe. "What does this have to do with learning to command?"

"I should have expected you'd be too dim to see it," Baraxis continued to needle. "It isn't enough that your people are slow witted in trade, you're ignorant to the things of strategy as well. 'Proud warrior people' you claim to be." Baraxis looked at Gwyn's sword. "I wonder where you *really* got that blade. You obviously didn't inherit it; your father's probably a swineherd."

Gwyn had revealed nothing of her past to the Sutherese, and she knew it was a trap, but her rage overcame her sense. With an inarticulate growl she launched herself at Baraxis, looking to bear him to the ground. Where Nafar, a year and a half before, had merely tripped her, the shorter, stockier Baraxis squatted low the moment Gwyn neared, driving his shoulder into her belly, heaving up with his legs and shoving back, over his head, with his arms. Gwyn flipped over him and slammed head-first into the ground. Her eyes bulged from the shock of it, her breath coming only in thin rasps.

"Do you hate me yet?" Baraxis asked, looking down at her. His tone was impassive.

It took several more gasps before Gwyn could speak. "I thought I was here to learn leadership," she choked.

"You will be," Baraxis countered. "But you cannot lead others until you have mastered yourself. Your anger is your strength. Fine. Do you think you're unique in that? *Use* that anger. Make it your weapon."

"I do," Gwyn rebutted, frustrated, rising once more.

"How can you use your anger when you can't control it? When *it* controls *you*?"

Gwyn scowled, then picked up her sword from where she had dropped it during the flip. She wiped the blade on her sleeve and leaned it against the corral fence, looking for a moment to the north. *Oh, Nafar*, she thought, *if you could see me now.* Squaring her shoulders, she met Baraxis' ebony stare and spoke two critical words. "Show me."

For the next three weeks the orcs rarely attacked, and never in strength. Every day Gwyn trained, sometimes with Shon but usually with Baraxis, never less than ten hours and sometimes fourteen, all in the late summer heat. At first the other men envied the special attention she received from leaders they so respected, but that envy quickly turned to pity when they realized the grueling pace demanded of her. One day late in the first week Ardos passed the training ring with a few of the other men. "What's all that about, anyway?" one of them asked.

"They mean her to command," Ardos said quietly.

"What's that got to do with Baraxis throwing her around the green?" another challenged.

Ardos pinned him with a withering stare. "He's honin' 'er, ye idiot. Ye see how she fights. I wouldn't care to stan' against her, but if I had to… If a man was smart enough not to match 'er strength fer strength, to just not be where 'er attack was when it landed, to flow past the reach o' that long sword. It don't matter how strong the enemy is if he never hits ye; you know that."

"You saying you could take her, Ardos?"

"I'm not sayin' *I* could, but Baraxis has been doin' it fer five days. Not fer much longer, though; ye can see she's gettin' better. If she can learn to add Baraxis' teachings to the boldness of 'er own style, instead o' just replacin' one with the other… If she can do that, that girl'll be unstoppable."

"I still think he pushes her too hard," the first man piped up again. "We weren't sure about her at first, and she's still an arrogant brute, but she's earned her place. I'd follow Gwyn the Savage, and I'm not alone, either." There were nods and grunts of assent.

"Oh, aye, but Baraxis knows what 'e's doin', lads. Today you'd follow Gwyn the Savage inta battle. By the time the lord major's done with 'er, you'll follow 'er into *hell*. Barefoot, mind ye, and thankin' 'er fer the privilege."

"You don't think too highly of her, do you Ardos?" one of the men jibed.

Ardos blushed to his ears. "Lads, if I was three decades younger'n not in love with my wife. As it is, I could think of a worse fate fer Daramis than to win that girl over."

The crowd laughed. "That boy's got more piss on his sheets than blood on his hands, old man."

Ardos eyed the speaker. "That's big talk, Royce, comin' from a man whose wife makes 'im wash 'is own pants after a big fight. Anyway, Daramis might have more guts than experience, but I'd take him over any ten o' you lot. An' a father can dream."

In the ring, Gwyn was disarmed and knocked down once again, launching into a string of profanity probably audible in the Capital two-hundred leagues away. No man there could imagine her settling into a home any time soon, not even Ardos. His friends clapped his back. "Keep dreaming, old timer. Keep dreaming."

While Ardos dreamed, he also began training Gwyn daily in archery, sometimes with the help of Daramis' younger eyes. While hand-to-hand fighting honed her sense of timing, reaction, and instinct, the bow taught her awareness, stillness, and focus. As the days passed, Gwyn slowly learned to take all these lessons to heart, learned to study her opponent and move past his defenses instead of always trying to batter them down, learned when to force calm and quiet and when to tap her passion. By occasional reminders Baraxis urged her to consider these lessons not only literally but as metaphor to the whole battlefield. During the third week Gwyn even consented to train with a weapon other than her sword and a lance for charges, finally bowing to the reality, though it took Baraxis hours of arguing and besting her in the ring to convince her, that her ancestral weapon was too large to be versatile from horseback. Rather than a smaller blade, she favored a light hammer with a back-spike for that purpose, preferring weight and power more reminiscent of the great sword. On foot, though, she became only the more devastating. She learned to take advantage of the speed the elf's enchantment lent to her weapon, adding grace and subtlety to her power, just as Ardos had hoped she would. Still she was bold, even reckless, but with that fearlessness she combined savvy and guile. Often she thought of Nafar and felt rare pangs of regret, remembering what a miserable student she had been and realizing how much she had grown since the Forest Campaign, though only sixteen months had passed.

On the last day of the third week, Baraxis and Shon both stood in the ring with Gwyn. Without warning, they charged. Gwyn stepped out of the way at the last moment, forcing her opponents to adjust. Baraxis went left, at Gwyn, while Shon went right to avoid the collision and attack by the best angle once it was done. Gwyn, however, reversed her dodge in a blink, avoiding Baraxis entirely and shoulder-checking Shon off balance. In another moment the smaller man was completely overrun, Gwyn's boot driving his body into the mud. Baraxis was on her out of nowhere, tackling her low and lifting her to her tiptoes; she had no purchase to resist his backward-shoving rush. She didn't try. Going instantly limp in Baraxis' arms, she forced the older man to stumble. As they both pitched toward the ground, she tucked her knees up and braced her hands, kicking Baraxis back to reel once more, now in the opposite direction. By then Shon was on his knees, so Gwyn planted a foot on his back, using him as a springboard to launch a flying tackle at Baraxis, driving the lord major to the ground with a heavy thud, then darting clear before he could counter.

"Did you see that?" Gwyn shouted, heedless of the pain her trainers were no doubt experiencing. "I did it! Finally!"

Shon staggered to his feet, clutching his chest where Gwyn had stomped it. "I saw it," he grunted, "though clearly not soon enough. I'm still not sure I *believe* it."

Baraxis, likewise, heaved his bulk off the ground and took a moment to steady himself, then strode over to Gwyn, looking at her squarely. He shook his head. "Gwyn," he said, "you still have much to learn about combat, but not from me. The foundation was there, and I've added everything to it that I know to add. If I was fool enough to believe every tavern tale and minstrel's song that's been told or sung this side of the Capital, you would *still* be among the best fighters I'd ever heard of, and you're easily the best I've actually *seen*. You've learned to separate heart from head and use them both as you aught. That's an unbeatable combination, Gwyn the Savage."

Gwyn's breath was heavy as fatigue caught up with adrenaline. Her success, and the obvious caring of these two men who had given so much to bring her to it, were humbling, even for her. "Am I finally ready, then, Lord Major?"

Baraxis nodded. "You are ready. Tomorrow, your training begins. Starting tomorrow, you learn to be a leader of men."

For the first time in her life, Gwyn was not hasty, not impatient. Baraxis had made clear from the beginning that mastering personal combat was only a means to an end; she was neither offended nor crestfallen that the real work was only now beginning. Indeed, she had learned so much in such a short time, had opened her eyes to so many new techniques that, if anything, she was saddened to know Baraxis could teach her no more. Still, a deeper camaraderie had grown with Shon and Baraxis that she knew would not easily be broken. She had been fired in the crucible of Baraxis' training, proving her willingness to accept a duty beyond any sellsword's contract, bringing her into a fraternity not even veterans like Ardos could enter.

After a moment of silence, Baraxis took a step forward. Gwyn started to crouch in defense, but hesitated as Baraxis rolled his eyes to the heavens. Then, unexpectedly, he threw his arms around her, crushing her in a hug that did honor to the bearskin cloak he often wore. "Well done, Gwyn. I never doubted you. Much." He released her, and Shon reached forward to clasp her wrist, which she reciprocated, now acclimated to the prickling surge his touch was certain to bring.

"Go get some rest, Gwyn. You've more than earned it," the captain said.

Gwyn nodded before retrieving her gear and heading to her bed, realizing she had found something she'd thought lost when she awoke last year to learn of Kellgore's death. Gwyn the Savage had found a purpose.

CHAPTER X

Two more months passed as Baraxis instructed Gwyn on the arts of leadership. Some days they spent closeted in his strategy room, poring over maps of old battles and picking them apart piece by piece. Gwyn showed zeal for these lessons, dredging her memories for any bit of knowledge she may have absorbed from Nafar's strategy sessions despite her best efforts to ignore them. In time she learned how to move people, how to use terrain, how to probe the enemy and fool him into exposing his weakness. Baraxis taught exclusively how to field small units, and that suited Gwyn well; she was eager to lead men directly but not to do so by proxy. She learned to break a platoon down into its four squads and command them through sergeants or veterans, but only as long as the pieces remained close enough for her to keep track of them and give her own orders if the situation changed.

Other days were spent in Baraxis' private study analyzing the finer points of leadership as a lifestyle. These lessons confounded Gwyn; she took easily enough to giving orders during combat but struggled to understand the importance of interactions with her men between battles. Finally, after another day of argument over the topic, Baraxis pinned Gwyn with a stare. "It comes down to this, Gwyn. If men fear you, they'll fight for you. If they respect you, they'll kill for you. But if they *love* you...*then* they will die for you. And that's the brutal truth of what we do. Every time you give an order, there will be a chance some of your men don't survive it. Sometimes more than a chance. You don't have to be their friend; in fact, you probably shouldn't be. But you *have* to let them love you, and *deserve* it from them. You'll owe them that much."

"Do I have to love them back?" Gwyn questioned.

"It isn't easy at first. Especially when they start dying and you realize what it takes from you. But in time, you'll find that you can't help it. When you've felt their loyalty, seen how eagerly they follow, you'll love them. I wouldn't be teaching you this if I didn't think you could do that. You can't always let it show, and you can't let yourself love them so much that you can't use them." Baraxis scowled, and Gwyn thought she spotted a twinkle of tears in his eyes. "It's an ugly business, disgusting really, sending men you love to die so the greater part can live. But I believe you can do that, too."

"I just don't think I can mimic your way of being so open. I thought you were a flippant bastard at first, but when it comes to it, you're just so...*nice* to people."

"Gwyn," Baraxis sighed, "I've done a poor job of this if I've led you to think you have to be like *me* in order to lead. You have your own way, and you'll only perfect it with experience. You just have to let them *see* you a little, that's all. You don't want to show fear or weakness. Just a little humanity."

"Too bad Windborne aren't really human," Gwyn answered with a grimace.

Baraxis scoffed. "There's that word again. What under the sky is this 'Windborne' business I keep hearing about you? People keep repeating it without knowing what it means."

Gwyn had to fight the urge to break back into Atlunding speech as she described something so unique to her homeland, but she managed. "Some say belief in the Windborne is just an old superstition, but the Wind is real enough. It blows in the coldest part of winter, sometimes six weeks, sometimes ten, depending on the harshness of the year. From sunset to sunrise it blows down out of the mountains in the north, freezing everything from the peaks down to the River Sharai. If it catches you outside for more than a few minutes it can be lethal. But the dead are the lucky ones. The Wind is charged with fell magics. Some say it isn't the movement of air, but chaos itself. Those who manage to find shelter after more than a minute of the Wind may survive, but their minds are warped, made paranoid and murderous. A Windtouched man will come home to tears of joy that he survived the ordeal, then the next night slaughter his whole family with a grin. Or wait until the height of the Wind and start shattering windows and breaking doors so it can touch his whole village. There is no cure but execution."

"No wonder my ancestors left," Baraxis said, horrified. "Still, how does a person come to be known as Wind*borne*? Surely a newborn could never survive exposure to such a storm."

"No, of course not," Gwyn replied, "but–as you might imagine–most children in Atlund are born nine or so months *after* the Wind starts. For those few born during the deep winter, it was a terrible bad omen for the birth to happen at night, while the Wind blew. It was said that at such a fragile time, even a draft leaking into a house could bring a lifetime of madness, especially in battle. Midwives used to do everything they could to rush a birth before sunset or delay it until dawn. There aren't many left who hold to such ideas now, but I've heard it all my life."

"And you believe it?"

"I used to. It was a tidy explanation for myself. Now... I don't know. I don't know that it matters."

"Well if you ask me, not that you ever do, it's rubbish," Baraxis said firmly. "We have no Wind here, and I've known men crazier than you. But if a Windborne human is all you can show to your men, then show them that. Be honest with them, and they will trust you. What they trust, they will follow."

Gwyn nodded. "I'll do the best I can."

"That's as much as any man can ask."

Gwyn's best lessons, though, came on the days the orcs still attacked. At first Shon continued to lead, but immediately following the battle he would review the details with Gwyn, explaining his tactics and answering her questions. Soon he allowed Gwyn to make the decisions herself, correcting mistakes before he transmitted the orders. Finally, as her errors became fewer and less damning, he took the role of acting sergeant and allowed Gwyn to command the unit directly. At the end of three more months, during which the mild winter passed and Gwyn's eighteenth birthday came and went without notice, Shon stepped aside entirely, giving Gwyn the platoon to lead as she saw fit, with Ardos as her sergeant.

Gwyn had only held full command of her platoon for a week when she and Shon met with Baraxis in his strategy room less than an hour after dawn.

"Lord Major," Gwyn began, "my scouts have returned. Something strange is threatening. A body of orcs *four hundred* strong is pushing north through the trees. We expect them to attack at midday."

"Another zil'bast?" Baraxis asked.

"Not that anyone saw," Gwyn answered.

"That's still the largest force in years," the lord major grunted. "Enough overwhelm the barricade if they're clever about it."

"I don't intend to let them, sir," Gwyn retorted, her eyes on Captain Shon. The smaller man nodded, urging Gwyn to continue. "Lord Major, nobody wants a force that large harassing us indefinitely, coming at us every day and only losing a dozen at a time, wearing us out and deciding for us when we're forced into a pitched battle. I propose to take a full company into the field before the orcs can array for the charge. There's always enough jostling and in-fighting beforehand. The orcs are complacent with Sutherset; they rarely send scouts, and those they do are easily distracted and late returning. We can silence them without raising suspicion. I will use the hill here," she pointed to a place on the map just east of the orcs' usual area of attack, "to conceal our presence, then drive into the enemy flank before they can charge."

"You'll be outnumbered four or five to one," Baraxis countered. "You'll collapse their flank, sure enough, but what happens when they turn to face you? You'll be out of arrow range from the barricade; they'll swarm you like locusts."

"That's where I come in, sir," Shon spoke up. "You know I've been training the new wave of recruits at horsemanship."

"I do," Baraxis was clearly suspicious.

"Properly arrayed, I'd expect the orc lines may hold and inflict severe losses, but charging against the new orcish flank, after they've redeployed to deal with Gwyn, I'm confident we can hit them with acceptable risk."

"You think they have the courage?"

"I think a charge at a surprised and disorganized foe takes a hair less courage than against a prepared enemy. I think we won't get a better opportunity to test them," Shon reasoned.

"What are you two playing at?" Baraxis finally asked.

Once again Gwyn hesitated to speak, and once again, Shon urged her on silently. "Lord Major," she began, "I believe you have been too cautious in your defense. My forays over the wall have forced some limited changes to orc tactics and increased their losses, but they continue to spend bodies here. It's my opinion–"

"And I've come to agree," Shon interjected.

Gwyn nodded her thanks to Shon before continuing. "It's our opinion that we can put the orcs away from here for good. Convince them with a decisive, bloody victory that your bridge will never be worth the taking."

"So there's been a conspiracy amongst my captains, then?" the lord major grumbled. "They think the old man's too timid."

"My Lord," Shon protested, "I don't mean–"

"Yes!" Gwyn interrupted him. "I mean no disrespect, Baraxis, and you know I don't say that lightly, but you *have* been timid. You love your men, and I admire that, but you aren't just *their* lord. You are a vassal to your king and a major in his army, and you hold the right flank. If we drove the orcs away from here, resources could be sent elsewhere; the front would not be spread so thin, to say nothing of the peace you'd buy for Sutherset's women and children. You owe it to your subjects and kingdom to at least try, don't you?"

"Between the archers and the palisade, our casualties are always light, sometimes nil," Baraxis countered. "Men are sure to die in the battle you propose. What of them?"

"All men die, Baraxis," Gwyn rebutted. "To free their families from the orcish menace for years, perhaps longer, my platoon will take that risk, and I'm sure others would as well. I ask nothing of them that I do not ask of myself. You know I don't lead from the rear."

Baraxis' eyes went distant, and Gwyn could all but see the thoughts flitting behind them, the calculation. The lord major was a man of deep passions, but they played no part in his warcraft.

Finally, he nodded. "I'm convinced, may Terillah forgive me. If you take your platoon and give the second to Ardos, who do you want for your third?"

Gwyn cleared her throat. "Daramis wants it. He says he's ready for a test, and he's done well on sorties."

"Only when Ardos is off duty," Baraxis argued. "I don't put the two of them in the field at the same time."

"I know," Gwyn sighed, "and I know why. But they won't stand down, Lord Major. I tried to keep Daramis out of it, but once he heard, he was first to volunteer. If he's to be kept back, the order has to come from you."

Baraxis submerged into his own thoughts again, then finally spoke. "Normally I would forbid it, but I have my own reasons to see what Daramis can do, and if your plan works this may be the last opportunity. Do it."

Gwyn and Shon nodded, then left the strategy room to assemble their men.

"And what of you, Gwyn the Savage?" Baraxis asked the air. "When no more orcs menace our doorstep and offer up their blood, how long will you stay with us in Sutherset?" The lord major shook his head once, then called for a scribe. "Listen well," he told the girl. "I need to dictate a message to the king."

~ * ~

Gwyn stood with her men halfway up the hill on the eastern edge of the plain as the orcs fanned out on the field. Her force, nearly eighty strong, could not see the orcs around the screening hill, but their battle cries and pounding feet were clear enough as the body worked into position. A few of the strongest archers on the walls took shots for range and windage, knowing the arrows would still fall short, and the orcs laughed derisively. Gwyn was surprised there weren't more arrows thudding down, and for a moment she worried she had pulled too much strength from the wall; they would be needed if the battle on the plain went wrong.

Finally Gwyn nodded to her company and started creeping up the hillside, knowing her men were behind her. Ardos would lead the left platoon, responsible for curling around to the orcish rear. Daramis, taking his first subcommand, would take the right, able to cut and run back to the wall if the battle turned against him. Gwyn had considered placing her least experienced leader on the left, where retreat was nearly impossible, in case he lost his nerve, but, to her surprise, found she didn't have the heart. Anyway, if the orcs managed to overmatch them, she knew she could trust Ardos to pull back quickly and guard their retreat, while Daramis might lack the presence of mind. Still, just like the young horsemen Shon should now be leading forward from the shadow of the wall, even Ardos' final son had to be tested sometime.

Gwyn could hear the change in the orcs' usual pre-battle infighting as they saw Shon's line of horsemen approaching. They quieted, and by the combined mass of low murmurs lofting faintly over the hill, Gwyn could sense fear rippling through their ranks. She wasn't surprised; she knew cavalry was common near the Capital, but here in the outlying territories her brief charge at the zil'bast had been one of very few attacks by horsemen. The plan was already shaping up nicely. A low, threatening voice boomed out from the orcish ranks. Gwyn had learned a few orcish words from Shon and Ardos; the primitive language was simple in structure, so it was easy to pick out the nouns and verbs: the commander was insulting his fighters' fear and reminding them they outnumbered their foes ten to one. Then it swore that the bridge would be theirs, promised them glory and opportunities for plunder. The orcs cheered their eagerness to pillage just as Gwyn crested the hill unseen, looking down at the sea of four hundred greenish troops. She looked quickly to the right. Shon and his horsemen were maybe a furlong away.

She raised her sword. Over seventy men readied their weapons with her, then swept down the hill.

The orcs were making so much noise and focusing so intently on the approaching cavalry that Gwyn's force was almost on top of them before they recognized the threat. A few turned to face the charge, but they were cut down almost immediately. Ardos, with perfect timing, wheeled his platoon to the left and charged back in, doing severe damage to the rear lines as Gwyn drove straight into the flank with two-dozen men at her sides, hewing down orcs with her great sword. They recognized the Hellwitch in short order, and most pulled back, trying to avoid her wrath while threatening to surround Ardos' platoon.

Now, Gwyn hissed in her mind. She had gone through the timing with her drummer a dozen times, but he was young. At last she heard the rhythm racing out through the battle only a pair of heartbeats too late, though it felt an eternity. A few moments after that, Daramis' platoon, previously hanging back on her right flank, wheeled out and smashed into the front of the orcish lines, now in disarray and facing to their side and rear.

Not even a minute had passed, but the orcs were taking heavy losses as Gwyn's charge smashed their right flank into a disorganized mob. Gwyn could hear no orders being bellowed from her enemy; clearly the commander was indecisive. Gwyn's forces were not, continuing to wreak bloody havoc on the enemy. Gwyn swung her sword powerfully, hacking one orc down and battering aside a second, then motioned the men on either side of her forward so she could breathe and take stock. Her right platoon under Daramis was driving deep into the orcish mob. She would need to push forward quickly to meet up and prevent them being surrounded; clearly any concern she had for Daramis losing his nerve was unfounded. Ardos' platoon was spreading out, not cutting as deeply but preventing the orcs from routing back to the trees. It would make them fight harder, but it was necessary to inflict maximum losses. Everything was going to plan thus far: the orcs were starting to turn toward her platoons, and Shon's cavalry was still advancing at a relentless canter. She only had to hold the orcs' attention for twenty or thirty more seconds. All this flashed through her mind during only two or three deep breaths, but the time for rest was over. Her men had become accustomed to her fighting alongside them, not flagging behind, and she could already feel them starting to hesitate.

"Sutherset!" she roared, charging through two ranks of her own men to savage an orc with her blade. Blood sprayed into her face, and she grinned with a hellish madness, the battle light sparking to life in her eyes. Even the most fearless orcs quailed before her laughing visage as she plowed through them, all but dragging her men behind. They quickly absorbed her energy, though, and soon her whole platoon was driving forward just as boldly.

They met up with Daramis' platoon on their right, the boy and Gwyn practically colliding in a few feet of cleared space. All the color had drained from his face, but his jaw was set, and his blade was bloody. "Come on, boy!" Gwyn yelled over the din as she spitted an unwary orc. "Let's go find your dad!" As one the platoons turned, gripping half a hundred of the enemy in a pincer across from Ardos and his men. Her platoon's sides were exposed, but the running count in Gwyn's brain told her that wouldn't be a problem for long, even as the orcs' main body wheeled and started throwing their considerable weight at Gwyn's right flank.

She wasn't wrong. Thunder seemed to roll from a clear, blue sky as Shon's cavalry broke into their charge, the crimson pennants of their lances whipping back in the wind. Gwyn's men continued to fight on, Daramis' platoon redeploying to defend the flank as Gwyn's kept up the pressure on her side of the pincer. Over the last twenty yards, Shon's lances lowered, dropping to target an instant before the impact. What was left of the orcish formation was thrown into utter chaos as the forty-strong contingent of horse hammered into it like a landslide, momentum carrying the riders three and four orcs deep into the mob, trampling those they didn't impale. Lances splintered or were dropped, and glinting steel flashed all down the line as they drew blades to continue their work, hewing arms and heads alike.

The orcish spirit was unbroken, however. They might fail to fully commit against a wall bristling with archers, but give them an enemy within arms' reach and their savagery was difficult to abate. The orcs had lost maybe a quarter of their number, and many more were broken into indefensible pockets, but half their force started to rally around their commander, preparing for a counterstrike. As Gwyn's and Ardos' pincer closed, leaving Gwyn in complete control of the orcs' right flank, she could already see the day would be bloody for the Southerners before all was done. The pale, late-winter sun shone down on the red-slicked field as Gwyn and Ardos eyed each other for a moment. Then they turned to throw their full weight behind Daramis' holding action.

Meanwhile, Shon struggled to redeploy his men, whose charge had penetrated so deeply that many were being cut off from one another. Gwyn's force was at a virtual standstill and couldn't form up with him immediately. The bulk of the enemy was still before him; he needed to reform so he could press them, keep the momentum of battle going in their favor. He had two horsemen on either side and urged them forward and to the left, cutting their way to an embattled comrade. They were too late; the lad was dragged from the saddle, the orcs hewing both horse and rider.

Ardos hacked off an orc's axe-hand, then spitted him, but the brute backhanded him with its remaining fist before dropping to its knees, spinning the older man's head and body around like a top heeling to the ground. Gwyn was forward of his position and didn't see him fall, didn't know his platoon was now leaderless. They continued to press, but less boldly, and Gwyn's left flank began to erode. That, at least, she did notice, but before she could consolidate her force, a strange rushing sounded overhead as a swarm of arrows fell into the orcish host like so many hornets. Hacking an orc down, Gwyn dared a look over her shoulder and saw Baraxis on the hill she had just come down, his bearskin hanging heavily from his shoulders as he pointed from Storm Cloud's back to direct the volleys of a full company of archers. They'd always been spread too thin on the palisade, but concentrated into one place, their attack was withering. Orcs in the reserve fell by the dozen, thinning the press of bodies and allowing Gwyn and Daramis to shove the orcish line back in bloody surges. The distraction and damage were more than Shon needed as well, and now his line closed steadily, all the while curling to the right, relentlessly drawing up the net.

Bloody minutes passed, and finally the surviving orcish force was so small Baraxis was forced to halt his archers for fear of hitting his own men. "Come on, Gwyn," he growled. "You know I'm back here, give them room."

Another moment passed, then Gwyn motioned to the left, ordering that platoon back. Most didn't see, but her drummer did, and a second later the order was beating out for all to hear. Baraxis readied his archers once more. Shon caught on as well and pulled his flank back, leaving a wide corridor back to the woods. Of the eighty orcs, more or less, that remained, some must have known it was a trap, but they were too desperate to care. Almost all of them ran, but only a few reached the forest, and even those few had wounds that would likely kill them before day's end.

Baraxis led his archers down the hill as men helped Ardos up from the body-strewn ground. Gwyn sought Daramis and put her hand on his shoulder. "Well done," she said, holding his eyes. Before that moment, Gwyn hadn't known it possible for a face so ashen yet to beam. Shon appeared, leading his bay horse, Cinnabar, through the wreckage of battle, many of his men behind him. "I have mounts," he said simply.

Gwyn nodded her grim understanding. "Daramis," she ordered, "see to our wounded. Ardos," she continued as the older man approached, bruised but otherwise unhurt, "see to theirs." Ardos nodded stoically and directed his men around the field, quickly silencing any groaning or screaming orcs. Meanwhile, Daramis' men helped the worst wounded onto Shon's horses, then led them back to the wall at an urgent trot. Others, thirteen in all, were tied ceremoniously to the saddles, their cloaks draped over them. Gwyn stood silent as she watched them go, but not with regret. They had done good work today, work that would save many lives and many families from war's desolation. Later she would mourn them, but she would not dishonor their sacrifice with self-recrimination.

At last the Atlunder addressed Baraxis as he rode toward her on the plain. "Just what in the hells was that, old man?" she demanded.

"I am *not* timid," Baraxis replied evenly.

"How many men did you leave on the wall?"

"Two dozen. Less."

"Baraxis! What if–"

"Today was to be all or nothing, wasn't it?" Baraxis replied. "By Terillah, Gwyn, did you think you'd *invented* the reckless gambit? I knew your plan could work. I also knew you didn't have the numbers to *make* it work without another trick in the bag. Not that I snatched victory from defeat, mind you, but I preferred to see success without burying half my men."

Gwyn nodded. "It was a good ploy, Lord Major, but only because it worked."

"And that, Gwyn the Savage, is the only measure I've ever found worth reckoning."

The Southerners started the long walk back to the wall, leaving the orcs to the crows.

Risky or not, their gambit *had* worked. Scouting was difficult too far into orcish territory; what intelligence the Sutherese had did not lead them to believe the loss of four hundred fighters would cripple the orcish left, but it seemed the decisive defeat had taken the fight out of the enemy, at least where Baraxis' lands were concerned. Every day the lord major's scouts ranged a little farther, uncontested, and every day their conclusions became more sure: the orcs were pulling out, moving east. After years of constant threat, Sutherset had a chance to breath. As early as the second day after the battle, Shon requested a week of leave to visit his family. It was evident any significant counteroffensive couldn't occur for at least that long, and Baraxis was now confident Gwyn could command the line against any skirmishers that might arrive in the meantime, so he agreed. As it was, not even such token forces appeared to harass them.

At first, Gwyn felt easy for the first time in years. Her thirst for blood was temporarily slaked, and unlike the sudden ending of the Forest Campaign, here she could take pride in a job well done. Moreover, here she had men that had entrusted her with the duty of command and allowed her take her full share of the glory, not stolen victory out from under her while she lay wounded and feverish. Gwyn celebrated with the Southerners, sharing in their joy and camaraderie.

After a week, however, and true to Baraxis' prediction, Gwyn grew restless. The orcs had cast not so much as an angry glance in their direction in all that time, and Gwyn missed the heavy pounding of her heart during the fight, the hot spray of her enemies' blood as she slew them. Baraxis could see the change in her almost instantly: She withdrew from the men, spent more time training and always more aggressively as she did so. She challenged Shon to spar barely an hour after he returned from his furlough and cursed him for a coward when he declined.

Shon fought the urge to respond in anger and instead sought Baraxis to inquire into their friend's state of mind. Baraxis didn't answer directly. He simply handed Shon a dispatch, which the captain examined without opening. The seal was broken, but the device impressed into it was unmistakable. "Are you sure I should see this?" he asked.

Baraxis nodded.

Shon unfolded the parchment and read, his eyes scanning quickly across the few lines, then finding Baraxis' gaze. "This isn't what you wanted," Shon said.

"I fear it no longer matters," Baraxis replied. "I've been reprieved from this fate longer than I deserved, and I can justify delay no longer, especially with the orcs in full retreat from here…and with no secret to the direction they're heading."

"Their final attack and withdrawal are much less mysterious now," Shon added. "I'm sure this is the least matter on your mind, all things considered," he continued, "but since it relates to my reason for coming up here in the first place: What will this mean for Gwyn?"

Baraxis sighed. "Suffice to say she won't be restless for long."

The next day Baraxis called an assembly of his captains and trusted sergeants. Ardos, Shon, Gwyn, and a pair of captains from the eastern flank, whom Gwyn had met but barely knew, gathered around the battle-scarred table in the strategy room.

"Men," Baraxis began, "I have news. Whether the first part be good or grave, that is for each of you to judge. I have been promoted."

Gwyn started to offer her congratulations, but the rest of the men at the table were stony faced, so she stayed silent. After a moment, though, when no one else spoke, her curiosity and frustration with Southern conversational vagueness got the better of her. "Is somebody going to tell the foreigner what she's missing?" she grunted.

"The Lord Major is the Lord General now," Ardos replied, as if this explained everything. Gwyn responded with an irritated look.

"Generals lead the armies of the king, Gwyn," Shon clarified at last, "the forces under the direct control of the

Capital. This promotion means Baraxis is compelled to leave Sutherset."

Gwyn leaned back in her chair, poleaxed. She had grown frustrated with the recent lack of action and even toyed with the idea of asking Baraxis if she could freelance somewhere for a few weeks, but she was utterly unprepared to have her new home crumble around her and see her new friends ride away to the Capital. For a moment a new shock layered over the first. *My new friends*, she thought. *By Terillah, I have friends*. Emotion welled up within her, but, appalled at the idea of showing such weakness in front of all these men, she choked down her sadness and replaced it with dignity. She rose abruptly, her chair grating back loudly over the stone floor.

"Lord General," she uttered formally, "it has been an honor to serve under your command, and I wish you–"

"Oh hells, Gwyn, would you just sit down," Baraxis ordered. "I shudder to think how the king is going to react to your Atlund 'manners' in the Capital."

Gwyn dropped back into her chair, events rushing by too quickly for her to interpret them all. "You mean–"

"Gwyn," Baraxis interrupted gently, his tone easy, "when I told you to sit down, that was also a none-too-subtle offer to shut up and let me tell it."

Gwyn closed her gaping mouth and nodded back.

"Thank you," Baraxis responded. "The king's orders are explicit. I've argued successfully against being removed from Sutherset on two previous occasions, due to the orcish threat here and the bridge within my holdings, but His Majesty no longer finds those arguments to be compelling. I'm to leave only a token force to the defense of Sutherset, left under the command of such captains as I feel can handle the task without oversight...for the remainder of current hostilities."

Ardos drew a breath. "Mother's bones!" he gasped. "Current hostilities? Our children's children could be old men before 'hostilities' are ended with the orcs."

"Then it will be our duty to ensure that isn't the case," Baraxis replied. "And speaking of our children, Ardos, I would like Daramis to remain behind as a sergeant on the defense. He's ready for the challenge, and I'd like to know he's keeping an eye on the general running of the holdings as well. He has proven his skill in battle, but you know I mean it only as an honor when I tell you he has the makings of a better seneschal than a sergeant."

Ardos nodded. "Thank you, Lord General." Everyone knew his unspoken thoughts: This young man's promotion would keep him clear of the worst fighting as surely as Baraxis' was casting him into it.

Next, Baraxis addressed the two eastern captains, giving his orders that they remain behind to lead the defenses. They were stout and determined men, but they lacked the boldness to excel in the pitched fighting surrounding the Capital. More importantly, both were knights already, enfeoffed by Baraxis to holdings within Sutherset, meaning they had authority to lead the subjects as well as the soldiers. The elder of the two had an objection, however. "Our levies are small, Lord General. How will we hold all of Sutherset if the orcs attack again?"

"They won't," Baraxis replied gravely.

"How can we know that? What makes the king so sure you're no longer needed here?" Gwyn asked.

"Because Sutherset has become irrelevant to the orcs' offensive strategy," said Baraxis.

The other Southerners gasped, save Shon, and Ardos hung his head in his hands. "No," he moaned. "No, no, no."

"It's true," the Lord General said. "The orcs have taken the King's Bridge just south of the Capital, securing free passage across the River Dr'Nai barely five leagues from the city. The king's engineers tried to destroy the bridge in the retreat, but it was built to withstand fire and flood, and the orcs gave them precious little opportunity. His Majesty is calling in reinforcements from every corner of the Southern Kingdoms, but the orcs are concentrating their forces as well. If something doesn't change, the Capital will be besieged before the spring rains.

"Ardos, Shon, I need you with me. We will be tested as never before. And Gwyn…the king ordered me to bring my best soldiers with me. Terillah knows that disqualifies you, but I also promised to bring him to the best *warrior* I have ever met. If I'm to contribute all I have to the war effort in the east, I can think of few better ways than to bring you along. I mean to introduce the king to Gwyn the Savage. And to introduce the eastern orcs, firsthand, to the Hellwitch."

Gwyn's shoulders ached to swing her blade as the battle light sparked briefly behind her eyes. "When do we leave?"

Chapter XI

The march east took weeks, and the closer Gwyn came to the Capital, the more congested grew the roads. Even with the great walled city still some days away, already Gwyn could turn her head to either horizon and see more troops in one place than she had in her entire life.

When finally they arrived, Gwyn stood awed by what she saw. The palace sat on the tallest of eight hills, spread with rolling vales in between. Trees thrust up here and there, but most of the space was carpeted with buildings of every size and shape, from palatial estates and fortified bastions on the hills to crowded slums in the narrower valleys. The city was more orderly than she expected, though, and Gwyn found her assumptions of squalor and poverty, taught to all Atlunders as they judged their more urban descendants in the south, to be largely incorrect. Still, the smells and sounds of a great press of humanity wafted to their position on a nearby rise, less from the city itself than from the massive armed camp that had grown up around it, thousands of soldiers bivouacked outside the outermost wall. Atlund historians taught that the Southern population had exploded after their initial settlement thanks to the milder climate and longer growing season in the south, but until she saw it with her own eyes Gwyn couldn't truly fathom it. If half the men of Atlund assembled in one place, she doubted they could have equaled the population in the camp, much less the city.

"This is unbelievable," Gwyn muttered.

"And all the barracks in the city will be filled to bursting as well," Baraxis added. "I only hope it's enough. Can I trust you to stay out of trouble? Not all the men are as decent as mine."

Gwyn grimaced. "You can trust me not to go *looking* for trouble. *Staying* out of it when it finds me, that's something else."

Baraxis nodded. "There's an idea I've been holding onto because I feared you would resent the offer. I have made you an officer of a sort, but that decision is not binding on my betters where it concerns hired swords. The same is not true of bound retainers. If you swear an oath of fealty to me, I can see that you get fair lodging and respect."

Gwyn's eyes narrowed. "This oath…does it make me a Southern subject? Would it mean I'm not an Atlunder anymore?"

"No," Baraxis reassured, "but it means that, legally, you are bound to my service until I release you. I give you my word I will do that when you feel the time has come, but you would have only my word for that. And it means that your service is no longer a matter of business, but a matter of honor."

Gwyn considered warily. "You offer this just to keep me away from the sellswords and strangers in the camp? To protect me?"

Shon, riding Cinnabar ahead of the main force with Gwyn, Baraxis, and half a dozen others, gave the rest a look, and they started back to the column at a trot. Baraxis was silent.

"Well?" Gwyn pressed. "Is that your reason?"

The lord general's face had gone solemn. "No, Gwyn. This is something I would have offered weeks ago only… I *would* have offered if I'd thought you would accept."

"Until we reached here, what would have been the point? What would it have changed? I believe your word is good, so if I'll be released at will anyway, what makes this any different from the contract I have now?"

"You're right," Baraxis concluded. "It was a foolish idea. I know you can handle yourself." He started to turn Storm Cloud, but Gwyn wheeled her horse around more quickly to block him.

"You didn't answer my question, Lord General." She managed to catch his gaze again. "Speak your mind, Baraxis."

"This oath: if you took it, you would become like Ardos or Shon. It would make you one of my household."

At last Gwyn understood, but she could only frame it in terms she knew as an Atlunder. "You mean," she clarified, "this would make us blood by choice? We would be family. You ask me to join your clan?"

Baraxis nodded once, and Gwyn could see by the uneasiness in his dark eyes how much such a thing would mean to him, how difficult it had been to ask. He never spoke of his past; she could only guess at the secret pain that made this such a weighty matter for the lord general, at the emptiness that she had somehow eased, without even knowing, when she came to Sutherset. She couldn't know why offering to accept such an undisciplined mercenary into his loyal retinue might become a matter of the heart and not of the head, but she could see that it was. Finally, she replied. "You do me great honor, Lord General. You know that our paths will not always run together. Do you accept that a time will come when I will ask that you release me, and expect you to remember your word?"

Baraxis nodded again.

"Then for as long as we fight together, I swear my sword and myself into your service, not as a paid woman, but as one bound to serve by a debt of honor, just as you are bound to lead." Gwyn had no idea if there were formal oaths that would have to come next, but she had spoken her own vow, and it was that one she would remember. Instead, Baraxis asked for no more words. He cut a strip of gold-trimmed, crimson cloth from the hem of his long tunic and tied it around Gwyn's right arm. Then he grabbed her shoulders and pulled her forward, kissing her forehead. The motion was brief and aggressive, but though Gwyn sensed its ceremonial nature, it was not wholly without affection.

"The other men will witness this," he said. "Wear my colors, and it will be known to all that the House of Baraxis is Gwyn the Savage's house."

Shon ordered the column to advance, and the force from Sutherset quickly crossed the ground to where Baraxis and Gwyn still stood. As they started down the hill, the young captain leaned closer to Gwyn. "Congratulations," he said.

"You must think mightily of Sutherset and yourself if you think congratulations are in order," Gwyn retorted.

"Gwyn, for you to willingly become a part of *anything* deserves congratulations, if you ask me."

"Well, I didn't."

"Noted and disregarded. Ardos will be sorry he missed it, though, but Baraxis wanted him with the rearguard again."

"If he had a better singing voice, or would just stop using the one he's got, he wouldn't get sent back there so much," Gwyn quipped.

"And the day the supply wagons start traveling at the front of the column instead of the rear is the day he'll take his first lesson," Shon joked back.

It was an hour later during the tedious waiting and line-jostling outside the Capital's west gates that word finally made its way back to the rear of the column and brought Ardos galloping to the head. Gwyn's horse nearly spooked, so forcefully he brought his own mount alongside, leaning sideways in the saddle to throw one arm about Gwyn's shoulders and squeeze her tightly. "The *weather* was dreary the day ye came to us, Gwyn, but the *day* was one o' the brightest these old eyes've seen, an' among the warmest in the memory o' my old heart."

"Ardos," Shon remarked. "That was nearly poetry."

The older man cleared his throat, his already-ruddy face blushing scarlet. "Well, I, *achem*… The midday report was due so I had ta… Where's Baraxis?"

Gwyn was still as unnerved as she was moved, but Shon, thankfully, did not hinder Ardos' clumsy attempt to change the subject. "He's up ahead, arguing with some drovers that are blocking the way," the captain replied. "Apparently this is the first time they've run herds to the Capital and don't realize the slaughter yards are on the *north* side of the city. Thank Terillah it's a small herd; even still they've been clogging up the road for hours."

At last Baraxis returned to the column. "We should be underway again directly," he said. "Shon, you'll be responsible for bivouacking the men as soon as we get orders on which scrap of mud belongs to us. A courier found me when I was dealing with the cattlemen; I've been summoned to the throne room. Gwyn will accompany me."

Shon nodded and rode back down the column to relay the lord general's orders to the sergeants.

"Ardos," Baraxis continued, "what are you doing here?"

"Midday report, milord."

"Everything secure and accounted for except what you've stolen and consumed yourself?"

"To the dram, sir!"

"Excellent. Now finish congratulating Gwyn and resume your post, man. And I want the midday report *at midday* tomorrow, not two hours 'til."

Ardos gave a lazy salute and turned his horse, following after Shon once he'd lavished another broad wink at Gwyn.

"'Congratulations' again," the Atlunder grunted. "You Southerners think so highly of yourselves it's a wonder you can see from up there."

"Proving our excellent vision," Baraxis snipped. "Now come on. The king awaits."

Gwyn gulped as they approached the massive stone walls, taller again than Baraxis' towers by half, and this outer wall was the shortest of the three. "I don't suppose your king is anything like mine."

"I do suppose that a king is a king is a king, to any of his inferiors. It isn't as though you *knew* 'your' king."

"He was my second cousin."

Baraxis chuckled. Gwyn didn't. The older man checked his horse and gaped at Gwyn. "By Terillah, you're serious!"

Gwyn nodded. "Once removed."

"Why did you never say so? All this time, and just now I learn you've royal blood?"

"Not really. My father and the king shared a great-grandfather in common, but the lines branched before the king's grandfather took the throne. Anyway, royal blood doesn't count for much back home. Heredity is just a matter of convenience; the heir apparent can't take the throne without support from the Conclave. That's the elders and clan chieftains."

Baraxis was already sifting Gwyn's words, though, trying to gain glimpses of her past as they waited for the last of the cattle to clear away from the western gate. "You said your father and the king *shared* an ancestor, not 'share' an ancestor. Even down here, we eventually learn of a monarch's passing in Atlund, so... Your father, then?"

Gwyn nodded.

"I'm sorry," Baraxis continued. "Was his death the reason you left home?"

"No," Gwyn began, but paused. "Well, in a way, perhaps. You don't need to apologize though; you haven't opened old wounds. I never knew him. He was killed before I was born."

Baraxis nodded to himself. "And the sword is all you have of him."

"Yes."

"If I'd known, before, with that elven mage–"

"What's past is past. I have enough of my own regrets, don't burden me down with yours as well."

At last the way was clear, and the pair proceeded through the gate, the guards waving them through without challenge in response to the royal courier's earlier instructions.

"If it was anybody else as young as you," Baraxis continued, "I'd say she hadn't lived long enough to have regrets, but there has always been something about you that says otherwise."

Gwyn shook her head. "If we are to be blood, now, then it may be you should know my story, and I yours, but I doubt there's time between here and the throne room, and you never answered my question. What is this king of yours like? What will be expected of me? King Vassin ate at my table and spoke to me as a friend and a kinsman, as easily as we speak to each other now. He was nothing like the stories I hear of the high nobles in your land." Gwyn hesitated long enough to swallow her pride before adding, "Must I go to this audience?"

Baraxis barked a short but hearty laugh. "Gwyn the Savage, is that fear I mark in your voice? Is she who charges headlong at zil'basts and orcs against five-to-one odds going into full route from a *conversation*?" His shoulders shook with mirth.

"Shut your cackling mouth, old man! I'm not running from anything. If I *am* nervous, it's your fault anyway, after months of mocking my manners."

"Alright, alright," Baraxis relented, stifling his laughter. "The best thing to do is keep your mouth shut. Just let me do the talking, and everything will be fine."

The buildings loomed up all around Gwyn, pressing in on her and crowding her very thoughts. Every curious face and barking dog amplified her apprehension. Her Atlund-bred horse took poorly to the city noise, twitching at every sound and smell; Gwyn was temporarily distracted from her anxiety as she fought to keep the animal under control. At last they reached the second wall, the gate guarded by a small barracks flying the royal banner.

Baraxis approached the guard on duty, who saluted smartly. The lord general handed the young man a dispatch, then dismounted. "We'll have to leave our horses in the care of these worthy guardsmen," Baraxis explained. "The inner districts are too crowded in places for mounts. We'll go on foot."

"You are expected," a guard captain said, emerging from the barracks at the younger guard's summons. "We will keep your horses here. I and my best men are to escort you to the palace without delay."

Baraxis handed his reins to the younger guard and motioned for Gwyn to do the same. "I suppose if you trust him with Storm Cloud, I can make an exception," Gwyn reasoned aloud, passing along her reins in turn, if reluctantly.

"You know I don't believe you've ever told me your horse's name," Baraxis mused as he waited for the captain to assemble their escort.

"I don't know it."

Baraxis laughed. "Another strange custom, no doubt?"

"No stranger than giving animals names they never wanted. The old tales tell of a time when horse and man could understand each other's speech, and horses would share their true names with trusted riders. It was a powerful bond, and an empty boast to give a horse a name when you hadn't earned the real one."

"And your people believe this?"

"Some do. Others don't, but tradition is what it is. Many long generations have passed since an Atlunder named a horse."

Baraxis muttered "barbarians" under his breath as the guard contingent moved out with him and Gwyn at their center.

"Fops," Gwyn snapped back.

In time Gwyn gave up counting the turns in the twisting inner streets, letting her mind wander as she and Baraxis traded stories and insults, her fear almost, almost, forgotten.

She remembered it immediately upon reaching the palace, a hulking mass of gray stone patrolled by crossbowmen and men-at-arms with halberds in their hands and swords on their belts. Gwyn had heard descriptions of luxurious, even decadent, estates to the north, farther from the press of war, but this was not one of them. Everything here was cold and hard and solid, a place forged by generations of warfare. Gwyn considered that she ought to be at home in such a place, but she couldn't put herself at ease. She decided it was the lack of character, no familiar trophies of victories or even the oddments of bustling habitation. It was as though nothing really lived here, it just brooded and waited for something unspeakably terrible to happen.

Soon a page had shown the pair to a small foyer outside the king's hall. Two stern guards, a generation apart, stood at the door, men that would have exceeded even Gwyn's high expectations, had they been the ones standing outside Baraxis' chamber on her first day in Sutherset. In at least one way, however, that day and this one proved annoyingly similar.

"The foreigner may not carry her weapon into the throne room," the younger, rightmost guard declared. His tone was neutral, but it brooked no argument. Fortunately for Gwyn, Baraxis wasn't in the mood for an argument either and spoke quickly to preempt one.

"Don't say 'foreigner' like an insult, Verrik, it only proves your ignorance. Your father's accomplishments might have impressed the court, but they don't impress *me*, and they wouldn't protect you from *her* if murder was in her mind. More important, she is a captain bound in my service and acting today as my personal bodyguard, which makes me the safest man in the Southern Kingdoms. Do you want to let us in as the king has ordered, or do you want to keep us standing here while the orcs push north, storm the place, and kill us all?"

The older guard, on the left, shook his head and stifled laughter. Finally he called, "Baraxis, you miserable old bastard, my boy's just doing his job."

Baraxis pulled a wry half-smile. "Actually, Farridix, he's doing *your* job. Does the Atlund lady scare you that much?"

"Hells yes! Even if captaincy didn't have its privileges, fatherhood still does. Delegation is a beautiful thing."

"Alright then," Baraxis continued, "enough talk. What's the verdict? His Majesty isn't used to being kept waiting, and I've been delayed too long as it is."

Farridix answered. "If you're vouching for her, Baraxis, then all is well. We hear most of the rumors hereabouts, but none that she'd sworn fealty to you."

"It's a recent development," Baraxis replied as Verrik stepped aside and pushed open the door.

At last Gwyn laid eyes on the king's audience chamber and throne room, a room that, if no more joyful than the rest, was at least somewhat brighter by virtue of the white marble floors and pillars and the blue royal banners hanging from the walls. The shuttered windows were open, and this far above the noisome city streets the breeze was the freshest breath Gwyn had taken in hours. She was distracted from this small relief, however, by the appearance of the king before her. He was tall and almost gaunt, with hollow cheeks and a shaggy gray head; its furrowed brow bore the weight of the simple, gold crown like a man pushing a millstone uphill. If the loss of the King's Bridge had hit Baraxis' captains hard, it had hit this man all the harder. Gwyn suddenly despaired for a Southern victory against the vicious orcs, for their leader had all the seeming of a man near his breaking point.

"Lord General Baraxis of Sutherset and Gwyn the Savage of Atlund!" a herald cried.

Baraxis bowed to one knee. Gwyn did not. The herald cleared his throat, but Gwyn ignored him, and the king had no time for formalities, in any case. Turning from the window, he impatiently motioned for Baraxis to rise, ignoring Gwyn completely. "How is the west, Baraxis?" the king said without pause.

"It is quiet for now, Majesty."

"That is good. I did fear to take you away. Know that the decision was not lightly made."

"I know, Majesty. Have you recalled the Mountain divisions as well?" Baraxis asked, apprehension lacing his tone.

"By Terillah, no. I won't repeat my grandfather's mistake; we can't leave the passes uncontested. Even with the bridge taken, the enemy may yet push north behind the wall of the Tunaris, but if they do, they won't take us unawares."

"I believe that is wise, Majesty."

"I appreciate your counsel, but did you really believe that I would leave the west that vulnerable, old friend?" the king consoled, softening.

"I hoped not, but I know the situation here is grave."

"So it is, and more than you know. There is a reason I called you straight here after so long a march. I have need of more than your counsel."

"You have only to ask, Majesty," Baraxis pledged.

"There is trouble brewing farther east. To the west, the orcs were focused on your bridge, and a few others, and they couldn't deploy more heavily there; the forage is poor south of the river, and long supply lines are not the orcs' strength. The east is quite another story. The orcs have rolled up our flank like a fancy rug, and even now they march to the Dr'Nai Pike south of the river, hastening to the fray here. If they can't be turned back, they must at least be thinned out and delayed. How would you do it?"

"What is their strength, Majesty?"

"Difficult to measure for certain. Our only reports come from men fleeing from them, and nothing multiplies the enemy like panic. Making allowances for such exaggerations, we reckon their number at several thousand, no more than eight."

"How many men can you spare?"

The king's voice was flat. "A short regiment, maybe a tenth of their number."

"Hit and run tactics, then," Baraxis reasoned. "Ambush, harass, and withdraw. Target scouts, flankers, foragers, make them fear to send out smaller detachments. That would slow the main body, forcing them to march blind and hampering their ability to gather provisions from the countryside. Then we can start hitting harder, if we're cagey enough."

On instinct, Gwyn shook her head and immediately regretted it.

"You have something to say, Northerner?" the king demanded.

Gwyn started to speak, then remembered Baraxis' advice and simply shook her head.

The king arched his eyebrows. "Does it speak, General?"

"It does," Baraxis answered as Gwyn's eyes burned into him. "Usually the challenge is in making her silent. *Speak* when spoken to, Gwyn."

Gwyn cleared her throat and focused on her manner, trying to sound formal but feeling the disadvantages of learning a new tongue mostly from uneducated fighting men. "This plan is good," she began, "but for a major weakness. Where can these attacks originate? You'll need to move along with the enemy in order to harry them, but many hundreds of men cannot be hidden. When they send a detachment of their own to deal with you or, Terillah forbid, turn to face you en masse, you'll need a place of strength to stand against them. More than one, if you're to keep attacking them all along their route."

"Your guard speaks truly, General," the king answered. "It would be folly to underestimate the orcs as wilderness fighters. In the hills and forests of the east, their scouts will almost certainly track your troops back to your camp, even if you can outrun them. What say you to that, Baraxis?"

The lord general nodded thoughtfully. "Can you spare a horse for every man, Majesty? They needn't be heavy warhorses, just quick mounts, surefooted and long winded. Mares, even, if that's what you can spare."

"I think I can arrange something. What are you working toward?"

"Captain Gwyn has spoken to me of the use of horses in the forest battles of her homeland. The terrain there isn't always suited to mass charges, but they've found great advantages in a lighter cavalry. While our heavy horses are brutal in a charge, they are slow and expensive in a long march, and require much in the way of foodstuffs. The Atlunders have learned that a lighter, hardier mount can be more flexible, offering unrivaled mobility and speed, especially in areas of good forage."

"We do have light cavalry, Baraxis, though perhaps we regard them too little. In any case, such a unit still needs training for both beast and man, and we have time for neither."

"I was considering the benefits of mobility only, Majesty, not fighting ahorse. Not a light cavalry so much as a mobile infantry. Mounted, even on mounts that had to be kept clear of the battle itself, our men could cover twice the ground and still arrive to the battle unwearied. With that kind of speed, we might only need two or three fortified positions from which to harass the orcish march, far fewer than if we went on foot. The thing starts to look possible."

"A worthy notion. By now I assume you've already considered the Craftholds."

"That was my very thought, Majesty."

The king shook his tired head. "You know I must order you to this, Baraxis, but I won't let you take any illusions as to the risks."

"I understand, Majesty. I am a poor liar, though. I can vouch for my own men. The rest will need to be equal to the burden as well. I will need the bravest soldiers you can spare."

The king nodded. "You may hand pick your force. Go."

Baraxis bowed, and Gwyn turned on her heel.

"Atlunder!" the king shouted.

Gwyn sighed silently, sure she would, at last, be chided for her lack of deference. She turned and still did not bow, trying at least to keep her eyes downcast. "Majesty?" she mumbled.

"Is it true what they say about your people?"

Always in the middle, Gwyn thought, but she resisted the urge to say it. "I'm afraid I must claim ignorance, Majesty."

"In these parts," the King responded, "it is said that Atlunding warriors can fight a dozen battles with a dozen wounds as long as nobody bothers to tell them that they're dead."

For the first time since entering the Capital, Gwyn smiled. "Actually, Majesty, that's understatement. I've been dead two years. Just don't tell me I said so."

The king returned her smile, and some of the creases on his forehead eased for a moment. He even chuckled a short, sardonic laugh. "With one such as you on our side, maybe we stand a chance after all."

Gwyn nodded and turned to leave, relieved in the realization that what she'd initially taken for a man near his breaking point seemed, rather, a man pushed well past it but refusing to break.

Yes, Gwyn thought as she followed Baraxis out of the room, *this one on the throne and me in the field may be all the chance we need.*

Once outside the throne room Gwyn was finally able to ask, "What are the Craftholds?"

"Four towns," Baraxis answered, "built by merchant guilds wealthy enough to afford solid defenses. Each one sits on a hill south of the Dr'Nai and overlooking the river. When the most recent spate of attacks began, the people evacuated with their tools and wares to the Capital, some out of fear, some to profit from the necessities of war. In any case, the towns are now quite strong and quite empty, and their positions along the orcish advance are good. Good enough, anyway. The one farthest east is called Dorn. We'll travel there first, by barge if at all possible. Once the orcs have passed that point, we will decamp from Dorn and travel west to Roon, the second Crafthold."

"And then on to the third?"

Baraxis gave Gwyn a hard look. "If we live that long, yes."

Gwyn was taken aback. "It isn't like you to be so dire, old man. Do you know more than you're telling?"

"Almost always," Baraxis quipped, but his smile did not reach his eyes. "This time… It isn't anything I *know*. The plan is good, and as long as the king's flotillas threaten the southern shore, we have a means of retreat if things deteriorate. It's more something I *feel*, like the morning before that second zil'bast came at us. I can't explain it, but I can't put it aside." Finally, he shook his head. "Perhaps I'm just getting too old and attached to life for soldiering."

But Gwyn knew it was more than that, and she had no reason to distrust Baraxis' instincts. Indeed, such warrior's forebodings carried great weight in the North. Gwyn thought the castle seemed colder still with the thought that the Lord General Baraxis might be afraid.

They rejoined their guard escort outside the castle and returned to the barracks where their horses were stabled, making the long, twisting walk in silence. Shon met them there and announced that Ardos and the sergeants were setting up camp and that he had reviewed their lodging assignments.

"Very good," Baraxis replied. "I assume I am in the palace?"

"Yes, sir," Shon confirmed, "and your belongings are being transported there now. Do you need anything else?"

"Not today, Shon, thank you. I would like to clear my head. Where can I find you tomorrow?"

"The men are camping in the northwest quarter; you'll see the banners from the wall. Gwyn, Ardos, and myself will be lodged in the Middle City, Ackras district, in the east wing of the Haddix family estate."

"Old Haddix has taken on boarders? He always bribes his way out of it."

"He's dead, sir."

Baraxis arched his eyebrows. "I guess that explains it. You're both dismissed. I will find or send for you when I need you."

With that, Baraxis rode off, leaving Gwyn alone with Shon in the strange city. Gwyn knew she could never find her way without help, but she blanched at the thought of admitting that weakness to Shon. As always, however, he was quick to help her avoid embarrassment.

"Well, Gwyn," he began, "it looks like we both have time on our hands. How would you like it if I showed you some of the city before we find the way to our lodging?"

Our lodging, Gwyn thought. *Just the one?* Of course, she wouldn't have been entitled to a place in the city until her oath to Baraxis that morning, and there was no way the stewards making preparation for their arrival could have known about that. Even if they had, it was unlikely there were enough women officers to warrant separate housing. Shon's description to Baraxis made the place sound big, but still. Even with Ardos as chaperone, her pulse quickened at the thought of sharing sleeping quarters with Shon.

After Gwyn's first, clumsy flirtation in the tavern, mortification had dampened her attraction, and it was easy to put such feelings aside when they'd been throwing one another about the training ring. Combat, after all, was combat, and Gwyn rarely felt unsure while in its sweet embrace. Her esteem for Shon had only grown during that training, however, and since its end, she'd found it harder and harder to overlook how kind and wise he was. Indeed, they were different in those and many other ways, but the moment she realized those differences were underscored by courage and skill as well, she had begun to desire them, to yearn for the way those cool, blue eyes bored into her, especially because she knew they weren't trying to. Occasional pangs of feeling had grown into a consistent want over the long march east.

She would never insult his honor by violating his marriage, and she knew Shon would never feel so much as tempted to such a thing. Away from the prying eyes of the men, however, she only barely trusted her own willpower, though in every other part of her life it never yielded. She knew if she did slip in her resolve and try to seduce Shon, not only would she make a fool of herself, but she would be forced to leave her new clan for good. She avoided his eyes, trying desperately not to blush. "That would be fine, thank you," she answered stiffly. "I don't think we'll be there long, anyway," she added, as much to reassure herself. "The king has already assigned Baraxis to the east."

"The rumors had it right, then," Shon replied as they led their horses away. "What do you think?"

"About what?"

Shon chuckled. "About all this, of course. The march here, the city, the mission east. Whatever."

"I don't think it matters what I think."

"Well, I know it matters to *you*, even though deeds are more precious to you than thoughts. I know it matters to Baraxis and to Ardos. And it matters to me."

Gwyn was glad the narrow street required her attention. *Why*, she thought, *did he have to say* that? "Alright," she bit back. "I think the march here was dull. I think the city is too big and too crowded and nothing at all like my home.

I never dreamed that would matter, when I left, but it does. I think the mission is straightforward enough, but Baraxis has a bad feeling about it, and that makes me uneasy."

"Well, who isn't uneasy, with so many orcs bearing down on us?" Shon tried to pass off the news, but Gwyn could see he was just as unnerved to hear of Baraxis' foreboding.

"You don't have to play cagey with me, Shon." She'd meant it to sound exasperated, but it came out simply neutral, which, on the scale of Gwyn's interactions, sounded altogether gentle. She cursed her treasonous heart as Shon replied.

"You're right. We are equals in all things, now, and we both could use a confidant. The truth is, I'm deeply troubled about the Lord General, even since before the march. The king has been trying to lure him away from Sutherset for years, but Baraxis never really believed he'd be ordered to it outright. He's been changing, day by day, since the courier came. Quieter, more withdrawn. He suffers under a great weight, and I don't know how I can help. It's so unlike him."

"That's what I told him," Gwyn agreed.

"Did he have an answer?"

"Not one I believed."

Shon nodded. "Your first day with us, when the zil'bast attacked, I put his life above my duty. That was wrong...but wherever it's possible, he *should* be protected; he means a great deal to his people. I've known other men who became convinced their time was nearing, and somehow fate or recklessness always obliges them." He paused to shake his head at memories Gwyn could only guess at. "Will you help me to see that doesn't happen to him?" he continued. "If we can't improve his spirits, we can at least watch his back in battle. He's no more likely to lead from the rear than you are, after all, general or no."

"I will do what I can, when I can. But we've still this war to win, as well."

"It's all a bit much for a day's work." Shon smiled weakly. "Even working together, perhaps we should figure more like a week."

Gwyn chuckled, but without mirth. "A week it is, then."

At last Shon left off such serious talk and began describing the workings of the city in earnest as they toured through its various regions. Starting at the outside, the poorest districts were beyond the protection of even the outer wall and went by many names: the Cheap Town, the Slums, the Outside, the Dog Markets, the list went on and on. These sat inside a ring of timber breastworks that had been erected a generation ago, and all now mingled, where not outright displaced, with transplanted soldiers and camp followers. Inside the outermost stone wall began the city proper. Those regions were a mix of indentured laborers and lower classes of freemen and artisans. Many wealthier craftsmen maintained shops there as well, even if they lived in more affluent areas. This ring of the city was usually called the Outer City or the New Town, even though the outer wall annexing it as a formal part of the Capital had been built over a century before. Next came the Middle City, inside the second wall. Five of the city's eight hills were in that ring, a place of palatial estates owned by aristocrats and wealthy merchants. There was little industry in the Middle City, but in more prosperous times money flowed freely there. Against such an immediate threat, most of the wealthier class had fled north, leaving the Middle City in the hands of a motley blend of boarding officers, middle class artisans, and guttersnipes. Finally came the Inner Districts, or Old Town as it was sometimes called. Inside the oldest, inner wall all the machinery of government was housed. Meeting rooms, servants' quarters, the homes of petty nobles at the beck and call of some more important personage in the castle, all these were built shoulder-to-shoulder, even directly on top of, scribes' quarters, alehouses, inns, and less reputable establishments. The streets were a twisting, barely navigable mess, and this was only partially accidental.

"Fire and such things are always to be feared, of course," Shon explained, "but any army trying to move from the inner wall to the castle itself without good knowledge of the terrain…"

"They'd be better off marching into a giant gristmill," Gwyn finished.

"It would be a quicker end, anyway," Shon agreed. By then they had reached the Ackras district, the western face of one of the southern hills in the Middle City. The lower slopes were terraced and held opulent row houses for merchants and artisans. Higher up, some of the city's few flashes of green showed through as the press of buildings gave way to wide lawns and gardens behind gates of wrought iron. The Haddix estate was one of these.

"Haddix the Elder was a cantankerous old miser," Shon explained as the gates were opened to them. "He spent just enough on the estate to keep up the family reputation; the rest he hoarded, save the occasional shrewd investment. His son is, how to put it? To say he is more indulgent would be the polite understatement. He fled north to the family's country estate years ago, and now that Old Haddix is dead, word tells that the son is preaching to his hangers-on that we're all doomed to fall to the orcs and have no future. At least, that's a ready enough excuse to spend all his father's money as quickly and pleasurably as he can."

"How do you know all this?" Gwyn asked, surprised his information was so comprehensive. "You're no gossip."

"No," Shon agreed, "but I've made nearly annual journeys to the city with Baraxis, and I am…innocuous. Politics in the south isn't always simple or reasonable, and the lord general can't always put his ears to the right doors without being noticed. But I'm quiet enough and common enough that most people don't remember me being places. I just find an alehouse where the right people are meeting to close a deal over a pint, or complain about this noble or that, and choose a nice, secluded table nearby. It almost always works." Shon paused with a shallow smile. "It worked well enough when Baraxis asked me verify the rumors about *you*, when word came you were headed our way."

The pair was ushered to the main doors, into a foyer that would have nearly contained Gwyn's entire childhood home, all marble and gold paint. "I'm Captain Shon, serving under Lord General Baraxis," the captain introduced himself to the steward on duty, handing him a dispatch bearing his assignment of chambers. "We are to be in the east wing."

"You should have ridden to the rear gate," the steward snorted. "That's the quickest route to the servants' quar—east wing, that is."

Shon's demeanor remained pleasant, but Gwyn saw something go cold at the corners of his eyes, and his motions were quick as he took back the dispatch and refolded it, creasing the edges. "I'm sorry to have inconvenienced you. Just the same, we are here now, so please direct us to our hall. We'll need another room prepared as well. Baraxis' contingent has grown by one."

"Impossible!" the steward huffed. "The house is full; you'll just have to triple bunk instead of double."

Shon cleared his throat. "Our situation is somewhat delicate. Do you know who this is?" He indicated Gwyn with a nod of his head.

"I don't believe I've had the privilege," the steward scoffed. His sarcasm was like darts of ice at Gwyn's eyes.

Gwyn had stomached enough of the functionary's condescension. Stepping forward, she snapped back in Atlund brogue as thickly as she could manage. "I don't care who you are, you worthless bootlicker. I've used the bones of better men than you to pick my teeth. I'd rather sleep in the stable than this glorified brothel anyway; I'd expect better conversation there from the help and better manners from the *residents*."

"What did she say?" the steward asked Shon.

Not missing a beat, Shon replied, "Gwyn the Savage, the warrior whose reputation has garnered some small interest at court, apologizes for the inconvenience of her gender and asks if it would be so very much trouble to ask if any pair of the kind gentlemen of this great city would consent to sharing a room so that a humble, foreign lady might safeguard her modesty."

Gwyn did nothing to shore up Shon's attempt at diplomacy, her glare boring into the steward.

In turn, the smaller man kept the corner of his eye on Gwyn as he answered Shon. "I could have sworn I caught something about bones picking her teeth."

"Merely a quaint, northern saying, I assure you. Now, about our rooms?"

"I'll see what I can do," the steward relented, "assuming you leave me to it. We've numbered all the rooms; yours is four-three, for now. Go straight back across the great hall, then down the passage and through the kitchens. I'm sure you're more than capable of finding your way." With that, he turned on his heel and left the foyer.

Shon glared at the man's retreating back and shook his head in disgust. "Useless toady," he muttered as he stalked through the hall, looking more furious than Gwyn had ever seen him. As they reached the kitchens, Gwyn salved her growing unease by nicking an apple from a counter before hazarding, "Is this trouble because of me?"

"What?" Shon replied, noticing her apple and holding out his hand for a slice as they walked.

"Well, obviously they weren't expecting a woman," Gwyn clarified as she pulled her belt knife to quarter the apple and handed a piece to her fellow captain, "but are they making it more difficult than it needs to be because I'm not a Southerner?"

"No," Shon reassured her, "this is something far older than your time here. These city folk, well, too many of the nobles, anyway, they're pompous ingrates. Useless aristocrats. No land has bled more for them than Sutherset, but many in the Capital still treat those from the far west like backwards hill-folk, not heroes keeping the war's depredations off *their* doorsteps. They see their taxes go up and think that *they* suffer while men and women like Ardos and Mona bury their sons and fight on without so much as a day to mourn."

Gwyn hesitantly reached up as they walked and finally let a hand rest on Shon's shoulder. It felt awkward, and she took it away. "You're right, it isn't fair, Shon, but you don't do it for *them*."

Shon's pace slowed somewhat. "I know. I don't need their gratitude, but a little less condescension wouldn't go awry."

Gwyn was relieved at the return of the level-headed man she so respected, but seeing the fire in his passion had warmed her blood in a way she couldn't afford to acknowledge. She changed the subject as quickly as she could. Shon seemed just as glad when she did. Could it be that he really had leaned into her touch for a moment, that she hadn't merely imagined it? And that skin-tingling feeling was there, stronger than ever.

"Before we met the Capital's most useless toady, you said something," Gwyn reminded. "You went out looking for knowledge of me before I got to Sutherset?"

"I'd been home on a long furlough, of sorts, surveying my and my neighbors' herds for potential war mounts. Rumor of your ability had reached Baraxis, so he sent a courier asking me to take a detour on the way home and see if I could make any firsthand judgment. How else do you suppose he knew about your big tavern fight when you arrived?"

"You were *there*?"

"What of it?" Shon challenged.

"You might have stepped in to help protect my honor."

"Didn't know at the time you had any to protect. Besides, I wasn't going to risk getting in your way. I like having *both* my hands."

Again Gwyn reflected on the past ten months and how much the camaraderie of these foreigners had changed her. "You're right," she answered. "I probably wouldn't have appreciated the help."

By then, the pair had arrived at the single room set aside for them. Shon's frustration flared anew when he saw the size and condition of the accommodation, but he only muttered under his breath instead of launching into another tirade. After inspecting the room, he turned back to Gwyn. "You stay here and refresh yourself; get some sleep, if you can. I'm going to hunt down that steward and see that this situation is remedied."

"We can both get some rest first," Gwyn tried to be accommodating. "I'm not soft, like you Southerners, I can just throw my cloak on the floor and—"

"No, Gwyn. This isn't Atlund; if it's known we share a lodging, people will assume the worst of both of us, and I won't have them whispering about you behind your back. Two-thirds of Baraxis' expedition to the east will probably be new soldiers who don't know you. You'll have an uphill battle leading them as it is, without rumors that you're lying with the other officers."

"Fair enough," Gwyn replied, allowing Shon to leave and close the door behind him. Gwyn kicked the bed's simple footboard in frustration, for even as ignorant as she was of such things, she was confident Shon's stated objection was not the whole reason for his hasty retreat.

CHAPTER XII

Apparently Shon could be extremely persuasive at need. Another room was made ready that afternoon, and the rest of Gwyn and Shon's week on the Haddix estate passed without incident, though their friendship deepened as they spent much of their off-duty time together. Shon spoke mostly of his family, and Gwyn found, to her surprise, a growing desire to meet them, to see what the household looked like of one who refused to sacrifice family and happiness for the sake of battle. She found the notion as intriguing as it was terrifying. Gwyn spoke little, but when she did, she spoke of home; mostly of Tehgil, at first, but remembrances of her mother, even her stepfamily, started creeping in as the days wore on, and she began toying with the idea she might even have a home worth going back to after she'd finished with the orcs. Then she thought of leaving her new clan and was overwhelmed by a sense of loss, reminding her that planning for a tomorrow which might never come was more painful and confusing than it was worth.

Their on-duty time passed more quickly; there was so much to do. Shon mostly ran errands for Baraxis, making preparations for the move east while the lord general was trapped in meetings of the war council. Ardos dealt with the quartermasters to ensure the new troops and their riding mounts were properly outfitted. Gwyn, on the other hand, was tasked with the critical job of reviewing companies to decide whether they should be short-listed for Baraxis' handpicked attack force.

Despite the relative rarity of female fighters in the south, most of the men had heard Gwyn's reputation and treated her with due respect. It was also possible much of their good behavior was in response to an incident on the first day when a bold and stupid soldier had tried to take liberties with Gwyn in the grappling ring. He was carried to the hospital tent with a broken wrist and "other undisclosed injuries." Baraxis learned of the matter that afternoon and, despite Gwyn's insistence that she'd seen to sufficient punishment for the offense, demanded the soldier be brought up on charges. When his captain came to the subordinate's defense, Baraxis cursed him for a letch and barred his entire fief from participating in the eastern campaign. Rumor had it the captain tried to challenge Baraxis to a duel for the insult, but his superior, one General Steract, forbade it, saying he couldn't afford to lose the man. The captain, in turn, took the order as an insult to his skill and attempted to resign his commission in outrage. The resignation was denied, but, like a ruined horse being put out to pasture, the captain was demoted to leading a guard contingent protecting noble estates to the north, troops that would never see combat unless all was already lost. General Steract was the rare commoner who had gained his rank purely from battlefield promotion, a commentary on his skill and initiative. Baraxis cautioned Gwyn that the general was also an arrogant man and unlikely to forget the trouble; moreover, in his own mind, he would probably lay the blame on Gwyn.

The rest of the selection went smoothly, and in eight days, all stood ready for the force's departure, by barge as Baraxis had hoped. Eight hundred men and mounts made for quite a flotilla, but they travelled with only a few supply vessels. Baraxis needed mobility, and he counted on the ability to resupply every few days from the river.

"If they outflank you and get around your north side, you'll be cut off from supplies," the king had countered in a strategy meeting.

"If that happens, Majesty," Baraxis had replied, "we won't live long enough to starve."

Gwyn had never spent any significant time on the water and quickly found river travel did not suit her. For one thing, it was dull, but more importantly, she couldn't swim. She hid her unease well, but Ardos noted it just the same as his barge drew alongside hers, and he attempted to offer comfort. "The current here's swift," he called, "an' there's quite an undertow. If the boat tips, even the best swimmer aboard is like as not ta drown."

"That's very reassuring," Gwyn shouted back.

Ardos saluted. "Glad to be o' help, Captain Gwyn the Savage, sir, lady, sir."

Fortunately, the barges were worthy craft with seasoned crews, and the force disembarked safely at Dorn two days after setting out, their movements hidden from orcish scouts by the row of hills south of the Dr'Nai. They took the rest of the day to settle the camp, but after that, Baraxis wasted no time. He called an officer council that night to outline his plan for a strike the following day.

"The main force under my command will hit the orcish rearguard," the lord general ordered. "They're strung out thin and not very disciplined; they're not expecting ambush, especially from behind where they've already killed or driven off any resistance. We should be able to smash the rear-most contingent and get out with minimal casualties. Shon, you will take a quarter of our force and strike the head of the column. The lead regiment will probably be well out ahead, but when those behind see the trouble, they'll charge you, so hit hard and retreat quickly. Their horde is stretched out over more than two miles, so my force won't be able to help you if you get into trouble.

"Gwyn, small unit tactics are your specialty, and I have something special in mind for you. The orcs should have a point squad about a quarter mile ahead of the lead column. I want you to wait until Shon strikes, preferably while terrain keeps the point force out of sight, then with a single platoon take them unawares and destroy them. As word of the two larger attacks moves up and down the column, there will be confusion. They'll call in the scouts to make reports and realize their eyes in front were already dead. The idea is to slow their march by causing uncertainty and fear, so we'll get to that right from the jump.

"Everybody else, see Shon for specific assignments. Dismissed."

Baraxis pulled Ardos aside before the crowd could disperse. "Old friend, I've assigned you to Gwyn's platoon, along with a young lieutenant from the Capital, a count called Sadax."

"Seems a lot o' officers fer only one platoon, sir."

"It is. I need to see what Gwyn can do with all the troops, not just Sutherset's, and I need to see it now. Two of the four squads I've assigned for her platoon include no Sutherset men, with the count lieutenant as their head. I'm as worried about *him* as I am about *her*. I need you with them, to watch them both."

"Watch and *what*, sir?" Ardos asked.

"Give counsel, provide a cooler head if there is disagreement. Just be yourself."

"Well, there's none better at that, sir."

"Knew I could count on you."

In some ways, Gwyn's role in the attack was the most difficult. Shon and Baraxis had all morning to get into position against huge targets, while Gwyn had to locate and shadow the orcish scouts and wait for Shon's attack without being seen. She had divided her force, twelve men under her command south of the road and another twelve under Count Lieutenant Sadax on the north. Given Baraxis' intent that no word of Gwyn's attack should reach the main orcish force, she'd been assigned one of the few squads trained to mounted fighting to ensure they could run down any of the enemy who fled. Though challenging to execute, the plan was simple enough: They kept extreme distance until the appointed time for Shon to be in position, then approached under the cover of heavy trees and waited for the sound of Shon's drums to start their own attack. Gwyn was to drive out first, in front of the scouts, then the lieutenant was to emerge behind and drive them to Gwyn. The pincer would ensure none of the enemy could escape.

Gwyn had moved her force into place and waited anxiously for Shon's attack to begin, her arms burning with the desire to unleash her sword after such a long, involuntary furlough, long enough, in fact, that even the war hammer she currently had readied seemed better than nothing. Sadax and his dozen should be hiding across the road, waiting, as she peered through the screening brush. The enemy scouts paced into view, she had only to wait for Shon to—

Suddenly, Sadax burst from the underbrush, driving his mounted force into the orcish flank. "What in all the hells?" Gwyn growled. She could see the count lieutenant's squad trying to fan out to surround the orcs, but the enemy was already scattering; he had no hope of containing them all if Gwyn didn't act quickly. "Ardos, go!" The older man led his dozen into the fray. Gwyn grabbed one of the Sutherese as they passed and ordered, "You, with me!" With that, she sped along a trail parallel to the road, heading east as Ardos directed his force into a wider, second ring to surround the orcs. Gwyn's Atlund-bred horse ripped through the yards of narrow, overgrown path, and the young soldier behind her, to his credit, kept the pace. After a few moments she drove left, out into the road. As she had anticipated, some orcs had broken free of the net. Three were sprinting back toward the main body, and still Shon's drums had not beat out over the intervening hill: if any orcs crested the rise to alert the main body, Shon may lose the element of surprise. One orc was well ahead of the other two, starting up that hill, and Gwyn pursued it, ordering her companion to intercept the others.

Gwyn's horse crossed the distance quickly, and a swing from Gwyn's hammer crushed the life from the orc's skull. The young soldier's mount was untested against the scent of live orcs and was giving him a hard time; as Gwyn wheeled her own horse, the boy was thrown from the saddle. Still, he rolled into a crouch, doing all he could to slow the enemy, forcing them to engage him. Gwyn crossed as much distance as she could but had no choice but to slow. If she attacked on the charge, momentum would carry her too far, and the soldier would be left alone. Instead, she reigned up next to the struggling trio, raining blows with her hammer. The Sutherese soldier thrust his blade desperately and slew the last orc, but even as he struck, the enemy's club connected with the young man's head in a sickening crunch. He cried out and went down; Gwyn dropped from the saddle to attend him.

She looked over her shoulder as she did to see the main skirmish already ending, the last few orcs being hacked down. She only needed a brief look to see that the boy's wounds were beyond tending. She pulled his cloak over his face before taking the reins of both horses and walking back to the squad.

Most of the men had dismounted, but the count lieutenant sat proudly astride his stallion, taking handshakes and congratulations from his men.

Gwyn reached up to Sadax with one hand, and the man ignorantly reached down to take it. Gwyn grabbed his arm and hauled him from the saddle, slamming his shoulder blades into the ground.

"Explain yourself!" she roared.

"How dare you?" he snarled back. "What did you expect, ordering me to flush the enemy to you like a dog, so some foreign bitch could–"

Gwyn expected something like "take all the glory" was supposed to follow, but she cut off the thought by slamming the lieutenant into the ground again. When his eyes stopped rattling, he grunted, "What are you complaining about? The plan worked."

"Three men lay dead. *They* might disagree, if they had the breath to."

"They might have died anyway."

Gwyn's fist swung into his face like a sledge. Trapped against the dirt, the lieutenant's head had nowhere to go; the impact exploded his nose into a fine mist of blood. He screamed as Gwyn berated him. "They're *dead!* And you're *arguing!* Do you have no regard for them? By Terillah, they were *your own men.* If we were back in Atlund I'd draw my blade and bleed you out *right here.*" She hesitated as her hand strayed to her dirk, and the men shifted uneasily. "You may wish I had, once Baraxis is through with you," she finished. Shoving off the lieutenant's chest, she stood, picking a Southerner, not a Sutherset man, at random as she did. "Bind him," she ordered the man.

She heard Ardos start to move to her right. "I wasn't talking to you!" she shouted without breaking eye contact with her original target. "You! Bind him, *now!*"

At last the man moved, and others stepped forward to put the bound lieutenant back on his horse and try to stop the bleeding from his face. Finally the sounds of drums and the clash of arms drifted from over the hill to the east.

"Ardos, see to our wounded and dead, and make sure none of the orcs will tell of this. We need to get out of here."

Gwyn headed east to the body of her fallen soldier and lifted him gently into the saddle before rejoining the men and leading them back to Dorn.

Baraxis found Ardos as soon as he returned. "How were they?" Baraxis inquired.

Ardos squinted one eye and rubbed the back of his head. "Well, Count Lieutenant Sadax is in irons."

"What!?"

"He was insubord'nate, Baraxis. Three men died. The young lieutenant was lucky Gwyn didn't kill 'im right there in the road. Prob'ly woulda been within 'er rights. She brought 'im back fer ye ta deal with."

"I will, and decisively. How was Gwyn?"

Ardos shook his head. "It was a trial by fire, an' she passed it flawless. She was magnificent, Baraxis. Magnificent. That woman is fearless."

"This is news?"

"Don' misunderstand, Lord, she's never been afraid ta *die.* But there's a zeal in 'er that wasn't there before. Now she's not afraid ta die, nor ta *live.*"

~ * ~

Later on, one Sergeant Rak sought an audience with Baraxis in the abandoned town hall he had converted into his command post. Rak was of average height and narrow build with a hardscrabble black beard and wavy hair, a smallish sword at either hip.

"What do you want?" the lord general asked sharply.

"The boys want to know what's to become of our lieutenant, Lord General."

"Count Lieutenant Sadax, you mean?"

Sergeant Rak nodded.

"I haven't decided," Baraxis answered.

"Two of the men wanted to speak for him, Lord General."

"Two out of the dozen that knew him?"

"Well, ten now, sir. The other eight want to speak for Gwyn," Sergeant Rak clarified.

"They don't need to. I have her word and Ardos', and that's more solid than holy writ."

"Understood, m'lord. I'll tell them." He waited to be dismissed.

Baraxis was shocked so many of the two squads who were strangers to Gwyn would take her side so readily, but he didn't show it. "What would *you* say?" he asked. "If you had to speak, I mean."

"Lord General, Gwyn the Savage is one hell of an officer, begging your pardon, m'lord."

"Granted. Go on."

"We all heard the stories, and we went to talk to some of your boys as soon as we got word you'd reached the city. Not all of us in the Capital look down on the west. Our squad comes from all over, anyway, and we got nothing but respect for the work you boys've been doin' out there. We wanted to see firsthand if this Gwyn the Savage was as good as the rumors, so we convinced the count lieutenant to have us reviewed for your campaign. We figured he only agreed so he could show Gwyn up, but we never thought he'd do something like this.

"Anyhow, Captain Gwyn did right out there. We'd have taken those orcs as easy as catchin' rats if our man hadn't fouled it up, and she kept her head and managed to save things. Then, at the end… She *cared* about our fallen, Lord. All just strangers, and poor folk, too, and them dying stoked up the rage in her like they'd been her own kin. There's a deadly mettle in her, Lord General, but there's a decency, too. We'd like to stay on with her, if you'll allow us. We've never met her equal."

"There aren't many to meet. I can't promise anything, and the captain will have no small say in the matter herself. Still, I will consider your words. But know this: If you or any of yours are playing false, hoping for a chance to avenge your lieutenant, you won't fool Gwyn, and she won't be merciful the second time. I've already spoken to her and given free rein dealing with insubordinates." Baraxis paused for a moment in thought. "I can't say she's ever killed a man in cold blood before, but I doubt it would trouble her overmuch."

Sergeant Rak was unflinching. "Whatever you feel is best, m'lord. Thank you for hearing me."

Baraxis nodded. "You're dismissed."

The lord general pondered Rak's report as the sergeant left. He'd seen the change in Gwyn but feared her respect might not extend beyond Sutherset to men she didn't know. In hindsight, he should have realized her esteem would always include the whole brotherhood of steel and blood. He shook his head. Steel and blood, these were his life, which should have been crops and livestock. He knew that was one of many ways he and Gwyn would always differ, for while he had to admit he loved duty even more than peace, Gwyn's love was always, only, for the battle itself.

He didn't understand that love, but he would use it for as long as he drew breath. Even that thought brought the dark murmurs of fear to the back of his mind, so he returned his attentions to his plans.

In the end, Baraxis decided against charging Count Lieutenant Sadax with treason. Some counseled to simply send him back to the Capital without charges, but Baraxis demanded more exacting justice than that. Gwyn offered no opinion on the sentence. "I can't fight with someone I can't trust," she said, "and if he wrongs me again, I'll kill him. Beyond that, he's in your hands. You have the burden to lead, remember?"

And so Baraxis stripped the man of rank and expelled him from service. He was allowed to keep his noble title, but his dishonorable ineligibility to serve would bring a crippling tax burden to his estate. Baraxis suspected he might go into exile rather than pay it, but that was the king's problem, not his.

Baraxis also agreed, with Gwyn's consent, to Sergeant Rak's request. The count's two loyalists were sent back to the Capital, and the remainder of the squads were assigned permanently to Gwyn. Rak proved trustworthy and capable, and Baraxis was able to redeploy Ardos to a unit that needed closer supervision. As other platoons took heavy enough losses to be dismantled, and Gwyn's targets became increasingly wary and tough, Baraxis added to her command. By the time they decamped from Dorn a week later, Gwyn led a short company of fifty men.

When the regiment arrived at Roon, the second Crafthold, Baraxis declared a day of rest, at least from combat. The constant movement and anxiety of ambush strikes, sometimes two a day, were taking their toll on man and beast alike, such that even Gwyn was grateful for a day without engaging the enemy. Still, there was more than enough work to do in setting up the new camp and making sure the defenses were secure, especially since Ardos, who usually saw to such things, was away taking a detachment down to the river to load in fresh supplies.

When Ardos returned that afternoon, Baraxis gathered all the men, just under seven-hundred remaining, at a stage in the town square to speak. "Southerners," he began, "the king is pleased with our progress!" A cheer went up from the crowd. "He sends his thanks. More importantly, he sends rewards!" Baraxis hoisted a small cask and tipped it back, sampling the contents, then handed it down to the nearest soldier. As the man drank and passed the keg, the lord general pulled the tarp from a wagon behind him, revealing a host of barrels and bottles. "The best ales, wines, and meads from the Capital. The nearest orc is fifteen miles away, the walls here are strong, and the booze is stronger. Drink hearty, men! Everyone is furloughed from duty for two nights and a day, starting as soon as that cask makes it back up to the stage."

An overzealous soldier heaved the half-empty vessel back at Baraxis, who laughed as he caught it, then backed away to avoid the coming onslaught as men stormed the stage to reach the wagon of libations.

Gwyn, standing near the back of the crowd with Rak, was glad to see Baraxis with some of his old zeal back, though even this display was strangely manic compared to the happy, easy man she had known in Sutherset. Rak cleared his throat anxiously. "One of us, I s'pose, ought prob'ly to stay out of the cups, make sure the boys don't get too out o' hand…"

Gwyn laughed. "Set to, Sergeant, you've earned it. You'll owe me one, though."

"Thank you, sir." Rak hurried to the stage.

Gwyn eventually made her way there, after the crowd had dispersed. Alas, there had been but little mead, it being the least popular libation in the south, and it was down to the silty dregs by the time she sampled it. With a wistful longing for that most traditional drink of her people, she pulled a flagon of ale instead. She drank slowly and kept a clear head, but she wasn't about to deny herself completely.

About an hour into the festivities, Gwyn ambled into the town hall and de facto tavern, impressed she'd only had to break up a pair of fights, and neither serious. Once inside, she scanned the room. It was half full of soldiers, a few playing dice games here and there, but most just boisterously trading war stories, and through the crowd she spotted a pair of familiar faces. Ardos, also mostly sober, sat at a table just inside the door, keeping an eye. Gwyn also saw Shon alone in a corner, as was his custom, but she was shocked to realize he sat before a firkin of mead with its head stoved in. It was clear the captain had not restrained himself.

"What's wrong with Shon?" Gwyn asked Ardos.

Ardos shook his head. "It's 'is annivers'ry. First one 'e di'n't get home for."

Gwyn started across the room.

"I wouldn't," Ardos cautioned.

"I would," Gwyn shot back over the din. "Shon, what are you doing?" she asked when she reached him.

"I'm getting piss-drunk, Gwyn. What are you doing?"

"I'm not rightly certain, but I think I'm trying to keep you from making an ass of yourself."

Shon snorted. "You're no expert on that, Atlunder."

"Maybe not." She sat. "What would Tira think if she saw you like this?"

"She's not here to see, Gwyn. S'kinda the point."

"That's right. She's home, safe, raising Karon away from all the blood and killing. That's reason to celebrate, not feel sorry for yourself."

"You've no right to judge." Shon lifted his empty tankard to dunk it back into the mead.

Gwyn grabbed his hand, stopping him, and held his ice-blue eyes with hers, though his were bleary. Even with Shon at his least admirable, she couldn't stop the shiver running up her arm at the touch, like sparks running through her blood. "I don't judge," she said levelly. "Terillah knows you're a grown man, and its safe enough tonight. I just know you well enough to be sure you'll think yourself a fool tomorrow if you keep this up."

Shon sniffed. "That's just what she would have said." He reached a hand toward Gwyn's hair, better kept than in her childhood but still wild and fiery. "You remind me so much of her."

Gwyn sensed events moving in a disastrous direction and fought off every burning instinct to let them. She leaned back from Shon's touch. "But I'm *not* her, Shon."

His eyes flicked away, but they came back, and they looked as though a fire danced in them. "What if…? What if, for a night, it didn't matter?" He leaned toward her, but not with drunken aggression. There was something weaving through the air between them, as though they were being pulled together. Gwyn could feel it, as soft as it was irresistible. Fighting against it was deadly; the conflict felt like battle, and that only bolstered her confidence and inflamed her passions. Shon was getting closer, and her body hummed with his nearness. She could feel the gravity of the moment washing over her, the knowledge that things had already gone too far, that whatever happened next, it would change everything and with no going back.

Gwyn reached up to Shon's face, briefly caressed his cheek, then grabbed a fistful of his short hair and jerked his head back. Still his eyes held her, and she knew her aggression had not killed the moment, that she was still in its grip. Even like this, she could bend her head and taste his lips, throw every scruple aside and never go looking for them again, make ultimate surrender to the one man she'd ever met who deserved to best her.

She drew a shuddering breath and hesitated as he stared into her.

He *was* that good, that was the trouble. If Gwyn gave in, she might one day forgive herself, or even decide she didn't need forgiving, but Shon never would. The man she so admired would be gone forever, broken, and she loved– *Terillah strike me down, it's true!*–yes, *loved* him too much to let that happen.

"How dare you," she grunted through clenched teeth, not trusting herself to anything more gentle. "How *dare* you, like this? A thousand times I've wished for you, and at last you offer yourself, half-drunk and pining for your wife? You love Tira, not me, but if you have even an ounce of respect for me, how *could* you?"

Shon's eyes misted over, and Gwyn knew the moment, at last, had broken apart. "Happy anniversary," she growled, "and you're welcome." She let go his hair with a shove, and his body slumped away as his shoulders tensed in silent sobs. He was miserable and alone, but he was still *Shon*, and that was what mattered. Even so, his loneliness was heart-wrenching, and Gwyn, reacting to some instinct she didn't know she possessed, reached out to him, pulling him to her not in a tender, lover's embrace, but in the crushing grip of friends who have faced death together. His touch still sent sparks dancing across her skin, but they no longer seduced her, instead binding her to him with a wholly different love.

"Damn this war!" he cried in her ear. "Damn it to all the hells; I hate it! I miss Tira. I miss Karon. Hells, I even miss my *horses*! I want to train them to plow and race and jump, not charge headlong into death! And when the time comes,

I'll train my own *son* no better! When will this nightmare end?"

Gwyn had no idea what to do or say, so she just stayed like that, holding him as he sobbed and babbled, loving him a little more with each word and tear, for each proved his kindness and innocence and, coupled with his unflinching duty, his courage and honor as well. Finally the man sobbed himself into slumber, and Gwyn arranged him over the table, his head on his arms. She picked up his flagon and refilled it, shunning her own ale, and leaned back, propping her feet on a second chair, nursing the drink as she kept watch, for most were still hours from ending their revel. Gwyn thought briefly of finding Sergeant Rak to redeem the favor he owed, or anyone else for that matter if Rak was too drunk, and taking him to a quiet corner to help satisfy the unfulfilled desires of her encounter, but the thought was distasteful. The only man she really wanted was the very one she'd resisted. She snorted humorlessly at herself as she took another sip of Shon's mead and settled in at the table. *Tomorrow is going to be a* long *day*, she thought, *without any orcs to take my mind off this madness.*

Across the room, Ardos decided the danger had passed. He nodded to himself, then drained his mug and went out to the wagon for another.

Gwyn was tending to her gray horse the next morning when Shon found her. "Gwyn," he said softly.

Gwyn started at the sound, so intent had she been at her work. She cursed herself for lowering her guard as she replied, "Morning, Shon," betraying nothing.

"Gwyn, last night…"

"I hope *you* remember what happened because I had far too much to–"

"Nice try, Gwyn."

She shrugged. "Not nice enough, I guess. I'm a better liar with most people."

"I appreciate the effort, truly, but…I acted horribly, and I am ashamed. If you hadn't stopped me–"

"I almost didn't."

"I could have done without knowing *that*," Shon replied.

"Sorry."

"Don't be ridiculous. You don't owe me an apology for *anything*. I owe you a great debt for your loyalty, and a great penance for my drunken foolishness. How can I make it right?"

"It wasn't drunken foolishness. Foolishness, maybe, but you weren't *that* drunk," Gwyn pointed out.

"I didn't think so either, until you touched my hand and then–"

"Like the air before lightning strikes."

"You feel it, too," Shon confirmed, amazement layered in his voice.

"From the day we met, and stronger all the time. I thought… I'd never, before…" Gwyn blushed to her ears and focused intently on her horse's mane. "I thought it might…be what…what love felt like."

Shon paused, raised his hand almost to Gwyn's shoulder, then hesitated, let it fall. "It isn't wholly unlike, in some ways, but I think it's something else," he finally replied. "Even the day you arrived, I felt it, weakly, and at the time I thought it best to send you away. And I *know* you thought little enough of me."

Gwyn was forced to nod. "At the time."

"It seems less like an emotion and more… You *provoke* me. I can't be indifferent to you; whatever feeling you inspire, you bring it to its fullest. It's funny. I hadn't thought of it before, but I see it in the men when they're fighting for you, not as strong, but similar."

Gwyn though for a moment. "I could use all those words to describe *you*."

"This is all crazy," Shon answered, shaking his head. "We're not sorcerers. But this thing, if it isn't only in our minds, if you're right, is no natural thing. It is the province of magic."

"What if it is? In Atlund, we know that magic can be anywhere. In the trees, in the blood, in the moons. In the Wind. Do you think nothing stranger than this has ever happened?"

"We don't even know what '*this*' is!"

"I don't care!" In that instant, Gwyn realized how true that was. She could imagine their past months together, even without this sensation, and it changed nothing of what her heart felt. "You asked what you could do to make it right. I know my price."

"Name it."

"Forget this happened. Bury it; never speak of it so long as we live. Just be my friend again. Be Shon. Don't ruin today what I sacrificed so much to save last night."

"But after what I did, and what you've said, or implied at least, how can we–"

"I don't know. But we will. And *you* will. I've named my price."

"You are merciful."

Gwyn scoffed. "We both know that isn't true."

"Perhaps. Do you need anything?"

"Yes, but not from you. Now go away; I want to think."

He left, and she watched him go. He did not turn back.

CHAPTER XIII

Shon was as good as his word. Within an hour of their conversation he behaved toward Gwyn as he ever had before the prior night. They ate and talked together as friends, and Shon betrayed no hint of embarrassment or unease, so much that Gwyn almost regretted the price she named, wondering if she'd made no amorous impression on him whatsoever.

It had become Gwyn's custom to take evening meals with her men, or as many as she could find in one place, but that night she sat alone under a budding peach tree, watching *Bia Creg* make her backwards journey over the western wall, the faintest glimmer through a haze of high clouds. Gwyn ate without tasting, her mind occupied with thoughts and her heart with feelings. She saw Rak across the green, his head turning from one side to the other as though he sought something. As soon as he saw Gwyn, he hustled over.

"Sergeant," Gwyn called without standing, "is something wrong?"

Rak finished his short jog and sat on the ground facing her. "I was about to ask you the same."

"I don't understand."

"A mob of us were at the supply wagons for evening ration, but you were nowhere about. Some of the men figured you were just giving us liberty since we're off duty, but I wanted to be sure."

"What for?" Gwyn asked.

"Well, we're partners."

"Are we?"

"Sorry, Captain, I know you're a proper officer, an' I didn't mean–"

Gwyn silenced him with a wave of her hand. "I don't care about all that. Where I come from, you'd be a captain."

"Really?"

She nodded. "Men follow you with respect, and in the heat of battle you can decide what to do with them. That makes a captain in Atlund."

Rak sat up a little straighter. "Maybe I should go north when my term is over, then."

Gwyn realized she knew no details of Rak's service. Baraxis owed the obligation to his king, and his men owed an obligation to him, at least one of honor. (As freemen, they could expect to be paid to fight for land that wasn't theirs. Gwyn had no idea how Baraxis would afford it, but that wasn't why his men followed him here.) Of Rak and his closest comrades, though, she had no idea. "Your term?" she asked.

He nodded. "I grew up in a king's orphanage in the Capital, well, a few of them. Bounced from one to another all the time, the house mothers trying to get me in front of new parents to adopt me." He laughed. "None ever did. Guess I was too ugly or, more likely, too lippy."

Gwyn chuckled. "I can relate."

"Well, if nobody picks you by your tenth birthday, or near enough to it as they can figure for an orphan, they send the boys north to an army camp. You get your room, board, and training for the next four years, then you owe twelve."

Gwyn thought for a moment of twelve years. Except for her childhood assumption she'd someday kill Kellgore, she'd never planned anything that far ahead. She'd been fighting for two years and, whatever it said about her, she still loved the thrill of battle. She couldn't imagine ever feeling differently, but did she want to do this for ten more years? Could she? As far as she knew she was the youngest officer in the regiment, but her old shoulder wound hurt when it rained in the same way she'd heard much older men complain. Apart from that, she'd been spared major wounds, but her hands were callused, her arms scarred. How much would be left of her in another decade? "Twelve years is a long time," she finally replied.

"I'm only halfway through," Rak added with a nod. "Even six years is a long time for people like me."

"People like us," Gwyn corrected.

Rak smiled. "You're no orphan, though. I can tell."

"No. But my father died before I was born, and my mother was...reserved, at least with me. I hated my stepfather without good reason. My oath-father was a great man, but other than that I knew my share of being lonely."

Rak looked around at the various soldiers going about the Crafthold on their various errands, then looked back to Gwyn. "No cause to be lonely anymore. Can't get away from your comrades even for a quiet meal alone, right?"

Gwyn smiled. "No cause at all. I wasn't doing myself or anybody any good sitting here ruminating, anyway." She stood with her half-empty plate. "Calling this tripe would be an insult to tripe. Do you want it?"

Rak stood and took the plate. "You don't have to ask twice, Captain. Anything that fills up the hole, I always say." He shoveled a bite into his mouth and swallowed. "Regardless, I know the fellah that always manages to hoard the best food in our company. Let's go track him down."

Gwyn shook her head, unsurprised. "Of course you do. Lead the way, Sergeant."

Three more days passed, with strikes at the orcs resuming. Every day their enemy grew cagier, reacting to threats more quickly and taking a heavier toll in every engagement. To do so, however, they were forced to slow their march, meeting Baraxis' objective in this theater of war. All that changed violently on the fourth day.

Evening had fallen just as Gwyn returned with the last guerilla band. An hour later, the captains had gathered with the lord general around a map table reviewing the next day's operations when a concussive *BOOM* shook the air, shattering the north windows and pitching Baraxis and Shon to the floor.

"What in all the hells was that!?" Gwyn bellowed above the ringing in her ears. Shouts and screams began filtering into her senses, and the night was suddenly aglow with flames from the wreckage of what used to be a merchant's house to the north.

Ardos grabbed Gwyn and pulled her outside. "Firestones!" he shouted as he pulled his mighty bow off his back and strung it. "The alchemists make them in the Capital: big, round urns, sealed off and filled with some kind of nasty stuff, lamp oil and something they render down from bat droppings and eye of some critter or other, if you believe the stories. They launch them out of catapults, blow up with noise and fire when they hit something."

"We're being attacked by our own people?"

"Impossible!"

"Something else, then? A zil'bast?"

Sergeant Rak ran toward them with a pair of Gwyn's men; one was armed with a bow. A great *whoosh* sounded from the north, followed by another sense-shattering explosion. This one hit the edge of the already-demolished building, though, lessening the second shot's destruction.

"No, that's a firestone, alright," Rak confirmed. "The orcs must have gotten their hands on some."

Gwyn ushered her ad hoc squad to the nearest wall steps, no plan in mind but to at least get sight of the enemy.

"They found 'em, fine," Ardos answered as they climbed, "but where'd they learn to *use* 'em?"

"They didn't." Rak answered, reaching the top. "Not well, anyway. Look." The sergeant pointed down at a pair of small catapults in the plain to the west. "They're too close. They must be launching with their arc too high, cutting their range. And they aren't pounding at the wall to open us up to attack; they're trying to get the buildings inside, but they can't even see them. They're just guessing."

"Going for the quickest kill, that's orc thinking alright," Gwyn reasoned. The enemies on the plain were busy loading another stone into the left catapult. "And you're right about them being too close; they're within a strong bowshot. Royce, give Ardos your quiver, then go get some rags and pitch."

"Gwyn," Ardos protested, "my old eyes, in the dark…"

"Just keep their heads down and get their range," Gwyn ordered. "When the time comes, we'll be your eyes."

Rak ordered a pair of soldiers to unsling their shields and form a small barrier behind the parapet that Ardos could use for additional cover. Others on the wall saw their tactic, and those with strong enough bows and arms joined in, confounding the orcs efforts to take a third shot. The big moon was nearly full, and all the while Gwyn watched the fall of Ardos' arrows to help him to find the range. A minute had passed when Royce returned with cloth strips and pitch, and others on the wall set to making fire arrows without delay. "Keep them light; just a thin coat of pitch," Gwyn ordered. "They don't need to burn long." As the workers completed each arrow they handed it to Gwyn, who had taken a torch from a nearby sconce and lit it. "You have their range?" she asked.

"Aye," Ardos replied.

"With the added weight of pitch, they're *out* of range," a younger Southerner protested.

"Not *his*," Gwyn answered, handing Ardos an arrow that he promptly nocked. "Place it a foot past your last shot."

"Light."

Gwyn lit the end of the arrow; Ardos drew and loosed, sending the missile on its way. It thudded into the left catapult's frame, but the flight had weakened the fire, and though it blazed up and consumed the shaft, it did little but blacken the heavy timbers of the siege weapon. The orc's raucous laughter could be heard as one more daring ventured from cover to approach the catapult's lever.

"Ardos, quickly!" Gwyn urged, handing him another arrow and stepping behind him. "Make ready." He raised the bow as if to shoot but did not stretch it. "Angle a hair to the left." He did. "Aim seven feet farther out." His bow raised slightly. The orc was reaching for the lever. Gwyn lit the arrow. "Now!"

Ardos flexed his mighty back, stretched his bow, and loosed again. The arrow burned through the night. It flew straight past the orc and slammed home into the firestone about to be launched.

The concussion was less than that of the stones that had smashed into the town as designed, but the arrow's flame touched off the volatile mixture in the loaded firestone with stunning effect. It burst the catapults to burning kindling and spewed flames in all directions, incinerating a twenty foot circle on the plain as a cheer went up from the wall.

Gwyn slumped behind the parapet. "Thank Terillah that's over," she sighed.

Ardos shook his head in sympathy. "Poor lass. You know so much of battle, but still so little of war. This is only just beginning."

"What's that?" Gwyn asked.

As their eyes recovered from the fiery explosion, the burning grass of the field illuminated a portion of the seething ranks of hundreds of orcs encircling Roon. Ardos looked back at Gwyn and answered, "The siege."

She craned her neck to look over the parapet at the jostling horde, and 'orc thinking' suddenly seemed much harder to disregard.

Thankfully the enemy had no more siege engines, but they had enough bodies to keep the Southerners completely pinned down. Orc bows were not well-crafted; they tended to be underpowered and inconsistent, so they favored thrown javelins for precision work. Neither could match Southern bows for range, but the orcs simply kept their distance or stayed in the cover of scattered copses to the south or the heavier woods of the northwest. If the Southerners tried to deploy or escape, they'd be overwhelmed in short order. The next day, Baraxis discussed the situation with his captains.

"The wells are holding out so far, and with this being a rainy spring we shouldn't die of thirst, but today was supposed to be another supply run to the river barges. We only have enough food for two days, three if we cut rations, and an army fights on its stomach. It will take at least a week for a force to arrive from the Capital to break the siege, so whatever we're going to do, we have to do it now. It may be that the barge captains will take news of it back to the Capital when we don't make our rendezvous, but we can't count on that. They could be attacked by the orcs when they try to dock or take the supplies meant for us and sell them on the black market. Even if word does make it back, anyone getting the news might just as easily assume we were overrun and are all dead already. And maybe we are…but not before we've tried everything we can."

"We attack, then?" Gwyn asked.

"Not exactly," Baraxis countered. "With only the main gate and two small posterns, we could never get arrayed before they charge us. I'm suggesting something less drastic, though no less dangerous. Someone is going to ride out of here, try to get to the river to warn the Capital. It's our only way to be sure the king knows what happened, that we're still alive and might be saved, and to give enough intelligence for him to send more than just a scouting party. Even if we aren't rescued, it must be known that our mission is at an end, that the remaining orcs will be advancing at full speed.

"I've written dispatches to the king. We will choose the rider by lot–"

"That won't be necessary, Lord General." All eyes were on Captain Shon as he stepped forward. "I volunteer."

Half a dozen voices cried out, all offering to take Shon's place.

"I'm the best rider here," Shon said, quieting them, "And Cinnabar the fastest horse. I'm surprised at you, Baraxis. You know the cost of this war, and you've never shrunk from it. Why do you not order me to go?"

"You know the danger. I was thinking of Tira and Karon as much as you."

"Tira knew the danger when she married me," Shon answered, his voice heavy.

"You think that's fair to her?"

"I think it more fair than returning to her a dishonored craven, which I shall be if another man rides in my place."

"You will not be dissuaded," Baraxis answered, no hint of question in his tone.

"I will follow orders, but you know that I'm right."

"Prepare yourself, then. Our prayers go with you, and we will do all we can to distract the enemy."

Shon nodded once and headed out to the stables.

An hour later, Gwyn stood on the northwest wall with Ardos and half a dozen bowmen. Baraxis had to keep the force small enough not to draw attention, but the few he could risk would provide all the cover they could until Shon was out of range.

To the south, at the main gate, two hundred Southerners gathered, the wall above bristling with archers. From the outside, it would appear they were preparing exactly the kind of mad dash Baraxis had refused, and already the orcs were weakening their net to concentrate at the south side.

The sun blazed brightly overhead; orcs having keen senses of smell, Shon would use speed more than stealth, and for that he needed light.

Shouts sounded from the main gate as the doors swung open, and the small foot-door directly beneath Gwyn opened quietly at the same time. For a moment her mind flashed back to her last conversation with Shon, only a few minutes before, in the stables.

"Let me go with you," she pleaded, "I'll watch your back."

"You're needed here. I'm just a rancher, remember. You're the warrior."

"Damn you. At least put on the coat of plates Baraxis gave you."

"Too heavy. If I can't outrun the orcs, the armor won't save me. Don't worry so much, Gwyn. I'll be back to raise the siege in no time."

"Unless the king won't spare the men. Unless the Capital is already surrounded, unless…"

"Unless I get killed?"

"Yes!" Gwyn exploded.

"Well, I don't plan on getting killed."

"Nobody ever does."

"Time is running short, Gwyn. This is not goodbye; I know you'd wish me luck if you thought I needed it. What else is there to say?"

"Nothing." Her thick tone belied her words. "Maybe if I was more… Maybe if I was a regular girl…"

"Maybe if that was true, we never would have met, and Sutherset would have been devastated by the first zil'bast that came our way. Neither of those thoughts are happy. You ordered that I must be Shon, remember? Then you must be Gwyn. Exactly as you are, not as any other would make you. *Gwyn et Sheevasa.* Now you'd best get on up to the wall. I want to know your arrows are flying to protect me."

She nodded and left. He watched her go, saw her hesitate and look back, but only for a moment.

Now Gwyn watched as Shon bolted through the postern, his sleek bay tearing through the grass as though running a race. Orcs armed with wicked javelins loomed up before him, but the Southerners' arrows did not miss. In the bright sun, Ardos' weak eyes were strong enough, and his bow never rested for a moment, picking off orcs so close to Shon's line of travel that the others feared to take the shots. Gwyn gave a good accounting of herself, relying on her quicker reflexes to drop more distant orcs the moment they appeared. Shon's speed was incredible, and even still he cut and veered, working always for the clearest path and ever closing the distance to the cover of the trees to the northwest. He was nearing the edge of arrow range and less than a hundred yards from the brush, and one more felled orc opened a clear path before him, all the way to safety.

Indeed, so intently were his friends clearing the way before him they failed to see the dozen orcs behind him, rising out of the grass like ghosts, covered in camouflage so perfect Shon had ridden right past them.

Gwyn saw them first. "Shon, behind you!" she screamed, re-aiming her bow. Their javelins reached him before her words did. The first struck him low on the right side of his back. He reached behind to tear it free and keep riding, but two more found his left lung before he could finish the act.

Arrows arced from the wall, but most fell short; too few found their mark. Shon leaned forward over Cinnabar's neck, and from the wall it almost appeared he was speaking in the horse's ear. Then he dropped from the saddle at full gallop and rolled when he hit the ground, the javelins tearing cruelly from his back.

The horse shot forward with impossible speed, faster than Gwyn had seen an animal move in all her days. She barely noted it, though. Shon's momentum had carried him out of range. All she could do was watch as he regained his feet and drew his sword. The orcs rushed him as one. Shon slashed one through the belly and skewered another, then they were on him. In the instant before he went to the ground, Gwyn saw an orcish spear point pierce his throat.

Her wordless scream shook the air, a sound of pain and rage that darkened the hearts of all who heard it. A chill wind hissed from the north, dragging a black cloud across the sun. She looked away until she heard Ardos' sickened whisper. "Damn them. Damn them ta all the hells, the butchers."

Gwyn looked back to see the orcs had not stopped their work when the job was done; their arms rose and fell in succession as they hewed Shon to pieces. Gwyn surged forward, and it took Ardos and two other men to hold her from flinging herself over the parapet to reach the enemy.

Just then, one of the orcs stood, roaring and raising a hand over its head in triumph, the blood of Shon's scalp dripping down his forearm.

Gwyn dropped her weaker weapon and tore Ardos' bow from his hand. The older man didn't restrain her. Gwyn took careful aim and drew the mighty longbow to full stretch, an impossible feat fueled by rage and hate. The first arrow had barely left the string when a second joined it in the air.

The first shaft ripped through the orc's wrist, knocking the trophy from its grasp, but it didn't have time to cry out before the second tore out its throat. The rest of the enemy fled in terror to the trees, but they could only escape Gwyn's arrows, not her hatred or her curse as she bellowed out in her native tongue. "You are all dead! Do you hear? You cannot hide from the Hand of Vengeance! You will suffer for this! Your blood is mine!" The chill north wind rose into a gale, impossibly cold in the southern spring, but her words cut through its howling, chasing the accursed enemy to the trees. She stood unflinching as the Southerners about her shivered.

Gwyn sprinted down the steps, leaping over the last three and turning toward the postern. Baraxis stopped her. "We need you at the gate, Gwyn."

"He's dead! They're tearing him apart!"

"I know."

"They have to pay."

"They will."

"Get out of my way, old man!" She lunged.

"No." Baraxis blocked her with a hand on her sternum.

Gwyn unslung her sword and drew it, the steel hissing against the leather. *"Get out of my way."*

"I need you at the gate, Gwyn. The ones you want are long gone. But they have friends. Do to them what they've done to you."

Her heart was sick with hate, but Baraxis' reason appealed to the brutal soul of Gwyn the Savage; she growled her grief even as she charged into the larger fray, shoving allies out of her way to get to the enemy at the southern gate. Already the Southerners were fighting in retreat, drawing the orcs to the wall where archers at pointblank range could thin them enough to close and secure the gate. So powerful was Gwyn's motivating presence on the line that none of the orcs had to make it through, but some did. None of those on the scaling ladders had to be allowed to reach the top, but some were. Those that, by whatever means, found themselves in the Southerners' hands didn't have to be tortured, butchered, and mutilated, their parts hung on display over the wall, but all these things were done, and for the first time in more than two years Gwyn's fang necklace gained new ornaments. Whatever it was that separated man from orc, it had quit the field with Shon's last breath, and for some, it would take a long time to return. For Gwyn, Shon's death was a wound that time alone could not heal. Even from the wall top, her enemies' insignia, their statures, their malformed faces were burned into her memory, images she knew would plague her nightmares until the day she had tracked down each one and her blade had tasted its blood. Only then could she rest. Only then would she mourn.

Even Baraxis was denied a measure of solace from his grief as conditions forced him to refuse repeated pleas by Shon's men to go out and retrieve his scattered remains. The area still crawled with the enemy, and everything Shon had been, inside, was gone forever. He could not dishonor

Shon's sacrifice by letting others risk their lives to drag back the ruined pieces of him. Baraxis' deep sadness was as far removed from Gwyn's rage as could be, but their thirst for retribution was alike.

Neither could additional riders be sent for help. The orcs had redeployed in response to Shon's attempt, and there was no hope now of getting past them that way. That night, three men in dark clothing and with soot-blackened faces were sent out on foot in the hopes of sneaking to the river. The following morning, defenders raged and grieved at the sight of two carcasses staked out on the field in full view of the north wall. There was no sign of the third, so the besieged regiment hoped he'd made it through, but whether or not this was true or would mean rescue they could not guess.

In a day or so the shock and numbness of Shon's death wore off, and those of Sutherset took what little comfort they could in one another, gathering to honor their captain's memory, meeting about a keg of ale and a brick oven in the room where, just days before, Gwyn had saved Shon's fidelity. Words were spoken, but to Gwyn's ears they were empty. Words could not bring back the dead. Girahl, Sudro, Shon: They were all heroes, and she would praise them as heroes for as long as she had the breath, but her praise wouldn't raise them. Praise might keep alive their memory, but only blood could honor it. Shon's comrades spoke in turn around the circle, but when Gwyn's time came, she only squeezed her necklace of fangs and gave a look that defied any to encourage her. Baraxis spoke last of all.

"Those of you who know me best have sensed a darkness in my heart for some time. Though it has only been replaced by a deeper pain, that first foreboding has lifted. I know now the unspeakable price this mission would require. And I am sorry, men. Had I known, I never would have let him go, I swear I wouldn't. I truly thought…"

He swallowed hard as tears glistened in his eyes. "It was *my* life I thought would be paid. When this feeling came over me, I thought the death was to be mine. He was like a son to me; I never thought… If I'd known, I never…" Baraxis' voice trailed off in weeping, and many pressed forward to console him. Gwyn sat unmoving, still squeezing the fangs. They pierced her flesh, and her blood ran like tears.

Rak and a few of his men approached Gwyn as she left the informal wake. "Captain, is there anything we can do for you?"

"Do?" she asked, her voice thick. "Can you give me my friend back?"

The sergeant didn't meet her eyes. "No, Captain."

"Then what could you possibly do to help me?"

"Nothing, Captain. We're sorry." Rak led the men away, and Gwyn stomped off to the stables.

That night she dreamed she lay in the field within sight of the trees. She couldn't breathe, and the top of her head burned like fire. She looked to her right and felt an odd sense of detachment at the realization that the lower third of her arm had been cleaved off.

She looked up again, and six orc faces looked down at her. One retched blood as an arrow ripped through its neck. The other five kept leering, their stupid, tusked grins making her boil with rage, but she couldn't move. She sensed a shadowy figure watching her from the northwest wall of Roon, far away, then awoke to the fiery pit that had become of her heart.

Five more days passed. Gwyn had never been so hungry in her life. The rations were gone. Rak's friend the food hoarder held nothing back, but while his stores were more appetizing their quantity could not make a dent in the needs of hundreds. Baraxis ordered parties to search every corner of the town for preserved foodstuffs, but the harvest from such efforts was meager. The lord general had expected as much and gave the orders mostly to keep the men focused on a task and curtail paranoid ransacking later on. These were strong men and resolute, under good leadership; after such a brief privation, no man boiled shoe leather or tried to dig up the graves of those slain in the skirmish, but the horses began to look appetizing. For their part, the horses themselves fared better for one more day as they were turned loose to graze on the tangles of wild growth that had grown up throughout the untended Crafthold. Gwyn took to sleeping in the stables with her gray, just in case, though she suspected the noncombatant mounts in the city quarter set aside as a corral would be the first eaten if men got hungry enough. After her first night with the horses, others took exception to her odor and avoided her all the more, which she did not consider a flaw in her plan.

Baraxis gathered his captains at the start of the sixth day, the third without food. True to his comment at Shon's memorial, the sense of strange foreboding had left his demeanor, though the current situation laid on him as heavily as on the rest. "If I knew rescue would come in a day or two," he began, "I'd order you all to put another hole in your belts and hang on. If I knew it would come in a week or two, I'd grit my teeth, wipe my eye, and start butchering enough horses to keep us upright. Since I can't be sure of either, we have no choice but to attack while we still have the strength. If we break for the river, at least some might–"

Horns blasted from the north wall, cutting Baraxis off. A chorus of shouts and the faint sound of orcish snarls followed. "By Terillah, they're rushing the walls," one of the captains deduced, his voice laden with dread.

Gwyn sprinted from the building, a couple other officers behind her. Rak lounged outside the meeting hall waiting for orders and followed the crowd as they rushed to the north wall. Gwyn mounted the stairs, but even before she reached the top she realized the cries of the watchers were not of alarm, and the sounds of battle rose to meet her. Peering over the parapet, she saw a hundred heavy horse pounding away at an orcish contingent halfway to the river. Infantry swarmed up behind the charge as more orcs rushed down the hill from around the walls of Roon.

"Rak," Gwyn ordered, "round up the men. Get them mounted and staged at the northwest postern; we need to get out there and fight." He hurried off to obey as Gwyn charged back down the steps, likewise calling out to any man in her company she happened to pass on her way to the stables. She heard other officers doing likewise, and by the time she reached the postern about half of her men were gathered. That was enough for her.

A soldier opened the door for them, then they filed out onto the field one by one, first Gwyn followed by a dozen men, then Rak leading fifteen more. They moved quickly to clear the opening, then fanned out. A few orcs running north to the battle saw them but didn't approach. As Gwyn arrayed her formation and charged, Baraxis opened the main gates and led the regiment out on foot to throw their weight to the rescue.

CHAPTER XIV

The orcs gave little resistance. Most of their force had already hurried on and by now must have reached the Capital, so the remainder left behind to keep Baraxis' regiment pinned down had already done their job. Once they saw they couldn't hold against the combined weight of both human forces, they formed up and made an orderly retreat to the southwest.

Gwyn found Baraxis in the field, ordering some men back to Roon to gather remaining equipment and others down to the river to begin boarding barges. A man with a major's insignia on his tabard approached as well and gave a report to Baraxis on the rotation of barges he had in command, then asked the Lord General's orders in aiding the evacuation.

"Just keep your men riding escort for us back to the docks," Baraxis ordered. "We can get ourselves out, but we're not in top shape to fend off an ambush."

The major motioned to his captains who stood nearby, both of whom then rode off to relay orders.

"Was it the boat men or the runner?" Baraxis asked.

The major shook his head but wore a thin smile. "Both, but also neither." Before Gwyn or Baraxis could voice their consternation with the reply, the major went on, "Both brought warning, but we were already hours into preparation when the boatmen came back, and your runner hailed us from the bank on our way."

"How then?" Baraxis demanded.

"I wasn't there to see it myself," the major cautioned, "but if you believe the story, four days ago a bay stallion comes charging through gaps in the orcish line and runs straight up to the main gates. The watchers managed to get him inside and took off his saddle and tack right away, since the poor animal was in an awful lather. In his saddlebags they find a sealed missive and rush it to the king. When he saw the date you put on it and asked how it got there so fast, he swore it should have burst the horse's heart."

Gwyn remembered Shon leaning over Cinnabar's neck and speaking to him at the last moment. *Shon,* she thought, *I told you there was magic in you.*

"Cinnabar," Baraxis uttered, bewildered. "Did the horse live?"

"As far as I know," the major answered, "and live in luxury at that. Word on the street as we left was that the king had kicked one of his own palfreys out of the royal stables to make a place for this mysterious steed." He paused. "We heard from your runner what happened to his rider. I'm sorry."

Gwyn turned her horse and galloped away from the conversation, back to Roon to gather the rest of her gear.

~ * ~

The boat ride back to the Capital was a journey of great sorrow. The mission had only partially succeeded, and at a cost of three hundred lives, each one a hero to someone, and one of them a hero to many. Gwyn turned most of her noncombat responsibilities over to Rak, and all camaraderie with her men vanished.

The night they reached the Capital, Rak held a secret meeting with the squad around his fire. "It could be everything changes once the lord general gets out of meetings with the king. It could be we get reassigned, anyway. If we don't, well, I know Gwyn isn't the same as when we got picked for her squad. So what do you boys think? Orders is orders, but if we think this grief on her will cause more than just bad manners, if we think she's not fit to lead no more, we got options. What do we say?"

"I say you shut yer mouth before one of us shuts it for ya," one of the younger men snapped back. "I never figgered you for a squawker, Rak."

"And I never did, did I, ya lunkhead? I'd take my grave before sayin' a word against the captain, but I'm *yore* sergeant. I'm just askin', is all."

"Gwyn won us over 'cause she cared about ours that fell. Now we're gonna ruin her good name 'cause she cares *too* much about *hers* that fell? That's a fool's sense if I ever heard it," a second soldier offered.

"Anybody disagree?" Rak asked.

No one spoke.

"Alright, it's settled, then," he concluded. "But she's gone cold, so be ready for it. I'll be the buffer as best I can, but when she's around, follow orders and stay out of the way."

Gwyn dreamed again that night. Her paralysis, pain, and dismemberment all ran the same, but this time after the first orc was slain by an arrow and disappeared, a second went from grinning to wide-eyed terror, and a Southern spearhead exploded from his chest. He sagged forward and disintegrated into mist as he hit the ground. The same, dim figure stood on the wall, gazing about, but she knew, somehow, it couldn't see her. She heard a woman's voice speaking from another direction but couldn't make out the words.

The next few weeks dragged by as spring ran into summer, increasing Gwyn's disgust at the oppressive heat and cloying humidity, and she knew the worst was still to come. By the time of her regiment's return to the Capital, the orcs from the eastern campaign had already arrived and deployed to add their strength to those already threatening the city. In but a few more days the Southerners were completely besieged; the poor still living in the Dog Markets were brought inside the outer wall, and those soldiers camped outside lived uneasily behind rows of trenches and breastworks, sleeping in shifts. Food and water were tightly rationed, undermining morale as the orcs lived freely off the fat of the countryside. Still, their lack of siege weaponry made the stalemate absolute. Gwyn spent seventeen hours a day on patrol, silent and brooding. Every day she requested permission to lead a sortie against the enemy, and every day Baraxis denied her, following his orders from the king. Any force venturing past the barricade would be immediately overwhelmed, so he refused to waste the men. Despite the Southerners' defensible position, however, the situation eventually became untenable, and the king called a council in his throne room. As Lord General Baraxis' bodyguard, Gwyn was allowed to attend, standing at the ready behind his chair three positions down from the king's right hand. Other generals lined either side of the long table, about twenty in all, the king's full war council, less only three whose places remained empty at the table's foot, nearest the door.

"We can hold out against the orcs until winter," the king began once all his generals had gathered, "but there is more at stake. Every day the enemy ranges farther and farther in search of forage to bolster their supply lines, or perhaps simply for the sport of it. Either way, the token defenses that were left cannot hold out for long. By winter, it won't matter that the Capital stands; my whole kingdom will be in flames."

The king paused, but the room responded only with grim silence. "Our last hope," he continued, "is with the mountain divisions. We have ten thousand men in the passes, all fresh for battle, and many on horse. If they can take the orcs by surprise, hit them hard in two or three places, they can throw the enemy camps into enough confusion to give us time to array our forces within the city. Then we can charge them with heavy cavalry, trap them between anvil and hammer, perhaps force a retreat."

"I'll go," Gwyn volunteered flatly.

Twenty pairs of eyes bored into her for speaking out of turn. Baraxis' were among them, but in his gaze she found not anger, but infinite sorrow.

"I see you need no help finding your voice this time, Atlunder," the king replied.

"Southerners talk too much and waste breath saying what everyone already knows. You were about to say someone needs to sneak a small force through the orcish camps to alert the mountain divisions. I volunteer myself and my first platoon."

Many muttered at her impudence, and General Steract, who had been looking for a chance to even the score since the business with his lecherous soldier and indifferent captain, stood aggressively, his chair grating back with a groan. "Majesty, this churlish lass goes too far. I care nothing for her reputation; she insults us with her words and unmans us with her action. I implore you, Majesty, let one of my captains lead the expedition."

The king's hooded eyes flicked from Gwyn to the general, then roamed the table of war leaders before him. "And each of you would offer a force of your own?"

There were unanimous nods and "ayes" of assent.

The king paused. "Then the Atlunder does what you have not. You offer up your men, but she offers *herself*. She is fearless, brash, and foolhardy, and it may be that she will win through by boldness where another would risk too little. *But*, she might also risk too much where prudence is required. I will not hang all our lives on so desperate a gamble. Three units will go. One will go south. The orcs are thickest there, but if they can be bypassed, the platoon could make it to the river and a swift journey west. Two others will go north and west."

"May I take the northern force, Majesty?" Gwyn knew a demand would be ignored, at best, so with some effort she made the request as civilly as she was able.

"As you wish," the king replied. "Call it your right as the first to volunteer. Now leave us, before you offend my generals any further. Prepare your men while we conclude our deliberations. You leave tomorrow night."

Turning to depart, Gwyn allowed herself the luxury of a predatory smile. She had been watching banners and insignias from the walls since the day she got back. She knew precisely where she was going.

Sergeant Rak awaited her in the palace courtyard. "Rak," Gwyn barked, "follow me." The sergeant fell into step beside Gwyn as she left the palace. Even after weeks of seeing them from the walls, the Capital's streets still mystified her, but the path from the palace to her quarters she'd learned well enough. "Pick a dozen men," she continued, "the most cunning warriors and woodsmen we have, and those who know best the western regions and the mountains. If there is anyone you trust amongst Baraxis' other battalions that you want, just take them. The general won't complain, but make sure there are no personal squabbles amongst your picks. The journey will be long."

"What's the mission?"

"Tomorrow night we breach the barricades and slip through the orcish lines to the north. Once we're clear, we turn west and strike out for the Tunaris. Our objective is to bring back the mountain divisions to break the siege."

"This is a dangerous task, Captain. Can I ask why you're so eager?"

Gwyn rounded on him. "You question my bravery?"

"Never, Captain. It all just feels a little familiar. Like maybe you're looking to succeed where Shon failed."

Gwyn's hand flew without thought, but she felt no remorse when it struck. Rak's head snapped to the left, his face red and quickly darkening where Gwyn's knuckles had struck him backhand in the jaw. "He didn't fail," she growled. "He saved all our lives. Never speak his name again."

Rak nodded vacantly. "I'll pick your squads, Captain." He saluted and left.

A few moments later Gwyn was stalking through the halls of the Haddix estate to her room, her eyes unfocused in defense against the bitter memories summoned by every corner of the place. One thing was certain: the estate was much less crowded than it had been when she first arrived. The intervening weeks had been unkind to the residents. Reaching her tiny room, she checked her gear, then sent a courier to Ardos to requisition supplies for the journey. They couldn't carry all they would need, but they would have to set out with at least enough provisions to sustain them until they cleared the land already picked clean by the enemy. They didn't require much, but in the tight rationing of the Capital it would likely take Ardos the rest of the day and most of the next to wheedle and finagle what he could get. Rak had probably already set Ardos to the task, but it did no harm to be sure.

The next morning, a quiet rap sounded on Gwyn's door. "Who's there?" she demanded.

"Baraxis," came the lord general's muffled reply.

Gwyn rose and opened the door.

"I brought the sealed orders for the generals commanding the mountain divisions," Baraxis announced.

"You could have just sent for me."

"I felt like the walk, and I wanted to talk to you."

"What about?"

Baraxis frowned, his eyes distant. "There was a time not so very long ago when there didn't have to be a reason."

"There was. But that was before, and this is now. So, what did you want to talk about?"

"You shamed me in the war council."

Gwyn laughed derisively. "If that's how you want to remember it."

Baraxis reddened. "Now what in the hells does *that* mean?"

"I didn't shame you. I *saved* you."

"How's that?"

"You weren't going to send me!" Gwyn snapped. "Every man in there was preparing to offer his best force. Except for you. Your silence *would* have shamed you, if I hadn't spoken."

"And I'm supposed to believe that's why you did it?"

"I never said that. Believe what you want. My reasons are just that: *mine*."

"Don't act like you're so unfathomable, Gwyn. You even requested the northern route. I see the enemy banners as well as you do. You don't give a damn about the mission, you're just looking for blood."

"I am the Hand of Vengeance."

Baraxis gave her a hard look. "I should bar you from going."

"Do that, and I will hold you to your word and leave your service."

Baraxis' eyes widened, and his face twisted. Gwyn couldn't tell if he was furious or sick. "What possible purpose–"

"I *need* this, Baraxis. Don't you understand?" she shouted. "For weeks, all I can see is him dying over and over, those murdering bastards–"

"Dammit, Gwyn! Stop!" Baraxis put his hands on her shoulders. "I know there was a connection between you. I don't understand it, but it was plain enough if you were looking. But do you think you grieve harder than I? He was like my son after my family died, *was* my son, my only family until..." He dropped his hands to his sides and turned away.

"Until what?"

" ... "

"Until *what*, Baraxis?"

"Until you came to Sutherset!" He turned back as he spoke, and his eyes shone with tears in the dim light. His voice was stretched and hoarse, but he took a shuddering breath that seemed to fill him, straightening his back so that Gwyn only then realized he'd been stooping, maybe for a long time. His voice was stronger as he continued. "My wife was second-generation Southern born after her grandparents immigrated to Sutherset. She was Southern-raised but strongly Atlund-blooded, and our daughter–" For a moment Baraxis' words caught in his throat, but he forced them out, casting off the weight of them. "Our daughter took after her mother. If not for the plague, she would look just as you do now. And she was vibrant and stubborn and strong." Baraxis even laughed, suddenly. "I'm lucky you're such an awful negotiator. Even that first day, I'd have given almost anything to make you stay, even half my fiefdom. Now that we've been in battle together, weathered all this… Leave my service if you must; it will change nothing between us. Not for me."

"You say all this to convince me not to go." Gwyn's tone lacked conviction.

"No. If there was anything I could say or do or give that I thought could make you stay, I would, but there is no such thing. I trained you to fight with your head, made sure you didn't *have* to hate them, but you *do* hate them, now. Whatever reckoning you find will not remove that hate, but I see now you have to learn that lesson for yourself. And maybe I'm wrong; maybe such things are different for Windborne Hands of Vengeance than for glorified farmers like me. And maybe most importantly, a part of me still *wants* you to do it, to make those murderers pay for what they've taken, to do what I'm not ruthless enough to do myself. Whatever the reason, I won't tell you not to go. But before you go, I'll have your oath that whatever happens out there, the mission has to come first. Untold thousands of lives, maybe the whole kingdom, depend on you and your men. I can't risk all that for your vendetta, much as I might want to."

"I so swear."

"And…will you promise to come back to me?"

"I'm a killer, not a martyr, Baraxis. If what you fear is that I seek my death out there, then your fear is wasted. I'll try to stay alive. Nor am I one to abandon my friends or my cause. I will return if I am able, to break this siege. After that? I've never made any promise, and I won't. I've already made one oath more than I care to today, and it requires one of you."

"Name your price."

Gwyn reached to the wall pegs by the head of her cot and lifted her sword, its ghostly sheen glowing in the lantern light. "This must be kept safe. Its great size on my back would hamper my stealth through the lines; worse yet, the risk of capture is too high. A day hasn't passed when it might not have been taken from my corpse, but I can't bear the thought of it in orcish hands and me left alive to know it."

Baraxis nodded and took the blade, then turned to go. He paused for a moment as though hoping she would stop him, but Gwyn had said all she meant to.

The night was black and starless as Gwyn led her men over the northern barricade, feeling exposed without the weight of her sword on her back. *Aridan* had not yet risen, and *Bia Creg*, wherever she was, glowed too dimly to pierce the clouds above. Humidity pressed in from all sides, making the darkness close and cloying. With silence fed by meticulous movements, two of Gwyn's men slid long planks over a trench filled with sharpened stakes and began crawling across, feeling their way forward in the dark. The orcish fires a furlong away flickered, showing enemies in silhouette but offering no useful illumination as Gwyn did her best with whispers and close inspection to regroup her men and make sure all were still accounted for. As she did, Rak pulled the planks toward him and slowly lowered them down into the trench. The only path back now went through the Tunari mountains. Satisfied, Gwyn led her men at a crouching hustle across the plain.

Progress was slow, but in several long minutes they reached the edge of the encircling orcish camps, targeting a gap where two clans, apparently, were in the midst of some kind of feud and refused to mingle their tents. Bordering the west side of this gap, as though marking a territorial boundary, a battle standard hung limp in the breezeless dark, it's firelit emblem seared into Gwyn's very soul. She yearned to stalk the camp until she found the four remaining of Shon's murderers, to bleed them like pigs and watch the life ebb from their eyes. She doubted she could survive the attempt, but she didn't care. Her promise to Baraxis weighed on her, but only lightly. Her standing devotion to him, though, and Ardos and all the other Sutherese who counted on her, urged her to press on.

Gwyn ground her teeth together in turmoil as she crept forward through the dark, then froze. Under the standard, backlit by a guttering campfire some yards away, a lone orc stood guard, staring across the narrow gap between camps.

Hells, Gwyn thought, *one disciplined sentry in the whole damn orcish army and it's right in my—*

The wind shifted, and the sentinel turned toward them, the firelight catching half its scaly face, a ragged ear, a scar, a broken tusk: a face Gwyn had seen again and again in her nightmares.

The whole squad had frozen as she did, and the orc's gaze was distant; Gwyn was sure they had been neither heard nor spotted. The wind was in their face, so she didn't believe the orc had smelled them, though with less certainty. Raucous laughter erupted from the campfire, and the sentry turned to look, taking a step toward the merriment. Its back was turned. She had to move *now*.

Gwyn motioned for Rak and the others to continue north. He paused when she didn't follow, but she could not see his expression. She repeated her hand signal, then turned away, creeping toward the orc. No love of comrades, nor any other force, could compel her to leave that orc alive when she was this close. She could have stayed with the squad, sent one of the others to deal with the guard. It would have been a reasonable enough order. But *she* was the Hand of Vengeance, *Gwyn et Sheevasa,* the last name

Shon had called her, the thing he had beseeched her to remain.

She crouched at the edge of the firelight now; stealth became a matter of swiftness instead of caution. She struck like a snake, springing up behind her foe, reaching with her left hand to clap it across the orc's mouth and preparing her dirk in her right to cut its throat. Her left hand was just darting forward when the orc opened its mouth to bellow some question or complaint to its comrades. Its mouth gaped wide, and Gwyn's hand slipped suddenly inside.

The orc did what any orc would do at the sudden intrusion. It bit down.

Gwyn knew few warriors more resistant to pain than herself, but even she couldn't completely stifle her cry, and for a moment her knife hand received none of her attention, long enough for the orc to open its mouth once more and bellow the alarm for all to hear. Silence now pointless, Gwyn thrust over and over with her knife, plunging it again and again into the orc's back, and its yells turned to screams as it died.

Gwyn turned to flee, desperate to at least draw pursuit away from her men, but by then the orcs were on her like a wolf pack, dragging her to the ground. A sharp pain stabbed through her skull, exploding starbursts across her vision that faded into all-consuming blackness.

The dream came again. The first two orcs died in the same way, followed by a third that opened its mouth wide, then spasmed repeatedly and coughed blood before disappearing as well. Only three were left, if she ever awakened to continue her vendetta. The woman's voice sounded again, still too distant to make out, but the tone was somehow familiar.

~ * ~

Gwyn had no idea how much time had passed when she awoke, but her head and left hand were throbbing pits of agony. Her eyes snapped open as the memories of her capture flooded over her. The sun was bright; she couldn't believe a day and a night had passed, so she guessed she'd been out for ten or twelve hours. She was upright, but realized she could barely feel her arms. Looking to either side, she saw she was bound between stakes, her body hanging from her wrists with her limp legs bent on the ground. She still wore her armor, but her weapons were missing, and her left hand was a swollen, scabrous mess. She panicked for a brief moment as she realized she couldn't move the fingers but then found the digits of her right hand were no more cooperative; it would be impossible to assess the damage while she was so cruelly bound.

"She's awake." The voice was behind her, grunting in orcish. Much of the tongue was known to her by now.

She gathered her legs under her, taking her weight and easing the sharp numbness in her arms. Looking forward, she realized she had been moved all the way to the south, her position now in full view of the Capital's main gates. Only a few ranks of orcs stood between her and the three-hundred yards of empty ground before the barricades. She was meant to be on display, then. That didn't bode well.

"Do we question her?" a second orcish voice asked.

"No!" replied the first. "This is the Hellwitch, not some sniveling man-whelp. Do not speak to her! Do you want her to steal your soul? I would gag her, but the enemy must hear her screams." That boded even worse.

Gwyn's ability to pronounce orcish lagged her understanding of it, but she didn't like the things she was hearing. She drew a ragged breath, doing her best to form the guttural words. "Cowards!" she growled. "Face me! I am the Hellwitch! If you would have my death, you must earn it!"

The orcs behind her muttered fearfully, but then another voice boomed out over theirs. "They *are* cowards! I am not. Cut her down! *I* will face her, and win rest for the souls she has damned."

After a few more moments of orcish shouting, the cords binding Gwyn's wrists were cut, and she sagged forward, stumbling. She willed her legs to hold her up, feeling their strength quickly returning, and turned as she straightened to her full height. Her arms hung down, still unfeeling and limp as rags.

Facing Gwyn across the ring formed by throngs of green spectators was the biggest monster of an orc Gwyn had ever seen. It stood head and shoulders over her considerable height, and its long arms hung almost to its knees, making for a staggering reach. In each hand it held an ax, one a hatchet that looked tiny and toy-like in its meaty fist, the other a huge, long-hafted weapon Gwyn doubted she could swing with both arms. A false mane of black horsehair ran from its bald head down its back, the mark of an orcish elite. Its features were unscarred, its tusks intact and honed to needle points; the orc before Gwyn had never known defeat.

Her opponent had offered no weapon for her to defend herself, and as it bellowed and hefted its axes, she was forced to assume it didn't intend to. *And it said it was no coward,* she thought. *Must mean something different in orcish.*

The orc charged. Gwyn dodged, keeping the stakes to which she'd been bound between her and the enemy, desperately biding time as strength and feeling seeped back into her arms. The wood spars halted the orc's charge for a moment, but it swung its large ax with a spiteful sneer and hacked one of them to the ground.

Gwyn was groggy, disoriented, and overmatched, scrambling about the ring like an animal at bay. Her mail might protect her body from the smaller axe, but even *if* the larger one didn't cleave through the rings, it would splinter whatever bones lay underneath. Even without weapons she trusted her skills, but whoever said size didn't matter in a fight had never seen the orc attacking her now. Unarmed, she had no hope against this massive beast. An alien sensation squeezed at her chest and the back of her head, but this time she had no reason to suspect a zil'bast slinking about to trick her. This fear was real.

The orc champion swung both its axes, and Gwyn jumped back. She landed off-balance, stumbled backward, and fell. The surrounding orcs jeered her weakness.

That was their mistake. The taunts sparked the fire of rage within her, these brutish creatures that had cringed in terror from her visage for almost a year now, cheering and mocking as though *they* were her betters. Bravery was easy to find when your enemy was wounded and disarmed. They should have mocked her less and watched her more; if they had, they might have noticed she was smiling. Not only had rage quashed her fear, but as Gwyn fell, instinct had thrown her arms backward to catch her. They had obeyed, and though pain shot through her left hand, her arms had held firm. The flow of blood was back, and with it strength. The battle light sparked in Gwyn's eyes as she jumped back to her feet and met the champion's gaze, giving it sudden pause. The other orcs could see only that she had fallen, but this one had the sense to see her change in stance and bearing, could see the strange light sparking ominously behind her eyes. Yes, this one was wise enough to sense the change, but just foolish enough to hesitate, giving Gwyn a few precious heartbeats to breathe and watch. As she stood, Gwyn took its measure once more, noticed an antler-handled knife hanging low from its belt on Gwyn's left, the curved grip sticking out just an inch farther than it should. That was it, then.

She leapt forward and to the right, luring the orc to react with a quick strike from its smaller ax. Gwyn dodged early, allowing the elite not to fully commit, then lingered for just half a heartbeat, holding herself in perfect position for a finishing blow from the great ax. She was ready when it moved, darting forward and left, allowing the momentum of the enemy's strike to carry it past her and slipping the knife from its sheath as she did. She lowered her stance and spun out to her right, shoving her empty hand at the orc's right kidney to check his counter-pivot and striking with the knife behind its right knee. She pressed with all her strength and felt the blade sever the tendons and rip into the joint, then pulled hard to tear the weapon free and prevent it from lodging fast in the wound.

The orc bellowed and flailed its arms as it dropped to one knee, trying to turn back toward its foe, but Gwyn was too quick. The knife flashed in the noonday sun as she buried it in the base of the orc's skull, twisting and angling the point downward as she stabbed; its eyes went vacant in death before it crumpled to the ground.

The crowd was stunned into silence as Gwyn tore the knife free with a sick, ripping sound. She transferred it to her left hand, throbbing and clumsy though it was, and pulled the smaller ax from her foe's limp grasp. Her eyes scanned the orcs between her and the Capital, finding one that shifted more nervously than the rest. She pinned him with her gaze, stalking toward him deliberately as the crowd vacillated between fight and flight. She had been a terror to them before, but now that she had slain this champion in such a manner, terror had grown into awe, perhaps even reverence. Everything about her, her poise, her confidence, her silence, most especially her sparking eyes peering out amongst the flecks of the champion's blood that stippled her face, all these things riveted the orcs in place, transfixed by the very idea of this legend walking among them.

For the rest of her life, Gwyn would wonder if she could simply have walked back to the city uncontested. Showing her back to the enemy was a risk she could not take, however, as the memory of javelins ripping into Shon's lungs flashed through her conscious mind. Having acclimated the crowd to her deliberate, plodding gait, she crossed the last few paces to the nervous orc at a sudden charge so that she seemed to stand before it in an eye-blink, her ax having appeared, as if by magic, in its forehead.

That broke the spell. Orcs struck from all directions as Gwyn took a short sword from her falling victim. She caught a blade on her knife, the impact jolting through her injured hand as she drove forward, sword-first, into the next rank of orcs. Sword slashes only bruised her beneath her mail as another orc fell to her assault. Her next block was too slow, too distracted by the sheer number of attacks, and a spear-point pierced the iron links and drove like white-hot pain through her right arm. A war club found the side of her left knee, and she dropped to a crouch from the buckling impact. She stabbed one more orc in the belly before it could deliver a coup de grace, then suddenly there came a resounding crash and a half-dozen horses thundering by. Her head swam as orcs bellowed and fled in all directions; she tried to stand, but her injured knee protested. Finally she heard her name shouted repeatedly and looked up to see Baraxis astride Storm Cloud, arrayed in heavier armor than was his custom, reaching a hand down to her in her half-crouch. She grabbed it and the back of his saddle, and between the two of them they managed to haul her up behind. Storm Cloud seemed barely to notice the extra weight as he wheeled at Baraxis' command and sped back toward the Capital with a dozen heavy horse at either side, crossing the barricade on a makeshift ramp and bridge of lashed timbers. Once past the defenses, Baraxis began to speak.

"They shouldn't have tried to make a show of you. We started moving the minute they staked you out there. You certainly have a way of stalling; men will be talking of that fight for–"

"Did they get through?"

"Did they what? Hells, Gwyn, are you in shock? You're arm's bleeding like–"

"What? No, not the orcs, old man, the runners! Did they get through?"

"Nothing's certain. If they had any more prisoners or bodies, though, they didn't show them. With you bringing half the orcish camp down on your own head last night, I suspect they had enough distraction to make good their escape."

"I did swear to put the mission first."

"Is *that* what you were doing?" Baraxis' tone was knowing.

"It would seem s–"

Baraxis felt Gwyn sag against him and shouted her name, his voice strained with fear. By then he had reached the gates, and willing hands bore Gwyn down from the saddle.

"She's alive," a medic reported as he laid her onto a stretcher. "We have a place prepared; we will attend her."

Baraxis watched as they carried her away, then handed Storm Cloud off to a page for stabling.

CHAPTER XV

This time Gwyn was surrounded by faces when she awoke. Baraxis and Ardos were known to her, but three others, a young man and woman and an old man with gray hair, also stood nearby. "Where am I?"

"Your quarters," Baraxis answered.

Gwyn looked up at the luxurious bed's canopy, the sunlight streaming through stained glass windows. This was a far cry from her dark room and cot in the warrens of the servant wing. "I must have got hit on the head harder than I thought."

"You've been given the best room in Old Haddix's estate," Baraxis explained, "and by the king's decree, no less. You're a hero, Gwyn. Half the men are saying we should forget the mountain divisions and launch a counterattack the minute you're well enough to lead the charge."

"And when will that be?"

"Another day or two," said the young woman in the room.

"That's all?" Gwyn experimentally flexed her left hand and right arm. They were sore and stiff, but otherwise seemed none the worse for her injuries. She bent her left knee beneath the coverlet and found its condition to be similar. "By Terillah, how long was I out this time?"

Ardos laughed as the young man spoke. "Only a day, I assure you. When Brosa and I–"

"Assistants to the royal physician," Baraxis clarified in a whisper.

"–found that two of your injuries would likely prove crippling, the king insisted that magical intervention was required."

The older man took half a step forward. His voice was stern. "Aedax, Wizard of the Crown. Your wounds are mended. You must rest for two or three days, or your condition may relapse, and magic will not improve it a second time. Now that you are awake, I must away. My duties are manifold, and my being is not. Be well." He left without further comment.

"Have you many such magicians about?" Gwyn inquired. "I've not seen them."

"Only a very few," Baraxis answered. "People are rarely born with the skill, and most burn out quickly with the war's demands. Perhaps four, and as many wandering elven mages. It's said elves all have the talent, but with rare exception they do not involve themselves in wars, however just."

"D'ye not have wizards in Atlund?" Ardos asked.

"Magic is thick in the land," Gwyn answered as she settled back on the cushions, "at least if the tales are true, but it's rare anyone can harness it on purpose. Maybe no rarer than here, person for person, but there aren't so many people in the north. There's an old saying that goes, 'In your life, expect to see three new wars, two new famines, and one new wizard, and pray the latter one is not cause for any of the former five.' The wizard born to the generation before mine turned against us."

"He must have done awful harm before he could be stopped," Baraxis mused, almost horrified at the thought.

"He killed my father," Gwyn replied. Everyone in the room was taken aback. "I must be tired," Gwyn added. "Give me some room; I want to sleep." She closed her eyes and heard them go, but she knew they would not go far.

Gwyn's experience proved to her that, for all her hatred and pain, she still preferred life to death. She knew the path she'd chosen often ended abruptly and thought little about the distant future, but even in the near term she had many debts still unpaid and resolved to see them cleared. From this determination she took satisfaction in her survival and hoped Rak and the rest of her men still lived, but she did lament the loss of her dirk, her first proper weapon. Ardos scoured the town for a replacement and found one functionally identical; indeed, leveraging Gwyn's heroic reputation the implement he'd acquired was most fine in make and materials, but it would never be the same.

The stalemate around the Capital continued for many weeks. Every day the Southerners saw more plunder carried back into the orcish camps and feared for their homes and loved ones, but there was nothing they could do but wait.

The orcs grew restless and began charging the barricades, but the archers always turned them back. Without siege engines, they lacked the punch to defeat Southern defenses. The Southerners spied a few attempts by the orcs to make their own machine, but they always ended in disaster, as did a pair of attempts to undermine the outer walls. The orcs captured several additional field pieces from Southern forces or stockpiles outside the besieged city, but they could never operate them effectively enough to strike the fortifications without coming under threat from the Capital's own wall-mounted weaponry, so they quickly lost interest and turned their attentions back to plunder.

Gwyn rode the barricades every day, encouraging the men, but her words felt hollow. Her strength lay aggression, and without it she had no zeal.

Sometimes Baraxis would accompany her, and on one such day, she finally asked the question that had been nagging at her thoughts for weeks. "Why don't they just swarm us? They could never hope to coordinate–that would be difficult enough for *disciplined* troops–but if they just came at us from all sides, they could overwhelm the barricades, get a ram to one of the gates."

"The cost in lives would be great."

"And the last time that mattered to orcs was…when?"

"Even if they got inside," Baraxis countered, "the street fighting would be a bloodbath, and they would get the worst of it, by far."

"But they don't *know* that."

Baraxis sighed. "If you're just going to contradict all my answers, then why ask in the first place?"

"I wouldn't contradict *good* answers."

"Fine. You want to ruin my efforts to reassure us both, then here you go: The farmer in me says they just don't want to die for nothing, that they started this war with no clear vision of how to end it, and now they're happy enough keeping us stuck here until they've cut all the fat of the land off the bone. The soldier, though? The soldier in me says they're *waiting* for something."

"Waiting for what?"

"I don't know," he replied, shaking his head. "Terillah help me, I don't know."

Nearly three months after Gwyn's capture, they had their answer.

Spotters on the south wall were silent at first. The train of wagons could have been just another supply caravan, should have been, looked for all the world like it was, if perhaps a bit better made. It wasn't until it stopped an hour before midday, and the passengers started disembarking, that the alarm was raised, rippling through the city like a wind of ill omen. Zil'basts. One after another after another came pouring out of the wagons until several dozen were arrayed behind the orcish lines to the south.

Gwyn and Baraxis were nearby on their daily tour of the defenses, and within minutes they had spotted the frantic runners heading up to the palace, tracked them back to their source, and climbed to the wall top to learn the cause of such commotion.

"Terillah save us," Baraxis muttered, "I never dreaded they could have so many." After a moment, he seemed to recover his nerve. He turned to Gwyn. "This is a strange feeling. I've been in my share of tight scrapes, but I've never really been *doomed* before. It's oddly freeing."

The sword hanging from Gwyn's shoulder, the weight she found so comforting, suddenly seemed a terrible burden. "Lord General," she said, "if I can get among them, I'm sure I can take a heavy toll before… I wager they aren't used to their defenses failing. My sword was made to this purpose, against my will, I grant. Best put it to use."

"Gwyn, what you talk of is suicide."

"I understand the cost, Baraxis."

He looked at the enemy. "It may come to that, and quickly, but not until we know it is the only choice. Your blade is warded, but you are not. How many could you take before they incinerated you? Not enough to make the difference, I fear."

A courier came panting up the stairs, his face red and hair matted with sweat. "Lord General," he gasped, "the King requires your presence immediately."

Baraxis motioned for Gwyn to follow, and they hastened away from the wall.

They heard the hum of anxious murmurs from the throne room even before they reached the antechamber. The guards and heralds had given up stopping and announcing anyone; runners came and went through the wide open doors, and only about half of the king's war council was present, those arriving early standing in pockets of two and three holding tense, hushed conversations. Gwyn broke protocol as soon as she entered, yelling aloud at what she saw. "Rak!" she shouted. "You're alive!"

The sergeant crossed the room to her at a brisk walk. "Captain! We thought you were dead."

"I was near enough. How did you fare?"

"Not as well as the southern force. They made it to the river and beat us to the prize by three days. Nobody's had any word from the platoon that went straight west. We had a skirmish or three; had to leave two friends where they fell. But we made it. The rest are with the reinforcements, hiding north of the hills."

"How did you get back into the city?"

"I had some help."

An elf in heavy, blue robes and a matching skull cap over shiny-black hair stood from the strategy table. He wore rings on most of his fingers and a small silver cuff high on his left ear. As he turned to face Gwyn, she remembered the face she'd seen only briefly in Baraxis' bailey. "Perhaps you don't remember me," the elf began, his voice almost hopeful. "Drax of the Western Vale, at your most humble service," he announced. "And you are the mighty Gwyn the Savage."

Gwyn narrowed her eyes suspiciously. "I remember. I don't believe I was properly introduced the first time."

"Well, your reputation certainly precedes you, or *follows* you, so to speak," the elf replied, pointing to the massive sword hilt standing above and behind her right shoulder.

Gwyn unslung her sword and slid off the scabbard. The royal guards tensed, then relaxed as they saw her intention. Gwyn placed the wrapped ricasso, where the runes glowed invisibly beneath the leather, under the elf's nose, which put the blade perilously close to his unarmored body. "Don't point your sorcerous fingers at my sword. I still haven't forgiven you for this *defilement*."

"I *beg* your pardon," Drax answered, undaunted. "If you believe there is a better enchanter in the Southern Kingdoms, I defy you to produce him, and while I admit my work has, from time to time, met with some small amount of, ah, stylistic criticism, none has dared call it a 'defilement'!"

Eyes around the room began to swing in the pair's direction as their raised voices cut through the tense whispers and atmosphere.

"I thought your service was 'most humbly' offered," Gwyn snapped.

Drax snorted. "You're still alive, and the blade is perfect. What more of my work would you see to realize even my boasts are humble, compared to the reality? Tell me your weapon has not perfor–"

"Enough!" the king shouted. "Everyone has arrived who's coming; we have no time for this nonsense. Be seated, all of you."

The assembly scrambled to find chairs; Gwyn found the seat to Baraxis' right taken, leaving only the position on his left. This, to Gwyn's chagrin, was right next to Drax. The elf smiled at her discomfiture. She sat, sheathing her blade and leaning it against the table.

"As you've no doubt heard, the mountain divisions are here," the king began. "In accordance with their sealed orders, they kept to the north, avoiding orcish scouts, and are hidden from enemy eyes behind the hills. They have just made a brutal forced march, and normally I would risk trying to keep them hidden for as long as was practicable, to rest. Unfortunately, as you have also no doubt heard by now, we have another problem. Master Drax, please elaborate on the situation."

The elf stood to address the assembly. "Scrying is not my specialty, but one of my fellow wizards who *is* so-gifted sent me a message a few days ago, warning that something, he couldn't be sure what, was gathering under a cloud, if you will, of magical concealment. The location was due south of here, so there could be little question as to the ultimate target. I came as quickly as I could to offer warning, and about midday yesterday, as I got closer, the movement of magical power became plain enough that even I could not fail to identify it in detail."

The king spoke. "My royal wizard, Aedax, collapsed at about that time yesterday. We believed he had simply taken ill; he is advanced in years, and he has been pushing himself harshly to heal our wounded and do what he can for the defense."

"No doubt he was targeted, magically," Drax explained. "As the enemy neared, they must have assumed that at least one wizard would be here and sought him out to silence him. He was probably only moments away from warning you himself when he fell. As for myself, the closer I came, the more sure I was that dozens of zil'basts could be no more than hours away, so I redoubled my speed. I discovered the mountain divisions on my way, early this morning. They asked if I could get a message inside, and Sergeant Rak here offered to come along to authenticate it. Your generals are ready, Majesty. They know of the threat and only await your signal to attack."

One of the generals at the table spoke up. "You spoke of a friend mage that sent you here. Why did he not come himself?"

"He was busying himself getting as far away as possible," Drax replied, "a place I've always wanted to visit as well, but I possess a, shall we say, a skillset that I dare say you will find most useful."

"Planning to carve up some more swords?" Gwyn muttered.

Drax spoke his reply to the whole room, though only he and Baraxis had heard her words. "Yes, I could enchant more weapons, but not enough to make the difference in what little time we are likely to have. I offer something a bit more immediate. The zil'basts' power is unnatural. My brethren do not know where it came from, but whatever the source, orc bodies were never meant to carry it. That is why the zil'basts' forms are twisted so. With the right conditions, a wizard with the right spells and knowledge, like myself, can turn that power inward. When they are close to one another like this, they will knit their power together for defense. The loss of one will weaken the whole, allowing the next to be overcome more quickly, and so on. If we strike suddenly enough, and with a little luck, they won't have time to adjust."

"You spoke of 'the right conditions.' What condition?" the king asked.

"If they are calm and focused, I'll never get past their wards. I need them startled, confused, off balance. Full panic would not be undesirable."

"How can we instill such fear in creatures so powerful?" one of the generals asked.

Gwyn sensed her moment had come. "I'll do it," she announced. "They fear me already, and my sword can harm them. I will go among them and...cause panic."

"Majesty," General Steract shouted, "why were we not made aware of the existence of such a weapon? The last time this woman volunteered for a mission she was captured, nearly killed, nearly cost men their lives in the rescue!"

Now Baraxis was on his feet. "*My* men *volunteered* for that rescue! It's no concern of this council!"

Talking over Baraxis, Steract continued. "*If* the weapon will perform as the foreigner claims, it should be seized for the war effort and granted to a more reliable soldier!"

Gwyn jumped to her feet so fast her chair flew backward, tumbling percussively to the floor as her hand found her sword hilt, though she did not lift it. "Try to take this sword from me and you won't *live* to face the zil'basts!"

"He'll have to get through me first!" Rak was shouting from his seat.

"Please, please, we must cooperate and act quickly," Drax urged through the shouting, though his voice was lost as other generals began speaking, lending their voices to one side or the other, or answering some perceived insult, the throne room roaring now with the sound.

A single *BOOM* pounded out above the noise, echoing out from where the king's fist had struck the table. The room went silent. The king's voice came as an icy whisper. "The next person who speaks without my leave is banished. Is that clear?" The table rippled with nods of assent. Most retook their seats, but Gwyn stayed put under the king's threatening glare, her fallen chair left on its side. The king let the silence drag for a few moments, daring anyone to defy him. Gwyn held his gaze until something in his eyes changed, so that it seemed he was no longer daring her but once again taking the measure of her, reading the mettle in her stare. At last, he spoke again. "The elf is correct. We have no time for this. Gwyn will go. I know of at least one other weapon so-enchanted here at the Capital. It will be held in reserve in case Gwyn fails. Now, Gwyn will need someone to watch her back."

Rak raised his hand silently.

"You have just made a long journey and risked much for your kingdom," the king stated. "Are you certain you want to do this? Speak."

"My place is with my captain."

"Very well. Gather your platoon. Master Drax, we have little enough time, but is there anything you can offer to protect them? I do not lightly send young men and women to the slaughter, but more importantly, their mission will fail if they are too quickly overcome."

Drax considered. "I will do what I can. How much time do I have?"

"Even now runners canvas the city carrying orders," the king replied. "Scouts from the mountain divisions watch for flags on the north wall. I expect to move in little more than an hour, and I begrudge every minute."

"With so little time, I can't do anything to help a whole platoon, I fear."

"How many *can* you help?"

Drax pointed at Gwyn and Rak. "Them. Barely."

The king looked hard at Gwyn once more. "Can you do this?"

"If the elf can get us to the zil'basts, we will do the rest. Better we attempt to get two warriors in and succeed than two-dozen warriors and fail."

The king muttered a curse under his breath. "Go now, then, the three of you. Strike no sooner than an hour, and after that as quickly as you can. The fall of the zil'basts is the signal for the rest of us."

As the trio left the war room, they heard the king launch into the strategy session. "If they succeed, we will get no better chance to strike than during the shock and disarray over the zil'basts' deaths. If they fail, we will have no *choice* but to strike before they can re-deploy. Either way, we must mobilize immediately…"

Once outside the throne room, Drax spoke quickly. "I'm sorry I can't support more men. It's a struggle just keeping my concealment up so the zil'basts don't detect me, and I have to save something for–"

"Spare us the wizard lessons," Gwyn griped. "Get to work."

"I'll need somewhere quiet and private," the elf explained.

"Baraxis' quarters will be empty until after the battle. Rak will show you there," Gwyn answered.

"Very well. I will also need some token or talisman from each of you as a vessel for the warding magic. I don't have the time or materials to enchant them permanently, but the stronger your bond with the object, the better the protection will work. Something worn is best, and something small."

Gwyn reached to her neck and reluctantly drew forth her fang necklace, handing it over to Drax with a frown.

He took it, arching his eyebrows. "Charming," he said sarcastically.

Gwyn's frown became a scowl.

"Now you," Drax continued, turning to Rak.

"Let's talk about that on the way to your new workshop," Rak answered. "Let's go; time is wasting."

"Meet at the gate in an hour," Gwyn called after them, then went to her own quarters to prepare.

~ * ~

An hour later, the trio met at the foot door by the main gate. No one was there to see them off; the whole city stormed with activity as the Southerners made preparations for the attack. "What's that contraption on your face?" Gwyn demanded.

Drax tapped the thin metal frame holding a piece of blue glass before each eye. They touched his eyebrows and cheeks and curved, like the surface of a glass bottle, around to his temples. "Elves see in the dark and live under a forest canopy. The high sun out here is a bit much. These take the edge off."

"Fine. Where is my necklace?" Drax handed it over, and Gwyn inspected it critically. "It doesn't look any different."

"No need to 'carve it up' for a temporary spell," the elf explained.

"How temporary?"

"Long enough for the job."

"Where's Rak's?"

The wizard and the sergeant traded looks.

"What's that about?" Gwyn asked sharply.

"I'm wearing mine. Don't ask, it's...intimate." Rak replied.

Gwyn shook her head and moved on. "So what will these talismans do?"

"They'll protect you from the zil'bast magic to start with. Then once I start my attack, the environment in the camp will become, ah, unhealthy. You'll be protected from that as well, at least as protected as I could make you."

"That's all?" Gwyn challenged. "How will we get to them in the first place?"

"Let me get in position atop the wall–"

"You're not coming?" Rak asked.

"If I go in there I'll be just as unsettled and unfocused as we want *them* to be. I'll do my work from the wall. Once

I'm there, go through the wicket to the barricade and make sure we can see each other. Once I give you the nod, you'll be invisible to orc eyes as long as I have you in sight, at least until you breach the wards around the zil'bast camp. That's an oversimplification, but I know you don't want the 'wizard lessons.' Just move quickly and avoid confrontation. If you physically run into anyone, well, the magic will hold, but orcs have ears and noses as well, better than yours, and they'll use them if they have a reason to doubt their eyes."

Gwyn eyed Drax with a dubious stare. "This had better work."

Careful not to point again, the elf gave a nod to Gwyn's sword, which she already held against her shoulder. "Trust me. It will." Drax turned to the wall steps and began to climb.

The door guard opened the wicket gate for Gwyn and Rak. They hustled to the barricade, and from there they could see that time was even shorter than they'd feared. The zil'basts were already milling about, organizing and spreading out subtly. It looked to Gwyn like they were starting a plan to disperse and surround the city. Gwyn paused at the outer breastworks and, looking up and back, spotted Drax's heavy, blue robes in silhouette against the pale sky, a glint from the glass on his face reflecting the sun. Autumn was quickly approaching, but it had rained the night before, and the air was muggy; sweat trickled down Gwyn's right temple. The seconds stretched interminably before the elf finally waved his arm at them. They waited not a moment longer before vaulting the barricade and crossing the trench on boards. Preparations for the Southern charge were already underway, and no effort was made to hide them.

They crossed the open field at a hard sprint, then slowed to a cautious walk before the sounds of their footfalls could attract notice.

Gwyn had to fight to control her breathing as they entered the edges of the enemy camp. She was not afraid, but watching pair after pair of orcish eyes pass over her, unseeing, was too uncanny for her comfort. Everywhere she looked she was surrounded by foes dowsing fires, sharpening weapons, sparring, or even just pacing from place to place. Clearly the Southerners were not the only ones preparing to strike. Gwyn looked to her left to see how Rak was faring and saw none of her unease on his features. His eyes were wide and excited as he marveled at each passing orc that overlooked his presence. And yet there was a strangeness in his gaze, an intensity, as though he tried to drink everything in.

She had little time to consider this, for by the time she had grown accustomed enough to the situation to notice his expression they were only yards away from the zil'basts' shell of protection. This was no mere shield of mystical heat as Gwyn had experienced before, but a wall of pure magic that she suspected would turn aside missile and spell alike, though Drax had given no reason to think they could not walk through it. If Gwyn turned her head away and glanced at it sidelong, she could almost make out the prismatic shimmer of it, but when she tried to regard it fully, it stubbornly eluded her gaze. Even without this faint visibility, its boundary was easy enough to mark: the other orcs avoided it like death itself, the ground where it touched was parched and brown, even the birds veered off rather than pass directly overhead.

At last Gwyn and Rak were only a step away, close enough to hear a faint crackling that surged in waves through the shield. At this distance, and seeing so many at once, Gwyn could recognize how warped the orcish sorcerers' bodies really were. Some had arms of unequal size, or shoulders humped up or twisted to strange angles. Others limped with turned-out feet or had the smoothness of their scales interrupted by spots or ridges of harder plates. Gwyn suppressed a shudder, but the sight provided at least some evidence of Drax's premises.

The elf wizard had implied his invisibility was forfeit once they passed the magical boundary, so the time for close caution was over. Gwyn caught the sergeant's eye and pointed to a zil'bast a few paces away along a clear path– not the closest to the edge, for Gwyn hoped to maximize the panic by getting immediately among them, but close enough to strike before the enemy could react to their sudden appearance. Rak nodded at her silent instruction.

Gwyn readied her sword and charged.

The king had put a full regiment under Baraxis' command, over a thousand men stretching around and behind him outside the northwest quarter of the city. The officers sat on horseback, but his force was infantry, and they stood in blocks and lines by battalion and company, awaiting the order to advance. A screen of cavalry had crossed the barricades ahead of them in case the orcs decided to attack upon seeing his deployment, but the enemy had offered no challenge. Apparently even an organized enemy massing before them wasn't cause for concern in the face of whatever their twisted sorcerers were planning to do. Seeing what a single zil'bast was capable of on two occasions, Baraxis was not inclined to criticize their confidence.

The Lord General looked over his shoulder to the wall, waiting for the signal flags ordering his attack. He'd never paced out the city boundaries with precision, but he knew Gwyn was at least a mile away on the south side, invisible from his position. She should be starting her attack any moment. He wondered whether she would live. He wondered whether he would.

Cries of alarm sounded as soon as Gwyn and Rak breached the magical wall, but that shock failed to materialize into practical action before Gwyn decapitated her first target. A second zil'bast stretched its hand toward her, but she turned and hacked it off before its intention, whatever it was, could be carried out. Now fear and outrage rippled through the horde as the enemy realized it was the Hellwitch and her fabled sword that attacked them. Guttural chants and incantations rose up from all around, but fire and lightning and scarlet bolts of light all washed over Gwyn and Rak with no more harm than an odd tingling and a surge of heat from her enchanted necklace. The air all around Gwyn began to shimmer with heat as zil'basts tried in vain to protect themselves from her. Meanwhile, Gwyn felled two more of the enemy. A third met her gaze, and by a nagging itch behind her eyes she thought it was trying to bewitch her somehow. The spell refused to form in her mind, and the sensation vanished when she spitted the monster on her blade.

"Gwyn, behind!" She heard Rak call out and turned to see a stouter zil'bast raising its staff to strike at her in more mundane fashion. Her blade was still lodged in her last victim, and in the moment it took to haul free, the beast struck. Gwyn dodged, but the creature was quick, turning its blow at the last second to deal a painful crack to Gwyn's shoulder. She moved into the zil'bast's reach and hacked its legs off at the knees before it could strike again. Another staff swung at her, but it missed completely as Rak tackled the aggressor to the ground, his swords still sheathed. Gwyn finished off the enemy and helped her sergeant to his feet; Rak promptly picked up an enemy staff and set to work. It burst predictably into flames, but only where it neared its target, and Rak managed a few heavy blows with the burning brand before he was forced to drop it and pick up another. Gwyn's enchanted blade flashed and felled all the while, until she and Rak stood back to back in a cleared space perhaps twenty feet across. The zil'basts drew back, too afraid to attack. *This is as startled and distracted as they get, Drax,* Gwyn thought. *Whatever you're planning to do, do it* now!

Just then, a bellow sounded from the orcish lines, and an avenue opened in the surrounding press of sorcerers. At the far end, an orcish elite stood at the head of a dozen warriors preparing to charge. Rak put himself in their path and drew his blades at last. "Come on!" he challenged them. The orcs charged. Gwyn chose a zil'bast near Rak's path and rushed forward. Before she reached it, its eyes went wide, then it doubled over in screaming agony. A moment later, Gwyn and enemies alike were shoved back by the force as the screaming zil'bast exploded.

CHAPTER XVI

The signal men on the wall began waving red flags back and forth over their heads with gusto. Baraxis nodded and urged Storm Cloud forward at a fast walk. His regiment moved with him, the muddled jostling of arms and mail resolving into a rhythmic *chunk-chunk-chunk* as they advanced, shields touching, spears pointed skyward.

In a minute they had crossed half the distance to the orcish camp where the enemy formed up to meet them. Baraxis thought he heard a sporadic pounding from the south and wondered whether it had something to do with Gwyn or some unit there had deployed field pieces with small firestones.

Baraxis held the far right, and he could see orcs from the north, at least double his number, mobilizing toward him. Still over a quarter mile away, for the moment he ignored them. At one-hundred-twenty yards from the enemy before them, one of Baraxis' majors ordered his battalion of archers to halt and make ready. As the other four battalions continued to advance, the first volley sailed overhead, falling among the orcs like iron rain. Baraxis heard rushing air and noticed a shadow to his far left, telling him a similar regiment there did exactly as he did. Predictably, the enemy refused to stay at such lethal range and charged immediately. Another volley fell as Baraxis ordered his battalions to stop and set spears. As the archers pulled to the north flank to winnow the orcs approaching there, the men in the front ranks overlapped shields and waited for the clash.

With intuition honed by a lifetime of battle, Baraxis felt as much as heard a disturbance from the south, a sort of ripple through the ranks that managed to register above the pounding of orcish feet and his heart hammering his ribs. He looked, and at the limit of his vision he saw a mob of orcs at the southwest corner of the city disperse, spreading southward away from the Southerners directly before them. Before he could suss the meaning of this, the orcs slammed against his spears, and the fight began.

The zil'basts' unstable power was being turned against them in far more dramatic fashion than Gwyn had imagined. Her necklace flashed hot for an instant, but no flame touched her, though those near her were singed and the zil'bast closest to the explosion flailed about, fully aflame.

The charging elite and his warriors cringed back in fear, and Rak pressed the slim advantage, keeping them away from Gwyn. Full panic, indeed, swept through the enemy ranks now, who must have thought Gwyn herself caused the conflagration. They bashed into one another trying to escape her. Gwyn's blade rose and fell, then she was buffeted by the wave of another explosion, then another. The heat was growing quickly, and zil'bast robes everywhere were starting to scorch.

Gwyn trusted Drax's quickly-made amulets only so far, and, as the elf had predicted, the more zil'basts fell, the more potent his attacks became, the more rapid the detonations. "Rak," Gwyn shouted above the roar of explosion and flame, "Rak, we're going! We've done enough." She ran to where he stood, and only as she neared did she realize his hair and clothes were smoking. "Rak," she called again. "Hurry! You're burning!" Rak started to run before a zil'bast not two yards away detonated, throwing them both to the ground. Now Rak's hair and clothes were fully engulfed. Gwyn rolled over to him and threw her body over his, but she knew even as she did that it was too late, for the reek of burning flesh overcame her nostrils. Miraculously, Rak didn't even scream. His scalp blistered and split, his mail seared against his flesh, but he didn't cry out. Instead, he met Gwyn's eyes for one last moment, and before the flames could reach his face, for an instant Gwyn was sure he smiled. Another zil'bast, fleeing in terror, stumbled over them just as he exploded, driving Gwyn down into Rak's burning form as the heat seared harmlessly around her, so hot that for a moment she couldn't even breathe. When she rose to her knees, a pile of charred armor and blackened bones were all that remained of Sergeant Rak.

Regaining her breath, Gwyn felt her necklace scorching her skin and clawed at it, pulling it outside her armor. The heat was beginning to reach her, so she knew that her protection, too, was beginning to fail. Zil'basts still incinerated all around her. The orc warriors were long gone, fled or burned to death, she couldn't be sure. Hastily grabbing Rak's swords, their heat painful to her hand as her talisman's protection continued to weaken, she sprinted from the zil'bast camp, a dark silhouette against the growing fireball.

Outside the conflagration, chaos gripped the orcish lines. The tents closest to the fire were already kindling into full flame, and the orcs were too occupied with flight to create any kind of firebreak. Elites and war leaders stalked among the fleeing hordes, trying desperately to order them into some kind of formation, *any* kind of formation, against the attack they knew must surely be coming.

Baraxis right flank was in serious peril. His bowman had thinned the northward orcs as best they could, but now the enemy had come too close. He was forced to pull his archer battalion back, and their quivers were likely all but empty anyway.

Shouting orders to Ardos, Baraxis rode to the north. Ardos repeated the order to a drummer, and in a few moments the back ranks began a redeployment in that direction in desperate attempt to keep the approaching enemy from crumpling their flank.

The archers in the regiment to the left had lent some support to Baraxis' southern flank, thinning the orcs there enough that the spearmen had managed to shove them back. The center churned at a bloody standstill, but Baraxis could spare no men there now. The wind shifted, blowing down from the north, and Storm Cloud snorted and tossed his head. Baraxis looked in that direction, and his heart sank. Behind the first wave of southward-advancing orcs, a horde just as large charged down a hillside, their mouths gaping with war cries.

The lord general spurred Storm Cloud to a gap in the front line, hacking and stabbing downward with his sword. If he died this day, he would not die alone. A mighty shout from the wall above nearly distracted him as he split an orc's skull. Fortunately no enemy jumped immediately into that one's place, for as the noise from the wall had threatened distraction, realization of its meaning stunned him completely. The shout he'd heard continued on, taking the form not of warning or lament, but of cheers. He looked once more to the north to see the nearest orcs had slowed their advance, the rear ranks milling about with clear uncertainty. Behind them, the second horde hurtling pell-mell down the hill were not charging. They were fleeing. Above them a mighty line of heavy horse pounded down the slope, their armor and spearpoints flashing in the sun.

"Hold, men!" Baraxis shouted. "Hold and fight! Help is coming!"

The distant horsemen rode through the orcish lines like a sharp scythe through grain, some turning to charge back, others standing to rain blows on either side. One rider managed to break away from the melee and gallop to the south, skirting the east side of the nearer orcs and coming behind Baraxis' regiment. He didn't stop even to salute the lord general but rode on parallel to the Southern lines, crying out again and again with all his might, "The north is ours! The north is ours! The north is ours!"

Gwyn could already hear fighting off to the north and west. The orcs' general avoidance of the zil'bast camp, now made absolute by the devastation, left her a clear path back to the city gates. Within a pair of minutes, Gwyn crossed the barricade to cheers and congratulations from the defenders. No one asked or seemed to care what had happened to Rak, and for a moment Gwyn's reputation tasted like gall in her mouth. *Do they even remember he was with me?* she wondered. *Everybody wants a hero. They see the glimmer of hope; they want a reminder of victory, not sacrifice. But who speaks for the fallen?*

By then Gwyn was being ushered through the wicket just as Drax came down the steps from the wall.

I am the Hand of Vengeance, Gwyn reminded herself. *I speak for them. And I act for them.* Drax limped toward her, his form bent. He smiled weakly as he met her eyes and started to say something.

Gwyn dropped Rak's swords to empty her right hand and wrapped it around Drax's neck, slamming his slight frame into the wall. "He's dead," she growled. "Your amulet didn't work. He *burned*, elf! He burned to death in my arms!"

"His…decision…" the robed elf gasped.

"Explain that!"

"Can't. Can't…breathe…"

Gwyn let go, and Drax dropped hard to the ground, collapsing to his hands and knees. He massaged his throat and tried to stand, but his knees buckled. Finally he leaned back against the wall and sat, sticking his feet out in front of him. He closed his eyes, and Gwyn realized suddenly how exhausted he looked. The part of her that could still smell Rak's burning flesh yearned for a justification to reach down and break his neck, but another part demanded a reason first, some meaning behind this fresh, sharp pain in her heart. Just when she'd decided the elf must have passed out, Drax opened his eyes again.

"After you left us," he began, "Rak asked me if I really had enough time to make two amulets. I told him that I did. He asked, 'Good enough to *survive* the mission, or just complete it.' I didn't answer, and he knew. Then I explained what would happen when I started getting past the enemy defenses, how deadly the air would be. He insisted that you had to live, no matter what, that his protection need last only long enough to watch your back. His pleas were in such earnest, I was inclined to assent, but he still hadn't given me anything to enchant. With the right object, I thought, maybe I could still save you both."

"What did he give you?" Gwyn asked. "Really?"

"That's just it. When I asked for some object he felt connected to, he had nothing to give. Did you know he was an orphan?"

Gwyn nodded.

"He said he was never allowed to keep things, that he'd lost everything he owned so many times he'd learned not to trust in possessions. That's what decided me. There was no way I could have protected him strongly enough without a true bond to his amulet. Not in time. He also said there weren't many *people* he trusted any more than he did things, but that you were one. So I honored his request. I put the warding magic on one of his boots as quickly as I could and moved on to your necklace. I barely had enough time as it was to ensure the mission. Before you walked out of the flames, I thought we'd lost you both. I'm not wholly callous, though. Dulling the senses is much easier than altering reality; I promised Rak his amulet would ease his pain. I could do that much for him, at least."

Gwyn nodded as she remembered Rak diverting her when she asked what his talisman was, the peaceful smile he wore in death. At last she put her own sword down on the flagstones, arranged Rak's next to it, and eased to the ground, leaning against the wall next to Drax. "Why would he do that for me?"

She hadn't really been asking the elf, but he did his best to answer. "We only spoke briefly after we made it into the city, but I know it grieved him when he believed you were dead. He talked about the officers he'd had in the past and what he felt serving under you. I think… I think, in your own way, you were the first person in his life he believed would actually *care* if he lived or died, might even carry on his memory if you survived. That's a powerful thing. Believe me."

"This is really what he wanted?"

Drax nodded, his fatigue obvious in his every move, and Gwyn could see he was telling the truth.

"I guess I shouldn't have tried to kill you, then."

Drax snorted, his eyes closed once again. "My throat would have liked it better, and the back of my head. Though I suspect you weren't trying very hard; if you had, I'd be dead. My magic is spent, and while I'm not helpless without it, I'm clearly no match for the great Gwyn the Savage."

"*Gwyn et Sheevasa.*"

"What?"

"My real name. *Gwyn et Sheevasa.*"

"Atlunding. Hand of Vengeance?" Drax translated.

"Yes."

"The necklace suddenly seems more fitting. And the bruises on my neck. Pleased to really meet you, *Gwyn et Sheevasa.*"

"I still hate you."

"I know. But that means you're alive to do the hating, so I can...live with..."

Drax's voice had grown weaker over his last few statements, and Gwyn looked over to see that, this time, he really had fallen asleep.

"If you're not responsible," Gwyn muttered, "then Rak's killers are dead. Not Shon's, though, and time is running out." She stood, and as chaos raged around the city, the Hand of Vengeance started heading north.

It took Gwyn the best part of an hour to make it to the north end of the city and through the stockyards to the outer wall. From the top, she saw the orcish standard she sought at the fringes of the battle toward the west. She could also see Baraxis' crimson banner some little distance farther to the south. The fighting in that whole quarter had become a surging maelstrom; there was no way she could get to him, at least not that she could see.

Instead, Gwyn joined up with a company of reinforcements about to enter the fray. They were more than happy to admit her, and by sheer force of will she persuaded the unit's lieutenant, who was leading well over his ability, to target the area she most wanted to attack.

Word seemed to pass from unit to unit through the Southern lines, news greeted by cheers wherever it went. The cheers were heard and interpreted by the nearest orcs, then that same word passed through their lines as well, and orcish hearts quailed at the hearing. Like winter Wind cutting through the enemy formations the knowledge rippled southward: Gwyn the Savage had taken the field.

Again she sighted the orcish standard that filled her thoughts, and she drove toward it. Before she could reach it, though, it flowed away like a leaf on a stream. From a low rise, Gwyn watched as the whole orcish contingent fought their way clear of Southern forces and hurried off to the west. "Cowards!" she screamed, her voice lost in the drone of battle to all but a few close by. "Murderers!" For the second time she cursed them, but this time Baraxis was not there to stop her pursuit. If she was quick enough, she could pick her way through the battle lines, start tracking them, find a riderless horse to start gaining ground.

"Captain?" The young lieutenant looked up at her, his eyes like gray pools of innocence and trust. The rest of the company, likewise, looked to her for guidance. They looked raw, untested. She had planned only to use them to get close to her prey, but in the process she had turned their leaders into followers, undermining their confidence. She looked again at the band of fleeing orcs under their cruel standard, gaining distance by the moment. What if they returned to the fight somewhere else? What if they turned to a river for escape, and she could no longer track them? What if…?

Gwyn looked then to the south, at Baraxis' embattled regiment. The lord general sat Storm Cloud on the front line, chopping and skewering as his noble mount reared to clout orcs with his hooves. Suddenly she heard Storm Cloud's piercing whinny cut through the noise of battle, and suddenly the steed bucked wildly, his saddle empty.

Mastering her rage and concern she turned back, and as her true enemies fled for the second time, she rallied her young company, leading them at a run toward Baraxis' regiment.

Hours passed. Human and orc alike bled and died. Horses screamed. Forces clashed and retreated, bodies surging across the field in waves. Somewhere in the midst of those hours, the battle in the northwest quarter came to an end as the last vestige of resistance was routed. For all her efforts, Gwyn never managed to join Baraxis' force, some obstacle or priority thwarting her at every turn. Now she didn't know if any of her friends were alive or dead. Gwyn's new contingent collapsed to the blood-slicked, trampled ground, gasping and weeping. Despite her worry for the Sutherese, Gwyn smiled grimly to her fighters. She hadn't the heart to order the men to their feet; truthfully, she'd have liked to join them, for she was weary to her bones. Instead, she made a quick count. More than half were here, still alive. A few others she'd sent limping back throughout the afternoon, nursing wounds she hoped they'd survive. She'd done all she could for these boys. She could only hope those who survived would believe it had been enough, enough to speak well of her when they told this tale someday to their grandchildren.

She nodded to the men, taking in their bloody armor and bruised, ashen faces against the backdrop of carnage, of broken bodies littering the ground and the sounds of battle still ringing to the south and, everywhere, the thick tang of blood in the air. "Well done, men," she said. "Well done. When you can stand, get back to the city. It sounds like the winds have turned in our favor, and you've done more than your part this day."

"You aren't coming with us?" one of them asked.

"No," she said flatly. She gave no other explanation as she strode toward Baraxis' scarlet standard.

She found Ardos sitting on a rock, the staff of Baraxis' banner leaning against his shoulder. His eyes were at the ground, staring straight through it. "Ardos?" Gwyn asked. He looked up at his name, but his gaze was blank. "Ardos!" Gwyn shouted. He blinked, then finally he focused on Gwyn's face. He smiled wanly, and it was as though he released the horrors of that day into the air, letting them pass over him in a way Gwyn knew she never could, slowly returning back to the compassionate farmer she knew.

"Gwyn," he sighed. "Thank Terillah ya live."

"Where is Baraxis?" Gwyn demanded. He hesitated. "Ardos, please, I saw him go down. Where is Baraxis?"

"I'm here."

Gwyn turned to see the lord general making his way across the littered ground toward her. His armor was dented and bloody, his face bruised, and his left arm hung in a makeshift sling of belts and torn cloth. He finally made it to Gwyn and put his good arm around her, overwhelming her with the smells of sweat and steel and gore.

Anxiety creased Ardos' face. "How bad was it?"

"Just wrenched out of joint. It's back in, now; I'll be fine. At least, my arm will mend, and all the other bruises and scrapes. Others will not be so fortunate, and I grieve for them. That wound will not so easily heal. To say nothing of…"

When Baraxis didn't continue, Gwyn looked to Ardos. "You saw 'im get pulled outta the saddle, but I guess ye missed the rest. Storm Cloud prob'ly could'a got away, but 'e stood over 'is master, kicking and biting like a mad beast 'til the very last. It's no small miracle we got there in time ta save Baraxis, and prob'ly wouldn't've, but it was too late fer Storm Cloud."

Gwyn could see the pain in Baraxis' eyes, the sparkle of unshed tears, but he cleared his throat and shook his head. "Dozens of my people will never see Sutherset again; I'll shed no tears for a horse."

"It isn't that the one diminishes the other, m'lord," Ardos reasoned.

Baraxis shook his head again. "Either way, I won't do it. There will be time enough to grieve when this is all over."

"*I* will not grieve until– Hells, I have to go!" Gwyn shouted.

"Where are you off to, lass?" Ardos called after her. She made no reply as she ran. "Where's she going?"

Baraxis looked sidelong at Ardos, keeping Gwyn also in view. "I think I know. I think you could guess."

Ardos considered for a moment. "Oh."

Baraxis nodded. "Aye."

They were both right. From the west wall, Gwyn surveyed all the land from north to south, from the battle lines to the horizon. The cruel standard was nowhere in sight. Either they had rejoined the battle and been destroyed, or–

"Gwyn," came a voice to the left, "I'm glad to see you alive." Drax, looking somewhat revived, was moving along the wall top toward her. The sun was lower and obscured by smoke billowing from the orcish camps, so Drax had removed his glass lenses to reveal his violet-tinged gray eyes.

"I'm indifferent to see you at all," Gwyn growled back. "How did you find me?"

"What makes you think I was looking? I've just been walking the wall, seeing what there is to see. And you?"

"I'm looking for something."

"Aren't we all?" Drax muttered, his tone rhetorical.

"Don't get philosophical," Gwyn spat. "I'm looking for a battle standard, orcish. I don't suppose…?"

"I'm better than I was, but the ground against the wall is not the most restful place, and scrying, as I said, is not my specialty. If you wanted somebody set ablaze or protected from hailstorms, I might manage something small before I collapsed from exhaustion, but if you need me to *see* something, I'm afraid you're out of luck."

"Damn," Gwyn cursed. "They could be anywhere by now." Gwyn turned and sank to the stones, leaning her back against the parapet.

"If I thought you were chasing me, I'd be anywhere but *here*," Drax reasoned as he also sat. "Do you want to tell me what this is all about?"

"Why should I?"

"Because I asked. I've noticed a lot of people around here idolize you, but I don't think anybody really *talks* to you."

"They know better," Gwyn grunted.

"If you say so."

"You think you understand an awful lot, considering you've known me for all of a few hours."

"We're not so different as you think," Drax commented. "Both a long way from home. Both selling our services in the war. And both doing it because we're killers by trade. Or do I miss my guess?"

Gwyn hesitated for a moment, then shook her head "no." "You have the truth of it," she admitted.

"So, would you like to tell me what this is all about?"

Gwyn sighed. "Before, there was someone, one of the few that did talk to me. Now he's dead."

"Not Rak?"

"No. Someone else. I saw the orcs that did it, but I couldn't get at them. At least a few are still alive, fleeing under that standard I'm looking for." Gwyn heard shouts and horn blasts from the south, signaling a new charge against the enemy. "We've broken this siege, and the orcs had so much committed here, I think the Southerners will finally have a generation or two of peace, or something like it. But for me, for me this war isn't over until those last few murderers are dead. That's what this is about. What it's all about."

"But how will you find them now? And what will you do if you can't?"

Gwyn pictured the trampled, bloody ground, terrain that would make her quarry impossible to track. She remembered the long ride home after the Forest Campaign, the empty, worthless feeling of being denied the vengeance she had so long vowed. The sound of victorious laughter drifted up from a tavern below the wall, and suddenly Gwyn felt cold and alone. What was wrong with her? What was so broken inside her that she couldn't simply let go of the past and join in the happiness of those around her? *Hells,* she thought, *what* am *I?* Her chin sank to her chest, and her eyes squinted tight.

Suddenly Drax's arm was around her shoulders. Her body tensed, but when he didn't immediately withdraw, she found herself ignoring the urge to shove him away. He was warm and he was close and, for whatever reason, he was there. Most importantly, she owed him nothing, had nothing to prove to him. She opened her eyes to glance along the wall, and, confident that no warriors were within sight, she leaned against the elf and sobbed a few deep, wracking sobs. She felt her eyes sting and, to her surprise, squeezed a few hot tears from between her squinted lids. After only a moment she leaned back, wiping her face as she drew a long, shuddering breath, feeling like herself again. "If you tell anybody about this, I'll kill you."

"You can trust me."

She turned to regard him more fully. "What is this manner you're taking with me? We aren't friends; you barely even know me. Why are you acting like this?"

"You seemed like you needed someone, and I was here. That's all."

"It's a lot more than I'd have done in your place."

"Well, maybe I'm just a better person than you are," the elf quipped.

"Get off this wall before I throw you off."

"As you wish." Drax rose and took his leave, continuing his rounds of the wall.

"As I wish?" Gwyn muttered. "What *do* I wish?" She was sure of only one thing, and on that she renewed her focus, to the exclusion of all the other possibilities that frightened and confused her so.

By nightfall, the orcs were through. Gwyn collapsed on her bed not long after sundown, and the nightmare came again. She lay mutilated, and the first three orcs died as before. One more dissipated to mist as a sword blade smashed through his collarbone and hacked down into his ribs. Two more continued their leering grins, and the dark figure on the wall still invisibly groped for her, its curiosity tempting and possessive. Now, though, her head didn't seem to rest on the hard ground, but on something softer. She looked up, and above her, shading the harsh sun as she looked down, was the face of a woman with soft, brown hair, a face that sparked memories Gwyn couldn't quite place. "Don't tarry too long, Little Gwyn," she said. "Don't tarry."

~ * ~

Gwyn woke the next morning well after dawn. She made her unhurried way to the palace where she learned Baraxis was in closed meetings with the king. Her presence was not required. Everywhere she went people cheered her and offered her food and drink from what little they had. At first she tried to be gracious in her refusals, but by the time she reached the outer wall it had become easier to simply ignore the accolades, though this seemed only to increase their frequency. At last she made her way to the Sutherset camp where Ardos directed a variety of activities with as little urgency as Gwyn felt. He welcomed her with an embrace and took a break from his activity to offer Gwyn the latest reports.

No orc reinforcements had arrived, nor any other last ditch tricks from the enemy. The Southerners, however, seemed to have done their job too well, if that were possible. Between the utter destruction of the zil'basts and the Southerners' surprise reinforcements, not a few orc units had lost their nerve completely. Though many did manage an orderly retreat back across the King's Bridge, where a small force held the Southern pursuit long enough for the rest to make a head start back to their homeland, early scouting suggested several thousand of the survivors had fled east and west, roaming the countryside in bands of anywhere from two- to eight-dozen orcs.

"What does that mean for us?" Gwyn asked.

"Too early ta say," Ardos replied. "Suspect we'll find out when Baraxis gets out of audience with the king."

Baraxis appeared after midday. Though he provided few details, the result was clear: None of them would be going home anytime soon.

CHAPTER XVII

The mop-up took weeks, and Gwyn and Baraxis rode out every day with a force of volunteers to harry the enemy. To ease his grief over Storm Cloud, Baraxis took to riding Cinnabar on forays. He was not the massive beast Storm Cloud had been and couldn't carry Baraxis as quickly in a gallop, but his slower gaits were so smooth the lord general often compared them favorably to a boat on calm water.

Gwyn saw much during these expeditions. All the lands for ten miles east and west of the Capital were a total loss, plundered or burned down to the very soil. Farther out, bandits had often claimed whatever the orcs had not, especially closer to the kingdom's northern border with the lawless wilds. Keeps and walled towns had fared better, but all throughout the land the Southern Kingdoms had become a place of fear and want, desolated expanses broken by only occasional pockets of safety and civility. Gwyn hoped Sutherset was far enough away to have escaped the worst desolation, but they'd had no word.

The one thing Gwyn did not see was the standard she sought. From every town they rescued, every band of refugees they escorted to safety, every orc and bandit survivor they questioned, Gwyn demanded reports of any orcs bearing this device, but not one answer gave any indication of where her enemy had gone. Almost every night the horrible dream repeated, sometimes with variation related to the dark figure or the mysterious woman but always ending with those last two orc faces mocking her. After weeks of searching, Gwyn was forced to the daunting realization that the orc regiment must have turned south just after she lost sight of them, making it across the bridge even before the bulk of the retreat. Her quarry could be anywhere, anywhere, at least, in enemy territory. Two months after the siege was broken, Gwyn spoke to Baraxis, convinced it would be the last time.

Gwyn sent word she wanted to meet, and according to Baraxis' preference he came to her in the lavish sitting room of Gwyn's new quarters in the Haddix estate. Ever since Gwyn had been moved there, Baraxis had taken every excuse to visit, for her rooms were more comfortable than those set aside for the generals in the cold, hard keep of the palace. Though Gwyn found Southern autumn to be comfortable even at its coldest, she lit a small fire out of deference to Baraxis and his less boreal sensibilities.

The lord general's manner was easy as he entered. He had grieved the fallen and found himself again, found joy in the prospect of going home soon in peace. He was once more the man Gwyn had grown to respect, though she saw in herself only the hard, distant mercenary that had first entered his employ. The lord general began gamely with the usual pleasantries, undaunted when Gwyn replied only with short words or grunts. At last, he relented to her obvious impatience and progressed to more serious matters.

"I am glad you asked to meet, Gwyn. I have something I want to discuss with you, but I assume you summoned me for a reason of your own, so you first."

"Thank you." Gwyn had spent a week working up to this conversation in her mind, but now that she truly came to it, she found the words difficult. She cleared her throat before pressing onward. "I have to go. I mean no disrespect or ingratitude, but I must ask to be released from your service."

"Very well. I'm as good as my word. I release you, at least in name. In fact, you may still wear my colors and eat at my table whenever you wish. I told you before that you are more than a retainer to me. Take your freedom back if you must. I don't suspect it will change anything."

"But it will. Didn't you hear me, Baraxis? I said that I'm leaving, Lord General."

"Lord Major," Baraxis corrected.

"What?"

"It seems this is the day for adjusting allegiances. I have reminded the king of a promise he made to me, similar to the one I made you. I have been demoted to my former station, which means I may finally return home."

"I'm happy for you, Lord Major," Gwyn replied. "I wish I could go with you. I find I would like to see Sutherset again, but my road takes me to a different end."

"None of us can see the end of the road, Gwyn. We are lucky if we can see a few stops ahead, and I'm certain our roads run together at least a little farther."

"You know where I'm bound, old man. Surely you don't think you can change my mind."

"I don't," Baraxis agreed.

"Then you know our roads must part."

"I said I was going home. I never said I wasn't stopping anywhere on the way."

"For once, old man, talk like an Atlunder and tell me plainly what's going on in that addled head of yours."

"They've been spotted, Gwyn. The orcs you've been seeking. Word has reached our ears that the whole orc race is suffering greatly. The war decimated their food stores and other resources, and though they plundered us heavily, little of that made it back to the home front. Many of the tribes most heavily invested are struggling just to survive. Some have started striking again, relying on the skills they know best to swell their larders. I have many friends and allies among the defenders, and there's little I don't learn of in time. Your standard has been sighted twice. I'm going after it."

"You aren't a vengeful man, Baraxis. You don't need this as I do."

"That's true. I have wept and grieved and said my late goodbyes to all those I'll never see again on this side of the veil. I thought that was enough...until the time came to return home. Then I imagined riding into my castle at the head of the triumphant vanguard, seeing the expectant faces of the wives and sons and daughters whose husbands and fathers are not behind me in the column. I thought of facing Tira, knowing what was done to Shon at the end, and telling her that the villains went free when it was within my power to bring them to account, and those words tasted like blood.

"The lord in me says I should not do for Shon what I cannot do for all my people that fell, but the father in me yells that Shon and Tira are special to me and that Shon must have justice before I can return home with a clear conscience. And so, we go together, you and I, as it should be: To *end* this war."

The next day, Baraxis gave orders to the Sutherese to begin preparations for the journey home. For every three men who had set out from Sutherset, one would never return. The rest were eager to be back, though, and despaired of being thought cowards when they did not accompany Baraxis to the south. Baraxis anticipated their loyalty and was equally eager for their homecoming, so he declared from the first that he would take only a small force. In the end, Ardos insisted on coming along over Baraxis' objections, along with a dozen others who had been most influenced by Shon's example. The group made their own preparations to set out the following dawn.

Winter had begun, and even in the south Gwyn could see her breath in the early morning chill as she rode her gray stallion out the main gate and toward Baraxis. He and Ardos waited for the rest of the band at a gap in the log palisade. The Southerners had great hope for the coming peace, but not so much to remove the outer defenses they'd kept as long as they could remember. The return of wealthy nobles from their northern estates had begun, pushing the homeless poor back out into the Dog Markets. Young Haddix had returned a few days earlier, but since Gwyn's chambers had been his father's rooms and not his own, the noble swayed with the political winds of the Atlunder's fame and allowed her to remain the short time leading up to her departure. Gwyn had overheard enough to surmise that Haddix, after the failure of his apocalyptic predictions, was embroiled in a domestic war with his numerous concubines to name a legitimate heir from the several bastards he had fathered on them, not that she cared. As she reached Baraxis by the barricade, he handed her a small, wooden box. "This came for you late last night," he explained. "It must have been a *long* time finding you."

Gwyn took the box, no larger than her hand. It had a sliding lid, and the seams were sealed with wax. Painted in fine letters on the top was her proper name and nothing else, with embellishments in the script even Baraxis could recognize as Atlunding. Far beyond that, Gwyn saw immediately in the letters her mother's practiced hand.

She swallowed a lump in her throat, her heart beating fast. She looked down at the box, then back to Baraxis. Finally she shook her head and reached behind her to open her saddlebag, placing the box inside.

She thought Baraxis would express surprise that she didn't open it, even challenge her to do so, but he didn't. He only nodded. In a few more minutes the last of the dozen Sutherese had arrived, and the band set out.

They journeyed south for a week, then finally they took firsthand reports of the standard they sought. Two days later, near sundown, Gwyn sighted a plume of smoke rising from behind a hill. She put spurs to her mount, and the rest of the band struggled to keep up as she galloped down the road.

Gwyn crossed the intervening mile in two minutes before she let her horse slow. She never had built up his endurance as she'd hoped. He swung about the curve of the hill at a fast trot, and Gwyn saw the ruins of a hill fort still smoldering at the top. Baraxis called to her as he caught up, and she forced herself to wait for her allies. The troop moved warily up the hill, but nothing moved against them. At last they passed the gate timbers and moved inside the small outpost.

The inner structures consisted of a tiny barracks and two plain outbuildings. All were half burned. A few orc bodies lay about, but no humans were in evidence.

"What happened?" Ardos asked.

"Possible one orc band took up in here and another fought them over it, but I doubt it," Baraxis answered. "More likely the noble who lost these lands to the orcs sent an advance squad to start scouting and see what's left."

"Then orc foragers attacked to take their supplies," Gwyn concluded.

"Where are the people?" Ardos asked. "Did they get away?"

"Maybe," Gwyn answered as she dismounted to make a proper search, "but we didn't pass them on the road. And the orcs are starving." She saw realization dawn on Ardos' face just as movement caught the corner of her eye. One of the orcs was not dead.

She leapt to the prostrate form and planted a boot on the narrow chest, and even in the failing light she recognized the missing left ear, the crooked nose, the short but intact tusks. It bore new marks now, a twisted knee and an oozing wound in its belly. Gwyn's weight on its ribs woke it with a howl, but its eyes had no more than opened before she had her dirk at its throat. She cut deep and turned away, then looked up at Baraxis, still astride Cinnabar. "One more. We should keep going."

"Most of these ashes are cold, Gwyn," Baraxis argued. "They're probably a day ahead of us, and we need sleep."

Gwyn turned away, muttering. Memories pummeled her: her nightmares, the sight of Shon hacked apart, her work on minions after her first fights alone in the woods. Part of her felt she'd killed the orc too quickly. She looked back to see Ardos had started ordering the camp, but Baraxis just watched her. "We'll get the last one, Gwyn. I swear it, no matter what."

"The days are too short," she retorted. "I'm riding out as soon as it's light enough to see."

"We're with you," the lord major confirmed.

Gwyn slept so little that night she didn't dream. Between bouts of half-sleep she tracked *Bia Creg* across the sky, then stared after the little moon waiting for the eastern horizon to gray. As soon as the stars began to vanish, she rose, stowing gear and preparing her horse by feel and the instinct of a thousand repetitions.

She set out, dimly aware the rest of the men were still struggling to rise behind her. She had the blood scent, and nothing would slow her down. Even in the twilight, the orc band was easy to track across the plain. After a mile they'd left the road and cut overland to the southeast, leaving a trampled swath through the dormant grass.

In another few miles the men had caught up. Baraxis let Gwyn set the pace, and she dragged the band behind her all day, challenging man and beast alike. As evening hastened toward night, the glimmer of campfires sprang up far out on the plain, in a broad cutting between the looming shadows of two hills against the sky. The camp couldn't be more than two miles away, and the Sutherese band reined in their mounts. Gwyn looked skyward to the big moon shining his gibbous face over the land and dismounted. "I'm going looking for sentries," she announced, keeping her voice low. With that, she ducked into the tall grass and crept away.

Two cold, tense hours passed before she returned, hissing to her own guards so she would not be mistaken for an enemy in the dark. "No sentries, no scouts," she reported to Baraxis. "I think they're celebrating something. Lots of laughing and mock combat, lots of drinking. There's maybe thirty of them. I need to get back to put eyes on the last one and mark which tent is his. I won't take the chance he gets away in the confusion if we attack."

"I agree," the lord major replied. "Get in position, but wait until they've worn themselves out in revelry. The rest of us will close in when the fires have burned low. If you wait to strike until dawn, we'll be able to see if he tries to run. Go now."

Gwyn melted back into the darkness. Baraxis turned to the men. "No tents, no lights, but try to get a few hours' sleep. One hour watches, the usual rotation." He drew a deep breath and sighed. "Now we wait."

~ * ~

A fiery dream melted into darkness as the sleeping orc snapped open his eyes, quickly absorbing all around him. Everything at the edges of his vision was as it should be, his gear, weapons, and trophies showing dimly in the dawn light that filtered through the seams of his tent. In the center of his view, however, staring straight into his bleary eyes, stood a vision of terror, a nightmarish demon spat up from the bowels of hell, or so his people believed. Still, it bore a human shape, a lithe woman with a mass of hair falling down her back, red and wild as flame. A heavy cloak of green and black shrouded her form, but the dull glint of mail beneath gave proof to her violent intentions. A flash of gold-trimmed scarlet tied about her right arm and the bloody gleam of a garnet in her cloak clasp matched a hellish, inhuman glow behind her piercing green eyes, eyes that held the orc's even as they cowed him. It was the battle light, sparked by the imminence of blood. For all the many rumors of this demon, the light in her eyes was unknown to all who faced her, for no enemy seeing that glint had lived to tell the tale. To the orcish captain, prostrate, unarmed, helpless beneath that burning stare, nothing could provoke more terror. His mind screamed for flight or battle, but those eyes held him, searing away his courage and replacing it with the certainty that any movement could only hasten his death.

"You know why I'm here, who I am," asserted the demon in a fair mimicry of the orcs' brutish tongue.

"I know *who* you are, Hellwitch," he grunted, biding his time while his mind scrabbled for anything that might save him, "but not *what* you are. If I'm dead anyway, tell me that secret."

The orc was denied even that, for the answer, the last words he would ever hear, came in a tongue he did not understand. The woman straightened to her considerable height, pointing a great sword at the prone orc's throat.

"I am *Gwyn et Sheevasa*," she proclaimed. "I am the Hand of Vengeance."

She swung her blade once, severing the orc's foul head from its body. Lifting the skull by the horsehair adhered to its bald pate, she stepped silently out of the tent, turning her gaze to a shoulder-high spear buried haft-first in the ground: a trophy pole, lashed with crossbars from which hung the trinkets and pieces of the orc's human victims. She slammed the orc's head onto the spearpoint, then, with a decisive jerk, removed a single ring of silver and crystal from the pole. Drawing her cloak more tightly about her shoulders, she mounted her gray stallion and rode slowly out of the sleeping orcish camp, sitting proud in the saddle, a ghostly figure in the gray light and mist that rise with the dawn.

After a few long moments she reached the line of soldiers in the field and their commander, Baraxis, a man she had grown to trust and respect over the past eighteen months, months which weighed like years. As Gwyn drew abreast to them, an older sergeant threw her a red towel on which she cleaned her gore-stained blade before wiping her bloodied hands. As she finished, she looked up to meet Baraxis' coal-black eyes, reading the unspoken question behind them.

She nodded her head, silent at first, then said, "It's done. I have avenged our fallen brother, as I swore I would the day he fell and every day thereafter. But there are more deaths unanswered, more scales yet to balance." She cast a backward glance at the orcish camp, her eyes narrow with contempt. "Burn it."

~ * ~

Some of the orcs died, screaming, in the flames, and some fled toward the Sutherese and were shot down with arrows. Most fled to the south, deeper into their own territory. Baraxis watched the tents burn until he was satisfied this warband was too damaged to be any future threat. Finally he flipped his reins and turned his mount to the north, leading his men back toward home. Gwyn lingered for a few extra moments, absorbing the sight, then spurred her own horse to catch up with Baraxis at the head of the small column.

The sun was well above the horizon when Baraxis finally spoke. "Well, Gwyn, how does it feel?"

Gwyn chewed her lip and guided her horse around a large rock in the path, trying to decide how to answer. "It feels…finished," she finally said. "I don't feel glad exactly; I don't want to celebrate. It was a grim task, and it's a grim satisfaction to see it done. I don't feel empty, though. Others warned that I might; you said as much yourself. It must be that way for most, but for me it's the opposite, like an emptiness has been filled. Knowing Shon was unavenged was like a hole inside me. I never told anyone this, but," she paused, gathering her words, "the last time I ever spoke to him, before he rode away, he told me to remain as myself. Then he called me by my proper name, the Hand of Vengeance. After he was killed, it felt somehow as if those words were a last request, like more tinder on the fire of my rage. Right or wrong, it was a fire only blood could quench. Now that it's done, I'm not sure what I'll do next, but I don't feel lost. I've finished what I started, fulfilled my vow. It feels right."

They rode a few more minutes before Baraxis spoke again. "*I* know what you have to do next."

"Let me guess," Gwyn answered. "I need to go back to Sutherset, hang up my sword, learn homecraft, and birth a dozen babies with Ardos' son."

Ardos, riding just behind, choked on his canteen and sputtered as the rest of the troop laughed.

"I long to give that advice," Baraxis answered, "and you could choose far worse, in more ways than one, but it isn't what I meant. Have you forgotten?" He pointed to her saddlebag.

In her commitment to avenge Shon, she *had* forgotten, at least in part. Gwyn's hand shook as she reached to her saddlebag and drew out the small box. Questions she'd suppressed on receiving it now surged to her mind. What could have happened to make her mother desperate enough to send for her, not knowing if she was even alive and that, even if she was, the package would likely never find her. Even if it did, it would take many months, and Lischa had to know that. Was she sick? Was Tehgil ill, or worse? When she'd left she never really planned to see them again, but now that she confronted that possibility, she almost couldn't bear the idea of either of them dead and her hundreds of leagues away and never able to say goodbye, to tell them she was alright, that she'd found a life. That she didn't blame them. Those thoughts rushed unbidden to her mind, and only in the thinking did she realize they were true, or that anything different ever might have been, so as to give that new truth significance.

She clenched her fist to still her trembling fingers, then finally slid the lid off the top of the box, the wax seals crumbling on either seam. Inside was a small piece of folded parchment. As her horse continued forward she unfolded the letter and looked at the text without reading it. Tehgil's clumsy signature was at the bottom, but like the lid's lettering the handwriting of the body was also her mother's. They, at least, were alive, or had been when the note was written. She let out an unexpected breath then started reading, beginning with the date. The letter was five months old.

Dear Gwyn,

Please come home. We need you. Trouble is afoot. King Vassin lies dying without an heir. Some suspect poison, and there have been strange dealings in the Conclave. Some clans seek proof of the treason. Others swear they will go to war even without it. Atlund needs all her daughters. Please come home.

–Tehgil

Gwyn was long silent. The news had been both easier and harder than she'd feared. Finally she remembered Baraxis was no doubt eager for news. "I'm going home," she said.

"I wish you meant Sutherset," Baraxis replied quietly.

Gwyn knew that a part of her did, too.

It was a three week journey back to Sutherset, and the bulk of Baraxis' force had brought word of his final quest and sent others to watch for him on the major roads south and east. Once the band crossed the border into the lord's holdings a crowd gathered, growing thicker with each mile. By the time they reached the bridge south of the keep, the bridge over which so much blood had been shed, the welcoming feast was already laid out.

Baraxis and Ardos pleaded with Gwyn to winter in Sutherset, but despite the hardships of such late travel, Gwyn relented to remain for but one more night, and she stayed up long into the evening remembering battles and trading war stories. She drank little though; morning would come early, and she meant to be off before the sun rose.

She entered the stable in the dark of earliest morning, her few possessions slung in a sack over her left shoulder.

"Good morning, Gwyn."

Baraxis' voice in the darkness startled her. The sack hit the ground as her left hand flung out in a defensive position and her right flew to her sword sling. She recognized the voice before the motion was finished. "Dammit, Baraxis. You made me drop my gear."

"I've never *made* you do anything. Besides, I think you've lost a step, letting me sneak up in the first place."

"If you say so. You just couldn't let me leave quietly, could you?"

"I only came down to help you on your way. Since we aren't strangers anymore, I didn't think you'd mind me taking care of your horse. He's all saddled up, ready to go."

Gwyn remembered her first day in Sutherset as she walked to her horse's stall. "You're right, and I thank– Very funny, old man." The gray stallion stood unburdened, his back bare and his tack still hanging from the wall. "Fine, what's the joke?"

"No joke." Gwyn started to motion to the barebacked mount. "Not *that* one." Baraxis whistled, and a powerful, black charger trotted into the stables through doors at the far end, doors that led to Baraxis' corral. "*This* one," he finished.

Gwyn shook her head. "No. No, Baraxis, I can't. I know that horse; he's Storm Cloud's last colt, by all rights–"

"I *know* that you know him, Gwyn. You've admired him since the day after you got here. Daramis and a few others worked on breaking him while we were away east. I'd always meant Shon to have a hand in that," he added, his words tinged with grief. "Anyway, now he is yours. If you must, think of him as a bonus, or a going away present. I'd rather you thought of him as a guide. However far you go, he'll always know the way home again."

Gwyn ran her fingers through the stallion's flowing mane, and he nuzzled at her shoulder.

"See," Baraxis said, "he loves you already. You can't refuse him now."

Gwyn's heart warred inside her, guilt over taking so fine an animal set against the desire to keep him. The look on Baraxis' face decided her, a look that said one refusal was gracious, but two would be hurtful. "Very well," she said. "This is the finest animal I could ever hope to ride, much less to own. Thank you, Baraxis."

"You are welcome. And he does have a name that he comes to readily enough when you call it. Tell your people it's merely a nickname if you wish, in honor of his father. We call him Thunderhead."

Gwyn looked intently at the horse. "Thunderhead?" He snorted and stamped, bobbing his head up and down. "Thunderhead it is, then." As Gwyn double-checked Thunderhead's trappings and stowed her gear, giving the stallion time to learn her scent between tasks, Baraxis saddled Gwyn's older horse, then led him from the stall. Finishing her work, Gwyn turned back to Baraxis. "I have nothing to give you in return."

"Actually, I was hoping there was something you could do. I expected to see Tira here when I got back, and I still owe her my condolences. I sent a runner ahead to her as soon as we crossed into Sutherset, but she likely couldn't get away. I sympathize; I want to go see her myself, but I've been away too long, and Sutherset demands all my time for now. Their place is two days north and east of here. Can you go there and check in on her and Karon, and extend my invitation that they come here to lodge for as long as they wish? Even permanently; I can appoint a steward to oversee their land and herd. I should send Cinnabar with you, but now you're already leading one, and too many riderless horses may attract cutthroats."

Gwyn knew another reason for Baraxis to hold on to the horse was to offer every incentive for Tira to make her visit soon, but she didn't make him say it. "Of course," she answered. "I meant to go there anyway and asked after directions last night. I have something for Tira."

Baraxis nodded. "Then I need nothing more. It is enough to have known you, *Gwyn et Sheevasa,* to have the chance to pass on my legacy to such a brave and cunning warrior. Your story will be told at my fire for as long as I have breath to tell it, and a place at my table and a room in my keep are ever yours, should you pass this way again."

Gwyn had no words to match the lord major's. She simply shrugged her cloak off one shoulder, showing Baraxis the crimson cloth she still wore around her arm. "It is an honor, Lord Major Baraxis," Gwyn said, extending her hand. They clasped wrists and held one another's gaze, Baraxis' bright with tears, then Gwyn mounted Thunderhead as the lord major handed her the gray horse's reins.

"Will we ever meet again, Gwyn?"

"I leave you now with the same words I left my family almost two years ago: Expect me...when you see me." With that she rode off to the east, Baraxis following slowly in her wake to watch her go. Finally he stood in the open gate, his mind wandering pensively as Gwyn urged Thunderhead up a hill in the middle distance. When she reached the top, she paused and turned back, and as the first rays of dawn's light crested the rise, she lifted her great sword high in salute, rearing Thunderhead onto his hind legs so that his forehooves pawed the air, horse and rider bathed in the sun's golden fire. Then she set Thunderhead back down, and the moment passed. Gwyn turned and rode down over the hill, disappearing from sight.

"How long were you standing there, old friend?" Baraxis asked as Ardos emerged from behind a cart of hay.

"Long enough, m'lord. Long enough ta see 'er go."

"You didn't want to say goodbye?"

"Nah. Goodbyes are fer people that aren't comin' back."

"You think she will?"

"I don't truly know, m'lord. But I wan' ta hope fer it. Every day, I'll hope fer it."

"Then I will hope with you, Ardos. We will hope."

APPENDIX A
ATLUND AND SOUTHERN KINGDOM MILITARY ORGANIZATION

In Old Atlund, even after the unification of the clans, anything resembling standard military organization was slow to develop. Each clan fielded warriors according to its own sensibilities and traditions, and limited force diversity delayed the need for more complex systems of arrangement. Communication between leaders generally referred to the relevant number of warriors directly, though in time the familial nature of unit organization developed into a sort of shorthand, with groups referred to as a "house," a "burg," and a "clan" representing the number of fighters an extended family, a small village and its surrounding crofts, and an entire clan could be expected to produce.

As more complex tactics and supporting standards did, inevitably, develop, Atlund units and terminology settled into the following hierarchy:

Unit Name	Size	Composition	Led by
Team	~6	Smallest unit	Veteran
Troop	~12	2 teams	Sergeant
Company	~50	4 troops	Captain
Brigade	~150	3 companies	Captain
Battle	600+	4+ brigades	Chieftain

Military ranks remained informal. Teams were led by warriors without formal command authority, their personal ties and lifelong relationships with the other members leaving little doubt as to the most capable leader. (Disputes and power struggles would play out in day-to-day village life long before battle, at least in theory.) Any warrior given authority to lead others by his clan chieftain or council, or by the king himself during wartime, was called a "captain." Captains of smaller units would defer to captains of larger ones; again, the local, even familial nature of Atlund army composition, with leaders knowing their warriors and peers personally, put little strain on such a short chain of command. Any warrior delegated to lead a smaller unit by a captain was termed a "sergeant." Units large enough to be designated as "battles" would be led by a clan chieftain (or direct delegate) or even by the king himself. These are the largest forces any individual could hope to control given the often obscured terrain of the north and the independent spirit of its warriors.

Initially this loose structure was brought to the Southern Kingdoms by the founding Atlund emigrants. Even as the southern population grew, skirmishes remained small, with little largescale warfare between the various Southern Kingdoms. Like the Atlund clans before them, different kingdoms created structures suited to their individual needs and philosophies, leading to a dizzying array of titles and unit configurations. War with the orcs changed all that. Two generations after the first High King established hegemony, a royal decree standardized unit terminology and target sizes to the following:

Unit Name	Size	Composition	Led by
Squad	6	Smallest unit	Veteran
Platoon	24	4 squads	Sergeant
Company	72	3 platoons	Captain
Battalion	216	3 companies	Major
Regiment	1080	5 battalions	General
Division	3240	3 regiments	Noble General
Army	6480+	2+ divisions	King

In addition to the ranks noted above, the rank of "lieutenant" also existed in a limited capacity between "sergeant" and "captain." As sergeants were almost universally commoners, nobles not yet considered experienced enough to lead companies were sometimes awarded the lieutenant rank as platoon leaders to further distinguish them as members of the peerage (in addition to the inclusion of noble titles preceding their military rank; see below). Even many in the nobility found this to be a matter of pure semantics, while most commoners considered it an attempt by aristocrats to claim an authority they had not yet earned.

It should also be noted that, given the limits on speed and accuracy of communication, the largest unit sizes of "division" and "army" were of great interest to campaign-level strategists and quartermasters but less so to engagement-level tacticians.

As the Southern Kingdoms' development of feudal nobility occurred in parallel with elaboration of its military organization, all ranks above sergeant were initially held only by those of noble birth. As the rise of professional armies swept through prosperous regions, and those units were integrated into command chains with more traditional, noble-led forces, the two systems inevitably required decoupling to prevent chaos. (In poorer regions, a similar transition took place when nobles were forced to free their serfs in exchange for military service and subsequently could not afford to overlook battlefield promotion for their most skilled leaders and tacticians.) This decoupling led to the practice of noble titles and military ranks being used in concert, with those of higher noble title being given priority in social and political situations, and those of higher military rank having authority in military action. Unsurprisingly, this policy proved less clearcut in execution, with offenses and feuds propagating during periods of relative peace only to be suppressed when the orcish threat amplified once again. The relative power of political maneuverers compared to loyal commanders tended to rise and fall in accompanying cycles.

APPENDIX B
SOUTHERN KINGDOM FEUDAL STRUCTURE

At its most fractured, the region now united under a single king contained no fewer than seventy kingdoms and principalities. These varied wildly in size, with the least vassals under greater kings sometimes holding more land than an entire kingdom across their border.

Naturally, the terminology used to describe feudal obligations across the many kingdoms and their various tiers of nobility encompassed a vast panoply of titles and ranks. Individual alliances attempted to resolve these discrepancies as they formed, but the naming of the first High King brought the confusion to a head. Titles of the same name across kingdoms may or may not be equivalent, and direct correspondence between ranks of different names couldn't always be established. The driving factor of the hierarchy had been, in effect, the number of feudal intermediaries between a landholder and the monarch, but this structure was of no use to the newly formed central authority in understanding the fighters and resources a noble could be expected to produce for the war effort.

In order to mitigate this inefficiency, the first High King replaced the inconsistent titles with a universal system which equated everything a fief could produce with an equivalent number of soldiers. Each armed fighter was counted normally; the amount of food required to feed that fighting man for a year gained similar consideration. Any arms and ammunition produced by a fief were converted directly to the number of soldiers they could arm for a year, while timber, ore, and other resources were converted more abstractly based on market exchange rates. The initial effort took nearly ten years, resulting in a hierarchy of four noble titles based on the size and prosperity of the holding as measured in equivalent soldiers: Duke, count, baron, and lord. These title changes had no impact on the feudal obligations between landowner and landholder, so a lord, for example, might hold land directly from a king. Naturally, that lord could wield significant political influence, but his rank in the peerage for social and legal purposes remained the lowest. Each new king taking the crown, if twenty years or more had passed since the last evaluation, was required to conduct a new census for the correct organization and defense of the realm.

At first these new titles were enforced only in communications to the High King or regarding comportment within his personal court, but as the culture of the Southern Kingdoms continued to homogenize, they eventually became the standard forms of structure and address for local matters as well. In time this practice also led to the organic development of a culture of primogeniture (in some regions even having the force of unwritten law) as dividing holdings between heirs inevitably led to a reduction of the family's noble standing in actual name, not only in perception.

The one original exception to this system was made for remaining royalty; the first High King held power over eight other monarchs, each of whom maintained their sovereign crowns. Various circumstances eroded these remaining titles (typically the heirless death of a monarch, upon which his most powerful vassal would petition the High King to recognize their ducal claim over the deceased king's demesne) and within nine generations the last of the lesser royal lines had disappeared.

A second exception, of a sort, developed subsequently, resulting in the creation of a new title below that of lord. During times when the orcish attacks approached the level of an existential threat, many nobles were required to spend increasingly long periods of time away from their actual holdings. Stewards from among the common classes typically took responsibility for managing lands in the noble's absence, but to invest these commoners with legal, decision-making authority beyond their station was believed to be a dangerous precedent. As a result, absent nobles initiated the practice of delegating power in their holdings to second sons or other family members possessed of noble blood but without title. Recognizing the value of this work, some of these delegates demanded compensation in the form of land, resulting in the creation of the "knight" as the new, lowest noble rank, responsible for legal administration and defending the land from incursions by outlaw bands or other local threats. A noble of any rank could create a knight, and the knight maintained this rank regardless of the size and prosperity of his fief. (Knightly titles were recognized in censuses, but the soldiers and resources associated with their parcels were credited to the granting noble.) Nevertheless, holding the rank did come with a variety of rights and privileges, and knights were often named as inheritors to a noble's lands and title if they produced no natural heirs. In a few notable cases a knight even received contiguous holdings from adjacent fiefs (having familial relations to both) and petitioned the crown to combine these holdings to become a full noble himself. Naturally, this was always a politically tumultuous proposition, as it typically resulted in one of the higher nobles losing land, but the wars in the south produced many desperate times and equally desperate measures.

A significant adjustment to the Southern Kingdoms' feudal system occurred over the last century of the orcish wars. As serfs in prosperous regions had been relieved of their military obligations by the development of professional armies, the laborers of poorer regions increasingly voiced their objection to risking their own lives without sharing fully in the land's profits. As casualties and disease put pressure on the population, the proportional value of each individual's work grew, improving their negotiating position. This eventually led to many nobles being forced to grant autonomy to their serfs, releasing them from their bonds to the land.

As far as the crown was concerned, those of common birth could not own land; however, the Capital did recognize what was, arguably, the most critical right of a freeman: the right to leave. Wise nobles allowed their freed subjects to enjoy the privileges of land ownership regardless of the king's position, and those who treated their subjects well often flourished. Foolish nobles continued to place injurious taxes or restrictions on their freemen, ultimately leading to mass exodus from their lands and an inability to meet their own feudal obligations, a failure that would cost the noble both land and title.

About the Author

Shane L. Coffey lives in Missouri with his wife and the multitude of characters trying to fight their way from his brain to his computer screen. He is a man of simple tastes, inexpensive hobbies, and little travel…but if anybody starts making plans for an expedition to Mars or Rivendell, he'll be very interested to know whether they require any skillsets he possesses (or could convincingly fake).